The Carnival Master

THE CARNIVAL MASTER

Craig Russell

HUTCHINSON
LONDON

Published by Hutchinson 2008

2 4 6 8 10 9 7 5 3 1

First published in Great Britain in 2008 by
Hutchinson
Random House, 20 Vauxhall Bridge Road,
London SW1V 2SA

www.rbooks.co.uk

Addresses for companies within The Random House Group Limited can be found at:
www.randomhouse.co.uk/offices.htm

The Random House Group Limited Reg. No. 954009

A CIP catalogue record for this book
is available from the British Library

ISBN 9780091921422 (Hardback)
ISBN 9780091921439 (Trade paperback)

The Random House Group Limited supports The Forest Stewardship
Council (FSC), the leading international forest certification organisation. All our
titles that are printed on Greenpeace approved FSC certified paper carry the FSC logo.
Our paper procurement policy can be found at www.rbooks.co.uk/environment

Mixed Sources
Product group from well-managed
forests and other controlled sources
www.fsc.org Cert no. TT-COC-2139
© 1996 Forest Stewardship Council

Typeset by Palimpsest Book Production Limited, Grangemouth, Stirlingshire

Printed and bound in Great Britain by
Clays Ltd, St Ives plc

For Holger and Lotte

Karneval in Cologne is a custom dating back to when the Romans founded the city. Its roots probably lie in the dark pagan past of the Celts who occupied the area before the arrival of Germanic and Roman invaders.

Karneval is a time when order is replaced with chaos, when the abstinence of Lent is preceded by abandon and indulgence. A time when the world is turned on its head. When people can become, for a few hours, someone else.

The Master of the Carnival is 'Prinz Karneval'. He is also known as 'seine Tollität' – His Craziness. Prinz Karneval is protected by the Prinzengarde. His personal bodyguard.

The German word 'Karneval' comes from the Latin 'Carne Vale':

'Farewell to Flesh'.

Prologue

Weiberfastnacht – Women's Karneval Night. Cologne. January, 1999.

Madness. Everywhere she looked was insanity. She ran through crowds of the demented. She stared around wildly, seeking an asylum: somewhere she could find refuge amongst the sane. The music thudded and screamed mercilessly, filling the night with terrifying cheerfulness. The crowd was denser now. More people, more madness. She pushed through them. Always away from the two massive spires that thrust up from the mayhem of the streets, black and menacing into the night. Always away from the clown.

She stumbled as she ran down the steps. Past the main railway station. Through a square. On and on. Still surrounded by the shouting, grinning, laughing faces of the insane.

She collided with a knot of figures gathered in front of a stand selling *Currywurst* and beer. The former German Chancellor Helmut Kohl stood in a nappy stuffed with Deutschmarks, laughing and joking with three Elvis Presleys. A medieval knight struggled to eat his hot dog through a visor that would not stay up. There was a dinosaur. A cowboy. Louis the Fourteenth. But no clown.

She spun around. Scanned the throng of bodies that now closed in her wake. No clown. One of the beer-stand Elvises staggered towards her. Blocked her path and circled her waist with his arm; said something lewd and latex-muffled. She pushed Elvis away and he collided with the dinosaur.

'You're mad!' she screamed at them. 'You're all mad!' They laughed. She ran on through a part of the city she didn't know. Fewer people now. The streets narrowed and closed in on her. Then she was alone in a narrow cobbled street, dark and tightly lined with four-storey-high buildings with black windows. She pressed into a shadow and tried to get her breathing under control. The sound from the distant city centre was still loud: madly cheerful music mingled with the raucous cries of the deranged. She tried to listen through it for the sound of footsteps. Nothing. She stayed pressed into the shadow, the reassuring solidity of the apartment building at her back.

Still no clown. No nightmare clown from her childhood dreams. She had lost him.

She had no idea where she was: one direction looked the same as the other. But she would keep heading away from the maniac sounds of the city, from the looming black spires. Her heart continued to pound but her breathing was now under control. She hugged the wall as she moved along the street. The raucous music and laughter faded further but suddenly there was a new blast as a door opened and yellow light sliced across the street. She shrank back again into shadow. Three cavemen and a female flamenco dancer burst out of the apartment house, two of the Neanderthals carrying a crate of beer between them. They staggered off in the direction of the other lunatics. She started to cry. To sob. There was no escape from it.

She saw a church at the end of the street. A huge church, standing crammed into a cobbled square. It was a Romanesque building that at one time would have sat grandly with fields and gardens around it. But the city had closed in on it over the centuries: now it was squeezed on every side by apartment buildings, like a bishop jostled by beggars. A parochial house nudged into its flank. A bar-restaurant at the other end of its meagre square. She would avoid the bar. She would seek refuge in the parochial house. She walked towards it, suddenly startled by the image of a small, frail, frightened, broken-winged fairy in the black shield of a butcher's shop display window. Her reflection. Her reflection hanging between pasted cardboard stars with special offers on beef and pork.

She reached the corner of the church. It loomed dark and austere into the cold night sky. She turned the heavy iron handle and leaned against the door but it would not give. She made her way towards the parochial house.

He stepped out in front of her from where he had been waiting, hidden, around the corner of the church. His face was blue-white in the dim street light, his over-wide painted smile dark crimson. Two flaps of green hair stood at a ridiculous angle from his otherwise bald head. She tried to scream but nothing came. She stared at his eyes: cold and dead and hard under the comical arches of his black-painted eyebrows. She couldn't move. She couldn't cry out. She couldn't find the strength to break free and run. His hand, gloved in bright blue felt, snapped up and grabbed her throat. He pushed her against the wall and into the shadows. Lifted her onto tiptoe. In a single movement of his free hand he produced a necktie from the huge patch pocket of his oversized coat and looped it around her neck.

Now she struggled. The necktie burned her skin, crushed the arteries in her neck, closed her windpipe. No breath came to her screaming lungs. Her head swam. Her world darkened. And as he tightened the ligature around her neck, all she could do was stare into his face.

His grotesque clown face.

Part One

CLOWN DIARY FIRST ENTRY.
DATED: 11.11A.M. 11ᵗʰ NOVEMBER.

IT IS ELEVEN MINUTES PAST ELEVEN IT IS THE
ELEVENTH DAY OF THE ELEVENTH MONTH I AM
AWAKE AGAIN *AWAKE* i am the *CLOWN* again and
i am awake IF THEY WANT CHAOS I WILL BRING
THEM CHAOS i am what i am ~~cows only eat grass~~
~~koalas only eat eucalyptus leaves pandas only eat bamboo~~
~~cows only eat grass koalas only eat eucalyptus leaves~~
~~pandas only eat bamboo~~ i only eat people I am what i
am i only eat what i eat i only eat people i've pasted
some pictures into this diary to remember lovely
pictures the flesh cut the flesh cooking the flesh
eating the flesh thoughts so many thoughts biting eating
eat kill eat today I am the CLOWN again awake again
strange to be awake again so long since last awake killed
the bitch then ate her ~~didn't fuck though never fuck~~
~~don't play with your food they want fucked but don't~~
~~want eaten~~ just kill and eat the bitch they're all bitches
bitches bitches if i'm awake it means KARNEVAL is
near soon soon *KARNEVAL* carnal carnage *CHARNEL-HOUSE*
CARNIVORE *THEY WANT CHAOS I WILL BRING THEM* CHAOS
i am the KARNEVAL CLOWN but nobody laughs just
afraid afraid when i paint my face paint my smile on big
wide biting smile they see the smile the big beautiful
clown smile and the teeth and they are burned by my
smile and they are helpless and wait to be eaten nobody
laughs at the CLOWN i watch them then watch them
then find a place to hide from them hide from them

then jump out at them and they see me and they
scream but don't laugh then i choke them and cut
them up and eat them and get strong so strong and the
stronger i am the longer i can stay awake i will kill again
and eat again and will wear the clown face and when
they look at the clown face they cannot run or move
they are so frightened they are in awe they are power-
less because the clown smile the clown smile is all
powerful and they are nothing _THEY BECOME MY FOOD_
i don't know how old i am i am old older i feel like i
have lived only for a day or a hundred years i have lived
and eaten for a long time but such long sleeps in
between i remember the last one the last meal karneval
is near in fact i'm sure of it i can smell it coming it is
like when you smell meat cooking somewhere in the
distance and the smell comes to you on the breeze and
you only smell it for a second then it's gone but it
makes you so hungry that's what it's like i smell
KARNEVAL getting closer closer asleep so long now
i'm awake and i'm the clown and don't have to share
I WILL BE AWAKE FOREVER AND IT WILL BE
KARNEVAL EVERY DAY and i will be the clown always
and always and i will feel real not like i'm watching
myself i have slept so long and so deep and far away
from the world but now i'm awake thinking clearer now
it is ~~me~~ i who am in control it is my time and the
other isn't in control anymore the other tries to deny
me pretend i don't exist and sometimes i feel i don't
exist but i do exist ~~and I have teeth~~ why do others
find what I do so repulsive find me so repulsive i am
the **CLOWN** and i am made of iron flesh and I eat
flesh i have teeth and a tongue and a gut and I would
die if I did not eat everything must eat to survive and
some can only survive by eating only one kind of _food_
cows only eat grass koalas only eat eucalyptus leaves

<u>pandas only eat bamboo</u> and i only eat people it's as simple as that if i did not eat the flesh of others i would grow weak and die i am the <u>CLOWN</u> and i must stay strong

it will soon be time for me to paint on the <u>CLOWN FACE</u> i will bring them chaos i have been asleep such a long time

and i am <u>**hungry**</u>

Chapter One

14–16 January

1.

The commander of the MEK tactical assault team looked surprised to see Fabel squatting next to him, taking cover behind the large armoured van.

'I was in the area and heard the call.' Fabel predicted his question. He looked up at the four-storey block of flats white against the blue winter sky. Pristine and cheerful. Balconies with winter pansies. Mid-range cars parked outside. Heavily armed, black-uniformed MEK officers were rushing the occupants of the block out of the main door and along the street to where the ordinary uniformed police had hastily erected the perimeter on Jenfelderstrasse.

'I heard you'd quit, Chief Commissar.'

'I have,' said Fabel. 'I'm working out my notice. What have we got?'

'Reports of a domestic disturbance. The neighbours called the police. The first local unit had just arrived when they heard shots. Then the guy inside took a pot-shot at one of the uniforms.'

'Does he belong to the building?'

The MEK commander nodded his helmet. 'Aichinger. Georg Aichinger. It's his flat the disturbance came from.'

'We know anything about him?' Fabel slipped on the body armour that one of the MEK team handed him.

'No record. According to the neighbours, never any trouble

until now. The perfect neighbour, apparently.' The MEK commander frowned. 'He has a wife and three kids. Or maybe had. There hasn't been much sound from the flat since the first gunshots. Four gunshots.'

'What's the weapon?'

'From what we can see, a sporting rifle. He's either half-hearted about it or he's a lousy shot. The idiot from the first patrol car to arrive presented him with the perfect target by running headlong up the stairwell. Aichinger missed him by a metre. More a warning shot if you ask me.'

'So maybe the family are still alive.'

The commander shrugged inside his Kevlar. 'Like I said, it's been pretty quiet since. We've got a negotiator on his way.'

Fabel nodded grimly. 'Can't wait. I'm going in to talk to him. Can you give me a man to cover me?'

'I don't approve of this, Chief Commissar. I'm not sure that I can allow you to put yourself at risk. Or one of my men at risk, for that matter.'

'Listen,' said Fabel. 'If Aichinger's family is still alive, then that could be a very temporary situation. If he's talking to me, then he isn't killing them.'

'They're already dead . . . you know that, don't you?'

'Maybe so, but we've nothing to lose, have we? I will just keep him occupied until the negotiator gets here.'

'Okay. But I'm not at all happy with this. I've already got two men positioned on the landing outside the apartment. I'll send another up with you. But if Aichinger doesn't feel chatty, or if there's any hint of things kicking off, then I want you straight out of there.' The MEK commander nodded across to one of his team. 'Go with the Chief Commissar.'

'What's your name?' Fabel examined the young MEK trooper: young, heavy-muscled bulk beneath the body armour. Eyes bright and hard with excitement. The new breed. More soldier than policeman.

'Breidenbach. Stefan Breidenbach.'

'Okay, Stefan. Let's go and see if we can talk our way out of you having to use that.' Fabel nodded towards the Heckler and Koch machine pistol clutched to the MEK man's chest. 'And remember this is a hostage negotiation and a possible crime scene – not a war zone.'

Breidenbach nodded sharply, making no effort to conceal his resentment at Fabel's remark. Fabel let him lead the way into the building and up the stairwell. Aichinger's flat was on the second level and there were already two MEK men positioned there, pressed against the wall, faces hidden by helmets, goggles and flash masks.

'Anything?' Fabel asked the trooper at the top of the stairwell.

He shook his head. 'All quiet. I reckon we've got a multiple. No crying, no movement.'

'Okay.' Fabel edged along the landing while Breidenbach trained his weapon on the closed apartment door.

'Herr Aichinger . . .' Fabel called towards the apartment. 'Herr Aichinger, this is Principal Chief Commissar Fabel of the Polizei Hamburg.'

Silence.

'Herr Aichinger, can you hear me?' Fabel waited a moment for a reply that did not come. 'Herr Aichinger, is there anyone hurt in there? Does anyone need help?'

Again silence, but a faint shadow moved across the frosted glass of the small square window set into the apartment door. Breidenbach adjusted his aim and Fabel held up a cautionary hand to the young MEK man.

'Herr Aichinger, we – I – want to help you. You've got yourself into a situation and I know that right now you can't see your way out of it. I understand that. But there's always a way out. I can help you.'

Again there was no reply, but Fabel heard the sound of the latch being taken off the door. It opened a few centimetres.

All three MEK troopers moved forward, keeping their aim locked onto the open door.

Fabel frowned a warning at the three MEK men.

'Do you want me to come in, Herr Aichinger? Do you want to talk to me?'

'No!' hissed Breidenbach. 'You can't go in there.'

Fabel dismissed him with an annoyed shake of the head.

Breidenbach inched closer to him. 'I can't let you make a present of yourself as a hostage. I think you should go back outside, Chief Commissar.'

'I've got a gun!' The voice from inside the apartment was tight with fear.

'We're very much aware of that, Herr Aichinger,' Fabel talked to the crack in the door. 'And as long as you keep hold of that gun, you are placing yourself in danger. Please, slide it out of the door and we can talk.'

'No. No, I won't. But you can come in. Slowly. If you want to talk, you come in here.'

Breidenbach shook his head vigorously.

'Listen, Herr Aichinger,' said Fabel, 'I'm not pretending it isn't a very *complicated* problem we have here. But we can solve it without anyone getting hurt. And we can do that in easy stages. I have to tell you that I have armed officers out here. If they think I am under threat they will fire. And I'm sure that if you think you are in danger you will do the same. What we need to do is move back from that situation. But we have to do that one step at a time. Agreed?'

There was a pause. Then: 'I don't want a solution. I want to die.'

'That's silly, Herr Aichinger. Nothing . . . no problem . . . is so hopeless that it's better to die.' Fabel looked around at the MEK men. In his mind he could see only too clearly that there would be three dead children and a dead wife lying in the apartment. And if Aichinger was determined to die, then this could end with 'suicide by cop'. All he had to do was run out onto the landing waving his rifle around and Breidenbach and his colleagues would gladly oblige him.

A phone rang somewhere in the flat. It kept ringing. The negotiator had obviously arrived.

'Shouldn't you answer that?' Fabel asked the crack in the door.

'No. It's a trap.'

'It's not a trap. It's help. It will be one of my colleagues. Someone who can really help.'

'I'll only talk to you.'

Fabel ignored Breidenbach's reproachful look. 'Listen, Herr Aichinger. The person on the other end of the phone is much better qualified to help you out of this situation than I am.'

'I said I'll only talk to you. I know that whoever is on the phone is just going to try to psychobabble me into believing he's my best friend. I'll talk to you. Only you. I've heard about you, Herr Fabel. You're the one who solved those murders last year.'

'Herr Aichinger, I want you to open the door so we can talk face to face.' Fabel paid no attention to Breidenbach's frantic signalling.

'They'll shoot me.'

'No, they won't . . .' But Fabel felt the need to look pointedly at Breidenbach. 'I'm ordering them not to shoot unless you do. Please, Herr Aichinger. Open the door.'

There was a long silence.

'Herr Aichinger?'

'I'm thinking.'

Another pause. Then the tip of Aichinger's rifle appeared as it nudged the door fully open.

'I'm going to come and stand where you can see me, Herr Aichinger. I'm not armed.' One of the other MEK troopers grabbed at Fabel's jacket sleeve as he moved towards the door, but he snatched it free. Fabel's heart pounded and he used every adrenalin-stretched second to take in as much as he could. The man standing in the hall was as unexceptional as it was possible to be. In his late thirties with dark hair cut short and gelled, he had what Fabel would have described as generic features: not so much a face in the crowd as the face of the crowd. A face you would forget as soon as he was out of sight. Georg Aichinger was someone you would never notice. Except now. Aichinger had a new-looking sports rifle in his hands. But he wasn't pointing it at Fabel. His arms were stretched taut and his chin pushed upwards as he jammed the rifle barrel under his own jaw. His thumb quivered on the trigger.

'Easy . . .' Fabel held up his hand. 'Take it easy.' He looked past Aichinger, along the hall. He could see, projecting into the doorway, the feet of someone lying on the floor of the living room. Small feet. A child's feet. Shit, he thought. The MEK commander had been right.

'Georg. Give it up. Please . . . give me the gun.'

Fabel's step forward made Aichinger tense. The thumb on the trigger stopped quivering. 'If you come near me I'll shoot. I'll kill myself.'

Fabel looked back at the child's feet. He felt sick at the sight of them. At that moment he didn't care whether Aichinger blew his own brains out or not. Then he saw it. Tiny. So tiny he could have missed it. But he hadn't. A small movement.

'Georg . . . The children. Your wife. Let us get to them to help them.' Fabel heard someone move into the doorway behind him. He turned and saw that Breidenbach had his gun aimed at Aichinger's head. 'Put it down!' Fabel hissed. Breidenbach didn't move. 'For God's sake, there's already one gun on him – his own. Now lower your weapon – that's an order.'

Breidenbach lowered the sights of his machine pistol slightly. Fabel turned back to Aichinger. 'Your wife . . . the children. Have you hurt them? Have you hurt the children, Georg?'

'Nothing makes sense.' Aichinger said as if he hadn't heard Fabel. 'I suddenly realised that nothing makes any sense at all. I suppose I've been thinking about it a lot recently, but then I woke up this morning and felt . . . well, I felt like I wasn't *real*. That I don't have a real identity. Like I'm just a character in a bad movie or something.' Aichinger paused, his brow furrowed as if he were explaining something that he couldn't fully understand himself. 'There was this person, in my head, when I was a kid. The person I was going to be. Then it turned out that I wasn't that person. I'm not who I was supposed to become. I'm someone different.' He paused. Fabel listened to the silence, straining it for any sounds from the room beyond. 'It's all mad.' Aichinger continued his tirade. 'I mean, the way we lead our lives. It's insane. The things that go on around us. It's all shit. All chaos. None of it makes any sense . . . Take your colleague there. Just itching to put a bullet in my head. You're here because I have a gun and I'm threatening to use it. He has a gun and is threatening to use it too. But that's acceptable. Why? Because he's a policeman. He's supposed to keep order. Except it isn't order.'

'Georg . . .' Fabel looked past Aichinger and down the hall to see if he could see the small feet move again. 'The children . . .'

'Do you know what I do for a living, Herr Fabel? I'm a "recruitment consultant". That means I sit in an office for the greater part of my waking hours and find people to fill other offices in other companies. It's the most pointless fucking waste of a life. That's *my* life. That's the *me* I became. I am one little hamster in his treadmill finding other hamsters for other treadmills. Supplying the meat to feed the big corporate mincing machine. That is what I spend my life doing. Where's the sense in that? Thirty-odd hours a week. I calculated it: by the time I retire, I will have spent nearly forty thousand hours sitting at that desk. Forty thousand. It's mad. I've always tried to do the right thing, Herr Fabel. Always.

What was expected of me. Play the game according to the rules. Everything else is chaos, I was told. But none of this makes any sense. Don't you see? All of the things I haven't seen. Places I've never been.' Tears streaked Aichinger's face. Fabel tried to understand what he was saying; to grasp what could have caused such monumental grief. 'It's all illusion. We live these ridiculous little lives. Live in boxes. Work in boxes. Give ourselves to senseless work. Then we just . . . *die*. All because that's the way we think it's supposed to be. We think that's stability and order. But one day I woke up and saw this world for what it is. Insane. There's nothing rational or real or vital about it. *This* is the chaos. *This* is the anarchy. Well, I've done it. I've turned it on its head. On its head. This isn't me. You've got to believe me: this isn't *me*. I don't want to be part of it any more.'

'I don't understand.' Fabel reached out his hand, slowly. 'Give me the rifle, Georg. You can explain it to me. We can talk about it. We can sort things out.'

'Sort things out?' Aichinger smiled a sad smile. It struck Fabel that there was a genuine but sorrowful gratitude in that smile. Aichinger's posture seemed to relax. The thumb on the trigger stopped quivering. 'I'm glad it was you, Herr Fabel. I know that when you think about what I've said, you'll understand it. At least you *do* something. At least there's some sense, some meaning, to each day that you wake up to. You save people. Protect them. I'm glad it was you who I could explain to. Tell everyone . . . tell them that I couldn't live with being someone else. Tell them I'm sorry.'

The sound of the shot was muffled by the flesh pressed hard against the barrel under Aichinger's jaw. There was a plume of blood, bone fragments and brain matter from the crown of Aichinger's head and his legs folded beneath him.

Fabel leapt across the body and ran into the living room. Towards the tiny feet in the doorway.

2.

Ansgar's meal was ready.

Ansgar Hoeffer's home in Cologne's Nippes district was modest and scrupulously clean and tidy. It was also unshared, unvisited. Over the years he had gradually withdrawn to specific places: home, work, the journey in between. He often felt that his life was like a large country house in which only a few rooms were used and kept in perfect order, the rest closed and shuttered and dust-sheeted in the dark. Rooms, Ansgar knew, it was best not to visit.

The kitchen of Ansgar's home was, given his occupation, surprisingly small but unsurprisingly well equipped; pristine and filled with light from the large window that looked out onto his house's slim fringe of garden and the blank side wall of his neighbour's house.

The oven chimed. The meat was ready.

The strange thing was that, when at home, Ansgar preferred to cook simpler meals. Uncomplicated dishes in which the true texture and flavour of the meat were allowed honest expression. As always, Ansgar had timed everything to perfection. The asparagus simmering on the hob would be cooked to the perfect consistency. He took the small dish of apple sauce from the fridge: it would reach the perfect temperature – cool but not chill – by the time he served the meat and asparagus. He poured half a bottle of Gaffel beer into a glass, the balance of body and foamy head exactly right. He removed the metal tray from the oven and unwrapped the single fillet of meat from its foil cocoon. Leaning forward, he sniffed the delicate scent of the tender flesh wrapped in thyme, his glasses steaming opaque for a second. He placed the meat on the plate, dressed it with a fresh sprig of thyme and some of the apple sauce. He drained the asparagus and laid it neatly beside the meat.

Ansgar took a sip of the Gaffel and contemplated his meal.

The first mouthful of meat melted on his tongue. As it did so, he started to think again about that girl at work. The Ukrainian girl who worked with him in the restaurant kitchen, Ekatherina. He frowned and tried to eject her from his thoughts. Another mouthful of meat. As his teeth sank into the yielding flesh she returned again to his mind. Her pale young skin pulled taut over her voluptuous curves. Even in winter the temperature in the kitchen would soar with the humid heat from the ovens and hobs. Ekatherina's pale skin would become flushed and moist with sweat, as if she were being slowly cooked herself. He tried to banish her and focus on his meal. But with each mouthful he thought of her buttocks. Her breasts. Her nipples. Her mouth. Most of all, her mouth. He continued eating. He frowned when he felt the tingle between his legs; the pressure against the material of his trousers. He sipped his beer and tried to compose himself. He ate some asparagus. He straightened the cruet set on the table. Another mouthful of meat. He hardened more. He felt sweaty moisture on his top lip. He thought of her pale flesh against the black T-shirts she wore. Again the swell of her breasts. Again, her mouth.

Ansgar's face was now sheathed in a film of sweat. He fought and fought to banish the images that surged into his mind. Those twisted, delicious images in which the chaos he had regulated from his life reigned. Those sweet, sick, perverted ideas that he had forbidden himself. And she was part of them. She was there, always, in those scenarios of tender, succulent flesh and biting teeth. He chewed the meat, unable to swallow. Ansgar Hoeffer thought of the sensual feel of the food in his mouth and again of the girl at work. He shuddered as he ejaculated into his trousers.

3.

It took Fabel four hours to go through the bureaucracy of death: all the form-filling and debriefings that gave Aichinger's senseless actions some kind of official shape. As he had so many times in his career, Fabel had stood at the heart of a human tragedy, burned by its raw emotional heat, only to go on to play his part in turning it into a cold, sterile statistic. But he would never forget Aichinger's final expression of sad gratitude. And he doubted if he would ever understand it.

Fabel sat on the edge of the table in the Murder Commission squad room on the third floor of the Police Presidium, Hamburg's police headquarters, drinking vending-machine coffee. Werner Meyer, Anna Wolff and Henk Hermann were all there: the team that, after fifteen years of leading, he would soon be leaving. Only Maria Klee was conspicuous by her absence. She had been on extended sick leave for the last month and a half: Fabel was by no means the only one who had been marked by the last three major investigations.

He sighed wearily and looked at his watch. He had been forced to hang around because his boss, Criminal Director Horst van Heiden, had asked to see him once he was through with the form-filling and the internal review questions.

'Well, *Chef* . . .' Senior Criminal Commissar Werner Meyer, a thickset man in his fifties with a grizzly bristle-cut, raised his coffee cup as if it were a glass of champagne. 'I have to admit, you like to go out in style.'

Fabel said nothing. The images of what had waited for him in Aichinger's living room still buzzed around his head. The emotions, too. The dread and the hope that had flashed through his mind and had tightened his chest as he had sprinted along the short apartment hall.

'You did well, *Chef*,' said Anna Wolff. Fabel smiled at her. Anna still looked nothing like a Criminal Commissar in the Murder Commission. She was small and pretty and more youthful-looking than her twenty-nine years; her dark hair was cut short and spiky and her full lips were deep red.

'Did I?' Fabel asked joylessly. 'I failed to disarm a mentally fragile man before he blew his brains out.'

'You lost one,' said Werner. 'One that was lost before you even arrived . . . but you saved three.'

'How is Aichinger's family?' asked Anna.

'They're fine. Physically, at any rate. But they're in deep shock. The shots the neighbours heard had been fired into the ceiling . . . and thank God that there wasn't anyone in the apartment above at the time.' Fabel had found Aichinger's wife, his seven-year-old daughter, his two boys, nine and eleven. Aichinger had tied them up and gagged them with parcel tape. Fabel would never know if Aichinger had done so to keep them safe, or for execution later. 'It's the little girl who's taking it the worst. Kids see the world so simply. When she woke up this morning, everything in her life was the way it should be. Tonight her world has been turned on its head.' Fabel paused as he realised he had just echoed Aichinger's own words. 'How do you explain what happened to a child of that age? How is she going to live with that memory?'

'The main thing is that she *is* going to live with it.' Werner sipped his coffee. 'They all are. If you hadn't kept Aichinger talking, they might all have ended up dead.'

Fabel shrugged. 'I don't know . . .'

The phone ringing interrupted Fabel. Werner answered it. 'You're summoned to the fifth floor . . .' he said with a grin as he hung up. The fifth floor of the Polizei Hamburg Police Presidium was where all the top-brass offices were, including the Presidial Department. Fabel grimaced.

'I better answer the call, then . . .'

4.

Taras Buslenko already knew where the meet would take place, if Sasha's intelligence was correct. But, of course, they didn't know that: they would run him all over Kiev before revealing his final destination and he would have to jump through all their hoops.

When the call came on his cellphone, Buslenko had been told at first to head for the Hotel Mir in Goloseevsky Prospekt and to wait in the car park. He'd been there ten minutes when a second call told him to head back to the city centre, park in the Kyivsky Passage and start walking down Khreshchatyk Street.

It was a Saturday evening: Khreschatyk Street was closed to traffic every weekend, allowing shoppers and tourists by day and clubbers by night the freedom to wander along it and appreciate its grandeur. Buslenko himself, as he made his way down the vast boulevard, couldn't help but think how beautiful it looked still laced with glittering Christmas lights. There had been a fresh but light fall of snow and the wide thoroughfare and the trees that lined it looked sugar-dusted in the crisp winter night. As he had been clearly instructed, Buslenko walked in the opposite direction from Independence Square. He had been there in November and December 2003. He had thrilled then at the sight of the orange banners, the air electric with the promise of change. He had felt part of something huge. Unstoppable. However, Buslenko had not been there to lend support: he had been in charge of a detachment of security troops ordered to the square, supposedly to prevent bloodshed between the 'Blue' supporters of Yanukovych and the 'Orange' revolutionaries supporting Yuschenko. The truth was more likely that they had been sent as a show of regime strength, but the police and intelligence chiefs had recognised a true turning of the tide and many within the security services, like Buslenko, were sympathetic to the Revolution. Buslenko's detachment had been stood down.

Buslenko made sure he walked past the Celestia nightclub without a glance. Maybe Sasha really had got it wrong. Or maybe the people he was supposed to be meeting were just being over-cautious.

He had almost reached the Central Universal Mall when his phone rang again. This time he was instructed to wait at the bar of the Celestia nightclub. Buslenko felt relieved. He had started to worry that he might be redirected to some more remote part of Kiev. The Celestia was good. Right in the heart of the city. More public. More difficult if you wanted to kill someone and dispose of a body.

The Celestia was one of the glittering symbols of the new Ukraine's aspirations: a glitzy place in Kiev city centre at the Independence Square end of Khreschatyk Street. Buslenko, despite his background, remained a solid supporter of Ukraine's new path: he had always been a patriot and now he saw the potential for the future that his country deserved. His heart had been with the Orange Revolution but places like the Celestia made him feel uncomfortable: they sought to reflect Western affluence and glamour, but something about them struck Buslenko as sham and borrowed, like seeing a ruddy-cheeked peasant girl in an over-glittery cocktail dress and inexpertly applied make-up.

There were two black-suited doormen outside the club. One was bull-necked and mutely massive; the second was smaller, leaner and friendlier, smiling at Buslenko as he held the door open. As he had been trained to do in every situation, Buslenko automatically assessed the risk the doormen presented. In a time too brief to be measured, he identified the smaller man as the main danger: he moved quickly and easily and hid whatever he was thinking behind a smiling mask. Buslenko recognised that the smaller man, unlike the cumbersome bodybuilder, would be capable of fast and lethal violence. A killer. Probably with a Spetsnaz background.

It was like looking in a mirror.

Buslenko made his way to the bar and ordered an Obolon beer. He was told by the unsmiling barman that the Celestia didn't have Obolon, or any other Ukrainian beer. Buslenko ordered an over-priced German Pils. The Celestia was busy but not crowded; populated with young, affluent customers who glistened under a sheen of Gucci and Armani. The bar was a long, sweeping arc of glittering black granite above rich walnut. The walls were illuminated by uplighters that projected sinuous, mildly erotic shapes onto their velvety deep red surfaces. To Buslenko, the Celestia looked like some contemporary designer's concept for Hell.

The best possible place, he thought, to encounter the Devil.

Buslenko became aware of someone at his side. He turned to see a young woman. She was tall and slender, with short blonde hair; her face was wide with high Slavic cheekbones, a broad pale brow and eyes that were a bright, glittering blue. It was a face that was truly beautiful and could not have come from anywhere except Ukraine.

'Hello, sir,' said the Ukrainian Beauty, with a perfect por-celain smile. 'You are expected. I wonder if you would follow me. Your party has reserved a private room.' She placed Buslenko's beer on a tray and turned from the bar with a glance over her shoulder to ensure that he followed her. Before he did, Buslenko scanned the bar around him as if to satisfy himself that he was not being watched.

The Ukrainian Beauty led him through a double doorway into a dark tunnel of a hallway, walled with black glass and illuminated by strips of tiny, bright spotlights that repeated themselves infinitely on the reflective obsidian. She knocked at a door before holding it wide for Buslenko to enter the large, plush private entertaining room. Four men were seated around the low table on an expensive L-shaped sofa. There were vodka glasses and a bottle on the table, along with a blue-covered file. The men stood up as Buslenko entered. Like the doorman, they had special forces written all over them and they all looked to be in their forties, which meant that they probably had real combat experience. Buslenko registered the dark glass wall behind them, which obviously divided this from the next entertainment suite. The room beyond was in darkness and the connecting door was closed, but some vague, deep instinct told Buslenko that it was not empty.

The man who had been sitting at the centre had prematurely white hair that had been trimmed to a coarse stubble on his scalp. A scar reached down out of the bristle, across his broad brow and down to the outside corner of his right eyebrow. Buslenko had done his usual split-second survey of the room and had already guessed the seniority of the scarred man from the body language of the others. But it wasn't Buslenko's instinct or training that told him that he was looking at a mean, dangerous son of a bitch. He had recognised the Russian as soon as he had entered the room and his chest had tightened. Kotkin. What was Dmitry Kotkin doing here? He was too senior in the organisation to be a recruiting sergeant. Buslenko also didn't need to turn around to know that there was now a fifth man behind him, at the door. But he sensed there was someone else. Someone who lay beyond the reach of Buslenko's skills; someone who waited, silent and unseen, behind the dark glass wall in the room beyond.

The Ukrainian Beauty put Buslenko's beer down on the table and left the room. He did not turn as he heard the door click shut behind him. The presence of the fifth man was academic: Buslenko was good and was perfectly capable of taking on four or five men in the right situation. But this was not the right situation and these were not the right men: they all had a similar background to Buslenko and, he guessed, had all killed before, more than once. At best Buslenko could take one or two with him. But he knew that if death were to come, it would come from behind and the man at the door.

'You're Rudenko?' Kotkin spoke in Russian. Buslenko nodded.

'Sit down,' Kotkin said and sat down himself. The other three stayed on their feet. The scarred Russian opened the file. 'You have a very impressive record. Exactly what we are looking for. Or so it would seem. But what I want to know is why you came looking for us?'

'I didn't. You contacted me.' Buslenko answered in Russian. He thought about taking a nonchalant slug from his beer bottle, but was afraid that his hand would shake. Not fear. Adrenalin.

Kotkin raised his eyebrows and wrinkled the scar unpleasantly. 'You went around asking questions. More than that, you knew the right questions to ask in the right places. That means only one of two things: you were advertising yourself or . . .'

Buslenko laughed and shook his head. 'I'm not a cop, if that's what you were going to say. Listen, it's as simple as this. Money. I want to make money. A lot of it. And I want to work abroad. You do want people to work abroad, don't you?'

'Let's not get ahead of ourselves.' The scar-headed Russian nodded to the others, two of whom approached Buslenko and gestured for him to stand up and raise his arms. One frisked him manually while the other scanned him for a wire with a hand-held electronic wand. Buslenko smiled. When they had satisfied themselves that Buslenko was clean, they sat down again.

'We know what we're looking for. You need to convince us that you're it.'

'I'm guessing it's already all in there,' Buslenko nodded towards the file. 'Twelve years' experience. As a paratrooper, then with an Interior Ministry Spetsnaz. I can handle myself and I can handle any job you give me.'

'I know the Spetsnaz unit you served with. Do you know

Yuri Protcheva? He would have served about the same time.'

Buslenko made a show of trying to remember. He had been through the files, through all the team lists, a dozen times. He knew right away that there had been no Yuri Protcheva: it was an obvious trick. Too obvious. Kotkin didn't want him to admit to knowing someone who didn't exist. He wanted him to deny it too quickly, revealing he had been rehearsed.

'No . . . I can't say I did,' Buslenko said eventually. 'I knew everyone, just about. But no Yuri Protcheva. There was a Yuri Kadnikov – could that have been him?'

'You say you got into trouble?' Kotkin ignored Buslenko's reply.

'Some. Not much. We had to bust up a prisoners' revolt in SIZO13 prison. I killed an inmate . . . Not a big deal, given the situation, but a prison official took one in the neck because he didn't do what he was told and stay out of the way. Not my fault. His. But his brother was a big shot in the Interior Ministry. You know how it is . . .'

'We're not looking for misfits or drop-outs. We're looking for soldiers. Good soldiers who can take and carry out orders.'

'That's what I am.' Buslenko straightened himself up in the leather chair. 'But I thought you were looking for people to . . . well, break the law.'

'The only law we follow is the soldier's code. If you join us, you will be a member of an elite. Everything we do is regulated by the highest military standards. It's no different from normal service with a Spetsnaz unit. The only difference is that it pays a hell of a lot better. But you're not in yet. I need you to answer a few questions.'

'Go ahead . . .' Buslenko shrugged nonchalantly, but his mouth felt dry and he had to resist the temptation to look over the Russian's shoulder to the black glass wall behind. His instinct now jabbed at him incessantly. There *was* someone in there. Watching. Listening. *He* was there. Sasha's intelligence had been right.

'Do you know what it is that holds a military unit together?'

'I dunno . . . obedience, I suppose. The ability to carry out an order as efficiently as possible.'

Kotkin shook his scarred head. 'No, that's not it. I'll tell you what it is. It's trust. The trust of true comradeship. Loyalty to one another and to your commander.'

'I guess so.' Buslenko detected something changing, like a sudden shift in air pressure just before a storm. He sensed the other three men on the long sofa tensing almost imperceptibly. But there was no change in the Russian's demeanour. Too professional. The files on Kotkin showed that he had been an interrogator, or torturer, in Chechnya or elsewhere on the fringes of Russia's crumbling empire. Maybe that was why he was there. Not as Buslenko's recruiter, but as his torturer and executioner. And still Buslenko's instinct nagged at him that there was someone watching and listening behind the glass wall.

'Loyalty. That's what holds a unit together. Brothers under arms.' The Russian paused, as if waiting for Buslenko to say something. The other three men stood up. Buslenko strained to hear the hint of any sound behind him.

'What's the problem?' Buslenko asked, trying to keep his tone even. It will come from behind, he thought again.

'We all share a common experience.' Kotkin continued as if he had not heard Buslenko's question. 'We are men of war whose lives depend on each other. What we fight for is secondary. What really matters is that we fight together. There is an unspoken, unbreakable bond of loyalty between us. There is no greater bond. And there is no greater treachery than when that bond is betrayed.'

As if responding to a cue, the other three men reached into their leather jackets and Buslenko found himself staring down the muzzles of three heavy-calibre automatics. But no one pulled a trigger.

'Your name is not Rudenko,' said the Russian. 'And you

didn't serve with the Titan unit. Your name is Taras Buslenko. You served with the Sokil Falcon organised-crime Spetsnaz units and you are now an undercover agent of the organised-crime division of the Interior Ministry.'

Buslenko gazed past the Russian at the glass wall. *He* was in there. Buslenko was sure of it. Close to the kill, the way *he* always liked.

'You're alone, Buslenko,' said Kotkin. 'You couldn't wear a wire and you couldn't come armed. Your people are outside but we are better than your people. By the time they get in here, you will be dead and we will be gone. In short, you're fucked.'

It was then that Buslenko heard the slightest hint of someone moving across the room behind him. He anticipated the next move perfectly. He had already worked out that they would want to kill him as quietly as possible and as soon as the loop of wire was whipped down in front of him he slid down in the leather chair. The wire dug painfully into his forehead before slipping off, having failed to hook under his jaw and the soft tissue of his throat. Buslenko rammed his heels into the coffee table. It was heavy and protested as it slid on the floor and it did not slam into the shins of the gunmen with the force he had hoped. He rolled sideways on the floor. Still no gunshots: it was clear that they were certain they could kill him without opening fire.

Buslenko rolled again but the fifth man, the one who had failed to strangle him with the high-tension wire, slammed his boot into the side of his head. It hurt like hell but Buslenko was not stunned as his assailant had intended and caught the boot as it came down again – expertly, edge first – towards the cartilage of his throat. Buslenko twisted his attacker's foot and swung his own boot upwards and into the other man's groin. Buslenko knew he was going to die. What the Russian had said was true: his support would not get here in time, but he sure as hell was going to take someone with him.

Now Buslenko moved without the panic of someone fighting for his survival; instead every part of his training came together in a perfect final performance. He leapt to his feet, spun his assailant around and in a single, continuous movement, snapped his neck and threw his dying body into the path of his attackers. The Russian feinted to the left and let the body fall on his companions. Buslenko saw something bright flash towards him and only just dodged the first thrust of Kotkin's knife. With a grace and skill to match Buslenko's own, the Russian changed his grip on the knife and brought it back in an arc. This time Buslenko did not move fast enough and, although he felt no pain, he knew the blade had sliced into his shoulder. The other three had now recovered their composure and a series of blows rained onto Buslenko. He found himself pinioned to the wall by his assailants, helpless against their combined strength. Kotkin moved close. He lifted the knife and jabbed the point into the side of Buslenko's throat. Buslenko knew what was coming next. It was a classic form of silent killing: forcing the blade in behind the windpipe then forwards and out. It was how they used to kill pigs on farms. No squealing. Just a breathless second of silence, then death. Buslenko looked straight into the Russian's cold grey eyes.

'Fuck you,' he said, and waited for the knife to sink deeper.

There was a cursory knock and the door to the entertaining room swung open. Everyone, even Buslenko, turned to look. The Ukrainian Beauty stepped in, a tray in her hands and started to ask if they needed more drinks. Her words trailed off as she saw the dead man on the floor and Buslenko pinned against the wall, a knife at his throat.

'Get her!' Kotkin barked at the others and two of them made towards her, leaving Kotkin and one other with Buslenko.

The girl dropped the tray, under which she had been concealing a Fort17 automatic. Calmly, she took Kotkin out first. Buslenko heard the round smack into the centre of the Russian's forehead, and felt a light splatter of fluid against his cheek. As the Russian dropped, Buslenko grabbed the knife from his grasp and arced it up under the jaw of the man who still held him. The knife sliced up through the soft tissue of his victim's underjaw, through his mouth and tongue and jammed into the hard palate of the roof of his mouth. There was a series of other shots and Buslenko knew that the other two men were dead. He shoved his last assailant, the knife still lodged in his jaw, away from him. As the man staggered back, Ukrainian Beauty fired two more rounds. The first hit the man in the body and brought him to the floor. The second, textbook style, hit him in the head.

She kept her automatic at locked-arm's length, scanning the room. There was a commotion outside and a troop of Spetsnaz burst into the room. Buslenko, clutching a hand-kerchief to the side of his neck where the Russian's knife had cut him, gestured towards the glass wall at the back of the room.

'In there! I think he's in there.'

Ukrainian Beauty walked over to Buslenko. 'You okay?'

'I think I owe you a large tip, waitress.' Buslenko smiled bitterly and looked at the body of the man he had stabbed and she had shot twice. He had wanted to take at least one prisoner alive for interrogation and thought Ukrainian Beauty's *coup de grâce* had been unnecessary. But considering she had just saved him from being slaughtered like a farm pig, he passed no comment.

The Spetsnaz commander came back from the other room. Like Buslenko, Peotr Samolyuk was a Sokil Falcon officer.

'It's clear.'

'What do you mean, "clear"? He was in there,' said Buslenko. 'Watching. I know it.'

Peotr Samolyuk shrugged black armoured shoulders. 'There's no one there now.'

'You sure it was him?' asked Ukrainian Beauty.

'Our primary fucking target was in there. I could feel him. And he's the only reason we're here. The intelligence we had that he would be with this group was as solid as it could be. But him . . .' Buslenko frowned and nodded down to where the body of the scar-headed Russian lay. A halo of dark crimson had oozed from the exit wound in his skull. 'He just doesn't make sense . . . what was Dmitry Kotkin doing here?'

'He's part of the organisation. Why wouldn't he be here?'

'Right organisation, wrong side of it. He's a Molokov man.' Buslenko was still looking at the black glass wall. 'And it wasn't Molokov in there behind the glass. Watching. It was the big guy himself. Vasyl Vitrenko. Some big business has brought him back. Something really big or he wouldn't have left himself exposed. Even Kotkin's far too senior to be recruiting thugs. He'd reached a level where he was becoming less and less visible.'

'All I can say is that we've got this place sealed up as tight as a drum. Whoever you thought was in there couldn't have got out.' Ukrainian Beauty followed Buslenko's gaze to the adjoining entertaining room. 'It was always going to be a long shot, Taras. Our intelligence was contradictory. We had information that Vitrenko was back in Ukraine and we had equally sound intelligence that he is still in Germany.'

'Well,' said Buslenko, turning to face the beautiful Captain Olga Sarapenko of the Kiev police militia, who had made such a convincing nightclub hostess. 'That was what my grandmother always said about the Devil: he has the craft to be in two places at the same time.'

5.

Fabel waited to be shown into Criminal Director van Heiden's office and thought about how he would soon become someone else. And how everyone except Susanne seemed to be doing their best to talk him out of it. He guessed that van Heiden might be about to try again.

The whole idea of resigning from the Polizei Hamburg had been to get away from death. His entire career as a policeman had been founded on its violent intrusion into his life. The young Fabel had never considered being a police officer; with the absolute certainty of youth, Fabel had had his entire career as a historian planned out for himself. But then death, in its most sudden and violent form, had shouldered its way, unbidden, into Jan Fabel's path.

It had happened while Fabel was still a student at the Universität Hamburg. Fabel had only been dating Hanna Dorn, the daughter of his history professor, for a few weeks when she had been randomly selected by a psychopath as his next victim. He knew that Hanna Dorn, in her own right, would not have made that much of an impression on his life. Without the trauma of her murder, she would have faded from his consciousness long ago. They would, no doubt, have had a relationship that would have lasted a while: they would have gone to parties, eaten out when they could have afforded it, met with friends. But every time Fabel thought back to her, he knew that they would not have stayed together and that Hanna Dorn would have diminished into the far distance of his memory. A name that would have to be prompted into his recall. It had not been Hanna's presence in his life that had marked Fabel for ever. It had been her sudden absence.

Fabel had moved on from trying to make sense of Hanna's death to trying to make sense of the death of strangers. Fabel had come to know so many names, so many faces of the dead. As head of the Polizei Hamburg's Murder Commission, Jan Fabel had spent his career getting to know people who were no longer capable of knowing him. He had become a master at reconstructing a life and a personality that was lost to everyone else; to walking in the footsteps of the murdered and understanding the minds of those who had killed them.

What had kept Fabel sane had been the fact that, throughout his career, he had always sought to keep death at arm's length. He had never been entirely detached: it had always been his empathy for the victims that had given him that critical edge. But since Hanna's murder, he had tried never to let death come too close to him. The last three cases had changed all that: one officer dead, one seriously wounded and mentally scarred. And twice more he had seen his officers placed in serious peril.

It was time to go. A chance encounter with an old school-friend had resulted in an offer of a job. More than a job. An escape into a normal life, whatever that was. To become someone else. It had been a monumental decision for Fabel. And now everyone was trying to talk him out of it. Everyone except Susanne. Susanne saw it as more than a change in Fabel's career; she saw the opportunity to change the basis of their relationship.

Fabel's superiors had, with great reluctance, agreed that he would leave the Polizei Hamburg's Murder Commission at the end of the so-called 'Hamburg Hairdresser' case. It had been this case, piled onto the three other serial-killer investigations he had undertaken, that had led Fabel to the final decision to quit. There was, he had decided, just so much horror and fear that one could experience, only so much bearing witness as foul, corrupted and sick minds opened themselves up in front of you, before you started to become more and more like the thing you hunted.

Criminal Director Horst van Heiden was Fabel's boss, in charge of Hamburg's Criminal Police, the investigative branch of the Polizei Hamburg. Fabel had been surprised at van Heiden's persistence in trying to persuade him not to resign. Fabel and van Heiden were, in many ways, opposites. Van Heiden was the typical career police officer, with a background in the force's uniformed branch. Fabel still saw himself as the accidental detective: an outsider. And he liked to think that he held little regard for the formalities of his occupation.

When Fabel entered the Criminal Director's office, there was a tall, lean man with prematurely greying hair whom Fabel didn't recognise waiting with van Heiden.

'Fabel . . . allow me to introduce Herr Wagner of the BKA . . .' said van Heiden. Fabel shook hands with the federal agent. The BKA was the Bundeskriminalamt – Federal Crime Bureau – the law-enforcement agency with a brief that covered the whole of the Federal Republic. Fabel had worked with them on several occasions, but he had never before encountered Wagner. Maybe this wasn't going to be all about van Heiden trying to persuade Fabel to remain in the Murder Commission after all. However, Fabel's hope was dashed with van Heiden's first utterance.

'I'm not going to beat about the bush, Fabel.' Van Heiden indicated that Fabel should be seated. 'You know my feelings about your leaving the Polizei Hamburg. I would rather see you in another department than lose you completely.'

'I appreciate that, Herr Criminal Director. But my mind is made up.' Fabel did not try to suppress the weariness in his voice. 'And, with respect, we've been through this before . . .'

Van Heiden bristled. 'I didn't bring you up here just to repeat myself, Fabel. Herr Wagner and I have something specific to discuss with you.'

'With the greatest respect,' said Wagner, 'I don't agree with Herr van Heiden that an alternative to you resigning from the Polizei Hamburg would be a transfer to another department. I know that you have successfully concluded four serial-murder cases in recent years.'

'It depends on how you define "successfully",' said Fabel. 'I have lost one officer and another has been so traumatised that she is currently on extended sick leave.'

'How is Frau Klee?' asked van Heiden.

'Maria's tough,' said Fabel. 'Very tough. I suppose in many

ways that's been her problem. She tried to simply work through what happened to her. Didn't give herself enough time to recover from either her physical or emotional wounds. That's why she's crashed now.'

'Frau Klee was seriously injured in the case in which Herr Fabel lost an officer.' Van Heiden clearly felt that Wagner needed an explanation.

'And a local uniformed policeman was killed as well,' said Fabel.

'Yes . . .' Wagner frowned. 'The Vitrenko case. Believe me, I am only too well acquainted with the exploits of our Ukrainian friend. Vasyl Vitrenko is at the top of our wanted list.'

'Added to that, Maria became . . .' Fabel struggled for the right word '. . . *involved* – albeit unknowingly involved – with a killer in another case. I'm afraid it's all taken its toll on her.'

'Fabel,' said van Heiden gently, 'it's more than a case of lost confidence and post-traumatic stress. Frau Klee has had a complete breakdown. We all know that otherwise she would be your successor. I hate to say this about an officer of Frau Klee's ability, but I very much doubt if she has a future in the Murder Commission.'

'I think that I should have a say in that,' said Fabel.

'But you won't, Chief Commissar,' van Heiden said. 'By the time Frau Klee returns from sick leave you will be long gone. Your choice, Fabel. Not mine. Anyway, I'm sure we can put Frau Klee to good use elsewhere in the Polizei Hamburg.'

Fabel said nothing. Eventually Wagner broke the embarrassed silence. 'Anyway, as I was saying, Herr Fabel, you have a natural talent for complicated murder cases. And your last case was rather . . . *high profile* to say the least. Your reputation now extends far beyond Hamburg. Whether you like it or not, you have earned a name within the police community throughout Germany as the most experienced and successful investigator of complex and multiple murder cases.'

'I certainly don't think that I have any special qualities or credentials,' said Fabel. 'It's more to do with bad luck . . . having four serial-murder cases in our jurisdiction. And the fact that I have a good team behind me and have had a few lucky breaks.'

'We all know luck has had nothing to do with it, Fabel,' said van Heiden.

'Listen, Herr Fabel,' said Wagner. 'There are a number of murder cases that come up every now and then in different parts of the Federal Republic that, for one reason or another, are more complicated than the usual run-of-the-mill killings.'

'Serial killers, you mean.'

'No . . . well, yes, but not exclusively. Everything is changing. We now routinely come across all kinds of more complex cases. Killings with some other dimension to them . . . political, organised-crime-related, professional murders. That kind of thing. Also cases where the geographical scope of the crime exceeds the boundaries of any single Federal State and the operational scope of any single police force. A contract killer in Bremen might be working for a gangster in Leipzig, for example. Or we might find ourselves faced with a serial killer who uses the autobahn network to kill across the Federal Republic. Or it could simply be that a case is so complex or unusual that the local force simply has no frame of reference for their investigation.'

'What's this got to do with me?'

'Well, as you know, the usual form with cases that extend across the Federal Republic is that the State Prosecutor of the Federal State where the first killing took place takes charge and the BKA provides coordination between the investigating forces. But we live in a much more complicated world. It isn't just business that is globalising. The Internet is providing a worldwide resource for sex criminals and organised crime is blind to national, far less federal borders.'

'The BKA want to set up a special unit to deal with such crimes.' Van Heiden took over. 'A Super Murder Commission, so to speak. And they want you to head it.'

'You would still be based here at the Hamburg Police Presidium,' explained Wagner, 'and you would still handle Hamburg cases as you have for the last fifteen years, but you would also be given additional staff and resources with which to build the special unit. Whenever there was a case that required your particular skills and perspective, your unit would respond.'

'I'm very flattered but—'

Van Heiden cut Fabel off. 'This is not about flattery. And it's not just about you. This is an opportunity for the Polizei Hamburg to gain Europe-wide – even worldwide – recognition as a centre of excellence in murder investigation, in much the same way as the Legal Medicine Institute in Eppendorf is a global leader in forensics.'

'But surely this unit would be a BKA unit?'

'You would remain a full serving officer in the Polizei Hamburg,' explained Wagner, 'but seconded to the BKA. There would be an increase in salary to reflect the increase in responsibility. If you wanted, we could leave things the way they are here, but use you in a, well, *consultative* role in other parts of the country.'

Fabel took a moment to consider what was being said. 'This is all very interesting, and it is an exciting challenge for any ambitious officer. But not me. I'm trying to get away from death on my doorstep. Not to take to the road to see more of it. I'm sorry, gentlemen.' Fabel stood up. 'I've made my decision.'

'It really is a unique opportunity,' pressed Wagner.

'Listen, Herr Wagner, I appreciate the offer. I really do. But it's time for me to move on.' Fabel paused for a moment. 'I've lost my way. When I first became a policeman, it was all very simple. I saw where I stood in the world, and that place was between the ordinary citizen and those who would do them harm.'

'That's a pretty good definition of what it is to be a policeman,' said van Heiden. 'And it's as true today as it was when you joined.'

'Maybe so,' said Fabel, with a sigh. 'But over the years . . . well, it's got more complicated. More *abstract*, I suppose you could say. The people I've hunted, the things they've done . . . I never saw myself getting involved with all that darkness.'

There was a pause. Then Wagner said, somewhat uncertainly: 'I mentioned earlier that I was only too well acquainted with Vasyl Vitrenko . . . I know that there is a certain amount of . . . well . . . *unfinished business* between you. I meant what I said about knowing Vitrenko well. He and his new partner Molokov are by far the most powerful figures in people-trafficking in Europe. They are selling women and children from Eastern Europe and Asia into sexual and other kinds of slavery. And they are using Germany not just as a prime market but as a gateway to the rest of the West. We have set up an interdepartmental task force dedicated to finding and taking Vitrenko out of action for once and for all. If you reconsidered your position, then your first task could be to help us nail him.'

'Why is it that everyone seems to feel they have an insight into what motivates me? What do any of you know about what happened out there when Maria was stabbed?' Fabel fought to keep the anger that flashed in him under control. 'This is real life, not some corny American movie. I don't burn with a desire for revenge and I'm not looking for some kind of final showdown. Vitrenko is not my problem. Not any more.'

'That's not the way we do business,' said Wagner and Fabel could see he had irked the BKA man. 'I'm not interested in personal grudges. I thought that as a professional investigator you would want to close a case that you have been so deeply involved in. And, from our perspective, you have a lot to bring to the table. No one has ever come so close to capturing Vitrenko as you and Frau Klee. Your insight could be invaluable. What I can also tell you is that we are much, much better off in terms of intelligence on Vitrenko than we were when you last crossed paths with him. For the first time ever we have an inside source on the Vitrenko–Molokov organisation and we've built the most comprehensive dossier ever compiled on him. With the help of our associates in the Ukrainian police militia we have succeeded in casting some light into the shadows. He's running out of places to hide.'

Fabel returned Wagner's gaze blankly, but he found himself wondering what was in the dossier. The truth was that as far as Fabel was concerned Vitrenko had ceased to be a person, a human being. He was a spectre.

'The Vitrenko Dossier has cost lives to compile, Herr Fabel. Much of the intelligence has come from Ukrainian undercover operations as well as from our own resources. We believe Vitrenko is aware of the dossier and would give anything to get his hands on it.'

'Why? It would only confirm what he can probably guess we know,' Fabel asked in spite of himself.

'Vitrenko is obsessive about loyalty. There are two versions of the Vitrenko Dossier. The master dossier and the working dossier. The main reason is that there is a limit to the intelligence we can share with our Ukrainian colleagues, which I know frustrates them. But the simple fact is that there is still a considerable amount of corruption within the Ukrainian security apparatus, added to which even the Ukrainians don't know how many of Vitrenko's people have infiltrated their own ranks. That's why the working dossier is the one that all members of the task force work with. It gives all the most important intelligence but doesn't identity the sources, which the master dossier does. But even if Vitrenko got his hands on just the working dossier, there would be enough clues in there for him to identify our sources within his organisation.'

'But surely there aren't any? Vitrenko's men are fanatically loyal to him.'

'That's very true. But when he merged his operation with that of Valeri Molokov, he compromised his security. Molokov has less noble ideas about his chosen profession. Like Vitrenko he is ex-security services, in his case Russian rather than Ukrainian, but he is a good old-fashioned gangster, plain and simple. There is no grand philosophy uniting his men. Just greed and violence.' Wagner paused, as if waiting for a reaction from Fabel.

'Well, as I said – Vasyl Vitrenko, his operation, his associates . . . it's all someone else's problem now,' said Fabel.

Van Heiden and Wagner exchanged resigned looks.

'Would you at least think it over?' asked van Heiden. 'I am prepared to hold your position open for a further three months. Senior Commissar Meyer has agreed to head the department in the interim. After that, I will have to replace you.'

'You can replace me now, Herr van Heiden. My mind is made up.'

'Listen,' said Wagner. 'I accept what you're saying, but in the meantime I wonder if you would look at this for me.' He handed Fabel a thick file. 'Just for your opinion. I understand that you won't want to be involved directly, but if you could look at it I'd be obliged. Just for ideas.'

'What is it?' Fabel took the file and eyed it suspiciously.

'It's from the Polizei Nordrhein-Westfalen . . . There's a Criminal Commissar Scholz working out of the Police Presidium in Cologne. He asked me if you would consider going down there to help with this case, but I understand now that that is out of the question.'

Fabel gave a cynical laugh. 'I see . . . a little bit of bait to see if you can reel me in.'

'I won't pretend that I wouldn't be disappointed if this case *intrigued* you enough to consider visiting Cologne and lending a hand. But I respect your decision. Nevertheless, I know that Herr Scholz would appreciate any comments or advice, Principal Chief Commissar Fabel.'

'Okay . . .' Fabel stood up, tucking the file under his arm. 'I'll take a look. But, as I said, that's all I can promise.'

Van Heiden walked Fabel to the door. They shook hands.

'We're going to miss you,' van Heiden said. 'I have to tell you that I don't see you as a computer salesman.'

Fabel smiled. 'Educational software, Herr Criminal Director. For universities around the world.'

'Whatever it is, you're not cut out for it. You're a policeman, Jan. Whether you accept it or not.'

CLOWN DIARY SECOND ENTRY.
UNDATED.

today i went to the church ~~today~~ *the church of bones*
i watched them like i always watch but they didn't
know it was me they couldn't see i was the clown
because they couldn't see the clown face or the clown
smile i watched them they are cannibals they fed on
flesh and blood they took flesh on their tongues and
swallowed blood from a chalice <u>they eat their god</u> who
are they to judge me when they eat their god <u>turning</u>
<u>bread into his flesh and wine into his blood</u> they really
want to eat each other **<u>THEY ARE ALL WILD</u>**
<u>ANIMALS JUST WILD ANIMALS</u> they feed on
flesh they look at it all the time pictures filthy talk in
their mouths filthy pictures filthy films on the internet
wild animals mountains of flesh without spirit without
mind without love and they wallow in it the internet is a
charnel-house flesh without taste or substance and
they would dare to call me sick they are the sick they
are the perverted fat old men looking at young girls even
children they are the sick and the women that do the
things they watch filthy whores they sell themselves as
meat the filthy cheap bitches i am the final justice for
them they burn their eyes on my clown smile if they
want chaos i will bring them chaos those hypocrites in
the church of bones they are all wild animals they have

all of these rituals to pretend they are not but they are all animals they eat their god i sat at the back of the church of bones sat and **THEY DIDN'T KNOW I WAS THE CLOWN** watched the priest speak stupid incantations the eucharist transubstantiation flesh became bread blood became wine bread became flesh wine became blood transubstantiation eucharist all shit all meaningless all they wanted to do was fall on each other and eat <u>so close I can't wait I can smell it i can taste it I can feel it in my mouth I can feel the strength in my body it will be soon so soon</u> *KARNEVAL* THE FEAST OF FLESH the chaos and the pleasure everything the other has forbidden me i will taste it soon **I REMEMBER THE LAST ONE** the frightened stupid bitch who begged and begged and wet herself with fear i choked her good with the necktie and her stupid face turned black and she pissed her pants and i took off her wet pants ~~off~~ and i turned her over and i cut out her meat and i took it home and cut off the skin and cooked her in oil and ate her it made me ~~happy dizzy~~ with ~~joy~~ ecstasy nothing tastes like it it fills the mouth it fills the gut it fills the soul **I AM SO HUNGRY** when i left the church of bones i saw a girl there and she was right for butchering ripe for it but it is not time I am awake and I am the clown but it is not time I will eat one at **KARNEVAL** have hidden this diary where no one will find it I will eat and eat and become stronger every one i eat makes me stronger i am so hungry but <u>IT WILL BE SOON</u>

Chapter Two

17–19 January

1.

Taras Buslenko sat in a steam bath in the Lukyanovka district of Kiev. There was only one other bather in the huge, porcelain-tiled steam room: a fat business-type whose paunch hung over his towel. Buslenko looked down at his own body and wondered if he too would end up fat and out of shape. An aged body was something he could never imagine for himself. His physique was hard and sculpted. A weapon. He ran his fingers over his scars. The most recent was the one on his shoulder, puckered with stitches and curved around the ball of muscle as if someone had tried to slice open an apple. The most noticeable was the bullet wound, enlarged by removal surgery, to the left of his stomach. He gave a half-laugh. It was no wonder he could not imagine his body older: the chances of him living that long were remote.

The steam bath was vaulted and Turkish in style. The walls and the floor were finished in ornate tiles and the bath itself had a distinctly Ottoman feel to it. The only things that reminded Buslenko that he was in Ukraine were the large porcelain panels, each identical, that punctuated the patterned tiles. The panels showed a man sitting cross-legged, Turkish fashion, under a tree, his weapons hanging from its branches. The man smoked a pipe and played a bandura. It was a representation of Cossack Mamay, Ukraine's national hero. Mamay was the legendary – probably mythical – protector of the Ukrainian people. The ultimate patriot.

The fat businessman on the far side gave a weary sigh, rose stiffly and left. After a few minutes three other men entered: a heavy-set middle-aged man and two younger men, both with the same hard, lean, muscled look as Buslenko. The two bodyguards sat near the door on the other side of the steam room. The older man sat down next to Buslenko.

'You missed him,' Oleksandr Malarek said, not turning to face Buslenko.

'If he was there at all, Deputy Interior Minister.'

'He was there. You know that.'

'Yes. I know that. Someone was on the take. One of ours. Someone broke my cover and allowed Vitrenko to organise an escape route.'

'Yes. Someone did,' Deputy Minister Malarek said without looking at Buslenko. 'It was Major Samolyuk.'

'The head of the assault team?' Peotr Samolyuk had been a Sokil unit commander with fifteen years' service. Buslenko had always considered him a solid man. 'Shit. Have you inter- rogated him? He could be the best lead we've got.'

'Not a lead. A dead end. A *very* dead end. We found him this morning. He had been tortured and castrated before death. They stuffed his genitals in his mouth.'

'He was going to talk? But he'd have gone to prison.'

'We'll never know. But if he had really been one of Vitrenko's men they wouldn't have done that to him. There is no betrayal in Vitrenko's organisation. They don't see themselves as crim- inals, but as a military unit with total loyalty to him. My guess is that Samolyuk took a massive bribe. Maybe he got greedy and asked for more to stay quiet.'

'Unlikely.' Buslenko still spoke to Malarek's profile. A bead of sweat gathered and hung on the tip of the older man's long nose. 'No one would be stupid enough to try to menace Vitrenko.'

'He's in Germany,' Malarek said, ignoring Buslenko. The

excruciating death of Samolyuk was clearly of no further interest to him.

'Vitrenko?'

'Our sources tell us that he is operating from Cologne.'

'I didn't think we had sources on Vitrenko,' said Buslenko.

'We didn't. We still don't, not directly. We have inform-ants who work for Molokov and that's as close as we can get.' Malarek wiped the sweat from his fleshy face with the palm of his hand. 'Vitrenko is selling our people like so much meat, Major Buslenko. He is a traitor of the worst kind. He debases Ukraine by debasing our people. His main centres are Hamburg and Cologne. But he travels back to Ukraine regularly. Part of the intelligence we have gathered is that Vitrenko has had extensive plastic surgery. The photographs we have on file are now useless, according to our sources.'

'Do you have any information on when he will next be back here? The next time . . .'

Malarek turned to face Buslenko. 'There won't be a next time. Vasyl Vitrenko moves like a ghost. He has so many contacts and informers here that if he does come back, he'll have evaporated into thin air again before we even know about it. That's where you come in, Major Buslenko. Vasyl Vitrenko's reign is an embarrassment to Ukraine. We cannot expect the world to take our new democracy seriously while we are seen as the cradle of the new Mafia. We need Vitrenko stopped. Dead. Do I make myself clear?'

'You want me to go to Germany without the knowledge or approval of the German government? That's illegal. Both here and there.'

'That's the least of your worries. I want you to take a Skorpion Spetsnaz unit with you. And just to make sure there are no misunderstandings, this is a seek-and-destroy mission. I don't want you to bring Vitrenko back to face justice. I want you to put him in his grave. I take it I have made my wishes completely unambiguous?'

'Perfectly. And I assume that if we get caught you will deny all knowledge of us? That we will be left to rot in a German prison?'

Malarek smiled. 'You and I have never even met. There is something else . . . I want it done quickly. The longer it takes to organise, the more chance there is for Vitrenko to find out about it. Unfortunately he has more militia in his pocket than I care to think about.'

'When?'

'I want you to be ready to go in a week or so. I know that gives you practically no time to select and brief a team, but it also gives Vitrenko less time to compromise it. Can you do it?'

'I know someone who can help me put a team together. Discreetly. But not just Skorpions. I want a mix of background and skill.'

Malarek shrugged. 'That's your thing. I just need to know if you can do it.'

'I can do it.'

After the Deputy Interior Minister and his bodyguards left, Buslenko sat alone in the steam bath and gazed again across the bath at the image of Cossack Mamay. Mamay stared out somewhat melancholically from his steam-wreathed porcelain panel, giving nothing away about how hard it was to be the Great Protector of the Ukrainian people.

2.

'This is a big step for you, Jan. I want you to understand that I do appreciate that.' Roland Bartz sipped the sample of wine, swirled it in his mouth and nodded to the waiter who then filled both men's glasses. 'And I understand that resigning as head of a murder squad is a lot more complicated than most job handovers . . .'

'But . . . ?'

'I've been waiting a long time now, Jan. I agreed to hang on till you tied up that last case of yours, but I really need someone to take over the foreign accounts now.'

'I know. I'm sorry for the delay. But, as I told you, I now have an official end date and I'll be sticking to it. You won't have to wait any longer.' Fabel forced a tired smile.

'You okay?' Bartz frowned with what Fabel thought was overdone concern. Bartz was the same age as Fabel. They had grown up in Norddeich in East Friesland together, gone to school together. Back then Bartz had been a gangly awkward youth with a bad complexion. Now his skin was bronzed, even in midwinter Hamburg, and his awkwardness had been transformed into urbane sophistication. To start with, Fabel had seen Bartz through childhood's eyes: recognising the similarities with the boy he'd befriended. But it had quickly become clear to Fabel that the Roland Bartz of today was a different person from Bartz the schoolboy. Fabel knew that Bartz had become a multimillionaire, but it had only been since their chance encounter and Bartz's offer of a job – and a way out of the Murder Commission – that Fabel had discovered just how vast his schoolfriend's wealth was. And now he was getting to know the businessman. Fabel preferred the awkward, spotty youth of his memory.

'I'm fine,' said Fabel unconvincingly. 'Just been a tough day.'

'Oh?'

Fabel related brief details of his encounter with Georg Aichinger, without giving any information that the press wouldn't already have by then.

'God . . .' Bartz shook his head in disbelief. 'Not me, Jan. I could never do that job in a million years. You're well out of it. But sometimes, to be honest, I don't know if *you* feel that way.'

'I do, Roland. I really do. When I was there today there was a young MEK trooper with me. Just itching to squeeze off a few rounds. You could almost smell the testosterone and gun oil in the air.' Fabel shook his head. 'It's not that I blame him. He's just a product of the times. What police work's become. It's time I got out.'

The restaurant was in Övelgönne and its vast picture windows looked out onto the Elbe. Fabel paused to watch as a massive container ship drifted silently past with unexpected grace. He had been here before with Susanne, on special occasions. The prices made it a special-occasion kind of place, but clearly not for Bartz and his expense account. It had been here that Fabel had had the chance encounter with Bartz that had led to his dramatic decision to change career.

'It's time for me to be someone else,' he said at last.

'I have to say, Jan,' said Bartz, 'you still don't sound one hundred per cent convinced that you're making the right move.'

'Don't I? Sorry. Being a policeman's been my life for so long. I'm just adjusting to the idea of putting it all behind me. It *is* a big step, but I'm ready for it.'

'I hope you are, Jan. What I'm offering is no sinecure. Admittedly it doesn't involve the stress or trauma of being a murder detective but I assure you it's just as demanding . . . just in a different way. It needs someone with your intelligence and education. Most of all someone with your sense of people. I just worry that you're having second thoughts.'

'No second thoughts.' Fabel hid the lie behind a smile.

'There's one thing about the job – a benefit we haven't discussed – that you should think about.'

'Oh?'

'What do you think being an international sales director for a software company means to people? I mean when you meet them at a party or a wedding or in a bar and they ask what you do. You know what it means?'

Fabel shrugged. Bartz paused to take a sip of wine.

'It means nothing. It's your job: it's not *you*. It doesn't define you. And people don't have an opinion about it. But if you say you're a policeman everyone has an opinion. Say you're a policeman and a whole lot of prejudices and expectations fall instantly into place. And they don't just see it as what you do, they see it as what you are. I'm offering you a way out of that, Jan. A chance to be yourself.'

At that moment the waiter arrived with their main courses.

'Ah . . .' Bartz smiled appreciatively. 'Now that the food's arrived, we can talk about your future . . . not your past. Eating and business, Jan. You can't separate them. We think we've come so far, that we're so much more sophisticated than our ancestors. But there's still some kind of fundamental intimacy that comes from sharing a meal, don't you think?' Fabel smiled. He couldn't remember Bartz talking so much as a boy. 'Think of all of the alliances forged, all of the deals done across the centuries, all discussed, bartered and sealed over feasts. It's something you'll have to get used to, Jan. You'll carry out most of your important negotiating across a dining table.'

They spent the rest of the meal discussing a life that somehow Fabel still couldn't see himself fitting into: a world of travel and meetings, of conferences and entertaining. And, for some reason, he couldn't get Georg Aichinger's desperate tirade against the futility of his life out of his head.

3.

Leave it, he thought to himself. Let it lie.

It had still been reasonably early by the time Fabel got home. Bartz had wanted to spend more time together at the bar after the meal, but Fabel explained that he had an early start in the morning. He had a report to write out on the Aichinger incident. Bartz had sighed and said, 'Never mind . . .' but had skilfully communicated a growing impatience with his soon-to-be international sales director.

Susanne had come over to Fabel's place after work. He hadn't seen her all that day: she hadn't been in the Presidium but had instead been working at the psychiatric department of the Institute for Legal Medicine in Eppendorf. He poured them both a glass of wine while he waited for her to come out of the shower. He gazed out of the tall window that looked out over the Alsterpark and the dark glittering shield of the Alster lake beyond it. He loved his apartment. He had landed it through bad luck and good timing: his marriage had collapsed just as the Hamburg property market had hit an all-time low. It had still been a stretch on his Principal Chief Commissar's salary, but it had been worth it. It had, however, been very much a place for one. His personal and undivided space. Now, with his change of career, had come another change: the decision that he and Susanne should sell their respective apartments, find somewhere new and move in together. Another decision that had seemed so clear at the time yet now lay shrouded in doubt.

Fabel watched the distant moving twinkle of car headlights along the Schöne Aussicht on the distant shore of the Alster. He thought of his meal with Bartz. Of his future. Of the file that lay dumped on the coffee table yet filled the room with its presence. If I pick it up, he thought, I'll be sucked into it all again. Leave it. Let it lie.

Susanne came into the room and Fabel placed a *Hamburger Morgenpost* on top of the file. He turned and smiled. Susanne was beautiful. Smart. Sexy. Her long thick hair was wet and hung over the shoulders of her white towelling bathrobe in glossy black kinks. She sat down on the sofa and he handed the glass of wine to her.

'Tired?' he asked, sitting down beside her on the sofa.

'No. Not really.' She smiled languidly.

'Hungry?'

'Oh yes,' she said and pulled him towards her, allowing the bathrobe to fall open.

4.

Timo had found the book dumped in a skip near the university, behind a house that was being renovated. It was an academic tome, an old copy, and its cover still felt gritty from the skip beneath Timo's fingertips, but it was similar to the one he used to have. The one he had sold along with so many of his other belongings. He had first read it while he had still been studying philosophy at Hamburg University. It was Émile Durkheim's *Rules of Sociological Method*: a treatise on social order; on the need for structures and forms to guide behaviour. Durkheim was considered the father of sociology, but Timo thought with irony how much more appropriate it would have been, given his current situation, if it had been Durkheim's later work, *On the Normality of Crime*, that he had uncovered.

Timo shivered in his inadequate jacket and leaned against the wall, gazing across at the store. It was getting dark and the lights in the store came on, turning the windows into warm embers in the January evening. Timo tried to read another page, but the light had faded too much. He sighed. The book had been a piece of his past that had fallen unexpectedly and unbidden into his present. It pained him to look at it: a reminder of a time when he had had hope, when his mind had been sharp and clear and organised. A time before. As if to snap him back to the reality of his current life, the gnawing pain in his gut intensified and the shivers that convulsed his body were not caused by the cold evening alone. He closed the book. He couldn't take it with him, but he didn't want to let it go. He didn't want to let his past go.

Max Weber, Ferdinand Tönnies and Émile Durkheim had provided the focus for Timo's studies. Max Weber's *State Monopoly on Physical Force* had been the basis for his thesis. Or at least the thesis he had started.

There were too many customers in the store. He'd have to

wait. The cold seemed to penetrate his flesh and chill his bones. Weber's hypothesis was that only the organs of state, the police and the army, should be permitted to use physical force; that otherwise anarchy reigned and the state was unsustainable. Timo had planned to posit, in his thesis, that such a monopoly could also be destructive to the state, as in the case of the Nazis.

A man in a business suit left the store, talking into his cellphone, followed by an older couple. The ache and the craving that burned in Timo's gut intensified. He slipped his hand into the pocket of his jacket and closed his fingers around the chill, hard steel.

Timo had also planned his thesis to balance this argument with a discussion of the United States, where the Constitution expressly allowed the citizen to bear arms, and therefore the means of independent physical force; consequently denying the state a monopoly on it. Yet the US existed and thrived as a nation.

He looked across the street. A car pulled up and a woman trotted into the store. She re-emerged a few moments later with a carrier bag and drove off. Timo felt a pang of something other than his body's craving. It was his grief, his mourning of his past-tense self: the disciplined, clear-eyed, organised philosophy student with the world at his feet. But that had been then. Before the drugs.

Timo stepped out of the shadow of the corner, his thin shoulders hunched against the cold, and made his way across to the store, his fingers closing around the gun in his pocket.

5.

After they had made love, Fabel and Susanne sat in the living room of his flat and looked out over the dark water of the Alster and the glittering reflections that played on it. Susanne leaned her head on Fabel's shoulder and he did his best to disguise the fact that for some reason he didn't want her there. The feeling surprised him. He felt restless and irritable and had, for a moment, an almost irresistible urge to get into his car and drive out of the city, out of Hamburg, out of Germany. He'd had the feeling before, but he had always put it down to his work; an urge to put the horror and stress of it all as far from him as he could. But wasn't that exactly what he had achieved? He had only a few weeks left to go and his escape would be complete. So why did he feel so panicky? And why was it, when he was supposed to be relishing a life free of murder, that he could not shake the call of the file he had half-hidden under the copy of the *Morgenpost*?

'How was dinner with Roland?' asked Susanne.

'Wordy. Bartz likes to chat. I don't know if he's that keen on listening but, boy, can he talk.'

'I thought you liked him.' There was an edge to Susanne's voice. Fabel had learned to be careful when talking about his new career with her: recently, any lack of conviction in his tone had been enough to start an argument.

'I do. I mean, I did when he was a kid. But people change. Roland Bartz is a very different person now. But he's okay. Just a bit full of himself.'

'He's an entrepreneur. It goes with the territory,' said Susanne. 'His company wouldn't be so successful – and he couldn't offer you the salary he's offering – if he was riddled with self-doubt. Anyway, you don't have to love the guy to work with him.'

'There's not a problem,' said Fabel. 'Honestly. And don't worry, I'm not having second thoughts about leaving the Polizei Hamburg. I've had a bellyful.' He took a long sip of Pinot Grigio, leaned back against the sofa and closed his eyes. The picture of sad, desperate, insane Georg Aichinger filled his mind. The same image that had haunted him throughout his dinner with Bartz.

'What's wrong?' asked Susanne in response to his sigh.

'I can't stop thinking about Aichinger. All that crap he talked before he shot himself. About waking up and realising that he wasn't real. What the hell was all that about?'

'Depersonalisation. We all get it to a degree at some point. Mainly through stress or overtiredness. In Aichinger's case, it could be that he was going through something more profound. Maybe even a full-blown dissociative fugue.'

'I thought that was when people lose their memory. Wake up in a new town with a new identity or lack or identity.'

'It can be, sometimes. People who suffer a great trauma can go into a dissociative fugue. To forget the bad stuff they dump their entire memory. Without a memory you can't remember who you are. You adopt a new identity without the biography of your real one.'

'But Aichinger hadn't lost his memory.'

'No. But if he hadn't killed himself he might have walked out of that door and disappeared. Not just from the world but from himself.'

'God knows there have been times when I've wished I could have disappeared from myself. Standing in front of Aichinger while he blew his brains out was one.' Fabel smiled bitterly.

'Well, you are, in a way. As soon as you walk out of the Presidium for the last time and put police work behind you.'

'Yeah . . .' Fabel took another sip of wine. 'And leave it all to the likes of Breidenbach.'

'Who?'

'The new breed.' Fabel sipped his wine.

6.

Stefan pulled up outside the all-night convenience store attached to the petrol station. He'd been at work until an hour ago. Now he felt good: freshly shaved and showered; wearing a brand-new shirt and his best cologne. He had phoned Lisa and she had agreed he could come and stay the night. This was the only store he knew that stayed open this late and it always had a good range of wines.

He had been seeing Lisa for a couple of months now. She was a great girl. A good laugh. Smart, and pretty with it. They had been drifting along in a casual manner and he genuinely had fun in her company, but Stefan was beginning to think that Lisa had ideas of it becoming a more serious relationship. He didn't want that. Or at least he thought he didn't want it. Things were fine as they were and he wasn't ready to get serious with anyone. Although sometimes the idea didn't seem so bad. But the fact was that, at the moment, the only thing Stefan had time to be serious about was his career. He had tried to explain to Lisa how important being a policeman was to him. He was up for his Commissar's exams in a couple of months and he had to get his head down to do some serious study. Not tonight. Tonight was going to be fun. But first he had to pick up the wine.

Stefan knew there was something wrong the instant he walked through the door.

The door chime drew the attention of the two men who were the only others in the store. A thin man with long, lank hair and dirty-looking clothes stood in front of the counter; the middle-aged Turk who ran the store was behind it. The two men were still. Too still, too tense. The young man turned suddenly to face Stefan. Stefan could see the fear in his eyes, the jerky motion as he swung his arm around to point his gun at him. Stefan held his hands away from his body.

'Easy . . .' he said. Stefan's training kicked in and he did a threat analysis. He took in as much as he could in as short a time as he could. The gun was an early Walther P8. Practically an antique. No, the barrel was too short for a P8: it was a P4, the type used by the Hamburg police after the war. Still, it was old and it didn't look cared for. Stefan wasn't entirely sure that it would be in working order, but it was impossible to tell for certain. 'Just keep calm,' he said, realising that the young man with the wild eyes and unwashed hair was the most frightened person in the room. Stefan thought back to the way Principal Chief Commissar Fabel had handled the situation in Jenfeld. 'Just take it easy.' Stefan saw the shake in the gunman's arm. The red rims to the wild eyes. A junkie. Desperate. Frightened. And Stefan's training told him a scared man with a gun is infinitely more dangerous than an angry man with a gun. Stefan did a mental calculation of the chances of the gun jamming and, if it did go off, of the junkie missing his target.

'Stay where you are!' the junkie shouted at Stefan.

'I'm not moving,' said Stefan calmly.

'You . . .' the junkie called over to the Turkish shopkeeper. 'Fill a carrier bag with the money from the till.'

The Turk exchanged a look with Stefan. He had served Stefan many times before and knew that he was a policeman. The Turk took what money there was in the till and put it in the bag. The junkie reached over with his free hand without taking his aim off Stefan.

'Okay. Get out of the way. I'm leaving.' The junkie tried to inject as much authority as possible into the statement.

'I can't let you do that . . .' Stefan said quietly.

'What the fuck do you mean? Get the fuck out of my way.'

'I can't do that,' repeated Stefan. 'I'm a police officer. I don't care about the money. I don't even care about you getting away. But I can't let you leave with that gun. I can't let you be a danger to the public.'

'You're a *Bulle*?' The junkie looked even more agitated. His shake grew worse. 'A fucking cop?' He snapped his aim from Stefan to the Turkish shop owner. 'What about this member of the public? What if I fucking kill him right now because you won't get out of my way?'

Stefan looked at the Turk. He had raised his hands but

Stefan could tell that he was more in control of his fear than the gunman was of his.

'Then you would prove to me that I can't let you leave. And I'd have to take you down.'

'With what? You're not armed.'

'Trust me,' Stefan kept his tone even. 'You pull that trigger and it's the last thing you do. I'm a specialist firearms officer. I know about guns. I know about the gun you're holding. When and where it was made. I can tell from the way you're holding it that you don't know what you're doing. And I know that you won't get us both before I reach you and snap your neck. But it doesn't have to be that way. Put the gun down. There's a way out of this.'

'Is there?' The gunman smiled bitterly. 'I suppose by restoring the monopoly on physical force?'

'I don't know what you mean.'

'Get out of my way!' He brought the gun back to bear on Stefan. 'Why do you have to do this? Why can't you just walk away? Just this once.'

'Because it's what I do. Just give me the gun.' Stefan took a step forward. 'Let's end this.'

'Okay . . .' The gunman's expression seemed to empty.

Stefan gave a small laugh. He had been wrong. The gun was old. It hadn't been maintained. But it didn't jam. And the junkie had been either a better shot than Stefan had thought or had just been lucky. The sound of the shot still rang in the confinement of the store as Stefan looked down at his brand-new shirt. At the hole punched through it. At the bloom that spread as his blood soaked into the fabric. A central mass hit. Almost a perfect shot. Stefan's legs gave way under him. He sank to his knees.

'Why couldn't you just have got out of my way?' The junkie's voice was filled with panic and hate in equal measure.

Stefan looked up at the junkie and opened his mouth to say something but found he hadn't the breath to spare.

'Why?' the junkie repeated plaintively and fired again. Then again. And again.

7.

Once more Fabel dreamed of the dead.

Fabel had had the dreams throughout his career. He had learned to resign himself to the sudden waking, the thunder of his pulse in his ears, the cold sweats in the night as part of his mental processes. He accepted that the dreams were the natural by-product of so many surplus thoughts and emotions circulating in his mind: those that he had learned to suppress as he dealt with the brutality of killers and, most of all, with the pain and misery of their victims. It was something he saw at every murder scene. The story. The history, usually written out in blood, of those last violent, sad moments. Someone had once said to him that we all die alone; that we can leave this world surrounded by people, but death was still the most solitary of acts. Fabel didn't believe this. The one element of each murder scene that burrowed its way into his brain, malevolently lurking there until he dreamed, had always been the cruelty of a murder victim having to share their last, most intimate moment with their killer. He remembered how he had once come close to smashing his fist into the grinning face of a murder suspect when he had boasted of how his victim, as she had died from the stab wounds he had inflicted, had tried to hold his hand, seeking the only human comfort available to her. The bastard had actually laughed as he talked about it. And Fabel had dreamt of the victim the same night.

Now Fabel dreamed he waited outside a huge hall. For some reason he thought he was perhaps in the Rathaus, Hamburg's government building. He knew he was being kept waiting for some reason, but that he would soon gain admittance. The heavy doors were swung open by two faceless attendants and he walked into a vast banqueting hall. The table stretched impossibly long and was lined with diners who stood and cheered as he entered. There was a seat for him at the distant end of the table and, as he walked past the other guests, he recognised almost all of them.

Fabel felt a vague sense of surprise that they recognised him. Each of them had, of course, already been dead before he had made their acquaintance. Fabel walked past the applauding victims whose murders he had investigated and took his place at the top of the table. To one side sat Ursula Kastner, who had been murdered four years before and who had visited previous dreams. She smiled with pale, bloodless lips.

'What is this feast in aid of?' asked Fabel.

'It's your farewell dinner,' she said, still smiling but using her napkin to dab a thick droplet of blood from the corner of her mouth. 'You're leaving us, aren't you? So we came to say goodbye.'

Fabel nodded. He noticed that the chair to his other side was empty, but he knew that the space was for Hanna Dorn, his murdered girlfriend from his student days. He turned to speak to Ursula Kastner again.

'I kept my promise,' he said. 'I got him.'

'You got him,' she repeated. 'But not the other.'

He turned back to see that the vacant chair had been filled. Fabel, in his dream-dulled mind, felt an attenuated shock to see it wasn't Hanna Dorn at all, but Maria Klee sitting there. Her face was gaunt and bloodless, her smile weak.

'What are you doing here? You shouldn't be here,' he protested. 'These are all—'

'I know, Jan . . . but I was invited.' She was about to say something else when another hollow cheer rose from the assembled guests. The chef had entered carrying an impossibly enormous silver platter capped with a huge silver dome. The chef's face was hidden, but he was massive, and his huge arms bulged. Nevertheless, it was only the eccentric physics of Fabel's dream that allowed the chef to carry the dish.

Setting it down as the centrepiece of the table, the chef pulled the dome from the platter. As he did so, Fabel saw a flash of bright emerald eyes and knew that the cook was Vasyl Vitrenko. Maria screamed. Fabel thought he heard Ursula Kastner beside him say: 'He is the other.' Fabel gazed mesmerised at the revealed corpse of a young woman lying on her back on the platter, her chest ripped open and the white picket of her ribs prised open and exposed. Her lungs had been torn from the body cavity and thrown over her shoulders. The wings of the Blood Eagle. The ancient Viking sacrificial ritual that had been Vitrenko's signature. Fabel, like Maria, was now screaming in terror but also found himself applauding with all the other guests. Maria turned to him.

'I knew he would come,' she said, suddenly halting her scream. 'We've waited for him to come for so long. But I knew he'd want to say goodbye to you.'

Vitrenko walked around to where Maria was sitting. He held out his hand as if inviting her to dance. Fabel wanted to get up to protest, to defend Maria, but found that he had lost the power of movement. He watched helplessly as Vitrenko led Maria into a shadowy part of the hall. The woman next to Ursula Kastner was bending down and searching for something beneath the table. She sat up, frowning.

'Lost something?' asked Fabel. He recognised her as Ingrid Fischmann, the journalist who had been killed by a bomb the year before. She laughed and made a 'silly me' face.

'My foot . . .' she said. 'I had it here a minute ago . . .'

Fabel woke up.

He lay in the dark, staring at the ceiling. He shifted his legs beneath the covers, just to prove that he could move. He heard Susanne breathing, slow and regular in her dreamless sleep. He heard the late-night sounds of Pöseldorf. The occasional car. A group of people exchanging noisy farewells. He swung his legs round and sat up on the edge of the bed, moving slowly so as not to disturb Susanne. His feet brushed against something. He looked down and saw another pair of feet. Black-booted. Massive. He looked up and saw Vasyl Vitrenko standing before him, his emerald eyes sparkling in the dark.

'Look what I found,' said Vitrenko, and held out a woman's dismembered foot.

Fabel woke up. He sat bolt upright, his face, chest and shoulders cold-damp with sweat. His heart pounded. It took him a moment to satisfy himself that this time he was truly awake. Susanne moaned and turned in the bed but did not waken.

He sat still for a long time but found that, when he laid his head back on the pillow, he couldn't sleep. So many things now buzzed around his head that he could not pin down what was pushing sleep away from his tired brain. He left Susanne in bed, went through to the kitchen and made himself a cup of Friesian tea. He took his cup through to the living room and sat on the sofa.

He had known as soon as he had got out of bed that he was going to read the file. He had known it all evening but had pretended to himself that he could leave it alone. He picked it up. He started to read.

8.

Oliver loved this time of night. The quiet isolation. Cologne glittering against his picture window. He listened to the slightly melancholic jazz that oozed expensively from his Bang & Olufsen system. He leaned back into the soft Italian leather of his chair and sipped at his Scotch and soda, ice tinkling against crystal. It was at this time of night that he could fully contemplate his life: a successful life; a life worth the envy of others; a life expressed through the designer furniture and original art, the twenty-year-old malt and the expensive architecture encasing him. Oliver felt good in his own skin: he had no problems with who he was or what he was.

His feet rested on the coffee table and the notebook computer on his lap. He rubbed his eyes hard with the heels of his hands. Enough was enough: he had spent three hours on the *Anthropophagi* site. Time in another world. There had been several answers to his personal advertisement and he had replied to them all. But he had committed to nothing. There was no doubt that there were risks in what he was doing: he had always before indulged his little foible through prostitutes. To have a volunteer to submit to it willingly and without reward was something he had only recently considered. But he had hesitated to make any firm arrangements or even to take things onto the next level. Out there in the real world he could cover his tracks. He had never used the same escort agency twice, never the same hotel twice, never anything under his own name. Here on the Internet he had remained without flesh, as insubstantial as a ghost. But placing the ad had changed things. Ironically, here in a universe of codes where flesh was formed from high-resolution pixels, he had become more detectable. He had to tread more carefully.

But visiting the site had served its purpose. An hors d'oeuvre. An electronic appetiser to sharpen his hunger for the main course. The real thing.

Tomorrow night. He had arranged everything for Friday evening. Maybe this was an agency he could deal with again. After all, the company's name seemed like a positive omen. What could be more fitting than an escort agency called *À la Carte*?

9.

What struck Fabel right away was that the file wasn't just about murders that had already occurred: it was also about a murder that was expected. That was of course true of any suspected serial killer, but in this case the Cologne police were not just expecting another murder, they even had a pretty clear idea about the day when it would take place.

Cologne's big thing was Karneval, the riotous celebration that took place before Lent every year. As a Protestant North German, Fabel found Karneval alien. He was aware of it, obviously, but he had never experienced it other than through the coverage he had seen on television. Even Cologne was a relatively unknown quantity to him: he had been there only a couple of times and never for very long. As he sank deeper into the case in the file, he found himself lost in an environment of unfamiliar landmarks. It struck him how difficult it would be for a unit such as the one proposed by van Heiden and Wagner to function effectively across the whole of Germany. One land, a score of different cultures. And if you considered East and West, two different histories.

Cologne's Karneval was unique. Further south there were the more traditional forms of Fasching and Fastnacht. In Düsseldorf, Cologne's great rival, or in Mainz, Karneval took a similar form but never quite matched the anarchic exuberance of the Cologne event. And Karneval in Cologne was much more than a date in the diary: it was part of the Cologne psyche. It defined what it meant to be to be a Cologner.

Fabel had already known about the case. Like all killings of their type, the two murders had all the ingredients of a good and lurid headline. The killer that the Cologne police were hunting struck only during Karneval. There had only been two victims: one the previous year, the first the year before that. But the investigating officer – Senior Commissar Benni Scholz – had recognised the modus of the killer as soon as he had arrived at the second murder scene. He had warned his superiors that another homicide could follow within the same Karneval season, fearing that the killer's serial offending might escalate. There hadn't been another murder, but Fabel agreed with the faceless Commissar behind the report that the killer would strike again. This year, during the coming Karneval.

Fabel laid the case files out on the coffee table. Both victims had been in their late twenties, female, single. Their backgrounds showed little commonality. Sabine Jordanski had been a hairdresser. Melissa Schenker had worked from home: some kind of software designer. Where Jordanski had been the life and soul of the party, Schenker had been quiet, reserved and almost reclusive. Jordanski had been native *Kölsch*, born and bred in the city; Schenker had been an outsider from Kassel who had settled in Cologne three years before. The investigation had revealed no shared friends or acquaintances. No links. Other than the way they had met their deaths.

Both women had been strangled. There was evidence of manual strangulation and then the use of a ligature: the male neckties that had been left around their throats as a signature by the killer. Scholz had explained the possible significance of this signature: *Weiberfastnacht* was a key date in the Cologne Karneval calendar. Always held on the last Thursday before Lent, *Weiberfastnacht* was Women's Karneval Day, when women ruled. Every woman in Cologne had, on Women's Karneval Day, the right to demand a kiss from any man. It was also a custom that women had the right, if they saw a man wearing a necktie, to cut it in half. It was intended as a symbol of overturning the traditional authority of men over women. In a more enlightened and equal cultural environment, the custom had become a bit of fun and nothing more. But Commissar Scholz expressed his belief that it meant a great deal more to the killer. He suspected that the killer was motivated either by a psychotic misogyny or a sexually motivated resentment of women. Scholz clearly felt that this view explained the post-mortem disfigurement of the bodies: approximately half a kilo of flesh had been excised from the right buttock of both victims. Fabel could see the Cologne officer's logic, but thought it premature. He suspected that there was more to this killer than met the eye.

Fabel had lost track of time and realised he had been sitting going through the file for a couple of hours by the time Susanne came through, rubbing the sleep from her eyes.

'I woke up and you were gone,' she said, yawning. 'What's wrong? Another one of your bad dreams?'

'No . . . no,' he lied. 'Just couldn't sleep, that's all.'

Susanne saw the file open on the coffee table. The pictures spread out. Dead faces. Forensic reports. 'Oh . . . I see. What's this?' There was more than a hint of suspicion in her voice.

'I've been asked to look at a case in Cologne. Just to offer an opinion.'

Susanne's face clouded. 'You cannot afford to get involved with another case, Jan. Roland Bartz has been more patient than anyone could reasonably expect. He's not going to wait around for ever. But there again, maybe that's what you're hoping for.'

'What are you talking about?'

'You know damned well. You've dithered and fluttered about like some reluctant virgin. I don't think you can go through with it. I think that's what all this is about. You can't commit to leaving the police.'

'That's crap, Susanne. I *have* committed to it. I've resigned. I even turned down an offer from van Heiden and the BKA today.'

'What offer?'

Fabel stared at Susanne for a moment. Her dark eyes burned in the soft light. He already regretted mentioning it.

'It doesn't matter.'

'What offer?'

'They want to create a new unit. A sort of Federal Murder Commission. A unit based here in Hamburg that could take on complex cases elsewhere in Germany. They asked me to set it up and head it.'

Susanne laughed bitterly. 'Great. Absolutely marvellous. I spend all my time worrying about your state of mind because of the crap you have to deal with here and you're off discussing how to increase your workload by seeking out cases across Germany.'

'I told you, I said no.' Fabel had raised his voice. He took a breath and lowered it. 'I said no.'

'What's the matter, Jan? Did you nearly lose your temper? Did you nearly lose control there?'

'Susanne . . .'

'Don't you realise that that is your problem? You're so buttoned up. You were never meant to be a policeman, don't you see that? If it hadn't been for the sainted Hanna Dorn being murdered it would never have occurred to you to become one. For the life of me I don't know why you felt you owed it to her to throw away your future and choose a job that otherwise you would never have considered. Everybody goes on about what a great detective you are. About all the cases you've cleared up. But it's screwed you up. I hear it, Jan. Every other night. The dreams. The night-mares. Don't you see that you're as bad as Maria Klee? You witness all of that horror and the crap that people inflict on each other and you screw it down deep inside. And if you don't stop, you're going to crack up. Big time.'

'You see the same things. You delve into their minds, for God's sake.'

'But don't you see that's different? I *chose* to be a crim-inal psychologist. I trained for it. Prepared for it. I took every step towards my career deliberately. I chose it because it was the direction in which my interests and skills took me. Not because I was diverted into it by some northern bloody Lutheran sense of crusade.' Susanne paused. 'The difference between you and me is that I can deal with it. I can keep it out of my private life.'

'I don't know why we're having this fight . . .' Fabel sat down again. His voice was tired. 'I keep telling you, I'm finished with the Murder Commission. With the Polizei Hamburg.'

'We're having this fight because you won't commit to anything.'

'What's that supposed to mean?'

'You know what it means, Jan. It was your idea for us to move in together, but we've been looking at apartments for months. It doesn't matter what part of town, what type of apartment, you just walk away shrugging your shoulders. You can't commit to changing jobs and you can't commit to me. Why don't you just admit it?'

'How many times have I got to say this, Susanne? I turned them down. Flat. And my resignation is final. In five weeks' time I cease to be a policeman.' Fabel stood up and placed his hands on Susanne's shoulders. 'And I can't help it if we haven't seen an apartment that I like. That doesn't mean I'm not committed to you. You know I am.'

'Are you?' She pushed his hands away. 'Then why have you been so distant? For the last couple of months. I don't know what it is I've said or done, but you've been strange with me. Cold.'

'That's nonsense . . .' said Fabel.

'Is it?' Susanne gestured to the case material on the coffee table. 'And what about this? Is it nonsense that you're taking on a new case when you're supposed to be finishing up?'

'Yes, it is. I told you. I've been asked to offer an opinion. That's all.'

'And of course you couldn't say no.'

'No, I couldn't. Whether you like it or not, Susanne, I'm a policeman for the next five weeks.'

Susanne turned and went back to bed and Fabel stood silently for a moment, looking at the closed bedroom door. Then he sat down and turned his mind again to a distant city and the deaths of two young women in it.

Fabel suddenly became aware that daylight was beginning to fill his flat and a leaden tiredness his body. He had been reading, comparing, taking notes for over three hours. It remained the assumption of the investigating officer, Scholz, that the two victims had been chosen entirely at random. But Fabel had noticed something as he had examined the morgue photographs of the victims: despite the difference in their heights, both women had slightly pear-shaped figures, with a fleshiness around their bottoms, lower belly and thighs.

Fabel read Scholz's notes:

There is no evidence of pre-mortem disfigurement. The comparative lack of blood loss from the site suggests that the victims were first strangled with a ligature, and fibres found embedded in the abraded skin on the necks confirm that the ties left at the scenes were the murder weapons. Inconsistent fibres were found on the tie used in the first murder. These fibres were unusual in colour and composition: blue felt. Once the victims were dead, the perpetrator partially stripped them, turned them face down in the pose in which they were found, and then, post-mortem, excised a quantity of flesh from the buttock or upper thigh of the victims. There is clearly a significance in this disfigurement. The perpetrator removes the flesh symbolically. A point of interest is the quantity of flesh removed. It is possible by exact measurement of the excised area to calculate accurately the weight of flesh removed. In the first case, 0.47 kilos were taken, and 0.4 kilos were cut from the second victim. The similarity in weight seems too close to be coincidental and would suggest that the killer has some expertise in measuring quantities. There is also no deviation from or correction of his incisions. These two facts would suggest that he may be someone used to working with quantities of meat and could be involved in butchery or meat rendering as a career. Similarly, he may be a surgeon or otherwise medically qualified.

The quantity of flesh removed may be significant in itself. In each case it has been extremely close to the 0.45 kilogram measure. This equates to one Imperial pound in weight, as used by the British. This is not to say that the killer is a foreign national, more that 'a pound of flesh' is intended (as in the Shakespeare play The Merchant of Venice) *and therefore is a metaphor for recovering justice from the victims. This could suggest that the killer was known to his victims.*

It is clear from the consistency of modus that the perpetrator of the first murder also carried out the second homicide. This, added to the symbolism of the tie left at each scene and the significance of Karneval, and the implied expression of psychosexual hatred of women all point to a serial offender.

Fabel leafed through the file. *Weiberfastnacht* had another name. *Fetter Donnerstag*. Fat Thursday. A day devoted to gluttony.

'No, Herr colleague,' Fabel said under his breath as he re-examined the scene-of-crime images. 'Our friend isn't interested in collecting mementos. He's hungry. His pound of flesh isn't a trophy: it's a meal.'

The phone rang.

10.

They stood and stared at the three clear plastic packages on Anna's desk: one containing an ancient-looking Walther P4 handgun, the other holding a carrier bag with cash and the third with a large dog-eared book in it. Each of them was sealed and labelled with a blue evidence tag.

'We found it outside the store,' said Anna Wolff, indicating the book. She was in charge of the case. 'Philosophy. That's what Tschorba studied – at one time, anyway.'

Fabel continued to stare silently at the evidence bags.

Anna ran through what had happened in the convenience store. The Turkish owner had said in his statement that Breidenbach had died bravely; that the young policeman had been determined that the robber would not go out into the street with a handgun. He also stated that he had got the idea to jump Tschorba from Breidenbach, who had told the gunman that he couldn't take them both. As Timo Tschorba had fired the fatal shots into Breidenbach's body, the shopkeeper had thrown himself at him. Tschorba was now in the cells, his swollen and bruised face bearing the marks of the encounter with the Turk. Once the shopkeeper had disarmed the junkie, he had rushed over to Breidenbach, but the young policeman was already dead. He admitted that when he had seen that, he had gone back and pistol-whipped Tschorba, who had cried like a child.

'I can't believe it,' said Fabel at last. 'He was there. I mean Breidenbach. He was there at the Aichinger incident. He was the MEK trooper who came up to the apartment with me.' He shook his head mournfully. 'I behaved like an arsehole . . . I treated Breidenbach as if he were less of a policeman than me. Just because he was a tactical weapons specialist. I was wrong. He was a police officer first and foremost.'

Anna went through the statement, including Tschorba's confession, the ballistics and forensics report and the initial observations from Möller, the pathologist. Fabel took in very little. It was the Murder Commission mantra of dry facts and figures, of times and causes of death, of wounded flesh and rendered fabric. He had heard it so, so many times before. His thoughts still held him on a landing of a block of flats in Jenfeld with a young MEK trooper just starting his career as Fabel was ending his. He found he could not forgive himself for making sweeping judgements about Breidenbach's motivations and ambitions. Fabel thought about Breidenbach's youth, about how fit he had been, and then imagined him lying grey and blood-drained on Möller's stainless steel autopsy table, sliced open, the vestigial warmth from his inner organs dissipating into the cool autopsy-room air.

After Anna's briefing, he asked Werner to come into his office. This had become an almost daily ritual since Fabel's resignation: the gradual transfer of responsibility to his friend. It had always been Maria that he had envisaged taking over, but that was simply not going to happen. He updated Werner on the caseload, confirming that Anna and Henk Hermann should see through the Breidenbach murder. When they were finished Fabel switched on his voicemail and took his jacket from behind the door.

'I'm finishing for the afternoon. Got shopping to do,' he explained to Werner. He indicated his desk, the files still lying on it from their meeting. 'Why don't you do your paperwork there? Might as well get used to it.'

II.

Ansgar busied himself in the kitchen. To an outsider, a restaurant kitchen would seem the definition of chaos: orders shouted over the sound of food sizzling or boiling, cookers and ventilators running at industrial noise levels, staff weaving between each other in a rushed ballet. But for Ansgar, his kitchen was the only place of true order that he knew. The dance of the kitchen staff, the rhythm of pan and oven: he orchestrated it all. No one ever had to wait too long for their order; no dish arrived under- or overcooked. His reputation was that of the artist tempered by the perfectionist.

Ansgar had never married. He had never met anyone who would have understood his *particular* needs. And those needs would have eventually emerged. There had been women, but again he had kept his behaviour within the range of that which should be expected. For the other needs, for his true needs, there had been the women he had paid. And he had had to pay well. But Ansgar's lack of a normal romantic life had meant he had no wife. The closest he had to a child was Adam, whom he was training. Adam was nineteen, eager and hard-working. Ansgar found in Adam someone to whom he could pass on the sacred knowledge of the *chef de cuisine*.

Ansgar had set the machinery of the kitchen in motion for luncheon. Each member of staff undertaking their preparatory roles. He took Adam to one side, taking this time to induct his protégé in yet another level of the culinary arts.

'I want you to prepare the *Wildschweinschinken*. It goes on the menu this lunchtime.'

'Yes, *Chef*,' said Adam eagerly. Ansgar had previously allowed him to prepare the leg of wild boar. He had carefully mixed the coating of herbs, spices and mustards, exactly to Ansgar's otherwise secret recipe, and had rubbed them into the boar flesh. That had been a month ago, and the wild pig's leg had been marinating and curing in the big storage refrigerator since then. Adam brought the boar ham from the fridge and placed it on the carving board.

'We will carve this slice by slice only as and when an order comes in,' said Ansgar. 'But I want you to practise carving a couple of slices from it. Also, I intend to serve it with a salad. I want you to suggest something appropriate.'

Adam frowned. 'Well . . .'

'No, not yet. First I want you to carve the meat. Examine its texture, its consistency.'

Adam nodded and, holding the leg with the carving fork, placed his blade against it.

'Wait,' said Ansgar patiently. 'I want you to think more about your cut. Not just how thick or thin to carve the slices. I want you to think about the beast this meat came from. Close your eyes and picture it.'

Adam looked embarrassed for a moment, then closed his eyes.

'Can you see it?'

'Yes. A wild boar.'

'Okay. Now I want you to think about where it foraged for food in the forest. About its shape, about the speed with which it could run. I want you to visualise that for a moment. Can you see it?'

'Yes.'

'Okay. Now open your eyes and carve. Then, without thinking any more about it, I want you to tell me what salad I should serve it with.'

Adam shaved a perfect flake of ham from the joint, placed it on a plate and looked at Ansgar, beaming. 'It should be served with wild mushroom, fennel, orange and rocket salad.'

'Do you see? Do you see what happens when you think beyond the food, beyond the meat . . . to the living flesh? Do that, and you will be a great cook, Adam. Do that, and you will always understand the true nature of the food that you serve.'

With that, Ansgar stole a glance across the kitchen at Ekaterina.

12.

Fabel wanted to buy a polo-neck sweater so he headed down to the Alsterhaus department store on Jungfernstieg, next to the Alster lake. Shopping in the Alsterhaus was a luxury he afforded himself perhaps a little too frequently, but he enjoyed browsing in its halls and treating himself to a morsel or two from the cheese bistro on the store's top floor. He had decided to walk into town and the promise of a fine morning had been fulfilled: the blanket of grey had broken up and the sky was a cold, bright blue.

As he approached Jungfernstieg, he heard music. Fabel noticed a group of about a dozen men and women harmonising in a language that you didn't need to understand to know that this was a song about pain and sorrow. The choir stood on the wide pavement a few metres from the deco-arched entrance to the Alsterhaus. Three men of Slavic appearance, like fishermen in a stream, were trying to hook the attention of passers-by. One of them approached Fabel.

'We're collecting signatures, sir. I wonder if I might trouble you for a moment.'

'I'm afraid I'm—'

'I'm sorry, sir, I won't keep you. But do you know anything about the Holodomor?' The Slav held him with a steady, inquisitive gaze. Fabel noticed the man's eyes. Piercing blue, and cold; like the winter-morning sky above them. He felt a lurch in his gut as he thought of another Slav he had known who had piercingly bright eyes.

'Are you Ukrainian?' Fabel asked.

'Yes, I am.' The Slav smiled. 'The Holodomor was the deliberate genocide of my people, carried out by the Soviet Union and Stalin. Between seven and ten million Ukrainians died. One quarter of the Ukrainian population. Starved to death by the Soviets between nineteen thirty-two and thirty-three.' He flicked open the folder he had been holding beneath his clipboard. It was filled with grainy black-and-white photographs of human misery: emaciated children, bodies lying in the street, huge communal grave pits being filled with stick-like bodies. The images were redolent of those that Fabel had grown to associate with the Holocaust. 'At one point, twenty-five thousand Ukrainians were dying every day. And practically no one outside Ukraine knows about the Holodomor. Even in Ukraine it was only after independence that we spoke about it openly. Russia still refuses to acknowledge that the Holodomor was an act of deliberate genocide. They say it was the result of incompetent collectivisation by Stalin's commissars.'

'And you dispute this?' said Fabel. He looked at his watch to check how much time he had before he was due to meet Susanne on the top floor of the Alsterhaus.

'It's a downright lie,' continued the Slav, undeterred. 'People starved to death all over the Soviet Union because of Stalin's insane collectivisation mania. That's true. But in nineteen twenty-seven we had started to Ukrainianise our country. We made Ukrainian, not Russian, our official language. Stalin saw us as a threat, so he tried to exterminate us by starving us. More than twenty-five per cent of the Ukrainian population were wiped out. Please, your signature will help us have this crime recognised for what it is: genocide. We need the German and British and other governments to do what Spain has already done and formally recognise the Holodomor as a crime against humanity.'

'I'm sorry. I'm not saying that I won't support your claim, but I can't sign this until I know more about what happened. I need to find out more about it for myself.'

'I understand.' The man handed Fabel a leaflet. 'This tells you where you can get more information. Not just from our organisation. But please, sir, when you have read all of this, please visit our website and add your name to our list there.'

When Fabel looked up from the leaflet the Ukrainian was already hooking another shopper from the stream on the pavement.

Fabel made his way up to the top floor of the Alsterhaus. Susanne wasn't there when he arrived, so he bought a coffee and sat in the café by the escalators and with a view of their agreed meeting place. He looked for a moment at the leaflet he had been handed by the Ukrainian. Fabel hadn't come across the name 'Holodomor' before, but he had heard of the great starvation in the nineteen-thirties. In the nineteen-eighties, the Ukrainian serial killer Andrei Chikatilo had cited the Holodomor as part of the reason he had turned cannibal. Chikatilo's brother had been murdered and eaten by starving villagers, but all that had been before Chikatilo's birth. One detail that the campaigners, quite understandably, had chosen to omit from the leaflet was that the Holodomor had resulted in mass cannibalism. The Soviet authorities had set up special tribunals to try and execute people found to have consumed human flesh. Distraught parents had had to find secret burial places when a child died because it was so common for the corpse to be dug up as meat. Worse still, there had been many instances of parents killing and eating their own children. Even today in Ukraine, there was an unusually high number of serial murders involving cannibalism.

But for Fabel, Ukraine had only one significance: that it had been the dark cradle out of which Vasyl Vitrenko had crawled. It was maybe this thought that prompted Fabel to take out his mobile and call Maria Klee. The phone rang a few times, then the tone changed as his call was redirected to her cellphone. Her voice sounded flat and dull as she answered.

'Maria? It's Jan. I thought I'd give you a ring to see how you are doing. Is this a bad time?' Fabel had had the idea that Maria hadn't ventured out from her apartment much during her sick leave. He took her not being at home as a positive sign.

'Oh, I'm fine . . .' Maria sounded taken aback. 'I'm just doing some shopping. How are you?'

'I'm okay. Shopping too, in the Alsterhaus. How's therapy going?' Fabel winced at his own clumsiness. There was a short pause at the other end of the phone.

'Fine. Making progress. I'll be back at work soon. It won't be the same without you.'

'Is that good or bad?' Fabel's laugh sounded fake.

'Bad.' No laugh. 'Jan . . . I think I might give it up too.'

'Maria, you're an excellent police officer. You still have a great future to look forward to.' Fabel heard himself repeat what had been said to him so many times by his own superiors. 'But it's your decision. If there's one thing I've learnt over the last couple of years, it's that if you feel you have to do something, don't wait. Do it.'

'That's exactly what I've been thinking. Recently . . . well, with all of the things that have happened . . .' There was something about Maria's voice – a detachedness, a remoteness – that emphasised for Fabel every centimetre of empty air it traversed on the crest of a microwave. It was the voice of someone lost and Fabel felt panic rise in his chest.

'Maria . . . why don't I come over later and see you? I think it would be good to talk . . .'

'I would like that . . . but not now, Jan. I'm not ready to see anyone from work. I think . . . you know, with my therapy and everything . . . Actually, Dr Minks has said it would be better for me to avoid contact with colleagues for a while.'

'Oh? I understand,' Fabel said, although he didn't. 'Maybe soon.'

They said goodbye and Fabel hung up. When he looked up he saw that Susanne had arrived and was scanning the Alsterhaus for him.

Chapter Three

19–21 January

Maria switched off her cellphone before slipping it back into her jacket pocket. She hadn't actually told Fabel a lie, but what she had done was effectively lying by omission.

The furnishings were typical budget hotel. She took her clothes from her suitcase and folded them into the cheap laminated chest of drawers, moving, as always, with economical precision. After Maria had unpacked, and with the same economy of movement, she hung up her jacket on a hanger, walked through to the small dimly lit en-suite bathroom, knelt down by the toilet bowl and inserted her long, manicured index finger into her mouth. Her vomiting was almost instantaneous. The first few times she had done this it had taken a long time: eye-watering, unproductive retching before she finally threw up. But now she had refined the action to a hair-trigger mechanism, allowing her to void her stomach with speed and ease. She stood up, rinsed her mouth at the washbasin and returned to the bedroom.

She went across to the window and swung it open. There was a lot of activity in the street below. Voices that were not German reached up to her: Turkish, Parsi, Russian. Ukrainian. This part of the city merged and mingled cultures rather than stitched them together in a patchwork. The hotel had six storeys and Maria's room was on the top floor; she looked out over rooftops huddled under the dark and heavy winter sky. Directly across was an apartment with a rooftop terrace. All the lights were on and Maria could see a woman cleaning the apartment. She was youngish with a mass of dark hair and a voluptuous figure. Maria speculated that the woman was Turkish. It looked to Maria as if she was singing as she vacuumed. Maria had no idea if the woman lived in the apartment or was merely a cleaner, but whatever her status or situation she looked to Maria as if she was someone totally comfortable with who, where and what she was. Maria felt a pang of jealousy and looked away.

It was sunny in faraway Hamburg, she thought as she gazed at the massive dark spires of Cologne Cathedral piercing the sullen sky.

2.

It was Susanne's deliberate cheerfulness that got to Fabel the most. He knew that she was doing her best not to let her anger with him reach boiling point again. Susanne was from Munich and culturally oriented towards the South and the Mediterranean. Fabel often envied her ability to let her emotions boil over and in doing so extinguish the flame beneath them. Fabel, on the other hand, was aware of his doubly northern mixed heritage. He kept a lid on things. Like a pressure cooker.

'What's that?' Susanne asked, pointing to the leaflet on the table. Fabel explained briefly about the encounter with the Ukrainian protester on Jungfernstieg outside the Alsterhaus.

'Oh . . . yes, I saw them. Didn't know they were Ukrainians, though. You know me, I just barge on through anybody I think is trying to sell me something.'

'It would have to be Ukrainians,' said Fabel gloomily. 'Why is it that so many Ukrainians have such striking eyes? You know, very pale, bright blue and green?'

'Genetics, probably. Didn't you tell me once that Ukrainians have a lot of Viking blood?'

'Mmm . . .' Fabel was clearly still struggling to wrap himself around jumbled, random thoughts. 'It's just something I've noticed. And of course . . .' He stopped himself.

'Vitrenko?' said Susanne with a sigh. 'Jan, I thought you'd laid that ghost to rest.'

'I have. It's just that he came to mind. You know, with meeting that Ukrainian outside.' Sensing the potential for another argument, he dropped the subject and spoke instead of his forthcoming weekend trip to see his mother, and how it was a pity that Susanne, whom his mother had always liked, couldn't come.

But all the time he spoke, something about the conversation he'd had with Maria nagged at him. He made a promise to himself to go and see her when he got back from his mother's. No matter what Dr Minks had said.

After lunch they headed to Otto Jensen's bookshop in the Arkaden, just a short walk from the Alsterhaus. Otto had invited them to come along to an afternoon book launch. Otto Jensen had been Fabel's closest friend since university. He was tall, skinny and one of the clumsiest individuals that Fabel had ever known, yet behind the clumsiness lay a razor-sharp intellect. Otto loved books, and his bookshop was probably the most successful independent in the city. But Fabel had often thought that his friend could have achieved a great deal in some other field.

Otto greeted them cheerfully but muttered under his breath that the book that was being launched was incredibly dull.

'Couldn't tell you that before,' explained Otto, 'or you wouldn't have come. Sorry . . . but I need you to pad out the crowd.'

'What are friends for?' said Fabel.

'Listen, the wine's not bad at all this time. You're half-Scottish, half-Frisian . . . I thought you'd do anything for a free drink.'

*   *   *

Otto had arranged a small reception after the event for the author and some of the guests. People stood in clusters, sipping wine and chatting. Susanne and Otto's wife Else had become close friends and were deep in a conversation about somebody that Fabel didn't know when Otto took him by the elbow and steered him away.

'There's someone I'd like you to meet,' Otto said.

'Not the author, please . . .' pleaded Fabel. He had found the event, and the author, as tedious as Otto had promised.

'No. Not at all. This is someone *infinitely* more interesting.'

Otto guided Fabel across to a shortish man of about fifty who was dressed in a beige linen suit that looked as if it had been worn every day for a week without making the passing acquaintance of an iron.

'This is Kurt Lessing,' explained Otto. The man in the crumpled suit extended a hand. He had an intelligent face that hid a certain handsomeness behind too-big spectacles that needed to be wiped clean. 'I should warn you that Kurt is quite mad. But really interesting to talk to.'

'Thanks for the introduction,' said Lessing. He smiled at Fabel. But his attention focused immediately on Susanne who had joined them. He gave a half-bow and raised her hand to his lips. 'It is my pleasure,' he said and grinned wolfishly at her. Fabel laughed at the deliberately conspicuous display of attraction. 'You are an extraordinarily beautiful woman, Frau Doctor Eckhardt.'

'Thank you,' said Susanne.

'I have to point out,' said Otto, 'that despite seeming to state the obvious, Susanne, it is actually an enormous honour for Kurt to say such a thing. You see, he is one of the world's experts on female beauty.'

'Really?' Susanne regarded Lessing sceptically.

'Indeed I am,' said Lessing, with another small bow. 'I have written the definitive work on female beauty over the centuries and across cultures. It is my speciality.'

'You're an author?' asked Fabel.

'I'm an anthropologist,' said Lessing, without taking his eyes from Susanne. 'And, to a lesser extent, an art critic. I have combined the two fields.' At last he turned to Fabel. 'I study the anthropology of art and aesthetics. I have written a book about the female form over the centuries. About how our ideal of beauty has transformed so radically over time.'

'Has it changed so much?' asked Susanne. 'This is something that interests me. I am a psychologist.'

'Beauty *and* intelligence. Now that has been universally attractive throughout the human experience. But to answer your question, yes, it really has undergone radical variations. What is particularly interesting is that our ideal of female beauty has changed more rapidly over the last century than at any time in human history. There is no doubt that mass media has played a key part. All you have to do is to compare the screen sirens of the forties and fifties with the stick-thin fashion models of today. What I find particularly amazing is the way that, within a given time, one will find different ideals of beauty running concurrently within the same culture.'

'What do you mean?' asked Susanne.

'No man finds the stick-thin catwalk model attractive. It is a woman's definition of female beauty. This imperative to be thin is a strange tyranny exerted on women by women. It is what differentiates us as genders that make us attractive to each other. Men like curves, women like angles.'

'But that contradicts what you said before,' said Fabel. A joke was a joke, but he was beginning to get fed up with the small man's preoccupation with Susanne. 'You said that the "ideal" of feminine beauty has changed throughout the centuries.'

'True, but within set parameters. If you look at the classical ideal of beauty as set out in Greek or Roman sculpture, it is pretty consistent with, say, the nineteen-fifties ideal. Then came a preoccupation with a large bust. However, if you look at Renaissance art, breasts were always small and firm. In those days, the big bust was associated with the wet-nurse: the lower-class woman who nursed babies for wealthier mothers determined to maintain their figures. There have been radical swings in fashion, the most extreme being the near-obese Titian model. But, generally speaking, there have been limits.'

Fabel thought about the murdered women in Cologne. About how they seemed to have fuller hips and bottoms.

'What about bottoms?' he asked. 'Have there been fashions in bums?'

'Obviously in the eighteen-hundreds there was a real fixation with them. The bustle exaggerated the bottom to an extreme and physically impossible degree. But generally the function of the hips and bottom has been to accentuate the narrowness of the waist. And that certainly was the intention with the bustle. It isn't a single body part that is important: it is its relationship with other parts. All fat women have full bottoms but obesity is unattractive. Men who are attracted to larger bottoms tend to look for the contrast with a narrow waist. It's part of our most primitive psychology. We assess the figure of another to judge their fitness and suitability as a sexual partner.'

After they left the event Fabel and Susanne took a taxi back to her apartment.

'I rather think he fancied me,' she said laughingly.

'Mmm.'

'What's wrong?' Susanne looped her arm through Fabel's. 'You jealous? He really wasn't my type . . .'

Fabel smiled. But his mind was still elsewhere, putting together an image of a woman in his mind. He knew exactly the type. The type the Cologne cannibal would target next, unless Scholz was able to get to him first.

3.

The couple in the corner kept distracting Andrea from her calculations. Every time she totalled the takings for the previous month a raised male voice would make her lose her place. Last month had not been as good as she had hoped. The café did good but simple food and she had put on a basic Christmas menu of traditional favourites and had decorated the place, but the café was just that little bit too far out from the city centre to attract the masses of tourists that came for Cologne's Christmas Market. Even the bank of flat-monitored computers that she had installed along the high counter at the back of the café had failed to pay for themselves. She was struggling to break even and it annoyed her that she needed her 'extra' income to supplement what she made from the café.

Andrea gave up on her calculations and checked her cellphone. There was a text message from the agency: two bookings. The one for tomorrow night was annoying because of the ridiculously short notice, but it was the second booking that froze Andrea's attention. A special date. *Weiberfastnacht.* Why would someone want to book Women's Karneval Night? Why did it have to be that date of all dates? She texted back to the agency saying she could make the booking tonight if they sent her details. The other one . . . The other one she would have to think about.

The sound of raised voices snapped her attention back to the café.

The couple had been building up to it. Or rather the man had been building up to it. They had only ordered coffee and the scene had all the hallmarks of them having sought out the café as nothing more than a place for them to sit and carry on the one-sided argument they had clearly been having outside. Andrea studied them: he was a loathsome little toad; she was surprisingly pretty to be with the likes of him. But soft. Andrea had begun by occasionally glancing in their direction; listening to the odd exchange as she had worked the tables. But as their argument became louder, it became impossible to ignore. And it was beginning to disturb the other customers. With a sigh, Andrea closed her accounts and crossed the café.

'Is there a problem?' Resting her red-fingernailed hands on the table, Andrea leaned in close and spoke in a calm, quiet tone. The couple had been so engrossed in their heated exchange that they had not noticed Andrea approach. The young man turned his acne towards her. His eyes traced the contours of her body. Andrea was wearing a tight black T-shirt with the café's logo on it. Her biceps bulged beneath the short sleeves, and her breasts were pulled into small, tight buns on her wide, taut pectoral muscles. There was a trace of a smirk on the man's lips.

'What's it to you?' The smirk ripened into a sneer.

'You're beginning to disturb the other customers.' Andrea kept her voice calm and low. 'That's what it is to me. I think you should leave. Now.'

'What about our coffees?' asked the man. The girl had her head down, letting her hair fall like a curtain to hide her face from the other customers in the café.

'You've drunk most of them,' said Andrea. 'Leave the rest. It's on the house.'

'Just what the fuck are you?' The young man with the acne now seemed aware he had an audience. He leaned back as if appraising her: the mane of platinum hair tied back in a ponytail, the heavy make-up, the deep red lipstick, the power-lifter shoulders. 'I mean, we were just trying to work that out – what you were born as. Male or female. Fuck knows I can't tell now. You a shemale?'

Andrea straightened up. 'Leave. Now.'

'What makes you think you can work here among *normal* people? I mean, they sell food in here, for fuck's sake. People *eat* here. You're enough to turn anyone's stomach.'

Still his female partner sat still and silent behind her curtain of hair.

'You've got two seconds to leave,' said Andrea, her calm tone belying the furnace of hate and anger that burned in her belly. 'Or I'll call the cops.'

The man got up and tugged at the girl's sleeve. She rose quickly, slid out from behind the table and slipped swiftly out of the café without making eye contact with anyone. The ugly young man eyed Andrea hatefully. He tried to push her out of the way but Andrea's body wouldn't yield.

'Fucking freak . . .' He laughed derisively as he was forced to squeeze past her sideways. Andrea watched them as they left the café and walked past the window, the man laughing through the glass at her, his companion still trying to be unnoticed. When they were out of sight Andrea took a deep breath and turned to the other customers with a broad smile of red lips and strong white teeth.

'Sorry about that,' she said. There were a few regulars amongst the customers and one of them said: 'Well done – that's the way to deal with trash like that.'

Andrea kept her smile in place. 'Could you spell me for a while, Britta?' she asked the other waitress and strode into the kitchen. Andrea swiftly exited through the back door onto the alley. She sprinted along the narrow lane to where a side street ran at right angles to Eintrachtstrasse, then up to the junction with Cordulastrasse. They were there. The girl still had her head bowed while the little shit berated her loudly about something. Their body language, his aggressive, hers submissive, expressed to the world the whole dynamic of their relationship; and Andrea could see that violence played a part in it. There were hardly any other pedestrians and only a few cars passed along the slushy-wet road, with the sound of waves on a shore. Andrea ducked back around the corner. The cold air turned the skin of her salon-tanned naked arms into gooseflesh. But inside the rage still burned.

The man was too busy shouting abuse at the girl to notice Andrea blocking his way. He looked startled as she grabbed the front of his coat and dragged him into the side street.

'What did you call me?' Her face hardened into sinew under the make-up. He didn't answer and she slammed him hard against the brickwork. 'I said: what the *fuck* did you call me?'

'I . . . I . . .' The little shit's expression betrayed his fear and confusion.

Andrea looked at his pasty, acne-covered face. Deep inside her, someone opened the door of the blast furnace of her hate. It surged up in her, white-hot. Her forehead slammed into his face and she felt his nose break. She let him go and he stared at her wildly, his face covered in blood. Andrea took advantage of his shock and slammed a boot hard into his groin. Gasping and retching, he sunk to his knees, clutching his crushed testicles. Andrea turned to the girl. She was staring, horrified, at her boyfriend as he keeled over and lay on his side on the pavement. Mouth open, a strangled scream in her throat, her eyes filled with tears.

'You're worse than him,' Andrea spoke to the girl in a disgusted tone. 'You're worse for playing the victim. For putting up with it. I despise you. I despise all women like you. Why do you let him treat you like that . . . in *public*? Have you no self-respect?'

The girl was still staring at her boyfriend. Shock and fear on her face. Andrea snorted, turned on her heel and strode back towards the café. As she did so, the girl's shrill screaming rang in her ears: 'You freak! You sick fucking FREAK!'

4.

Maria sat on the edge of the hotel bed and assessed her plan: she knew that the only way to conquer chaos was to have a plan.

The idea had come to her when Liese had phoned her just after all the trouble with Frank. Liese was an old school friend from Hanover with whom Maria had kept in touch. She knew all about Maria's problems and had always been supportive. Liese had offered Maria a chance to get away from it all: to come and spend a few days with her in Cologne. Maria had thanked her but had said no. She would need more than a short break in Cologne for what she had planned. Then it had all come together: Liese had phoned Maria and told her that work meant that she had to go to Japan for three months. The opportunity had come up unexpectedly and had caught Liese somewhat on the hop and she was worried about her flat lying empty. Maria would be doing her a favour if she stayed in the flat. Liese knew that Maria needed a change of scene, so the arrangement seemed ideal. But Liese had found it a little strange when Maria asked her to tell only her immediate neighbours about the arrangement, and even then only to give them Maria's first name.

'I need to be anonymous for a while,' Maria had explained. The flat was in the Belgian Quarter near one of the gates that were remnants of Cologne's old city wall. Liese had told Maria that the Dresslers, the only neighbours on the same floor, were a young professional couple without kids who were out at work all day and were also often out in the evening. There were a couple of families on the floor below and on the ground floor there was a younger man whom Liese never really ran into, as well as another young professional couple. It was perfect. But it would not be enough on its own: she would need more than one safe house. In any case, Liese would not be leaving until the end of the week. Maria had decided to check into the budget hotel for a few days. She might even keep the hotel room for a while after she moved into the flat.

She took her laptop from her briefcase.

Sitting on the bed, Maria opened up the files she had

accessed from the BKA database before she took her sick leave. There had been a limit to what her clearance as a Hamburg Murder Commission detective had allowed her to access and the information was general, but there were enough pieces of the picture to give her a starting point. She had even endured a lunch appointment with a woman she had been at the Landespolizeischule academy with and who was now a hotshot with the BKA Federal Crime Bureau. Maria had noticed the look of alarm on her table companion's face when she saw how changed Maria was. Maria had been able to establish the existence of a much more detailed dossier on Vitrenko, but then the BKA woman had become reluctant to discuss it further. Maria suspected that she had become concerned about Maria's state of mind.

Maria knew she was not well. It had only been after several sessions with Dr Minks that she had come to recognise that her behaviour had become odd; that she had slipped into a world of bizarre rituals and obsessions, one laid over the other and obscuring her view of what was normal in life. Since the stabbing she had struggled most with aphen-phosmphobia, a morbid fear of physical contact with other human beings. Since the affair with Frank she had suffered a severe depression and had developed an eating disorder. Now, Maria could barely look at herself in a mirror without a sense of revulsion. But she did look in a mirror often: she would strip naked and stand before a full-length glass for an hour, her self-loathing intense and vast. She would look at herself and despise the flesh of which she was composed. And, most of all, she would stare at her image and wish she could be someone else. Anyone else. It was all part of the mental chaos through which she had to stumble just to get through each day. But enough of the old Maria, the organised, meticulous, efficient Maria had still been there for her to assemble her own detailed dossier before she took her sick leave.

It had been the day she had heard that the Ukrainian investigator Turchenko had been killed in a road crash that she had decided to gather all the information she could on Vitrenko and his organisation. Turchenko, a quiet, polite, highly intelligent lawyer turned investigator, had passed though Hamburg while on the trail of Vasyl Vitrenko. Turchenko had asked Maria to describe in detail the events that had led up to Vitrenko stabbing her. She had tried to explain to the Ukrainian detective, as she had tried to explain to the counsellors and psychologists after the event, that what had really destroyed any feeling of self-worth that she might have had was the way Vitrenko had not intended to kill her. Instead, he had used his expertise to place the knife where it would leave her hanging onto life by a thread. All Maria had represented to Vitrenko was a delaying tactic. Vitrenko had known that by leaving Maria alive but critically wounded Fabel would have to give up his pursuit. She had been used. Her body had been defiled by Vitrenko just as if she had been raped by him.

And now Maria couldn't stand the sight of her own flesh, or the touch of others. The therapy hadn't helped. Talk. Maria wasn't someone who believed you could solve things by talking them to death.

Maria knew that, comprehensive as it was, the information she had compiled was not complete. She felt frustrated at the idea that, right now, there was a secret investigation going on that involved a number of Federal and local law-enforcement agencies. It had been brought to her attention when she had been reprimanded by the BKA in the presence of Fabel and Criminal Director van Heiden. Maria had been photographed by their surveillance operation talking to key figures. She had, they said, seriously compromised the operation. Maria had gained the partial trust of a young Russian prostitute working the rougher end of the Hamburg trade. Nadja had given Maria information and had disappeared immediately afterwards. The BKA had made a point of high-lighting that Maria's clumsiness had probably cost Nadja her life.

But she wouldn't make the same mistakes again. Maria knew that the surveillance operation was probably still active, but this time she would work around it. Large police operations like that always looked at the bigger picture, building connections, establishing command structures, identifying key locations; hundreds of experts working on the detail while the investigative management stood back to see the whole. But the core of Vitrenko's operations was people trafficking. These weren't stolen cars, the licence numbers of which could be logged and filed. These were people and at the heart of each statistic lay a human tragedy. That would be Maria's way in. To start with the victims and work back. And because she was here unofficially – without authority or even legitimacy – she could work with the gloves off. It was something she had to do alone, but she found herself wishing that Anna Wolff was there. Anna was no great lover of rules, but Fabel and Werner were both sticklers for procedure. Anna would be willing to break heads and bend rules; Maria was going to have to work the same way.

Maria placed her SIG-Sauer service automatic on the bed next to the laptop. And then the other gun: a 9mm Glock 26 Compact. Maria had studied law before becoming a police officer, all set for a high-flying career. The law had been everything to her, the thread that held the fabric of society together, that gave order to the world. In obtaining this other gun she had, for the first time in her life, broken the law. Maria was still a police officer. It would be her training and skills that would lead her to Vitrenko. But then . . . then, if she were to get that far alive, it would be the Glock in her hand. Maria had no intention of arresting him.

She went through the files on her computer again. The Farmers' Market: that was what the organised sale of humans from Ukraine, Russia, Poland and elsewhere in the East was called. Not a title invented by the investigators, but the name given it by the criminals who organised it. A fitting title for the sale of people as meat. She opened up a spreadsheet document on which she had plotted all the salient points of the investigation. It was a view of a torn spider's web: as many connections missing as there were present. There was practically nothing for Maria to go on. Vitrenko's organisation was supremely well constructed: layers of management and production, just like any corporate structure, but engineered in such a way that each level operated without knowledge of who was on the tier above or below. Even on the same organisational level, 'cells' often operated without knowledge of each other. Each cell was led by a *pakhan,* or boss, who took his orders from a 'brigadier' who ran as many as ten *pakhans.* The foot soldiers never knew who the 'brigadier' was who transmitted their orders to them through their *pakhan.* Added to this was the use of freelance specialists who were not full-time members of the organisation and who were often not Ukrainian or Russian. In this way, the Ukrainian Mafia had a completely different form from the Italian Mafia. It was also infinitely more difficult to investigate and prosecute than its Italian counterpart.

But Maria didn't need to find evidence. She wasn't interested in building a case. All she wanted to do was find Vitrenko.

Maria laid another file next to the other items. A face looked out from a military service photograph. Colonel Vasyl Vitrenko, formerly of the *Berkut* counter-terrorist Spetsnaz. Maria had stared at this face so often, so intensely, that it should have lost its power to churn her gut. It hadn't. Every time she looked at the bright green Ukrainian eyes, the high, broad cheekbones and wide forehead framed by thick butter-blond hair, she felt a twinge in her chest, just below the breastbone. Where her scar was.

Of course, Vitrenko would probably look nothing like that

now. Turchenko, the investigator who had been killed on his way to Cologne, had been certain that Vitrenko would have changed his appearance radically, probably by cosmetic surgery.

'But you can't change those,' Maria said to the photograph. 'You can't change your eyes.'

5.

The bar was dimly lit and Annett Louisan played in the background. The décor was conspicuously trendy, the clientele well heeled and the drinks expensive. Oliver realised that this was going to cost him a fortune before they had even left the bar. He sat on a bar stool, leaning on the counter, drinking a cocktail made with white rum and looking at his reflection in the smoked-glass mirror behind the bar. He smiled a knowing smile to himself. Things were never what they seemed to be; *people* were never who they seemed to be. Oliver was handsome; his clothes were as trendy and expensive as any in the bar; he certainly was intelligent, highly educated; he was a respected professional with an excellent income; and since he'd arrived in the bar he had caught the eye of several attractive women. If anyone knew that he was here to meet a *professional* companion, they would have found it difficult to understand. But Oliver understood. And he was quite comfortable with the reasons why he found himself in a situation like this. His needs were so *specific*.

He reflected on this for a moment as Annett Louisian held a particularly breathy note in the background. Oliver had never had to spend anguished hours trying to isolate some subliminally erotic encounter that would explain his 'predilection'. It was all so classically *Freudian*: involving, as it did, a female cousin, a particularly languorous summer by the sea, and a singular moment in which his understanding of what it was to be a creature of flesh had been born.

Oliver's cousin Sylvia was two years older than him. She had always been there somewhere in the background of the family landscape but, because his uncle and aunt lived far out in the country near the coast, she had not figured much in his early consciousness. Oliver's first real awareness of Sylvia had been an awareness of her curves; when he'd been fourteen and she sixteen. Sylvia's figure had been full but not fat: she was voluptuous but firm, sturdily, lithely athletic. She was the daughter of Oliver's mother's brother, but she had borne no resemblance to their side of the family: she had had her mother's red-blonde hair and freckled skin. Sylvia had always been an outdoor girl. Adventurous, robust; but even at sixteen too charged with feminine sexuality ever to be considered a tomboy. Despite her being naturally pale, Sylvia's complexion had been burnished a light gold-bronze and the freckles darkened by long summers under the seaside sun. More than anything else, Oliver remembered her figure: perfectly rounded breasts and, most of all, her big, beautiful, glorious bottom.

There had been a group of them that day, including Oliver's younger brother and sister and Sylvia's three giggling, stupid sisters. Oliver had been annoyed that so many other younger children had come along. Instinct told him that he needed to be alone with Sylvia, without telling him what he actually should do if they did find themselves alone.

It had all happened during a family holiday far up in northern Germany: a shoulder of land near Stufhusen separated the exposed western shore from the Wattenmeer mudflats and a broad, sweep of golden sand scythed into the North Sea and sparkled under a cloudless sky. It was an idyll for a child: an environment almost empty of people and consequently without the interference of grown-ups, the houses scattered across the low, flat landscape.

There was, perfectly for children hungry for adventure, one source of menace. At the far end of the beach an old house with a vast thatched roof stood elevated on the dyke. This was where the 'Old Nazi' lived: a cantankerous old man whose rejection of contact with his neighbours bordered on being a hermit. He was certainly old enough to have been in the war – and in the Nazi Party – but the epithet of 'the Old Nazi' had been given him by one of Sylvia's younger sisters after overhearing her parents describing the recluse as such. From this unsubstantiated snippet, the children had built an entire history for the old man, including a rationale for his anti-social attitude: he was, they had worked out, hiding from Nazi-hunters who had scoured the globe for him, from Sweden to Brazil. He sat sullenly, they had decided, under a tattered and dusty photograph of Adolf Hitler and waited for the Israeli snatch-squad to break down his door and whisk him off, drugged and in a cargo crate with a Tel-Aviv dispatch note on it. The old man himself did not seem to represent that much of a threat, but the danger lay in his dogs: two snarling, barking beasts, one an Alsatian, the other a Dobermann, who kept anyone who wandered too close to the house at bay.

All this mystery and menace, of course, gave the old house at the far end of the beach an irresistible attraction for the children, who would taunt 'the Old Nazi' and his dogs with their presence. After the incident on the beach, there had been accusations that 'the Old Nazi' had deliberately let his dogs loose, commanding them to attack, probably in the same way he had ordered his men on the Russian Front. The truth was a little more prosaic.

There was a small nick in the dyke, where a finger of sand penetrated the rough reeds and grass and offered a little shelter from the brisk sea breeze. The smaller children had been playing down by the water, building sandcastles. Sylvia's nascent feminine intuition had clearly picked up on Oliver's interest in her body, and she had been doing her best to taunt him with it. She had encouraged him to come and splash around in the water. He had been reluctant at first but she had made a pout that had given him a tingle down below. The water made Sylvia's T-shirt cling revealingly to her breasts and the white cotton shorts cleaved to her ample backside. After a few minutes she complained that it was too cold and ran back to the nick in the dyke. It had taken Oliver a while to follow as he waited for his erection to subside even a little. In the end he had walked, his hands clasped in front of his groin as casually as he could manage, to join Sylvia. She was sitting, leaning back on her elbows and arching her back as she let the sun play on her face. Oliver looked at her, savouring every curve, every swell of firm flesh. She turned to him and looked down at his groin. Wordlessly, she placed her hand on where his erection protested against its confinement by his shorts.

At that moment the snarling head of a Dobermann appeared above them, over the edge of the dyke. Oliver didn't move: he was still overcome by what had just happened with his cousin, and the ghost of her touch brought the heat in his loins to boiling. But she jumped up, screamed and started to run. Her fleeing figure awoke the attack instinct in the Dobermann and it leapt from the dyke. After a couple of bounds, it clamped its jaws on Sylvia's backside. Oliver saw the dog's teeth sink into the firm flesh of her buttock and her still-damp cotton shorts became blotted with blood. Simultaneously, Oliver shuddered in intense orgasm.

The 'Old Nazi' had come running and shouting after his dog. It was clear to Oliver that he had simply been walking his dogs along the dyke and the Dobermann had become startled by the unexpected presence of two young people half-hidden in the grass. The injury to Sylvia's rump had been a lot less severe than everyone had at first thought, although it was expected that there would be a scar. The mark left on Oliver, however, had been much more permanent.

Oliver had met Sylvia again only two months ago at a

family wedding. It was one of the greatest moments of disillusion he had ever experienced. It wasn't so much that his North Sea Venus, his icon of femininity, had crumbled before him. It was more that she had partially melted. The firm, full flesh had sagged; the round glory of her breasts had succumbed to twenty years of insistent gravity; the summer-burnished golden gleam had faded and her complexion had, perhaps because of so many summers outdoors, aged prematurely and had assumed the same pasty, blotchy paleness that Oliver remembered in her mother. And, worst of all, the firm, full roundness of Sylvia's large, beautifully sculpted bottom had given way to a generalised, waistless bulk. Oliver had wondered, as he chatted to her about nothing in particular, if she still had the scar, and the image of it, dimpled and white in a mass of soft, formless flesh had made him feel sick. But the encounter had not cured him of his strange obsession. The idol might have been shattered but the zeal had remained.

Oliver was sipping his overpriced cocktail and contemplating the fall of his idol when he became aware of someone by his side.

'Are you Herr Meierhoff?' she asked in a foreign accent that Oliver took to be Russian or Polish. He smiled and nodded but his heart thudded in his chest. If it had not been for the accent and the lack of a summer tan, she could almost have been the Sylvia of his youth. No – she was actually much prettier. But prettiness wasn't the criterion that she had to meet for Oliver. There were plenty of pretty girls whom he could have. The girl beside him was about twenty-two, Oliver figured. She had reddish-blonde hair, crystal-blue eyes and a fresh complexion sprinkled with pale freckles. Oliver found himself involuntarily scanning her from head to foot. She was wearing a blouse that hung loose around a tiny waist yet which was stretched taut by the fullness of her upper arms and breasts. She turned slightly sideways, smiling coyly, knowing what he wanted to see. She wore a pencil skirt which narrowed towards the knee yet which accentuated the fullness of her upper thighs and her magnificent, massive buttocks.

'Am I what you were looking for?' she asked. 'Do I please you?'

'You, my dear,' said Oliver with a broad, handsome grin, 'are sheer perfection.'

6.

Having travelled down to Cologne from Hamburg by train, Maria didn't have her own car with her. It was part of her strategy: her car was an older Jaguar XJS – in an uncharacteristic moment of flamboyance she had bought it deliberately to turn heads. And that made the XJS far too conspicuous for the type of surveillance work that she intended to carry out. Maria had therefore spent much of her first morning in the city looking for a rental car. Even the small economy models were too obviously new and shiny. Cologne had been sulking under a leaden sky that refused to unburden the snow it had been threatening all day. Maria's mood matched the weather and her feet hurt. She could simply have phoned around from her hotel room but she knew she needed to see the car that she would use.

It was about three in the afternoon and the sky was already dimming from dull to dark when she left the last rental place. It wasn't one of the main national or international rental companies and was attached to a servicing garage and second-hand car showroom. The girl behind the rental counter was confused when Maria asked her if she could rent the dark blue Citroën Saxo parked on the lot. A phone call brought to the office a salesman who looked to Maria as if he should still have been at school. He explained that the car could not be rented; it was for sale. Perhaps it was because Maria glanced out at the car through the rental office window that he decided to launch into his pitch, promising Maria that it was an exceptional car for its age. When Maria asked him the price he began his prepared build-up.

'Never mind the crap. How much is the car?' Maria fixed him with a withering gaze. The salesman blushed behind his freckles. After she had taken the Saxo for a test drive, she told him he'd take seven hundred Euros less than he'd asked. An hour and a half later, with all the documentation sorted out, Maria drove in the Saxo back to her hotel. She parked in the car park around the corner. The car was perfect: completely anonymous and ideal for surveillance. The paint-work was dark blue but had dulled and there were no dents or trims that would mark it out and Maria removed a colourful sticker from the rear window.

She left the Saxo in the car park and walked to the Karstadt store in Breite Strasse, where she sought out the clothing equivalent of the Citroën: grungy tops and jeans, a knitted hat and a couple of heavier jackets, one with a hood. All the clothes were in muted dark colours. As she ran the cheap clothes through the scanner the assistant at the till cast a surreptitious eye over Maria's expensive lambswool coat and designer handbag.

'A present for my niece.' Maria smiled emptily.

7.

It was as good a hotel as Oliver could pay for in cash without arousing suspicion or undue attention. He had booked in before meeting the amply bottomed escort girl in the night-club and had used a false identity, as he always did. So when the escort agency telephoned the hotel and asked to speak to Herr Meierhoff, to make sure that he was genuinely a guest there, they were put through to his room. It also meant that there was no embarrassing or conspicuous fumbling with wads of Euros when he brought the escort back. While still in the nightclub, he had passed her an envelope containing cash to the pre-agreed amount. All done calmly, with Oliver's easy smile never faltering.

Oliver had been his usual chatty, charming self all evening and he could see that his professional companion was a little confused about why a man as attractive and urbane as he was would need to pay for sex. But, there again, he had been quite specific about his requirements. In the taxi, however, Oliver fell silent and watched Cologne slide by, occasionally glancing at his companion and smiling. She had explained that her name was Anastasia, and he had commented on what a beautiful name it was, while thinking to himself that it was probably as genuine as Meierhoff. Oliver's comparative quiet came from his need to anticipate the fulfilment of his desire. He considered these moments to be the most delectable of all, almost better than the fulfilment itself. It was the perfect combination of a growing, hardening lust and the mouth-watering anticipation of a fine meal, whose aromas had already reached him. He became intensely aware of the pressure of Anastasia's wonderfully full and firm thigh against his.

He gave the taxi driver a reasonable but not lavish tip. Oliver was doing his best not to be remembered by anyone too clearly. He and Anastasia walked straight past reception and to the lifts, again as inconspicuously as he could manage.

'We'll have a little nightcap in the room,' Oliver explained in the elevator. 'Anastasia' smiled at him with contrived mischievousness and placed her hand on his groin.

'Maybe that should wait for after.' She closed her fingers around him a little. 'By the way, if you really like what you get tonight, it's quite in order for you to give me an extra tip.'

The curtains were still open in his hotel room and the main railway station and the massive profile of the cathedral loomed dark against the night sky. Oliver returned Anastasia's smile as he closed the hotel room door behind him.

I hope, he thought to himself as he dropped the door's night-bolt lever, that she doesn't scream. Like the last one did.

8.

Everybody needs to be someone else sometimes, even if it is only for a couple of hours becoming lost in the flesh of another in an anonymous hotel room. Andrea always held that thought at the front of her mind during the first few moments of meeting a client. She didn't see herself as a prostitute: she would never allow herself to be sold as just so much meat. She was not, after all, what was normally considered feminine. But not everybody had the same ideal of femininity: the work she got through the agency was for a niche market. After all, she was no ordinary woman and the men who paid to be with her were not looking for ordinary sex. Andrea was well aware that the agency she worked for specialised in the more unusual end of the sex industry and she didn't like to think about what other tastes they probably catered for. She had always suspected that *À la Carte* was run by gangsters, but her contact with them was confined to the calls they made to her cellphone and the envelopes she mailed them with their percentage of her fees. She knew they had come looking for her, or someone like her.

The first contact had been in the gym where she had been preparing with a few of the other girls for a local competition. It had been a sleazy-looking man called Nielsen who had made the approach. Nielsen had been dressed like a businessman but had had the thick, thuggish build and face of a gangster. He had spoken to Andrea and another three girls. Andrea had noticed that the girls Nielsen spoke to were the only others with the same amount of muscle mass as Andrea had. Nielsen had at first said the work was photographic modelling. He had been quite specific about the type of modelling and it had not bothered Andrea. She was used to parading in a bikini that strained to contain her heavily muscled body: being gawked at without it didn't unduly bother her. It was after the second photo session that Nielsen had mentioned that *À la Carte*'s main business was providing escorts. Escorts for an especially discerning clientele.

Cologne had been the first German city to levy a tax on prostitutes' incomes, but *À la Carte* was less than assiduous when it came to record-keeping. This had meant that Andrea had successfully managed to avoid being registered as a part-time sex worker and therefore was not taxed on her 'extra' earnings. The money from the escort work was more than useful, supplementing the income she made from running her café; but Andrea knew that she didn't do it just for the money.

Andrea had been booked for two hours and the agency knew she would phone back to confirm that she had been paid and was safely away from the client. Not that anyone worried seriously about Andrea: it was more than evident that she could easily look after herself. But, she knew, if she were ever to experience difficulties, a couple of heavies were on call.

She always thought of her clients as small men. They probably thought of themselves that way too. It didn't have to do with height – this client was at least 180 centimetres tall – it had to do with the way they saw themselves. How she saw them. The client was in his forties, thin and pale; his suit was middle-budget, as was the hotel room. He sat on the edge of the bed, his expression a mixture of nervousness and excitement. Andrea did nothing to put him at his ease, which was as it should be. She confirmed his name and demanded the envelope with the money: Andrea always asked for cash. She checked the amount and stuffed the envelope into her bag.

'Strip,' she commanded and removed her raincoat, jeans and baggy woollen top. Beneath she was dressed in an assembly of black leather straps and buckles that left her breasts and genitals exposed. As usual she had done a full workout before coming out to her client and her oiled muscles were hard and sleek. The man on the bed gazed at her with an expression of awe. He was now naked and Andrea looked down at his erection with an expression of contempt.

'Stand,' she ordered. He obeyed. 'You can touch me.'

The client ran trembling fingers over her body. Not her breasts or her pudenda, but her arms, her stomach, her thighs. She stood solid, firm and unresponding. The truth was that Andrea enjoyed her work; she enjoyed the feeling of power, of control, that it gave her. She knew that Cologne was full of dominatrixes, but this was something else. Her clients didn't get off by being ordered around to clean toilets and polish shoes. This was less psychological and more physical. Her clients lusted after her body; wanted to touch her. Sometimes it would end in penetrative sex. Other times, like this, the client had asked for something very particular.

The client removed his hands but his eyes still ranged over her bulk.

'Are you ready?' she asked. He nodded.

'But not the face . . .' he said and his voice trembled.

'Not the face,' she repeated. 'I know.'

There was a short pause. Andrea filled her mind with the image of the acne-faced youth who had created a scene in her café and then she slammed her fist into the client's naked belly. He gave a gasp and buckled slightly. Andrea realised that she hadn't hit him hard enough; that he wasn't getting his money's worth. She placed another image in her mind: a much older image. She hit her client again and he doubled over, suppressing a cry of pain.

Andrea pushed him onto the bed, straddled him and hit him again. And again.

9.

It took nearly four hours for Fabel to drive from Hamburg to Norddeich, slightly longer than usual. It was not a journey that he liked to make much in the winter, unless he took the train. But his mother's recent heart attack and advancing age meant he felt the need to make the trip more often; and the idea of six hours of solitude in the car there and back had appealed to him. Time to think. However, as the skies grew darker, that appeal started to fade. Friesland is flat; it is hill-less and lies defenceless against the temperaments of the North Sea. As Fabel crossed the landscape he had grown up in, a wind from the west, unopposed by anything resembling a hill, tugged at his steering wheel and the rods of rain against his windscreen became beaded with sleet.

Fabel drove without the radio or the CD-player on, frowning through the rain at the grey ribbon of the A28. He needed the thinking time. He had decided to spend the journey imagining two futures for himself: the one that Bartz had offered, where Fabel's expensive tastes could more easily be met and where he would be free from a world of horror and violence; but the other offer, made by van Heiden and the BKA, was a lot more attractive than he liked to admit. It was flattering, no matter how much he tried to deny it, to be considered the leading expert in his professional field. Fabel tried hard to view each future objectively. As he did so, he fought to keep something else from his mind: the Cologne file. A distraction he didn't need. But it kept creeping back into his thoughts.

Fabel got a shock when he realised that he had no recol-lection of the last half-hour of driving, as if he had been on some kind of autopilot while his mind had wandered over his future, his relationship with Susanne, and a faceless killer in a city he hardly knew. Suddenly he realised that Norden had taken a monochrome form around him. He continued

along Norddeicher Strasse towards the North Sea and his
mother's home.

10.

Maria Klee walked by the restaurant again. She had done
so a dozen times over the last two days, wearing something different each time. She had even donned scruffy jeans
and a sweatshirt, tucking her blonde hair into the knitted
cap that she had bought at Karstadt. She had learned her
lesson. If this restaurant was under any kind of federal
surveillance, then the frequency of her passing by it would
not be noticed.

The owners of the Biarritz were not Ukrainians, but the
restaurant had been one on a twenty-page list of German
businesses included in the BKA file that were suspected of
using Ukrainians trafficked by Vitrenko's outfit. Maria felt
at a disadvantage. In Hamburg – Hanover, even – she knew
the lie of the land. But here she was hunting across an
unknown landscape. She felt exposed. She was after dangerous
quarry and she could just as easily find herself becoming the
hunted and not the hunter. She had found a way to get to
the back door of the Biarritz: a circuitous route of lanes and
alleys. She knew that the Ukrainian boy did the most menial
tasks and that in a restaurant kitchen there is always trash
to be taken out and sorted. She watched the rear of the restaurant from an alley lined with waste and recycling bins. The
back of the Biarritz was windowless on the ground floor and
the fire door was heavy and sheeted with metal. This security meant that the management had clearly felt that a CCTV
system was unnecessary; and that allowed Maria to approach
him without the encounter being recorded or even witnessed.
If she wanted the Ukrainian to talk, he would have to feel
safe. That was if she could get him to talk.

It was cold. Maria had wrapped up well. She had grown

to hate the cold, something that had never bothered her before *that* night. As she had lain in the long grass, with Fabel's face close to hers, she had felt a chill like no other she had ever experienced. She had fought to stay awake and her breathing had been short and shallow. Fabel's breath had been warm on her cold cheek and Maria had realised that Death is cold. Since then, she had made sure that she never felt cold.

The restaurant's rear door opened and a skinny man in his early twenties appeared. He was wearing a white T-shirt, along with a stained apron that hung from his waist to his shins. He cast a glance over his shoulder back into the kitchen before lighting a cigarette and leaning against the wall. He looked tired and gaunt and smoked the cigarette with the appreciation of someone snatching a precious and rare private moment. He stood up when he saw Maria approach. He turned to go back into the kitchen.

'Wait!' Maria called. She held up her oval bronze Criminal Police disc. 'Police . . .' She was relying on the young Ukrainian not challenging her and asking to see her police identification card, which would, of course, reveal that she was several hundred kilometres outside her jurisdiction. The young man looked startled. Afraid. 'It's okay,' Maria said, with a tired smile. 'I'm not interested in your status here. I just need to ask a few questions.'

The Ukrainian nodded tersely. Maria took her large black notebook from her coat pocket.

'You are . . . ?' Maria made a show of searching for his name in the notebook, as if she had it recorded somewhere, which she hadn't.

'Slavko Dmytruk . . .' said the young Ukrainian, seeming eager to cooperate. He still stole a peek back into the kitchen to make sure no one could see them. He stepped out a little from the doorway and pulled the fire door almost closed. He fumbled in his pocket for his ID card and handed it to Maria.

It proved he was illegal: the ID card was not German, his photograph was captioned in Cyrillic writing and the yellow trident on a blue field identified the card as Ukrainian.

'I have not done anything wrong,' said Slavko; his German was almost impenetrably accented. 'I want stay in Germany. I good worker.'

'I didn't say that you had done anything wrong. I just want to ask you a few questions,' said Maria.

'About what?'

'About how you got here.'

Slavko's unease shifted into genuine fear. 'I don't know what you talk about.'

'How you got here from Ukraine,' said Maria in as soothing a tone as she could manage. She could see that Slavko was becoming more and more agitated. She found herself wishing she had Fabel's knack of putting people at ease. 'There's no need to be alarmed, Slavko. No one will know that it was you I got the information from. I promise. But, if you don't cooperate, then I will be forced to inform immigration.' Maria spoke slowly and in simple German, giving him time to take in what she had said. 'Do you understand, Slavko? I need to know who arranged your transport here, got you the job, somewhere to live . . .'

'I don't know . . . very dangerous man. Very dangerous people.' The young Ukrainian glanced back towards the crack in the door.

'Most of them are, Slavko. But I need to know who got you this job.'

'I work hard.' Slavko looked close to tears. 'I work so hard. I want send money back to family in Ukraine. But I can't. I work all day and most of night and I have to give half to the man who brought me here. Then he take half of what left for where I sleep. It not fair. Not fair at all.'

Maria noticed Slavko trembling. She began to feel sorry for him. She also began to regret fooling him into believing that she had some official clout. She knew that she was exposing him to danger from which she couldn't protect him. Or herself.

'Slavko, all I need is a list of names. *A* name. You know this isn't right. This isn't work, this is slavery. These people will have you working for nothing for ever. And you're one of the lucky ones. Think of the women and children who have been sold into God knows what.'

Slavko gazed at her intently. He seemed to weigh up his options.

'I was brought here by container lorry. From Lvyv to Hamburg. Then they took us in middle of the night in van. We were dropped at different places in Cologne. I was brought here, to restaurant. It was middle of night and I was told wait here, at the back, until the morning and someone came to open up. Then I have to work for fifteen hours and after they take me to the apartment. Eight of us. Two bedrooms. We take turns sleeping.'

Maria nodded. So there was still a Hamburg connection. Vitrenko's empire hadn't withdrawn from the city, just from visibility.

'Who arranged it all?'

'There is man back in Lvyv . . . all I know him as is Pytor. I don't know names of any of other people who collected us from the container in Hamburg. Except man who drive minibus . . . we see him every week. His name Viktor. But at the first stop we made here in Cologne, a big black Mercedes was waiting. Man got out and gave orders to minibus driver. He was tough-looking man. Like a soldier.'

Maria scrabbled in her bag for one of the scaled-down copies of Vitrenko's photograph.

'This man . . . could this man be the soldier?'

Slavko shook his head. 'No, soldier-type much younger. Thirty. Thirty-five, maybe.'

'Ukrainian?'

'Yes. I hear him speaking. Not what he say, but I hear it was Ukrainian.'

At that moment a tall, slim African came out with a pail of scraps, which he put into one of the bins. On his way back in he looked suspiciously at Maria.

'Boss is looking for you,' the African said to Slavko.

'I come right now . . .' Slavko was clearly concerned at having been seen talking to Maria. 'I have to go.'

'Then I'll have to come back,' she said.

'I told you everything. I don't know no more.'

'I can't believe that. Who takes the money from you for your accommodation?'

Slavko looked confused.

'Your apartment,' said Maria. She really did feel sorry for him. But she needed a lead. 'The man who brought you here in the minibus. Viktor. You said he takes your money.'

'Oh . . . him.' Again Slavko looked anxious. 'If you talk to him, then they know it me who talk.'

'I'm not interested in him. It's his bosses I'm after. He won't even know I'm onto him.'

'All I know is his name Viktor. I don't know last name.'

'When do you see him? How often?'

'Friday is when we get paid. Most of us work until late Friday nights and sleep on Saturday because we work again Saturday nights. Viktor comes to collect money Saturday and Sunday. Around lunchtime. Some people working Saturday lunchtime so he makes second call Sunday.' Slavko shook his head despondently. 'He leave us nothing. Says we have to pay back all expenses in getting us here. Viktor bad man. Everybody frightened of Viktor.'

'Do you think Viktor is an ex-soldier, like the other man?'

'He don't look like soldier to me. Gangster. One day one of the men in the apartment say it not right Viktor take everything. Viktor hit him with heavy piece of wood. Beat him bad. Next day the man gone. Viktor say he send him back to Ukraine and keep his money.' The memory of the event seemed to disturb Slavko further; he stole another glance back at the door the African had left wider open. 'I go now. I don't know nothing else.'

'The address . . .' Maria ordered. 'Give me the address of your apartment.' Seeing Slavko's alarm she held her hands up in a placatory gesture. 'Don't worry, no one will know anything. I'm not going to visit your apartment or send other police or the immigration people. I just want to see what Viktor looks like. That's all. You've got to trust me, Slavko.'

Again Slavko hesitated, then gave Maria an address in the Chorweiler part of the city. She tried to remember where it was from the maps of Cologne she had sought to memorise.

Slavko went back into the kitchen. Two other Slavic types looked up from their work and eyed Maria suspiciously through the open door. As she walked away, Maria could still see the fear in Slavko's eyes; his timidity and his hungry gaunt look. Most of all she thought about how she had given him assurances; how she had told him to trust her. Just like she had told Nadja, the young prostitute in Hamburg, to trust her. Just before Nadja disappeared.

Chapter Four

21–25 January

I.

Buslenko had arranged for the team to assemble at the hunting lodge on the Monday afternoon. He himself had arrived in Korostyshev two days early. Buslenko had been born in Korostyshev and, since it was a hundred and ten kilometres west of the capital, it was far enough away from Kiev for him to feel reasonably satisfied that he could carry out a secure pre-mission briefing. The city lay under a blanket of thick crisp snow as if the buildings were dust-sheeted furniture waiting for summer visitors. The sane inhabitants of the city were indoors or traversed Chervona Plosha with definite purpose: dark bustling smudges over the Plaza's white expanse. But Buslenko did manage to find a *pirog* vendor who had been enterprising or mad enough to set up his paraffin-heated stall for the occasional passer-by. *Pirog* was bread baked with meat inside, and Korostyshev *pirog* was famous throughout Ukraine.

Buslenko wandered down between the naked chestnut trees to the War Memorial. Behind the obelisk stood a row of sculpted granite commemorative stones, each carved with the face of the officer whom it honoured. He had come here as a child and his father had explained that these were the men who had died saving Ukraine from the Germans. Fourteen thousand had lost their lives defending the city. The young Taras Buslenko had been hypnotised by the remarkably detailed faces, by the concept of being a defender of Ukraine, just like Cossack Mamay. He had been much older when his father had gone on to explain that many more had also died in Korostyshev in nineteen-nineteen, unsuccessfully defending Ukraine against the Bolsheviks. There were no memorials for them.

Buslenko sat on a bench and contemplated his *pirog* for a moment before taking a deep bite into childhood memories. He dabbed his mouth with his handkerchief.

'You're late,' he said, as if talking to the graven likeness of the long-dead Red Army lieutenant facing him.

'Impressive . . .' The voice came from behind Buslenko.

'Not really.' Buslenko took another bite. The meat inside was hot and warmed him all the way down. 'I could hear you coming across the snow from twenty metres away. You stick with your job pushing paper round and snooping on adulterous politicians and I'll stick with mine.'

'Killing people?'

'Defending Ukraine,' said Buslenko, his mouth full. He nodded to the memorial sculptures. 'Like them. What did you get, Sasha?'

Sasha Andruzky, a thin young man in a heavy woollen coat and with a fur hat pulled over his ears, sat down next to Buslenko and hugged himself against the cold.

'Not much. I think it's genuine. From what you told me there will be absolutely no official sanction for what you've been asked to do. But unofficially I think that taking out Vitrenko is a government obsession.'

'Malarek?'

'As far as I can see, our friend the Deputy Interior Minister is clean. If he has another agenda, then it's pretty well hidden. But, of course, that's exactly what you'd expect if he were involved with Vitrenko. But I don't follow your logic . . . Why would Malarek send you on a black mission to assassinate Vitrenko if he's on Vitrenko's payroll? It doesn't make sense.'

'It doesn't make sense unless I'm being sent in all packaged up as a present for Vitrenko. Maybe I'm the target and Vitrenko's the one with his finger on the trigger.'

'Then don't go.' Sasha frowned. The cold had pinched his cheeks and nose red.

'I have to. I don't think it's likely that it's a set-up. But it's possible. Anyway, I'm acting out of pure self-interest. There have only been three people who have got close to nailing Vitrenko. Me and two German police officers. We're three loose ends that Vitrenko will eventually tie up. He's nothing if not neat. But that's also his one weakness. Despite all his efficiency, if it's a target that's important to him then Vitrenko likes to be close for the kill. Really close. He's like a cat who plays with his prey before killing them. And *that* is the only time he's exposed. Anyway, did you do a check on the three names I gave you?'

'I did. But again I don't get it. You hand-picked those three because you know them personally. If you trust them, why get me to check them out?'

'Because I thought I knew Peotr Samolyuk.' Buslenko referred to the commander of the assault team who'd been there when they'd missed Vitrenko in Kiev. 'I would have trusted him. It would seem that every man has his price.'

'Well, I did check them out.'

'And no one knows you've been through their records?'

'If you want to know who's been accessing the Ministry's records,' Sasha shivered despite the layers of thick clothing, 'I'm the one you come to. Don't worry, I've hidden all my tracks. Anyway, all three are clean, as are the three I picked out. No one served with Vitrenko or under an officer who served with Vitrenko and I can find no hint of any other connection.'

'And have you found me the other three?'

'I have.' The cold chilled the brief satisfied smile from Sasha's face. 'I'm rather proud of my contributions. All three meet your criteria exactly. I've included one woman. Someone you already know . . . Captain Olga Sarapenko of the Kiev City Militia's Organised Crime Division.'

Buslenko was surprised at Sasha's choice. He thought back to Ukrainian Beauty and how well she had handled herself in the Celestia operation. 'You reckon she's up to it?'

'She understands Vitrenko, Molokov and their operations. She's one of the best organised-crime specialists we've got. She's clean and I believe you've seen how handy she can be in a tough situation. Like I say, it's a good, solid team.'

'The only thing that concerns me is that we've pulled them together from such a wide range of units,' said Buslenko. 'Wouldn't have it been better to pick exclusively from Sokil?' Buslenko himself was a member of the Sokil – Falcon – Spetsnaz unit. That made him, technically, more of a policeman than a soldier. The Falcons were an elite police Spetsnaz under the direct command of the Interior Ministry's Organised Crime Directorate. The rest of his team were drawn from other Interior Ministry Spetsnaz units: Titan, Skorpion, Snow Leopard and even one Berkut, the Golden Eagles, in which Vitrenko himself had served. There were also two members from outside the Interior Ministry: they belonged to the SBU Secret Service's Alpha Spetsnaz.

'I wanted to put together the best team for the job. Each one of these people has special expertise. The thing that worries me is that maybe Vitrenko has a better team.' Sasha stood up and stamped his feet on the compressed snow. He handed Buslenko a document folder that he had tucked inside his overcoat. 'The details are there. Look after yourself, Taras.'

Buslenko watched as Sasha made his way back towards Chervona Plosha, his dark frame hunched as he walked.

'You too,' said Buslenko, when Sasha was too far away to hear.

2.

Fabel's mother was delighted to see her son. She embraced him warmly at the door and steered him into the parlour, taking his raincoat from him first. Fabel's mother was British, a Scotswoman, and he smiled as he heard her richly accented German, influenced as much by local Frisian as by her native English. It was an odd combination, and Fabel had grown up continually aware of another dimension to his identity. She left him by the tiled *Kamin* to warm up while she went to make tea. Fabel had seldom drunk coffee while at home. East Frisians are the world's heaviest consumers of tea, leaving the English and the Irish in their tannin-hued wake.

Fabel had spent so little time in this room during the last twenty-five years, but he could still close his eyes and picture everything exactly where it was: the sofa and chairs were new, but they were in exactly the same positions as their predecessors; the reproduction of *The Nightwatch* by Rembrandt; the bookcase that was too big for the room and was crammed with books and magazines; the small writing table that his mother still used for all her correspondence, having let the world of e-mails and electronic communication pass her by. As well as its contents, the very fabric of the house was still so familiar to Fabel. The thick walls and heavy wooden doors and window frames always seemed to embrace him. He had a strange relationship with Norddeich: he came back to it only to visit his mother, and he felt no real affinity with the place. Yet this was the only world he had known as a child. It had formed him. Defined him. He had left East Friesland in stages: first studying at the Carl von Ossietzky University in Oldenburg, then at the Universität Hamburg.

When she came back into the parlour with a tray set out with the tea things, he shared the thought with his mother.

'I never thought I'd end up being a policeman. I mean when I was growing up here.'

She looked surprised and a little confused.

'It's funny that now, at my age, I'm giving it up and going to work for someone who grew up right here in Norddeich.'

'That's not strictly true,' said his mother. She poured some tea, added milk and dropped a *Kluntje* into the cup before handing it to Fabel, despite the fact that he hadn't taken sugar in his tea for nearly thirty years. 'You were always such a serious little boy. You always wanted to look after everybody. Even Lex. Goodness knows he got into so many scrapes and it was always you who got him out of them.'

Fabel smiled. His brother's name was short for 'Alexander'. Fabel himself only narrowly missed being called 'Iain', his Scottish mother finally compromising with his German father and calling him 'Jan', which had been 'close enough'. Lex was the older of the two, but Fabel had always been the wiser, more mature one. Back then, Lex's carefree attitude to life had annoyed the young Fabel. Now he envied it.

'And that painting . . .' His mother pointed to *The Nightwatch*. 'When you were tiny you used to stare at that for hours. You asked me about the men in it, and I explained that they were patrolling the streets at night to protect people from criminals. I remember you said, "That's what I'm going to be when I grow up. I want to protect people." So you're wrong. You did think about being a policeman when you were young.' She laughed.

Fabel stared at the picture. He had no recollection of expressing any interest in the painting, or in the occupation of the people featured within it. It had become just an unnoticed, taken-for-granted element in his childhood environment.

'It's all wrong, anyway,' he said and sipped his tea without stirring it, letting the sugar dissolve and settle on the bottom of the cup. 'It's not even a night scene. It was the varnish that made it too dark. And they're nothing to do with a nightwatch. They're civil militiamen under the command of an aristocrat. It was just that the original painting had been stored next to another titled *de Nachtwacht* and the titles were confused.'

Margaret Fabel shook her head, smiling reproachfully. 'Sometimes, Jan, knowledge isn't the answer to everything. That painting is what you think it is when you look at it. Not what its history makes it. That was another thing about you. You always had to know things. Find things out. You becoming a policeman isn't really the great mystery you think it is.'

Fabel looked again at the painting. Not night, day. Not police, an armed militia. A few days ago he would have said that it had more to do with Breidenbach, the young MEK trooper, than with Fabel. But Breidenbach had died defining what it meant to be a policeman: placing himself in harm's way to protect the ordinary citizen. They changed the subject and talked about Fabel's brother Lex for a while, and how his restaurant on the island of Sylt was doing its best business for years. Then Fabel's mother asked about Susanne.

'She's fine,' said Fabel.

'Is everything all right between you two?'

'Why shouldn't it be?'

'I don't know . . .' She frowned. Fabel noticed the deepening creases in her brow. Age had crept up on his mother without him noticing. 'It's just that you don't talk about Susanne so much these days. I do hope everything is all right. She's a lovely person, Jan. You're lucky to have found her.'

Fabel put his cup down. 'Do you remember that case I was involved with last year? The one that took such a terrible toll on Maria Klee?'

Margaret Fabel nodded.

'There was a terrorist connection to the case. I got involved in investigating anarchist and radical groups that had kind of faded into the background. Raking up the past, I suppose you'd call it.'

'But what has this to do with Susanne?'

'I was sent a file. Background information more than anything. One of the photographs was of a guy called Christian Wohlmut. It was taken about nineteen-ninety, when German domestic terrorism was on its last legs. Wohlmut wanted to breathe new life into it. He sent parcel and letter bombs to US interests in Germany. Amateur stuff and most were intercepted or failed to go off. But one was professional enough to maim a young secretarial worker in an American oil company's office in Munich. That's where Wohlmut was based. Munich. And that's where Susanne studied.'

'It's a big city, Jan,' said his mother. But her frown indicated that she was already ahead of him.

'There was a girl in the photograph with Wohlmut. It was blurred and she was only ever described as "unknown female".'

'Susanne?' Fabel's mother put her cup back in the saucer. 'No! You can't believe that Susanne could ever have been involved with terrorism?'

Fabel shrugged and took another sip of tea. He had forgotten the sugar at the bottom and got a mouthful of nauseous sweetness. 'I don't know what her involvement with Wohlmut was. But I do know she's very defensive, almost secretive, about her student days. And there was some guy in her past who she says was manipulative and domineering. It was I who suggested we should move in together . . . Susanne was wary at first because of some bad experience she'd had.'

'And you think it was this terrorist, Wohlmut?'

'I don't know.'

'So what if it was? What does that matter now? If she didn't actually do anything wrong – I mean, break the law?'

'But that's exactly it, *Mutti* . . . I'll never know for sure that she wasn't actively involved.'

'You're not seriously thinking about confronting her with this?'

'She knows something's wrong. She keeps on at me to find out what it is. Things aren't so good between us and she knows I'm stalling over moving in together.'

'Susanne works with the police, Jan. If her political views in the past were so radical, I don't see her doing that.'

'People change, *Mutti*.'

'Then accept her for who she is now Jan. Unless . . .'

'Unless what?'

'Unless you are simply using this as an excuse for you to get out of the relationship.'

'It's not that. It's just that I've got to know. I have to know what the truth is.'

'Like I said, Jan,' his mother smiled at him in the same way she had when he had been 'such a serious little boy' and she had sought to reassure him about something, 'knowledge isn't always the answer to everything.'

3.

The British had bombed Cologne to a pile of rubble. So much so that there had been a serious suggestion at the end of the war that the city shouldn't be rebuilt. Just moved. But the cathedral had remained standing to remind everyone that this was Germany's oldest city and deserved a new life. So they had rebuilt Cologne. Unfortunately, whole chunks of the city were brought back to an artificial and sterile form of life. Chorweiler was a perfect example of the kind of place architects and city planners at dinner parties would boast about creating, but would never themselves contemplate living in.

When Maria thought about Slavko and his countrymen, she couldn't believe that they thought that Chorweiler, with its towering clumps of multi-storey apartment blocks, was really the end of the rainbow. Chorweiler lay to the far north of the city and Maria reckoned that Viktor would start his Saturday pick-up run here and work his way back toward the city centre. She was pretty sure she had worked out which of the high-rises contained Slavko's flat and she parked the Saxo some distance down the street from the block and sat with the engine switched off.

Contrary to its depiction in American movies, surveillance from a car was not always the best way of keeping tabs on someone's movements. Most of the time people would walk by a car and not notice anyone sitting in it, but once they did they would notice *every* time they passed. Maria was dressed in her grungy clothes and she had slumped slightly in the driver's seat so that her head did not project above the headrest. Her main disadvantage was that she had no photograph of her surveillance target. She didn't even have much of a description of Viktor from Slavko to go on. At about eleven-thirty an Audi pulled up and a big-built man of about forty went into the apartment building. Maria noted down the time and the make, model and licence number of the car. She had brought a small digital camera with a half-decent zoom, and she took a photograph of the man as he went into the building, then again as he came out with a younger man. Maria could tell that this was not her man and she didn't follow the Audi when he drove off. She settled back down. The clothes she had bought were too big for her, but they were warm and comfortable. More importantly, the body she hated became lost in their bagginess.

It was about twenty past noon when Viktor pulled up. Maria was in no doubt that this was Viktor. He had 'organised crime, lower echelons' written all over him – his clothes, his car. It sometimes felt as if Vasyl Vitrenko and his lieutenants were spectres, without form. It had only been at the very end of a long and detailed investigation that Fabel and

Maria had actually come face to face with Vitrenko, and then only for a few deadly minutes. It was through people like Viktor that the Vitrenko organisation had form and visibility. Conspicuous visibility as far as Viktor was concerned. He was a large man, over two metres in height. He wore a long black leather coat that strained to contain his massive shoulders and his hair was dyed bright blond. The vehicle he double-parked outside the apartment block was a vast 1960s American ocean liner of a car. Maria took several photographs and made her notes. She guessed that Viktor would not be in the apartment building long, so she turned the key in the ignition of her own car and readied herself.

As it happened, Viktor was in the building for nearly half an hour. A delivery van came along the street and could not pass Viktor's Chrysler and the driver blasted his horn several times impatiently. When Viktor did eventually emerge, carrying a package bound in black plastic, the driver leaned from his cab window and berated the Ukrainian loudly. Viktor ignored him completely, walked round the Chrysler, opened the cavernous trunk and dropped the package in. Then, in the same unhurried manner, he walked over to the delivery van, wrenched the door open, pulled the driver from his cabin and head-butted him with such force that the back of the man's head slammed into the side of the van and he slid unconscious onto the road. Viktor calmly took a handkerchief from his pocket and wiped the blood that had splashed on his face, walked back to the car and drove off to where the narrow residential street joined the main road, the Weichselring, that looped around Chorweiler like a restraining lasso.

'That's my boy,' Maria said to herself. 'You're definitely Viktor.' She pulled out and realised that she now had the same problem that the van driver had had: the van now prevented her from following Viktor's car. She looked at the van driver lying crumpled on the ground. In the same situation in

Hamburg she would have given up the pursuit and made sure that the driver was okay. But this wasn't Hamburg. Slamming the Saxo into reverse, Maria cut up a side street. On the way in she had driven up Mercatorstrasse, the main route into Chorweiler and guessed that Viktor would be heading along Weichselring in its direction.

She took two rights, which she reckoned would bring her out onto the Weichselring. It didn't. She cursed and looked wildly around for some landmark that would give her a clue to which direction she should take. She floored the accelerator and drove at high speed towards where the street swung left. She took the next right and saw the traffic on Mercatorstrasse. Maria had bypassed Weichselring completely. She reached the end of the street and was stopped at a red light. She scanned the Mercatorstrasse in both directions but could see no sign of Viktor's distinctive Chrysler. The lights changed but she still had no idea which way to turn and didn't move off. A car had come up behind her and the driver sounded his horn. She looked in her mirror to mouth a curse. A colossal American car with a colossal Ukrainian driver. She held her hand up in apology and pulled out onto Mercatorstrasse, turning left and hoping that Viktor would do the same. He did. Maria had no idea how she had managed to beat Viktor to the junction, but now the target she had intended to follow was following her. Her mouth became dry at the thought that it might not be coincidence but intention. Could he have spotted her outside the apartment block? Viktor did not look to Maria as if he was the most highly trained of Vitrenko's goons. He was all thug and no soldier, she thought. But, there again, most Ukrainian and Russian gangsters had a Spetsnaz background and the way Viktor had dealt with the van driver had certainly been expert if a little unsubtle. She pulled up at the next set of traffic lights, looking in her mirror to check if Viktor was indicating a turn. He wasn't, so she went straight on. He followed. Up ahead there were a couple of free parking bays. Maria indicated and pulled into one. Viktor drove by without looking in her direction and Maria let another couple of cars pass before pulling back out. She sighed with relief. As far as she could see the anonymity of her car had protected her from detection and she fixed her attention on the ridiculous tail fins of Viktor's 1960s Chrysler, three cars ahead of her.

They drove south through the city for about fifteen minutes without going back onto the A57 autobahn that had brought her to Chorweiler. Viktor made two stops to collect, both in run-down areas. After the second stop Maria became concerned when she found herself immediately behind Viktor, the two previously intervening cars having turned off at different junctions. She held back as much as she could, but whenever they stopped at traffic lights she ended up bumper to bumper with Viktor. If he looked in his rear-view mirror, he would see her face clearly. She tugged her woollen hat further down over her brow. Maria no longer had a clue where she was, but she tried to make a mental note of the road endings she passed. They were still within the city but the architecture changed from residential to industrial and she became painfully aware that there were fewer cars on the road, making her tailing more conspicuous. Eventually they passed under the autobahn and came into another residential area indicated by a yellow *Stadtteil* sign as Ossendorf. She noted the name of the road they passed along, Kanalstrasse, and followed Viktor as he turned along a street lined with four-storey apartment blocks. Now her and Viktor's were the only cars driving along it. Maria decided to break off rather than risk Viktor identifying her as a tail. She took the next on the left, did a U-turn to face the road she had left and parked at the kerb.

Maria cursed under her breath. She took the Cologne street plan from the glove compartment and checked Ossendorf. Her instincts had been right. This was a residential area and not a short cut to anywhere else. Either Viktor lived here or he was doing another pick-up. She would wait half an hour. If it was another pick-up, then he would probably come out of the area before the half-hour was up, and more than likely by the same way he had come in. And if she were unsuccessful either way, then she would watch Slavko's apartment every day and pick up his trail again.

Maria was hungry. She hadn't eaten since her insubstantial breakfast of coffee and toast. And with the engine off she couldn't switch on the heater. Her lightly fleshed frame felt chilled to the bone. That old feeling. The cold made her scared. She looked at her watch: three-fifteen. Already the sky was dark with more than the clouds. If it got any darker she would have significant trouble locating Viktor's car. She remembered her shock at finding Viktor's car behind her at the traffic lights. What if it hadn't been a coincidence? What if he had been onto her from the start? All kinds of irrational fears began to well up inside her. Suddenly an idea came to her and she spun around suddenly to make sure that Viktor's car wasn't there, sitting behind her in over-styled American menace. It wasn't. She turned to face front again. Pull yourself together, she told herself. For God's sake get a grip.

It was then that she saw the improbably long profile of Viktor's Chrysler glide past the road end. She had been right: it had been a collection and he was heading back. Maria switched on the car lights, started the engine, and headed after him.

4.

Thirteen . . . fourteen . . . fifteen . . .

Andrea counted each one silently and focused on her breathing, each inhalation hissed through tight-drawn lips.

Sixteen . . . seventeen . . .

She had added two kilos to the bench press. If she did

twenty reps, three sets, that would mean that by the end of her routine she would have lifted an extra one hundred and twenty kilos.

Eighteen . . . nineteen . . .

She felt the muscles around her jaw set hard with every push. No need for a facelift if you did this kind of thing. It was called radiated stress. The whole idea was that with each exercise you isolated one part of your body, one set of muscles, to maximise the benefit to that area. But the muscle and sinew of neck and jaw always strained under the effort. The first sign of someone beginning a weight work regime wasn't on their bodies, it was in their face.

Twenty.

Andrea eased the bench press slowly back to its resting position. It was the great thing about multi-gym equipment: you didn't need a spotter to buddy you through your routine. But Andrea knew that when it came to building bulk and definition, it was the free weight that worked best: the system used since the gymnasia of the Greeks and Romans. But using this high-tech equipment freed her from the need to engage with anyone else in the gym.

She took a slug of water from her bottle, sprayed the bench seat and back with anti-bacterial spray and wiped everything down. The etiquette of the gym. She liked coming at this time of night. It was always quiet. Few people, no noise, no chat. Even the usual dance-track muzak was switched off.

Andrea moved across to the leg-extension machine. She performed a set of stretches to elongate and align the tendons of her legs before adjusting the seat and the cushioned shin bar. She pulled the pin from where the last person had set it and added ten kilos.

One . . . two . . . three . . .

Andrea felt the tight tingle that she knew was the signal that lactic acid was being released into the muscle tissue to lubricate and ease strain. It felt good. Sensual. A thrill ran through her limbs and chest. She knew these feelings came from her endocrine system releasing endorphins to combat the pain.

Four . . . five . . . six . . .

Her thighs were good. They responded to each abduction with a rope-ripple of muscle beneath her dark tanned skin. Yes, she was happy with her thighs. Her abs were probably her best feature, along with the stone-carved definition of her arms. It was her glutes that she was still disappointed with: both her medials and maxes. She spent hours working on them, but seemed unable to rid herself of the sheath of soft fat that cloaked their musculature.

Ten . . . eleven . . .

Andrea had six months until the competition. She had a good chance this time round, but her glutes would let her down. She had to work them harder. She would do an extra hour's running tonight. Anything to try to burn off the last vestiges of the old Andrea. Soft Andrea. She thought of the couple in the café. About the girl and how she had let her boyfriend talk to her, treat her. The anger she felt whenever she thought about it drove her on harder. Another lift.

Twelve . . . thirteen . . . fourteen . . .

Andrea scowled through the pain of the lifts as a man came into the gym. She caught him staring at her. She met his gaze and he turned away to start his warm-up on the treadmill. Andrea was used to people looking at her. Some, like the man who had just come in, did so with an expression of part awe, part revulsion. And some, of course, just like the little shit in the café, with disgust.

Fifteen . . . sixteen . . .

What Andrea liked most was that moment when some men looked at her and were totally confused about their own reactions. In those faces she read a mixture of distaste and confused lust. And, of course, there was the way women looked at her. Andrea was proud of the body and the face she had sculpted for herself. Andrea the Amazon. She had added to the impact of her physical presence by dying her thick mane of hair platinum blonde. And she always wore expensive make-up: deep red lipstick and dark eyeshadow to emphasise the fire in her blue eyes.

Seventeen . . . eighteen . . .

It was one of those things that people didn't like to talk about. That there were men who found a form like hers beautiful. Erotic. She had even been paid good money by Nielsen to pose nude. And, of course, there were the men who came to the competitions. Eager little men with eager little eyes.

Nineteen . . . twenty.

The last extension lift was tough and despite the restrainer across her thighs and the padded shin bar isolating the effort as much as possible, her whole body tensed and strained. Her neck and jaws became made of cable and wire; her arms, tensed against the lateral grips, tautened and swelled simultaneously. She saw the man looking at her again. This time he could not look away. It was there: the revulsion. But what was also written across his threatened expression was that he was looking at something awesome.

Something magnificent.

5.

Maria followed Viktor to two more pick-ups, each time noting the addresses as well as she could. It had been dark for a couple of hours and that gave her some protection from detection, but she was still taking a risk: Viktor might have already spotted her on his tail. In which case she would find out soon enough.

The Chrysler made its way back to what Maria now knew to be the Nippes area of the city. He berthed the American cruise ship at the kerb and locked it up. Maria pulled in further down the street and got out. Viktor walked about fifty metres before entering an apartment building. Maria had watched him do this so many times during the afternoon and evening, but Viktor was calling it a night and this was obviously where he lived. After half an hour of standing in the cold, Maria was satisfied that the giant Ukrainian wasn't coming out again and she checked the names on the door buzzer panels. There was a Turkish name, two German, no Ukrainian. But one panel had been left blank. That was it. Third floor. The street Viktor lived in was reasonably busy. There was a bar across the road, a small supermarket with window stickers marked up in Cyrillic, and an electrical store. Maria's options for surveillance seemed limited; she would probably have to resort to sitting in the car again. First, though, she would camp out in the bar across the street. It had a window from which she could watch the apartment.

She knew it was a mistake as soon as she entered. The customers in the bar were almost all men, apart from a scattering of brassy-looking female types, some of whom were dressed ten years too young for their ample figures. Maria, her body cloaked in the baggy pullover and jeans, was revolted by their exhibition of age-puckered flesh. She sat by the window that she had selected. A couple of men at the bar followed her progress, exchanged muttered remarks and burst into laughter. The waiter came to her table and she ordered a beer.

'Nothing to eat?'

'Nothing to eat.' Maria paid for the beer as soon as it arrived. She was aware of the glances being cast across at her by the men at the bar, as well as the hostile, bottle-blonde glares of some of the women. She decided to watch the apartment from here for only a few minutes, and then from the car. Two patrolling policemen passed the window. Unlike the Polizei Hamburg, who had switched to new blue uniforms, the North-Rhine-Westphalia police still wore the nineteen-seventies-designed green and mustard. It made Maria feel strange watching the police officers go by; they seemed like alien creatures. Something, she knew, had become broken inside her and could not be repaired. Hamburg and her job as a detective seemed so very far away from her now.

'Y'awright, darlin'?'

Maria knew without turning that it would be one of the drunks from the bar. She didn't reply.

'Asked if you was awright, darlin'?' the man repeated, then added something in a thick dialect that she took to be *Kölsch*.

Maria left her beer untouched and stood up to leave. The man in her way wasn't particularly tall but he was heavy, with a vast belly stretching his checked shirt. He stood too close to her. She felt her panic rise.

'Excuse me,' she said, avoiding eye contact with the drunk.

'What's the matter?' he said in an offended manner. 'I just asked if you was all right. My friend and I would like to buy you a drink.'

'I've got a drink. And anyway, I'm leaving. Get out of my way, please.'

The heavy man stepped to one side with a shrug, but without allowing her much room to pass. Maria squeezed past him, fighting the revulsion that rose within her at the idea of physical contact. She simply wanted out of the bar: the scene was attracting a fair bit of attention and the barman was clearly considering intervening on her behalf. This was all wrong: surveillance meant keeping the target visible and yourself invisible. As she passed the drunk, she smelled the thick odour of stale beer on his breath. He winked at his partner at the bar. It was then that she felt his hand on her backside.

'Not much there . . . he said loudly and laughed. 'But you'll do!'

The explosion of revulsion, hate and panic within Maria was immediate.

'Don't *touch* me!' She screamed into the drunk's face so loudly and so fiercely that his smile gave way to shock. The laughter in the bar died. 'You FUCK!' she screamed again.

Her arm arced so fast that no one saw it coming. There was an explosion of glass, beer and blood on the side of the fat man's face. He staggered sideways and Maria, now clear of the table, slammed her heavy boot into his groin. She looked at him and laughed as he doubled over. A shrill, not entirely sane laugh. Then she looked at everyone else in the bar. No one met her eye. Probably for the first time in years, the brassy bar blondes were trying not to be seen. Maria noticed the barman reaching for the phone. He was going to call the police and she'd seen a foot patrol just two minutes ago in the street. It was all fucked up. Her anger surged again and she kicked the fat man in the face as he lay on the floor. She grabbed her coat and headed for the door.

'I won't be back,' she said to the barman as she did so. She eased her pullover up from the top of her trousers just enough for the barman to get a glimpse of the automatic tucked into her waistband. 'But if you call the police I will.'

He put the phone down.

Maria turned to the door and found a couple standing in her way. The girl was a younger version of the other women in the bar, dressed gaudily and with a gold stud in her nostril. He was tall and massive, wearing the same long leather coat he had worn all day while she'd been following him. Viktor looked at the groaning fat man lying in a pool of blood and beer on the floor, at the barman with his hand still on the phone, and then at Maria. He beamed an amused grin and stood politely to one side.

Maria stormed out of the bar. As soon as the cold night air hit her she started to cry in silent sobs, and headed down the street in the opposite direction from where she'd parked. She'd have to come back for the car later, in case Viktor or the barman noted her licence number.

She walked for a number of blocks before taking a taxi. Once she was back at her hotel she changed swiftly into a completely different outfit and then took a second taxi back to where she had left the car. Maria didn't look in the direction of the bar or Viktor's apartment until she was sitting in the dark of the Saxo.

Fuck, she thought. It's all completely fucked up. She could hardly have done more to bring herself to Viktor's attention. She had done so well in tracking him to his apartment. She had addresses or partial addresses for the pick-ups. But she hadn't been able to see the crucial next stage in the process: when it was Viktor's turn to hand over the cash. He wouldn't hang on to that amount of cash for long. Someone would come to him, or he would go to someone to hand it over. Regularly. But now Maria's face was known to him. In Hamburg, with an *official* surveillance, it wouldn't be an issue: there would be a constant circulation of cars and faces. Being followed by a team of five is five times more difficult to detect. She wished she could have called Anna Wolff, who worked with Maria in the Murder Commission in Hamburg. But there was no way of getting Anna, Fabel or anyone else involved. This was Maria's solo crusade and she had messed the whole thing up. She would have to find a way herself.

Maybe Viktor and his tart were still in the bar; she could sneak up to his apartment, break in and see if she could find something, some connection between Viktor and the next step up in Vitrenko's organisation. Maria bit her lip and gripped the steering wheel tightly. She was thinking like an amateur. She was worthless. She was a worthless bag of shit who had failed as a police officer and would now never achieve anything more in her life.

She started the car and drove without any sense of destination. She crossed the Zoobrücke bridge to the other side of the Rhine. After about half an hour she found a service station with an all-night American burger bar attached. She ordered a massive portion of burger and fries and shovelled the food into her mouth, swallowing huge chunks without chewing properly and washing it down with cola. When it was all gone, she went up and ordered the same again, defiantly staring down the waitress.

When she had finished the second portion, Maria went into the burger bar's washroom, knelt down at the toilet bowl and pushed her finger into her throat.

6.

Senior Criminal Commissar Benni Scholz was not someone who frowned often, but his broad brow creased beneath the mass of dark hair as he watched the television screen. This was probably the most important, most publicly visible task he had undertaken since he had become a police officer fifteen years ago. Every single officer in the Cologne police department would judge him on how well he handled it. Stress like this was something to which he was totally unaccustomed. So much pressure.

Scholz's office was in darkness, other than for a single small desk lamp and the flickering light from the TV. A tall, lean uniformed Commissar sat next to him, his attention also fixed with a frown on the images on the screen.

'Who was behind this, Rudi?' Scholz asked the uniformed officer without taking his eyes off the television.

'Hasek.'

'Hasek!' Scholz turned to Rudi Schaeffer with an expression of disbelief. 'Hasek organised this? That wanker in the Ops Room?'

Scholz turned again to watch the screen. An elaborately decorated carnival float, capped by a black Model-T Ford with the word 'POLIZEI' painted clumsily in white on the side and flanked by twenty or thirty men and women dressed as Keystone Cops, slowly progressed along a crowd-lined street. The 'Keystone Cops' continually bumped into each other, tripped over, spilled buckets of fake tinsel water over onlookers and hit each other over the heads with oversized rubber batons while others threw handfuls of candy into the crowd, all in carefully choreographed mayhem.

'That was three years ago. He won awards for that float,' said Rudi unhelpfully.

'I knew it had won an award,' said Scholz. 'But I had no idea it was bloody Hasek who had been the organiser that year.' His mood darkened even more. Everybody had been so certain that Benni Scholz was the man for the job. Everyone knew him for his sense of fun. His wacky humour. The ideal choice as organiser of this year's Cologne Police float for Karneval. He would rather have taken on another dozen murder cases.

'Did you get the dummy heads sorted out?' he asked Rudi. The services of Commissar Rudi Schaeffer of the city's traffic division, and an old friend of Scholz's, had been volunteered as assistant organiser. It had been Scholz who had volunteered them. No point in suffering alone, he had thought.

'Sure did.' Rudi smiled good-naturedly. 'I've got the *proto-type* outside . . .'

Scholz watched, despondently, as Hasek's perfect, award-winning float continued its flawless progress. Rudi reappeared, his head encased in a mass of painted papier mâché.

'What the fuck . . .' said Scholz twisting around in his chair. 'And allow me to repeat for the sake of clarity . . . what the *fuck* is that supposed to be?'

'It's a bull . . .' said Rudi, plaintively, his voice muffled by the dummy head. 'Just like you asked for. You know, big joke, we all dress up as *Bullen*.' Rudi referred to the derogatory nickname in German for a police officer. The Americans and British called their policemen '*pigs*'; the French '*les Flics*'; the Germans called them '*Bullen*'.

Benni Scholz was considerably shorter than Rudi Schäffer and had to reach up to put his arm around his colleague's shoulder. Rudi turned his huge papier-mâché head toward him.

'Rudiger, my dear friend,' said Scholz, 'I fully appreciate that you are from Bergisch-Gladbach. And I do make allowances for that . . . I really do. But I'm pretty sure that even in your formative years, you never saw a bull, cow or any form of cattle that remotely resembled whatever the hell that thing on your head is supposed to be. Unless, that is, Bergisch-Gladbach is twinned with Chernobyl.'

'It's only a prototype . . .' replied Rudi defensively from within the cavern of the dummy head.

At that point a young detective came into Scholz's office. He paused for a moment, staring at Scholz with his arm around a uniformed officer wearing a bizarre head. Scholz removed his arm.

'Can you guess what this is meant to be?' Scholz asked the young officer.

'Dunno, Benni . . . the Elephant Man?'

Rudi slunk out, his massive dummy head bowed.

'What is it, Kris?' Scholz asked the young detective.

'The Biarritz restaurant on Wolfsstrasse. One of the kitchen staff has been turned into mince by some guy with a meat cleaver . . .'

7.

The Teteriv river was beautiful at this time of year: crusted with ice but still flowing and free of the thick viscous algae that sleeked it in the summer. The lodge was wide and low and had its face to the Teteriv. It was fringed by forest, the trees thickly iced with frozen snow. Along one side of the lodge was a large wooden frame on which hunters would hang and gut their kills.

The others had already been there a day by the time Buslenko arrived. The road from Korostyshev was ancient, probably first forged by ox-driven *chumak* wagons four hundred years before. The deep snow had made the road all but impassable, but the drivers of each of the three Mercedes four-by-fours had been trained to negotiate every type of condition, from arctic waste to desert. As Buslenko approached the lodge, he was cheerfully greeted by a thickset man in his early forties, a sporting rifle slung over his shoulder. Buslenko smiled to himself at Vorobyeva's seeming casualness. Vorobyeva was a member of the Titan Spetsnaz and would have had Buslenko's four-by-four in his sights for the last ten minutes, only lowering his high-powered rifle when he was satisfied that it was Buslenko behind the wheel. And that he was alone. The Titans were specially trained to provide close protection for individuals as well as guarding key Ukrainian government sites. In the spirit of the free enterprise that the government had so enthusiastically embraced, they were even available for hire on a contract basis. If you were rich enough.

When Buslenko opened the door of the lodge the warm, rich odour of *varenyky* being cooked on the wood-burning stove embraced him.

'Smells good . . .' he said.

'You're just in time, major.' The man stirring the *varenyky* was Stoyan, the Crimean Tatar, whose dark good looks spoke of the blending of Mongol and Turk a thousand years before. 'Want some?'

'You bet. You'd better take some out to Vorobyeva too.' Buslenko took off his outer wear and greeted the group that sat at the heavy rough-hewn wooden table playing *Preferens*. Buslenko joined them and they joked and laughed their way through the meal, complimenting Stoyan on his cooking skills. They could have been any group of people in thick knitwear and hiking boots, gathered around a hunting lodge's hot stove, eating dumplings and drinking vodka and taking a break from their dull jobs to gather for a weekend's fishing or hunting in the wilds. But they weren't.

As soon as the meal was over, the dishes were cleared away

and everyone's attention was sombrely fixed on Buslenko. He took his laptop and several document folders and laid them on the table.

'This is a "Greater Good" operation,' he began without preamble. 'As such, we are being asked to carry out a mission that is illegal, under both Ukrainian and international law. But it is an operation that is fully in the interests of justice, internal order and the external reputation of Ukraine. Some of you may feel that the illegality of this operation is incompatible with your roles as law-enforcement officers. I also have to tell you that there is a considerable chance that we may not all come out of this alive. And if any of us are caught, we will go to prison abroad and without the recognition or intervention of the Ukrainian government. So if any of you feel that you don't want to take part in the operation, now's the time to say. You can leave now and no one will think any the less of you for it.'

Buslenko paused. 'I also have to tell you this mission isn't just black, it's wet.' A 'wet' Spetsnaz mission was one where blood was spilt; where people died. Buslenko's audience remained silent, their attention fixed on him and waiting for him to continue. He grinned and carried on.

'Okay, now that that crap's out of the way, let's get down to brass tacks.' He turned the screen of his laptop in their direction. He used a wireless mouse and the handsome face of a middle-aged Ukrainian officer appeared on the screen.

'This is our target. I know you all have heard of him. Colonel Vasyl Vitrenko, formerly of the Berkut counter-terrorist unit.' Buslenko nodded an acknowledgement to Belotserkovsky, the Berkut member of the team. 'I want you all to take a moment to think of the most dangerous person you have ever come across in your career.' Buslenko paused. 'Now imagine someone twenty times more dangerous and you're beginning to understand Vitrenko. He was nearly caught in Hamburg, Germany two years ago. He was being tracked by his own father, also a former Spetsnaz officer, as well as the Hamburg police. Vitrenko arranged a little spectacle for the Hamburg cops. He wired his own father up to an anti-tank mine and put it on a timer so that the investigating cop could bear witness to Dad being splattered across half the city. When it comes to killing, Vitrenko sees himself as a poet. An artist. He has a taste for the symbolic and the ritualistic. Before he took up his command post in the Berkut in nineteen-ninety, he'd already had a distinguished Soviet career in Afghanistan and had then volunteered to help our Russian cousins in Chechnya. The story is that he went renegade, converting the loyalty of his men from the "Motherland" to personal loyalty to him. This group forms the basis of the criminal organisation he has built. Vasyl Vitrenko is as skilled a killer and torturer as you are ever likely to experience. Like I said, he sees himself as an artist . . .' Buslenko clicked the mouse and another image filled the screen. It took a moment for the explosion of blood and meat to be recognisable as the remains of a human being. 'He believes that Ukrainians are descended from Vikings, which is partly true, so one of his specialities is to copy the Viking Blood Eagle ritual. He tears the lungs from victims while they are still alive and throws them over their shoulders as the wings of the eagle.'

Buslenko paused to let the image sink in. But this wasn't an audience to be easily shocked. Buslenko clicked the mouse again. Another face replaced Vitrenko's.

'Now say hello to Valeri Molokov. Russian. Forty-seven years old. Ex-cop. Former member of the Russian OMON special police Spetsnaz. Turned the people he was supposed to be hunting down into business associates. For a while he was considered to be a highly effective OMON operative, because one way or another he was taking down so many of Russia's key targets in organised crime. Turned out he had been steadily eliminating his competitors, or carrying out

contract killings for other crime bosses with whom he coop-
erated. It soon became known that if you wanted someone
taken out nice and cleanly, then Molokov was your man.
Despite having served with *OMON* and their history in
Chechnya, Molokov is known to have very strong links with
the *Obshchina* Chechen mafia. Wanted in Russia for smuggling, drug-trafficking, seven counts of murder, eight counts
of conspiracy to murder, rape and false imprisonment.'

'Any traffic convictions?' asked Stoyan with his handsome
Tatar grin. Everyone laughed, including Buslenko. A little
laughter in the face of enemies like these couldn't do any harm.

'Molokov is the only member of Vitrenko's senior management we've been able to identify. He has his own team within
the organisation and that's Vitrenko's first and only weakness: Molokov's security isn't a patch on Vitrenko's. It was
a hasty marriage of convenience . . . Basically Molokov was
made an offer he couldn't refuse by Vitrenko. Molokov's
activities were encroaching on Vitrenko's, so Vitrenko intercepted several consignments of Molokov's and set fire to the
container lorries.'

'What was the cargo?' asked Olga Sarapenko.

'It was a people-smuggling operation . . .'

'Fuck,' said Belotserkovsky. '*That* was Vitrenko? The thing
on the Polish border?'

'I thought it was an accident,' said Olga.

'That was the version put out for the media,' said Buslenko.
'A few kilometres further on and it would have been the
Polish police investigating and the whole thing would have
come out. It was kept quiet to buy us time to track Vitrenko.'

'So Molokov got the message?' asked Belotserkovsky

'He handed control over to Vitrenko – grudgingly – but
was left in charge of the people-smuggling operation. The
main difference is that he has no competition any more. He
works for Vitrenko and if any smaller-scale operation starts
up, Vitrenko ends it.'

'So why is this a black mission?' asked Stoyan. 'Ukrainian criminals, Ukrainian police and security. Ukrainian victims.'

'It's a black operation for two reasons. Firstly, our mission is to intercept Vitrenko with maximum prejudice. We're not coming back with a prisoner. The second reason is, as I said at the start, that we are operating outside Ukraine.'

'Specifically?' asked Olga.

'Specifically the Federal Republic of Germany.'

There was a outburst of expletives. 'Germany?' said Belotserkovsky. 'I've never been to Germany. My grandfather went there, though. Nineteen forty-four . . . with the Red Army. I think I may have German cousins.'

More laughter to defuse the tension.

Buslenko went though all the intelligence they had on Vitrenko and his operation. Buslenko told his team that Vitrenko was believed to have his base in Cologne, and still controlled much of the vice in Hamburg. The scope of his operation was vast, covering everything from luxury car rings to protection to electronic fraud. Buslenko wound up the briefing by laying out a map of Cologne marked with the three properties from which they would run their operation; a second map highlighted known Vitrenko-controlled operations. He then handed each member of the team a folder containing their individual mission objectives and responsibilities.

'By the way, Vitrenko would kill you for the information you now have in your hands. He is desperate to find out how much has leaked to us from the Molokov side of his organisation and from other sources. He is on a traitor hunt.'

'Is this everything we have on him?' asked Olga Sarapenko. She was sitting by the lodge's window and the light accentuated the blue of her eyes. When Sasha had recommended that she be brought on board Buslenko had seen the value, but now he found increasingly that her beauty distracted him.

'That's everything we've been given,' he said abruptly. 'The

Germans have more information. A lot more, probably, but they are reluctant to share it with us. Like most Westerners they believe "Ukrainian" is synonymous with "crooked". They're worried about leaks.'

'You can't entirely blame them,' said Olga. 'We could have nailed Vitrenko in Kiev if Peotr Samolyuk hadn't sold us out.'

Buslenko nodded, but he still found it difficult to believe that the Spetsnaz officer had betrayed them for money.

'Before we wind this up,' he said, 'there are two wild cards in the pack that you should know about. They're not likely to be an issue, but it's best that you're aware of them.' He clicked the mouse. 'This is Senior Criminal Commissar Maria Klee of the Polizei Hamburg . . . and this . . .' he clicked the mouse again, 'is her boss, Principal Chief Commissar Jan Fabel, chief of the Hamburg murder squad. These two are the only people to have come close to nailing Vitrenko. The price they paid included Vitrenko using Klee as a delaying tactic, leaving her with a near-fatal wound that Fabel had to deal with. And Vitrenko left two dead cops behind him.'

'But you don't think they're still after Vitrenko?' asked Olga Sarapenko.

'The price you pay for coming close to Vitrenko is high,' Buslenko said, closing the lid of his laptop. 'Jan Fabel has quit the police and Maria Klee is a basket case.'

8.

As he entered the kitchen, Benni Scholz paused to dip a spoon into one of the large pots on the huge brushed-aluminium cooker range. It was a split-pea soup that was still warm despite the hobs being switched off. A number of other pans had been knocked over, their contents splashed against the wall and across the floor where they mingled with other splashes – of blood. Scholz sipped the soup.

'Are you deliberately trying to contaminate this crime scene,

Senior Commissar?' An attractive young woman in a forensics coverall scowled up at him from where she knelt in the
centre of the kitchen floor.

'I've told you many times before, Frau Schilling.' Scholz's
dark eyes twinkled mischievously. 'Any time you want to
collect a DNA sample from me for elimination, I'd be more
than pleased to supply one. But I think we should have dinner
first. This place any good?'

'I have a feeling they'll be closed tonight,' the forensics
chief said flatly and unsmiling, turning her attention again
to the mass of lacerated flesh on the floor before her. 'In the
meantime, please don't touch *anything* else.'

Three other forensics technicians were working in the
kitchen, each on a different area. There were also two other
Criminal Police detectives from Scholz's department: Kris, the
young Criminal Police Commissar who had accompanied
Scholz to the scene and Tansu, a young Turkish-German
officer. The junior detectives lingered uncertainly at the
doorway that led from the main salon of the restaurant to
the kitchen. Both looked decidedly unwell, particularly Kris.
Scholz scanned the kitchen. Everywhere there were signs of
violence. The spilled pots. Blood smeared on the door frame.
A stool upset. Pools of blood on the floor. The epicentre of
the violence was the lump of meat that Simone Schilling now
examined. It was also the cause of the nauseated look on the
face of Kris Feilke.

'What's the story?' Scholz asked.

'Ukrainian,' Kris said at last. 'A kitchen worker. More than
likely an illegal. There were three other staff in the kitchen
at the time. Two Ukrainians and a Somalian. The Ukrainians
won't say a word . . . scared shitless. But the Somalian said
that three masked men came in and started shouting at the
victim. Not in German, so I'm guessing they were Ukrainian
too. Specially as the two Ukrainian kitchen staff have been
struck dumb. One of the masked men picked up a meat

cleaver . . .' Impossibly, the young detective's pale complexion paled further. 'Anyway, he did that to him.'

Scholz moved over towards the body. Simone Schilling stopped his progress with another cute scowl.

'I suppose it's too early to ascertain a cause of death?' Scholz grinned. It was difficult to see the features of the figure on the floor. One side of the face gaped open where the meat cleaver had sliced cleanly through skin, muscle, sinew and bone. Similarly, a straight-edged flap of flesh had separated from the upper arm, just below the cuff of his T-shirt. The cleaver's sharp edge had made the wounds unnaturally recti-linear. Scholz reckoned there were at least a dozen slashes on the body. 'But I'm guessing it wasn't a gunshot.' Scholz laughed at his witticism. Simone Schilling didn't. She stood up.

'You'll get a full report from the pathologist. Herr Dr Lüdeke will be carrying out the autopsy.'

'He's got his work cut out for him . . .' said Scholz and laughed, alone, at his joke.

Simone Schilling cast her eyes around the floor, where her team had tent-flagged various bloody smears. 'His attackers certainly didn't care about leaving evidence. We've got half a dozen bootprints in the blood. Clear patterns.' She looked at Scholz with disdain. 'Mind you, half of them are prob-ably yours by now.'

Scholz looked at the body again. Four or five of the slashes on the forearms. Palm split open, exposing bone. Defensive wounds.

'Do we have a name?' He called to the two detectives by the door.

'Slavko Dmytruk,' said Kris. 'Or that's the name the restaur-ant have for him. The owners reckon he's about twenty-three or -four.'

'Are you okay?' asked Scholz.

'Never been good with this side of the job . . .'

'What's not to be good with?' Scholz nodded to the corpse.

'That's not a person any more. It's nothing but meat. Whoever Slavko Dmytruk was, whatever made him who he was, has got nothing to do with what's left here. You've got to get past that. If you don't, you'll walk into a murder scene and find some little kiddie dead and you'll go to pieces. It'll be your last day on the job.'

Kris was looking at the partially dismembered corpse and did not look at all convinced.

'Have you had anything to eat?' asked Scholz. 'It's always worse if you've got an empty stomach.' He turned and dipped a ladle into the still-warm soup. He held it out to the young detective. 'Try some of this . . . it's really good. Split pea . . .'

Kris turned suddenly and bolted out into the restaurant, in the direction of the toilets. Tansu Bakrac scowled disapprovingly at her boss. When Scholz turned back to Simone Schilling, she was staring at him in disbelief.

'What?' he said defensively, the ladle still extended. 'I was trying to help him feel better . . .'

'Not everyone is as insensitive to human suffering as you, Herr Scholz.'

'Call me Benni.'

'Okay. You can call me Frau Doctor Schilling.' She nodded in the direction of the departed detective. 'Shouldn't you check that he's okay?'

'He'll be fine. If not, he's in the wrong job. Anyway, I'm not insensitive to human suffering. I feel for the victim. Horrible death. But I don't lose my lunch every time I look at a stiff. Like I said, they're not people any more. Just meat. No one knows that better than you.'

'You're right,' said Simone Schilling. 'A corpse isn't a person to me. It's a store of evidence. But it took years to become accustomed to it. Now I look at them professionally, not emotionally. But you . . . you're just an insensitive pig.'

Scholz smiled. He liked it when she insulted him. 'I'm not insensitive. Just practical.'

The young detective reappeared.

'You okay, Kris?' asked Scholz. He turned to Simone Schilling. 'See? Sensitive.'

'I'm fine,' said Kris. But he still looked pale.

'Right, then tell me about what happened here. Were you able to get any more out of the Somalian or the restaurant owners?'

'Not a lot,' said Tansu. 'The Somalian was being very helpful but then he suddenly dried up. I reckon the two Ukrainians told him who they thought the hatchet men were. Probably Ukrainian Mafia. Anyway, the three of them have been taken into custody by Immigration. The restaurant owners aren't too chatty either. Immigration is all over them as well.'

'So the answer's nothing?' Scholz asked impatiently.

'Not completely,' Kris said. 'Before the Somalian shut up, he said that there had been a woman around talking to Dmytruk. Tall, thin, expensively dressed. He got the impression she was Immigration. Or police.'

9.

Maria woke at six a.m. and listened to the sounds of the city sluggishly stirring in the dark winter Tuesday morning. She hadn't eaten since her binge on Sunday evening and her gut ached from having been force-fed and then forcibly emptied. She still felt chilled. But something had changed.

She placed herself in another place and another time. Maria never fully understood why she did this. So much of her recent past had been devoted to trying to put what had happened behind her. But she did this regularly: lay in the dark and imagined herself back in the field that night near Cuxhaven.

Until that night they felt they had been pursuing a ghost. The team had succeeded in cornering Vitrenko and a couple of his key henchmen. Vitrenko had escaped by throwing himself through a window and into the night. Maria had been in the field with two local Cuxhaven officers. Spread out. Vitrenko had probably not even broken step as he had sliced open the first officer's throat. Maria remembered Fabel screaming warnings to her down his radio. She had seen nothing. Heard nothing. But Vasyl Vitrenko had been brought up since boyhood to be a soldier of stealth. There had been a sound behind her and she had spun around but still had seen nothing. Then Vitrenko had suddenly loomed up from the long grass less than a metre away from her. She had swung her gun round but he had caught her hand with insolent ease and held her wrist in a crushing grip. It had been then that she felt him punch her in the solar plexus. But when she looked down she realised that he hadn't punched her. The handle of a broad-bladed ritual knife had jutted from her body, just below her ribcage. She had looked into Vitrenko's face. Into his cold, glittering, too-bright green eyes. He had smiled. Then he was gone.

The night had been cloudless and she had lain gazing at the stars. The pain had subsided, although she was aware of the knife as an alien object in her body. She had found she could only breathe in rapid, shallow gasps and had felt that terrible, gradual chill fill her being. It had seemed an eternity before she heard Fabel's voice calling her name. It could only have been a couple of minutes, but to Maria it had seemed so long that she had actually begun to wonder if she was dead: if this was what death was like, your final moment stretched out infinitely. But then Fabel had been there, bending over her, touching her, talking to her. He had been her link to the living. Fabel her boss. Fabel the father of his team.

But Fabel was not here now, in Cologne. And anyway, he was giving up his career as a policeman. Maria knew that she would never go back to duty. She would resign too. Or she would die here. It was not a thought that troubled her too much. Maria knew that Vitrenko had really already killed her, three years ago in that field. All he would be doing now would be to exorcise Maria's tortured ghost from the world. Maybe it would have been better if Fabel hadn't found her. Death would have been better than the hell she'd endured.

And then there had been Frank. Maria knew it was as close to love as she could have come. He had helped her through the worst times. He had been gentle, loving, kind. He had been a killer.

A car passing along the street outside the hotel sounded its horn and temporarily brought her back to the present and Cologne. Maria thought of Frank and wept. Not just for him, but for herself. He had been her last chance for salvation.

Maria felt empty and aching and old. But there *was* something else. The idea. The idea had been there, fully formed in her mind as soon as she woke up. And with it came a strength and sense of purpose she thought she had lost for ever.

Maria showered, changed and tore the page she needed from the telephone directory. She was about to go straight out, again skipping breakfast, but she checked herself. She went into the dining room and forced herself to eat some muesli and fruit. The breakfast and the coffee she drunk seemed to fuel her instantly. And this time there would be no trip to the toilets to void her gut. She headed purposefully out of the hotel. There had been a light fall of snow during the night that had turned into a mucky grey slush. She left the car and walked into the city centre. She found the hairdresser's first. Maria's hair was never particularly long and she usually spent a small fortune on expensive Hamburg stylists. This salon was the standard sort of place with a limited range of styles and an even more limited range of skills. A girl who looked as if she should have still been at school shampooed Maria's hair and asked her what she wanted done. Maria took a photograph from her handbag.

'That,' she said. 'I want to look like that.'

'You sure?' asked the hairdresser. 'Your hair has a lovely natural colour. Most of my customers would kill for hair your shade of blonde. They keep asking me but I never manage it, of course.'

'Can you manage that?' asked Maria.

The hairdresser shrugged and handed back the photograph of Maria and her friend and colleague Anna Wolff. 'Easy. If you're sure that's what you want . . .'

An hour and a half later, Maria was out on the street again. Despite the cold she didn't put her hat back on. The chill air nipped at her newly exposed ears and every now and then she would stop and look at her reflection in a shop window. Her hair was now a very dark brown, not quite as dark as Anna's and not quite as spiky-short, but it changed her appearance considerably.

The cosmetics assistant in the department store on Hohe Strasse was a little puzzled as to why her customer seemed so unsure about what went with her colouring, but a few minutes later Maria, who had always been conservative with her make-up, had a bag full of strong colours in eyeshadow, blusher and lipstick. The next store she went to, she described exactly the make-up she had just bought and claimed that she'd been wearing those shades for years and she wanted something completely different.

Before she found the next shop, she had to stop a couple of times to take the page she had torn from the telephone directory from her pocket and check the address against her street plan of Cologne. It was about lunchtime and, although her belly felt swollen to her from her unaccustomed breakfasting, she had a light lunch of soup and bread in the restaurant across the street. Maria now felt totally bloated and imagined her stomach distended, but she fought back the urge to make herself sick. It was all part of the plan.

It was a middle-aged and clearly gay man who took her

through the selection of wigs. Maria told him that she was an actress and was always looking for something to change her look. It was clear that the salesman had doubts about her story, but she explained that she often had to supply her own wigs and costumes. It was, she explained, a very specific form of acting she did, mainly for the DVD market. The salesman smiled knowingly, and took her through a range of styles, short and long, brunette, blonde and redhead. Maria bought five wigs, which delighted the salesman, although she was horrified at the cost.

'We could always put one back . . .' suggested the salesman tentatively.

'No . . . it's fine. I'll take them all.'

Maria called into another couple of clothes stores on her way to the hotel and arrived back in her room laden with shopping bags. She drew the curtains and stripped naked, standing with all the lights on in front of the mirror. She had been dreading this moment, knowing that after eating two meals in one day for the first time in months she would see how hideously bloated and fat she would have become. But she didn't. For so long Maria had been used to regarding her naked form with loathing, seeing the flesh swollen and fat. But not this time. It was as if her decision to become someone else had shifted her perspective and she was looking at someone else's body. So much damage. Maria had always been shapely, but slim. Now, after months of binging, purging and weeks of semi-starvation, Maria's body looked emaciated. Her ribs showed through the skin and her thighs seemed thinner than her knees. Her upper arms were stick-thin and the knife scar beneath her shrunken breasts contrasted pink against her pale, lifeless skin. Her face, beneath its new crown of near-black, short-cropped hair, looked gaunt and drawn. What had she done to herself?

She dismissed the thought: she would separate herself from the flesh of which she was composed. Her body would now simply be a canvas that she could use to create a dozen different Marias. The idea had been there when she had woken up: she had wished she could have brought in Anna to help her with the surveillance. Well, she could: by making herself into Anna and anyone else she chose to be. As the thought had evolved from an idea to a strategy to a plan, Maria had rediscovered a sense of resolve and direction. Instead of trying to dissolve into the background with her grungy clothes, she would *become* other people.

10.

Oliver drank his coffee and gazed at the blank white-tiled wall opposite him. But he wasn't seeing anything. Instead his mind dwelt on what had happened in the hotel room. It had been five days now and he had heard nothing. But he knew it would take the police some time to trace him, if ever. He had been extremely careful in his planning; in ensuring that his tracks were covered. She had made so much fuss, so much noise. She had known what he had wanted, that he had *special* needs: so why had she started to scream? Why did the stupid sluts always scream when they knew all along what he had to do to them? Oliver had had no choice other than to shut her up before someone in the hotel heard her.

He took another sip of coffee. No. He had nothing to worry about. He would never use that escort agency again and he would lie low for a while. And if he needed to exercise that deliciously dark side of his nature, then he would travel to another city.

Oliver drained his cup. He pulled on surgical gloves of a particularly heavy latex and snapped the cuffs around the sleeves of his protective gown. He went through the door and into a room flooded with a cheerless, harsh luminescence from neon strip lights. The steel tray was already set out with all the blades and tools he would need.

The taint hung faint but growing in the air. Oliver knew the causes of it, understood the science behind it: the smell of cellular degradation escaping from the large open wounds, the pooling of stagnant blood in livid blotches in the lowest points, the odour leeching out through the skin. But no matter how scientific the explanation or professional the understanding, it was still quite simply the smell of death. He took a deep breath, picked up a large-bladed scalpel and held it poised for a moment as he looked down on the corpse, already split with large gashes, before him.

Chapter Five

25–26 January

1.

There was no such thing as a slow day at the Speisekammer and Ansgar Hoeffer always arrived at the restaurant early for his shift. He was the Head Chef and saw his duties extending beyond when he officially clocked on and off. It was, after all, his reputation that had been behind the Speisekammer's growing success. The restaurant was doing the best trade it had known in its ten-year history. When Ansgar had first taken over the kitchen the Speisekammer had closed on Wednesdays. Now it did brisk midweek business for both lunches and evening meals. People came from across the city and beyond to savour Ansgar's fusion cuisine which combined the best of German dishes with influences as varied as Thai, French and Japanese. And that was quite an accomplishment in Cologne: there were thirty or more world-class restaurants in the city. Even the delicatessen attached to the Speisekammer was benefiting from what Ansgar had done to elevate the restaurant's reputation amongst Cologne's discerning diners. Not that this had gone unnoticed or unrewarded. Ansgar was amongst the highest-paid chefs in Cologne and the owners, Herr and Frau Gallwitz, had even talked about making him a partner. Ansgar had responded positively but cautiously to this suggestion: he had enough common sense to realise that the Gallwitzes' offer was as much motivated by sound commercial acumen as by any fondness for Ansgar who, even by his own admission, was a rather cold and distant man whose entire passion seemed concentrated on food. Everyone knew that if Ansgar moved to another restaurant, the greater part of the clientele would move with him.

Ekaterina, the Ukrainian *sous-Chef*, was waiting with breathless anticipation when Ansgar arrived. She hadn't changed into her whites yet and was still wearing her crop-top T-shirt. The T-shirt accentuated the swell of her breasts and her midriff was exposed: Ansgar tried not to look at the stud that pierced through the flesh of her navel. She looked up at him with her pale blue Ukrainian eyes that sparkled even brighter with morbid excitement.

'Have you heard about the Biarritz?' she asked in her heavily, sexily accented German. Ansgar shook his head. He knew of the Biarritz, but it was in the *Gulaschsuppe* league: tourists and business-lunch specials.

'What about the Biarritz?' he asked and stole a look at Ekaterina's breasts.

'One of the kitchen staff has been murdered. The day before yesterday.' She nodded her head gravely as if this added credibility to the statement.

'Oh?'

'Chopped up,' Ekaterina said. Deliciously.

'What do you mean?' Ansgar felt his heart begin to race. He looked into Ekaterina's electric-blue eyes. Why did Ukrainians have such bright eyes?

'Someone cut him up with a meat cleaver.' Ekaterina was clearly excited.

No, thought Ansgar. No, not that. Anything but that. Don't talk to me about that.

'It was awful,' said Ekaterina. 'And in the kitchen, too. There were bits of him all over the place. Like meat.'

Ansgar had taken his coat off and held it draped over his arm in front of him, hiding his erection.

'Did they catch who did it?'

'No. And it was a Ukrainian who was killed. But he was an illegal.' Ekatherina said this with another solemn nod. Ekatherina was proud of her legal status. She had been in Germany for five years and viewed the more recent arrivals from the East with some disdain. 'Horrible, though, isn't it, Herr Hoeffer? I mean, with a *meat cleaver . . .*'

Ansgar nodded curtly and headed into the kitchen, his coat still held before him.

2.

Maria sat outside the bar. She guessed that, living so near, Viktor would be a regular. She was not disappointed. She took a note of the time he left the apartment with his tarty girlfriend; it was almost exactly the same time that he had come into the bar on Sunday. Maria felt sick. The weight of the food she had eaten sat heavily in her gut. She had taken dinner in the restaurant before coming out and that, combined with the two other meals she had eaten that day, was causing her unaccustomed body to protest. But it was nerves more than anything that was making Maria nauseated. She could not believe that she was about to do what she was about to do. She had spent the entire afternoon experimenting with her new palette of cosmetics and trying on different wigs and outfits. But instinct had told her to go with her first idea in its purest form. She now looked like Anna Wolff. Anna, of course, was petite and had dark brown eyes, but Maria had successfully transformed herself into a taller version of her friend and colleague. She had applied a fake tan to her face and body and had given her newly dyed and cropped hairstyle the waxed, almost spiked look that Anna often had. She had filled out her lips with the same shade of fire-truck-red lipstick that Anna used and had emphasised her eyes with a quantity of shadow and eyeliner that she had never before in her life used. It was disconcerting to feel so much make-up on her face. Maria had even bought herself a biker-style leather jacket that hung too big over her thin frame and she had used a padded bra to boost her insubstantial curves under the black T-shirt.

This was it. This was the biggest test she could undertake. She got out of the car, locked it, and crossed the street to the bar.

Maria was shocked that the first two faces to turn to her as she walked into the bar were those of the two drunks from the last time. The one she had hit with her beer glass looked at her sullenly, a gauze pad taped to his distended and discoloured cheek. Her heart sank: this could mean that her little adventure would end before it had even begun. The two men eyed her and then turned back to their drinks. They were obviously chastened by their experience of the night before. Either that or they weren't yet drunk enough to have the courage to molest a female. But it was clear they hadn't recognised her and Maria felt a small thrill of satisfaction at the sight of the lingering injury she'd inflicted on Fatso. The barman was by far the greater challenge. Unlike the other two, he was sober and the same barman who had been on duty on Sunday. Instead of sitting at a table as she had before, she took a stool at the bar. She was relieved to see that the looks she received from the brassy-looking blondes in the bar were even more hostile.

'What can I get you?' asked the barman.

Maria smiled widely. She had good teeth and had been surprised just how much Anna's shade of lipstick accentuated them; made her mouth look sexy.

'A vodka and coke, please.' Maria did her best to sound less Hanover and more Cologne. 'I'm here to meet a friend. He said this bar but I couldn't find it so I'm late. Did he leave a message?'

'What's your name?' asked the barman.

'Anna . . .'

He checked with another member of staff.

'No. No message. Still want the vodka?'

'Why not?' Maria smiled again. The muscles in her face reminded her of just how unused to it she had become.

Maria sat and sipped her vodka, feeling no less conspicuous than she had the night before, but this time she felt in control. Her anxiety began to ease. There was a decent enough crowd scattered around the tables, at the bar and even standing in groups talking loudly. It was dense enough foliage for her to remain as concealed as much as a young woman on her own in a bar like this could be. Maria became aware that quite a few of the conversations were taking place in a Slavic language. Whether it was Polish, Russian or Ukrainian she didn't know; they all sounded the same to her.

She stole a glance across at the two men who had accosted her on Sunday night. The man with the injured face still looked pretty sorry for himself and his drinking buddy looked equally as glum, but seemed to be trying to console him.

Maria casually swung round on her bar stool. It took her a while to locate Viktor. He was sitting at a table in the far corner, wreathed in blue cigarette smoke. Maria felt a thrill when she saw he was talking to another man while his girlfriend sat looking gloomily bored. There was something about Viktor's body language that suggested Maria had hit the jackpot: Viktor's companion was clearly someone he was more than a little afraid of. The man had his back to her but she could see enough of his profile, build and hair colour to be confident she could ID him when he left the bar. She drained her glass and got up.

'What about your friend?' asked the barman.

'Sod him. His loss,' she said with a grin and left the bar.

3.

It was Wednesday the twenty-fifth. Buslenko had been able to give his team three solid days of briefing. It still wasn't enough, but he knew that Vitrenko had so many informers and double agents in place across the Ukrainian security apparatus that moving quickly and surprising him was their one advantage.

Buslenko was impressed, however: Sasha had done well with his choices. After only three days, it seemed as if the eight members of the team had worked together for years. The only slight exception was Olga Sarapenko. Her background as a Kiev city militia policewoman set her slightly apart from the others. Sasha had recommended her and Buslenko had agreed. There was no doubt that she was tough enough but Buslenko struggled to see her that way, continuously pushing aside the way he felt attracted to her.

But the team had to contend with another enemy that was even more unpredictable than Vitrenko. The weather had taken a turn for the worse and more snow had made the track impassable. Buslenko had always known that choosing such a remote location in the middle of the Ukrainian winter carried the risk of this happening. He had allowed himself a couple of days' leeway in setting the start of the mission. That said, they were going to have to start digging their way out if it snowed any more.

Buslenko decided that the third evening should be free of talk of the dangerous mission they had to undertake. Stoyan, the Crimean Tatar, reheated the leftover *varenyky*. They ate and played cards, taking turns to take lookout duty in the cold night air. Buslenko always felt more secure when Vorobyeva watched their backs. He was one of the team members personally selected by Buslenko and was going to handle the security for the mission. Vorobyeva's background in a specialist Titan unit meant that he could read any environment and identify exactly where threats were likely to come from. It was as true in an otherwise unknown German city as it was here in a snow-covered forest. Vorobyeva had been out on a two-hour duty and was a couple of minutes late.

Olga Sarapenko, wrapped up in her fleece coat, came back into the lodge. She had said she wanted some fresh air and had taken a cigarette outside.

'Did you see Vorobyeva?' asked Buslenko.

She shrugged. 'No. But I was only out on the porch. Maybe he's further down the drive.'

Buslenko looked at his watch. 'He's late. He's never late.' He picked up the two-way, hit the transmit button and called Vorobyeva. Silence. He called again. Still no reply.

Buslenko didn't need to give the order. Tenishchev and Serduchka unzipped the large canvas holdall in the corner and started passing out brand-new Ukrainian *Vepr* assault rifles and clips before taking a couple of AK74Ms for themselves.

'Lights!' Buslenko said, unholstering his Fort17 handgun. The night filled the lodge. The moon was not yet full, but reflected brightly off the snow. It traced the snow-smoothed edges of the drive and Buslenko followed its sweep round to where it disappeared into the dense forest. No fresh footprints. He looked at each one of his team in turn. Now he would find out how good they were. He signalled to Tenishchev who passed him the night-vision scope. Buslenko scanned the forest and the fringes of the drive for movement. Nothing.

He used hand signals to order the team to spread and search. He indicated that Olga should stay in the lodge.

It was impossible to move without making a noise. The snow had stopped falling, but the night-time drop in temperature had given it a sparkling crust which twinkled in the moonlight and crunched underfoot. Anyone waiting for them would be able to see and hear them. Buslenko's mind raced. He knew something was wrong. Vorobyeva was now well overdue. He sent two teams of two out on either side of him: Tenishchev and Serduchka to the forest side of the track, Stoyan and the Berkut officer, Belotserkovsky, on the river side. He walked along the middle of the track, exposed, while the others covered him, their weapons sweeping from side to side. Buslenko strained the night for any sound of an enemy hidden in the forest, the sound of the river to his left became deafening.

He followed the track around the corner. The river was now behind him and thick forest on either side. He waited until the others flanked him, sheltered on the edges of the forest. About three hundred metres down the track he found fresh bootprints in the snow. Vorobyeva's: he was the only member of the group who wore Russian *OMON* boots. Buslenko crouched down and signalled for the others to follow him twenty metres behind, on either flank. He followed the bootprints into the forest and deeper snow. He could tell that Vorobyeva had swung across here to check something out. Buslenko felt his heart pound. He was only a few kilometres from his old home town, yet he knew he was at war. Clearly Vitrenko had decided not to wait until Buslenko travelled to Germany before finishing him off. He froze. About twenty metres ahead was a clearing in the forest, illuminated like a stage by the moonlight. He took aim at the figure kneeling at the edge of the clearing, not moving. He drew closer, trying to minimise the sound of his progress through the snow and the forest debris, always keeping his aim locked on the kneeling figure. He was ready to fire if any sound he made caused the man at the edge of the clearing to turn. Buslenko's foot sunk into a snow-filled hollow, making a slow crunch that the kneeling man must have heard. But he didn't move. Buslenko moved further forward; from this distance he could recognise the black parka, its hood pulled over the man's head.

'Vorobyeva!' he hissed. 'Vorobyeva . . . are you all right?'
Still no answer. He moved further forward. 'Vorobyeva!'

He signalled for the others to join him. Stoyan and
Belotserkovsky appeared like ghosts from the undergrowth.

'Where are Tenishchev and Serduchka?' Buslenko asked.

'They were there a minute ago . . .' said the Tatar.

Buslenko scoured the forest to their right. There was no
sign of the other two Spetsnaz. No sound.

'Cover me,' said Buslenko. 'We've definitely got hostiles.'

Buslenko crawled through the snow. He reached the
kneeling figure.

'Vorobyeva!'

For the last three minutes Buslenko had known what to
expect. The snow in front of the kneeling Vorobyeva was
stained dark. Buslenko touched the figure's shoulder and
Vorobyeva toppled backwards. His throat was gashed open
and glistened a cold crimson-black in the moonlight.

'Fuck!' Buslenko turned his attention like a searchlight on
the fringes of the clearing, scanning them for any sign of the
enemy. He moved back to where he had left Stoyan and
Belotserkovsky.

'He's dead. Vorobyeva was one of the best in the business.
Whoever's taken him by stealth must be even better. We're
in trouble.'

'Vitrenko?'

'God knows how he tracked us here, but that's who's behind
this.'

'What about Tenishchev and Serduchka?' asked Belotserkovsky.
'Them too?'

Buslenko suddenly remembered Olga Sarapenko. 'We've
got to get back to the lodge. Now!'

4.

He looked down at the corpse on the table.

For Oliver, death held no mystery. He had become accustomed to it: so many dead over the years. He could still recall his first, how he had looked into her face and had seen the person instead of the flesh; someone with a history, who had had a life and a personality, who had dreamed and laughed and felt the sun on her face. He had seen the stretch marks of distant pregnancies, the scar on her knee from an even more distant childhood injury, the lines around her mouth from a lifetime of laughing. Then he had pushed his knife into her and had begun to cut her up and she had ceased to be a person. After her, after his first, it had become so much easier. He still looked *at* a face before he started to cut, but he never looked *into* one. Now they were all simply so much cold flesh: doubly chilled from death and from their refrigerated storage until Oliver was ready for them.

He drew a deep breath before starting. The dismemberment of a human body was much harder work, physically, than most people imagined. Deprived of its vitality, a corpse was a heavy, dead mass, its density varying radically from the almost liquid, to gristly, to the solid and unyielding. Organ and bone, skin and fat, cartilage and sinew: cutting through the material of a human corpse required robust tools, some even power-driven. Oliver had all he needed to hand. Breadknife. Electric saw. Hand-held saw. Shears. Scissors. Knife.

He started as he always did, walking around the table and observing the lifeless body. The dead man was still fully dressed and Oliver noticed that some of the material from his blood-soaked T-shirt and kitchen overalls had been forced into the deep gashes. Oliver counted the cuts out loud, some of which gaped open, exposing the subcutaneous layer of pale marbled fat and the darker, denser mass of sinew and muscle beneath.

Some of the slashes exposed white bone and as Oliver leaned
closer to examine the wounds he saw where the bone had
been chipped by the cleaver, the primary evidence of sharp-
force trauma.

There were two other men in the room; together they helped
Oliver turn the cadaver onto its belly. He examined its back.
There were fewer wounds there, but they were still signifi-
cant.

'Let's get him undressed,' Oliver said and the two other
men helped him cut and remove the dead man's clothes. After
the body was naked, Oliver repeated his observational circuit
of it, again speaking his thoughts out loud.

It had been one of the first things Oliver had learned as a
forensic pathologist: to take time and use his eyes. To make
observations. He had often compared his work to that of an
archaeologist, where technology, science and professional
skills combined to uncover a complete history. But first, like
an archaeologist viewing a landscape and identifying a likely
dig site, you had to know where to look.

'Deceased is male, early twenties, light build. There are
multiple wounds indicating sharp-force trauma . . .' As he
looked at the corpse, Oliver voiced his thoughts into the
Dictaphone. 'Incised wounds and lacerations suggest the
deceased was in motion for much of the attack and are pri-
marily anterior but with several posterior.' Oliver nodded to
the technician and the other attending pathologist and between
them they used a tape to take the body's measurements. He
took his time, examining every mark, every bruise, and noting
it out loud into the Dictaphone. The man on the table had
been hacked to death but Oliver saw no horror, no pain, only
injuries and traumas to be methodically and individually
enumerated, location on the body noted, and their length and
depth measured. For Oliver in his work, death had become
nothing more than a point in time: a moment that divided
every injury, every mark, into ante-mortem, perimortem or

post-mortem. Within seconds of death occurring, a whole new chronology began: cells started to break down; blood that had been pumped on an endless cycle for a lifetime sank to the lowest points of the body and empurpled the skin with post-mortem lividity; the chemistry of the muscles became altered causing rigor mortis; bacteria in the blood and organs began to produce gases that inflated cavities and soft tissues.

Oliver started at the head and worked his way to the feet, talking his way across the topography of the body. Observing, remarking, measuring. He marked on a body map each of the incised wounds, where the cut had been clean and sharp-edged, and lacerations, where the weapon had sliced through the flesh but had caused tearing to the wound edge. To a forensic pathologist, there was always a distinction. When he had finished he nodded to the technician who lifted the corpse's head and eased a body block under the neck.

As he worked, Oliver thought back to his childhood and remembered his father carving meat. A long time ago. The technician swept a scalpel in a U-cut around the base of the scalp while Oliver began slicing a T-shaped incision into the body: one cut across the upper chest, from below the outer edge of one collarbone across to the outer edge of the other; then he made a long steady slice from the throat to the groin. He peeled back the skin and the subcutaneous tissue to reveal the ribcage. The process was a lot more awkward than usual because of the numerous other slashes that had been made to the body by the attackers. He also couldn't free himself of the butterfly flutter in his chest whenever he thought about what had happened in the hotel. He picked up a pair of shears that looked as if they should be used to prune rose bushes and started to snip through the ribcage. Two cuts: one right and one left of centre along the mid-clavicular lines where the ribs were composed of carti-lage. He lifted out the sternum and exposed the pericardial sac which he in turn cut open with the smaller scissors.

Oliver knew he would get caught eventually. He was an intelligent man, and his work brought him into contact with the police all the time. He knew they weren't stupid, and he also knew that every time he did what he did the chances of arrest increased exponentially. He used the long sharp knife, known as the bread knife, and cut out the heart. The pathologist assisting Oliver sucked out some of the blood from the heart with a syringe and placed it in a sample tub. Oliver eased back the skin of the neck. One of the blows from the victim's attackers had sliced into his neck, so Oliver opened up the throat, cutting from the jugulum up to the chin. He could see where the cleaver had severed the sternomastoid muscle almost completely. Here lay the immediate cause of death. The victim had died by exsanguination, resulting from the multiple incised wounds, but the slice into the subclavian artery had been what had caused him to bleed out fast. Oliver imagined the death, something he was not normally inclined to do: the victim would have been in extreme shock, would have felt extremely cold, and unconsciousness and death would have come pretty swiftly.

Maybe the police already had their suspicions; maybe Oliver had said something or done something or had left something behind that would lead them to him. Maybe they were watching him. Waiting for him to do it again.

He made a midline incision into the peritoneal cavity and used the bread knife to sever the organs of the neck and removed the victim's tongue and throat. Then he carefully lifted out the slippery mass of the lungs, bronchi and aorta, all of which were left connected. Oliver took great care while cutting free from the mesenterium the seven metres of upper and lower intestines and removing them from the body. He had learned from experience that a rupture could result in content escape, the stench of which was somewhere between that of vomit and excrement combined and ten times as potent. He then excised and removed the liver, pancreas, spleen and stomach from the upper abdomen, again keeping them connected. No, he thought, it doesn't make sense. If the police suspected him then he would have been immediately suspended from work.

While the assistant carried out weighing duties, Oliver removed another connected set of organs, this time the kidneys, urinary bladder and abdominal aorta. The subject's body cavity was now empty and the grey-white of his spine was exposed. Oliver turned his attention to the head, removing the brain and inspecting the inner aspect of the skull. Once the exenteration was finished, Oliver cut sections for histology and later microscopic inspection, dropping the samples into formaldehyde. There was no need for the whole brain to be fixed in formaldehyde and sliced in two weeks' time for detailed study: there were no significant cranial traumas, so he took slices from the brain to be sent for toxicology along with the body fluids. It took Oliver another hour to lift the skin from around the slice wounds for detailed inspection.

After the autopsy was completed, Oliver washed up and drove home to his flat. The city slid by, glistening-wet dark in the night. He smiled to himself. The butterfly sensation had gone. A voice deep inside seemed to reassure him: no, he said to himself, they won't catch you. You're too clever for them. And soon it will be Karneval.

5.

It was about half an hour before the man whom Maria had seen Viktor talking to left the bar. He came out alone, but Maria recognised him. He was shorter than Viktor and not as heavily built, but there was something about his physique and the way he moved that told Maria that this was the 'soldier' Slavko had talked about. Maria had made an in-depth study of Soviet and post-Soviet Spetsnaz soldiers. Vitrenko was the devil she had had to get to know. Part of the selection criteria was that the men chosen were never particularly tall or muscle-bound: they had to be able to dissolve into the background, whether that was in a desert, a jungle or a city. But there was always something in the way they moved that identified them. Maria had no doubt that she was looking at an ex-Spetsnaz. And that she had just taken a significant step up in Vitrenko's organisation.

Maria felt afraid. She knew that tailing this man was a whole different ball game. Unlike Viktor, this guy would have been trained to spot surveillance. She would only have one shot at this.

The Ukrainian got into a mid-range BMW and drove off. Maria waited until there were several cars between them before she pulled out into the traffic. She would have to risk losing him rather than have him detecting her too close on his tail. They headed out of Nippes. Maria struggled to steer with one hand while stealing glances at the Cologne city plan in her other. They seemed to be heading along Kempener Strasse towards Neu Ehrenfeld and she guessed they might be destined for the autobahn. It started to rain heavily and Maria had to switch the wipers on to the fastest setting. Her head ached after the adrenalin rush of testing her new look in the bar and from concentrating through the dark and rain on the distant tail lights of the Ukrainian's BMW.

They joined the autobahn heading north. Maria relaxed a little. She could drop back even further, accelerating only as they approached an exit, in case he took it. Eventually Cologne's silhouetted skyline disappeared from the edges of the autobahn and they seemed to be heading towards Düsseldorf. The BMW suddenly veered off the autobahn without indicating. Maria felt a tightness in her chest. Was there a significance in him pulling off without signalling? She put her indicator on and followed him off the autobahn. As she followed the circular sweep of the exit, she found she had lost sight of the BMW. The rain still pounded on the windscreen and the unlit arc of road seemed crowded in by trees. The road straightened and she came to a junction. She could see as far along the road in both directions as the darkness and the rain would permit. No tail lights. She stopped. There were no cars behind or in front of her – she was isolated in the tiny universe of her car and the silver rods of rain caught in her headlights. She sighed. She accepted she would have to lose him rather than stick too close and if she had to pick up his trail every night at the bar where he obviously had a regular meeting with Viktor, then that was what she would do. She put the car back in gear and drove off.

Maria knew she would get lost if she blindly followed the road, so she decided to turn and head back in the direction of the autobahn. She reckoned that the Saxo's turning circle would be tight enough for her to swing round without finding a junction to turn in. She checked her rear-view mirror. Clear. Maria swung the Saxo around and, apart from the right front tyre mounting the verge a little, did a perfect turn. It was then that the headlights of the BMW came on full beam, blinding her. The Ukrainian's car was on the wrong side of the road and she realised that until that moment it had been heading straight for her at high speed, its lights switched off. Maria pulled hard on the steering wheel and the BMW flashed by, but it caught the rear right wing of the much lighter Citroën and sent her into a sideways skid. Maria's training took over from her instinct and she straightened the Saxo. She floored the accelerator and the little car surged forward faster than she had anticipated. She checked the rear-view mirror: the BMW had been forced to do a three-point turn, giving her time to open up a precious lead on it.

Maria's mind worked hard and fast. Bastard, she thought, you were hiding with your lights out in that entrance to the woods. She knew what he had intended: to knock the Saxo off the road, then probably smash her head in and make it look like she'd been killed in the crash. Maybe that's what they had done with Turchenko, the Ukrainian investigator who had come after Vitrenko. Maria was aware of the nauseating fear that gripped her, but there was also a sense of exhilaration. And defiance. There was no way this prick was going to chase her to her death.

She saw the headlights of the BMW behind her. A couple of cars passed in the opposite direction, then nothing. He had known that this was a relatively deserted stretch of road and had led her here deliberately. The BMW was still some distance behind, but she calculated that he was closing. If there had been more bends on the road she would have stood a better chance: the Saxo was quick to accelerate and handled corners well, but on a straight stretch like this she was no match for the BMW's horsepower. Maria kept her foot pressed hard to the floor and tried to achieve the same with her mental processes. He was a soldier. A Spetsnaz. He could probably kill someone with a paper clip in a snowstorm, but that didn't necessarily give him an advantage in this environment. There was a gentle bend ahead; he would lose sight of her for thirty or forty seconds. She took the bend fast, the rain now driving hard against the windscreen. As she did so she unbuckled her seat belt and killed her lights. She swung the Saxo round in the road as fast as she could without losing control on the rain-sleeked tarmac. The BMW was already round the corner by the time she had completed her turn. Maria braked hard, leaving the Saxo on the wrong side of the road, hit the lights and jumped from the car.

6.

The three Spetsnaz made their way back along the edge of the Teteriv river. Buslenko had calculated that, in this moonlight, anyone approaching them would be silhouetted against the sky. When they reached the lodge it was still in darkness, the door wide open. Buslenko sent Stoyan around to the back, got Belotserkovsky to cover him, and swung his aim into the lodge.

'Captain Sarapenko?'

'Here,' said Olga, and switched on a table lamp. She was aiming her automatic at him. She eased the safety catch back on and lowered the weapon.

'Very good . . .' Buslenko smiled. 'But switch the light off. We've got trouble.'

'Vorobyeva?'

Buslenko shook his head. 'And we think Tenishchev and Serduchka too.'

Belotserkovsky swung into the lodge and closed the door. Stoyan came in from the back. 'Clear at the rear. But there's bad news there as well. Someone has disabled the vehicles. If we want to get out of here, then we have to walk.'

'That should make it easy for them,' said Belotserkovsky grimly.

'Enough of that,' said Buslenko. 'I'm not going to let that bastard Vitrenko fillet me the way he did Vorobyeva.'

'So you think he's out there?' asked Olga.

'Oh, yes. If the prey is special to him, he likes to be there for the kill.' Buslenko paused, frowning. 'Funny . . . I said exactly the same thing to someone just yesterday.' He felt a sudden panic in his chest as he thought about Sasha. Sasha was no soldier. He was an analyst. A soft and easy target. The thought must have registered in his face.

'What's wrong?' said Olga.

'The guy I got to put the team together . . . He was the only person who knew we would be here. They must have got to him.'

'Bribery?'

'No . . .' Buslenko shook his head. 'Never. Not Sasha. They must have . . .' He let the thought die.

Belotserkovsy rested a hand on Buslenko's shoulder. 'If it

was him, Taras, he's not in any pain now. They wouldn't have kept him once they knew we were here.'

7.

The BMW braked as it came around the corner and found Maria's Saxo head-on in its path, but the tyres aquaglided on the wet surface. The driver corrected by accelerating and swinging the BMW to avoid the Saxo. By the time he passed Maria where she stood at the side of the road, she had the illegal automatic aimed at the flank of the speeding car. She fired six rounds in rapid succession as it passed and the side windows shattered. The BMW swung from side to side, straightened, then accelerated away. Maria fired three more rounds at the rear of the car as it disappeared into the distance.

Maria watched the BMW for a moment, then took a second clip from her pocket, rammed it into the grip, snapped the carriage back to put a round in the chamber and stood, arms locked before her, waiting for the BMW to come back. It didn't. Her heart pounded. The rain plastered her newly darkened hair to her scalp and she was chilled to the core of her being.

And she felt better than she had in months.

The bastard had seen her as an easy victim. She had seen herself as an easy victim. But now the hunted was the hunter. Nine rounds into the body of the car: she must have hit him somewhere. Maria ran back, spun the Saxo around in the road once more, and headed off after the BMW.

8.

They had been in the lodge for three hours. They had not allowed themselves a light, nor the comfort of food or drink.

'I don't get it,' said Buslenko. 'Why don't they just get it over with? There's only four of us in here. We're kilometres away from civilisation. They could use finish us off with silenced fire and no one would be any the wiser. Where are they?'

Stoyan nodded. 'It doesn't make sense. And they've covered their tracks pretty well.' He peered out of the window into the moonlight. 'Maybe they're waiting for us to try to get out.'

Belotserkovsky suddenly looked agitated. 'Maybe there's no one out there,' he said at last. 'Maybe it's the enemy within we should be worrying about.'

'What are you talking about?' said Buslenko.

'Maybe there's no Vitrenko force out there. Maybe we're dealing with an infiltrator.'

'That's crap,' said Stoyan, but he looked uneasy.

'Taras is right that only his friend knew about this location,' said Belotserkovsky. 'That is *outside* all of us.' He looked at Olga Sarapenko. 'She's not one of us. How do we know she isn't in Vitrenko's pay?'

'That's bullshit,' said Buslenko.

'No . . . no, wait a minute,' said Stoyan. '*She* was outside immediately before Vorobyeva was killed.'

Buslenko's face darkened. 'Enough! Are you trying to tell me that *she*,' he indicated Olga with a nod of his head, 'was able to sneak up on the best personal security specialist I've ever worked with? No offence, Captain Sarapenko.'

'None taken,' she said. 'Even I know my limits. But maybe this is why they haven't finished us off. Maybe they're waiting for us to come apart at the seams.'

'Good point.' Buslenko's expression suggested that he had made a decision. He looked at his watch. 'It'll be light in two hours. I want us out of the woods by then. Get kitted up. We're going for a walk.'

'Stoyan, you take point.' Buslenko looked up at the sky. The moon was low, caressing the bristling tip of the forest. He found himself blessing the few clouds that had drifted in from the west. 'Captain Sarapenko, I take it you know how to use one of these . . .' He tossed a *Vepr* assault rifle to her.

'I can handle it.'

Buslenko pointed to the river to the left of the hunting lodge. 'Same as before – we use the bank as cover. Keep low and keep together. If we're going to encounter opposition, it'll come from the forest, where there's more cover. They'll have to expose themselves to attack. The one thing we have to watch out for is grenades. Or they've maybe predicted our route and set booby traps. Watch out for tripwires.'

Buslenko gave Stoyan a gestured countdown. On one, Stoyan rushed out of the lodge, across the drive and down the river bank. He ran crouched low but fast. Buslenko waited. No gunfire. Stoyan indicated the all-clear and Buslenko gave Olga Sarapenko the order to cross, then Belotserkovsky. Still no attack.

It didn't make sense. Now would have been the time to pick them off. It seemed as if they were running from ghosts. Maybe Belotserkovsky had a point. Maybe it was one of them. But there was no one in the remaining group that he could have imagined taking out Vorobyeva with such ease. Certainly not the woman.

Buslenko scoured the fringe of the woods with the night-vision scope he had attached to his *Vepr*. Finally, he bolted across the snow-encrusted track and down the river bank.

9.

Maria spent three hours searching for the BMW. She had been sure she would find it slewed off the road, the Ukrainian slumped over the wheel. She was vaguely shocked at her lack of concern for the driver. She could be pretty certain that she had just either killed another human being or seriously injured him. But, there again, he had tried to kill her and death was something these people traded in. Maria backtracked to check for turn-offs she might have missed: there were none. He had got away. She checked the fuel gauge: she was running low and she was not entirely sure which way would lead her back to the autobahn and Cologne. And it was as if she herself was running out of fuel; the leaden, aching tiredness of her system was draining the adrenalin that had flooded it during the chase. Eventually she came to a junction which indicated Düsseldorf, Cologne and Autobahn 57. She turned onto it and headed back towards the city.

10.

They had covered five kilometres in the last hour, by Buslenko's reckoning. Not bad considering the terrain and the darkness. There had been no booby traps, no ambush. And, Buslenko was beginning to believe, no enemy waiting in the woods. The woman, Olga Sarapenko, had done particularly well, considering she hadn't had to go through the same rigours in training as the rest of them.

'Take a rest,' he ordered them.

'I'm telling you . . .' Belotserkovsky dropped down next to Buslenko, resting his back against the frozen river bank. 'There's no attacking force. It must have been one of us.'

'Where are you going?' Buslenko called across to Stoyan, who had started, crouching low, to climb up the river bank.

'I'm going to take a look around, boss. I'll be careful. Then I'm going to take a leak.'

Buslenko nodded and turned back to Belotserkovsky. 'It can't have been one of us. I've been working it out. The four of us here had no opportunity. Captain Sarapenko was outside for less than ten minutes. It would have taken her that long to reach Vorobyeva. You, Stoyan and me . . . we were all inside.'

'We don't know for sure when Vorobyeva was done,' said

Belotserkovsky. An owl hooted in the woods and suddenly flew over their heads, its wings clapping the air. They both swung their weapons to bear on the owl. After a moment they relaxed.

'We're getting jumpy,' said Buslenko. 'And yes, I do have a rough idea when Vorobyeva was killed. His body was still warm. In these temperatures that means he died just about the time he was supposed to head back to be relieved. And he wasn't killed by ghosts, so it's best to keep our wits about us.'

At the top of the river bank, Stoyan kept low and scanned the length of the river. He could see the lights of Korostyshev in the distance. It would take them less than an hour to get there, but the sky was lightening and it would be the trickiest part of the journey. His eyes traced back up the front edge of the forest. The first three ranks of trunks were visible, then blackness. It would stay night in the forest for hours yet. He decided to recommend to Buslenko that they should quit the river bank and use the trees as cover. It would be slower going but safer. He gestured down the bank to Buslenko, pointed two fingers of one hand to his own eyes, then indicated his near surroundings with a sweep of his hand. Buslenko nodded, signalling that it was okay for Stoyan to recce the immediate area.

Stoyan crossed the narrow expanse of open ground between the river bank and the forest. He pressed his back to the bark of a tree, took out a small monocular night-vision scope and surveyed as far into the forest as he could. He could see nothing. Literally. Even the night-vision scope couldn't penetrate the blackness of the forest's interior.

'Stoyan!' He spun around and aimed the scope in the direction from which he had heard his name called in a loud whisper. 'Stoyan! Over here!'

Stoyan didn't reply. He tried to locate the voice near enough that a burst from his assault rifle might hit whoever was there.

'Stoyan! It's Tenishchev!'

Stoyan moved closer, keeping low to present as small a target as possible, and keeping his *Vepr* aimed at the source of the voice.

'Here,' said the voice. Tenishchev appeared above some bushes at the edge of the forest. He looked ragged and dirty and had no weapon. The dark stain on the side on his face looked like blood. 'Come here . . . but keep low. Serduchka is somewhere around here. He's been shadowing you. Serduchka is a traitor. He killed Vorobyeva and he tried to kill me.'

Stoyan ran across to the bushes and they both dropped behind them. Tenishchev looked afraid. His parka was torn and when Stoyan touched it, it felt wet. Stoyan looked at his fingertips – they were slick with blood.

'Are you okay?' Stoyan asked. Tenishchev nodded, but Stoyan put his rifle down and eased back the parka where it was soaked in blood.

'You say Seruchka killed Vorobyeva?'

Tenishchev nodded again. Stoyan was worried: there was a lot of blood but he couldn't find the wound that was causing it.

'Seruchka is one of Vitrenko's men?'

'Yes . . .' said Tenishchev. 'It's hard to believe, isn't it? Do you know what's even harder to believe . . . ?'

Stoyan stared wildly into Tenishchev's eyes. He found that he couldn't breathe. He looked down and saw where Tenishchev had rammed his hunting knife up and under Stoyan's sternum.

'. . . So am I,' said Tenishchev into Stoyan's already dead eyes.

11.

Buslenko and Belotserkovsky had been lying flat, scanning the forest fringe for fifteen minutes. The sky was now dangerously light.

'We're going to have to move on . . .' said Buslenko.

'We can't just leave Stoyan behind,' protested Belotserkovsky.

'Stoyan's dead,' said Olga Sarapenko with sudden authority. She was below them, down by the river, watching the opposite bank. 'And so will we be if we don't get out of the wilds. There's a reason why Vitrenko's targeted us here . . . either he is simply making sport of us as if we were a herd of wild boar, or he's decided that we represent too much of a threat to him if we get to Germany.'

'We'll never make it to Germany,' said Belotserkovsky dully.

'He's not going to get us here,' said Olga defiantly. 'I'm going to watch that son of a bitch die.'

Buslenko smiled. He turned to Belotserkovsky. 'You ready to roll?'

Belotserkovsky nodded. Something drew his attention upwards to the brightening sky.

'Take cover!' he screamed.

12.

Maria had planned to sleep until mid-morning. She had put the 'do not disturb' notice on the doorknob of her room and had thrown herself onto the bed and fallen asleep almost immediately. When she awoke she was annoyed to find herself still fully dressed – her unbrushed teeth and mouth felt coated. She lay for a moment not knowing, not remembering what it was that was causing the nauseating ache in her chest. Then it came back to her: the crushing remembrance of firing into the car. She had probably killed someone. Maria had committed the crime that she was supposed to prevent, to solve. She could probably quite legitimately claim in a court that she'd been acting in self-defence. But the gun was illegal. And so was the intent: Maria had fired into the cabin of the car and had wanted to kill the Ukrainian. She no longer had the right to call herself a police officer. She was a vigilante, nothing more.

She went to the window and pulled back its curtains. There was no light from the apartment opposite and the curtains there were drawn across the glazed doors that opened out onto the roof terrace. The sky was a dull glimmer above Cologne's rooftops. It was barely dawn but Maria knew she wouldn't sleep again. She looked blankly at the growing light in the sky and it looked blankly back at her. Time to move on.

She stripped and showered and packed her bags. She went down to reception and checked out. The hotel was good enough for her purposes, but she had used her own name and credit card, added to which the hotel staff had looked somewhat surprised at her sudden change of appearance. Maria's plan was to check into another hotel in the same area. She would pay cash and stay a couple of nights. After that, she could move into the flat of her friend who was working in Japan.

She carried her bags out of the hotel and into a bright winter morning, without the slightest idea of how she was going to get back onto Vitrenko's tail.

13.

There had been no cover to take. They had all seen the dark, round object arc through the sky towards them and had thrown themselves in different directions, scrabbling on the frost-hardened ground and waiting for the blast to finish them off.

It didn't come.

Buslenko saw the object dark against the snow and crawled towards it. It was a head. He grabbed the hair and turned the face towards him. Stoyan. Belotserkovsky was next to Buslenko now and looked down at his friend's dark, handsome Tatar face.

'Bastards! I'll kill the fuckers!' Belotserkovsky turned towards the river bank but Buslenko seized his sleeve and pulled him down.

'Don't be a fucking amateur,' he said. 'You know what this is about. Don't lose your cool now. We're moving out. And we'll take our chances along the river. I need us to move fast.'

Belotserkovsky gave a decisive nod and Buslenko knew he was fully back in the game.

'Let's move.'

They moved in a half-run, covering a considerable distance in a short time. The forest on either side of the river had begun to thin out, offering less cover for their pursuers. Added to which the dawn that Buslenko had dreaded now worked in their favour. Maybe they were going to make it after all.

The only thing that worked against them was that the Teteriv river was wider and shallower here, and they had lost the cover of a steep bank. Buslenko heard a cry behind him and turned to see Olga Sarapenko fall, her rifle clattering on the stones.

'You all right?' he asked.

She sat up and cradled her ankle. 'Nothing broken.' She got up with a struggle. 'It's badly sprained, but my boot saved it from anything worse.'

'Can you walk?'

'For now,' she said, with an apologetic expression on her face. 'I'll slow you down.'

'We stick together,' said Belotserkovsky. The big Ukrainian threw his rifle to Buslenko and then hoisted Olga Sarapenko onto his shoulders as if she were a deer that he had bagged hunting. 'We're nearly there. You have to keep us covered, boss,' he said to Buslenko.

Buslenko grinned and shouldered both Olga's and Belotserkovsky's rifles. At his command, they made off again towards the houses on either side of the river that marked the outskirts of Korostyshev. But Buslenko was focused on more than making it alive to the town of his birth. Instead he was fixed with grim determination on a goal far to the west: a strange city in a foreign country. Where he had an appointment to keep.

Part Two

KARNEVAL

CLOWN DIARY, FIFTEENTH ENTRY.
UNDATED.

i am hungry so hungry when ~~i was the other~~ i was
small little and weak and i the other could do nothing
to change ~~my the other's~~ my world to control my world ~~i the~~
~~other always~~ i always had to eat everything on the plate
and be quiet and not talk at the table my daddy was so
<u>angry</u> all the time angry and i had to eat everything we
lived in the country on the farm and we had <u>rheinische</u>
<u>soorbroode made from horsemeat soaked in vinegar and</u>
<u>wine and spices and blood sausages</u> and i saw him i saw
him do it he killed the pig i was only tiny and i saw it
he held it between his knees and cut its throat it
<u>SQUIRMED AND SQUEALED AND THERE WAS BLOOD</u>
<u>EVERYWHERE AND IT WAS BLACK IN THE SOIL</u> and
the pig ran around a bit then fell down and all of the
blood soaked into the dirt and it was black i could
smell it i cried for it i cried for the pig and my daddy
smacked me and told me don't you know where your
food comes from don't you know what you eat don't
you know it has to die before you eat it i didn't think
about it then he made me eat the pig after mummy
cooked it and <u>it was good but i kept thinking of it</u>
<u>running around and the blood gushing</u> and it twitching
and twitching when it died but i liked the meat <u>i cried</u>
<u>but I liked eating it</u> but that isn't what made me

what I am no it was the other thing the later thing
that happened to me then i knew that he was me and
me was he and that i come to life when it is karneval i
can smell it coming *KARNEVAL* then they will see
then they will know what chaos is they took me to
church when i was small i was frightened all the time
they took me to church and i was told i was bad and
they told me all the things that happened to bad people
for ever forever i will not be locked up i will not be
kept away i will KILL THE OTHER and i will make it
KARNEVAL all the time all year round <u>I will give them
their crazy days</u> i am the <u>CLOWN</u> and i am awake <u>IF
THEY WANT CHAOS I WILL BRING THEM CHAOS</u> i am
their judgement and they shall burn their eyes on my
smile and I will <u>EAT THEM</u> i shall eat them all

Chapter Six

1–3 February

I.

Fabel put the phone down. It all made sense now.

Something had been nagging away at him for days and he hadn't been able to put his finger on what it was. It had unsettled him, because every time he had had a feeling like this in the past it had turned out to have a solid foundation. He understood the process behind it: little scraps of seemingly unrelated information that he had picked up coming together in his subconscious to start an alarm bell ringing. There had been nothing unusual about the telephone conversation that he had had with Maria, but her claim that her psychologist had said she should cut herself off from her colleagues for a while had rung false with him.

And now, two weeks later, Minks had called him at the Presidium and everything had fallen into place.

Fabel had come across Dr Minks as part of a previous investigation. Minks was an expert in post-trauma stress and phobic behaviour. As such he had set up a specialised Fear Clinic in Hamburg. The Polizei Hamburg had brought in counsellors to help Maria, but the main element of her treatment was now provided by Dr Minks. Minks had been one of Susanne's lecturers at Munich University and she rated his skills very highly.

'Obviously I cannot go into the specifics of Frau Klee's treatment,' Minks had said on the phone. 'But I know that she values your . . . *guidance* . . . very highly. I mean not just as her professional superior. That's why I thought I'd give you a call.'

'What's the problem, Herr Doctor?'

'Well . . . I really felt I was getting somewhere with Frau Klee and I think she is making a big mistake in breaking off her therapy. She is far from well. I was hoping that you could get her to see sense.'

'I'm sorry, Dr Minks,' said Fabel. 'I don't understand. Are you saying that Maria hasn't been keeping her appointments?'

'Not for the last four or five weeks.'

'Tell me, doctor, did you suggest it would be a good idea for Maria to avoid contact with me or any of her colleagues for the time being?'

'No . . .' Minks sounded puzzled. 'Why would I say any such thing?'

Fabel had promised to speak to Maria about returning to therapy and hung up. Maria had lied to him. Not just about the therapy: she had lied about her whereabouts. And now Fabel knew exactly where she was.

He sat for a moment, his hands pressed flat on his desk, staring at them absently. Then he snatched up the phone and made the first of the three calls that he knew he had to make.

2.

Benni Scholz was growing to hate Karneval. There were hotels just outside the city that had started to offer sanctuary from Cologne's carnival madness and compulsory bonhomie: places where order remained unchallenged and where a serene sanity was guaranteed until Lent. He had never before understood why some people sought out these places, or why many Cologne families took a holiday away from the city at Karneval time. Benni had always felt that, as a *Kölner*, Karneval defined who and what he was. But now, with deadlines looming and the police Karneval committee hounding him with e-mails, texts and phone calls, Scholz found himself wishing he had been born in Berlin.

But now there was something else to add to his stress. He had just over three weeks until Women's Karneval Night. He knew that the Karneval Killer would strike again. Another woman would die unless they got a lead on the murders of the previous two years. Files lay scattered across his desk and in an untidy arc on the floor. Scholz had the feeling that there was something he wasn't seeing in the available evidence. He had learned about serial killers. At least the theory. But this was the first time he'd ever been involved with a case and he felt out of his depth. He had called the Polizei Hamburg again, but had been told that the Murder Commission boss, Fabel, was leaving the force and really wasn't interested in taking on Scholz's case. He was going to have to think the Karneval Killer case through again, alone, without the assistance of some Hamburg supercop. Fuck him, thought Scholz, stuck-up *Fischkopp*. Scholz had been to Hamburg only a couple of times. Beautiful city, shame about the people. And the food was crap: all they ate was fish or that shit *Labskaus*.

He turned from the files and looked out of his office window in Cologne's Police Presidium but didn't see anything of the city that lay grey dark under the moody winter sky. Scholz turned his thoughts from the murders he was investigating back to his other problem: getting this bloody Karneval float and costumes organised. Scholz had studied so many books and researched so much stuff on the Internet about Karneval. Its origins, its significance, what had changed and what had stayed the same throughout the centuries. Maybe that was where he was going wrong: he was over-thinking it all.

It was while Scholz was in this doubly darkened mood that the phone rang. He was surprised to hear that it was the Hamburg cop, Fabel.

'Aren't you supposed to be leaving the force?' said Scholz. 'I didn't think I'd hear from you.'

'I *am* supposed to be leaving the force and you *are* hearing from me,' said Fabel. That famous northern charm, thought Scholz.

'Have you looked at the files I sent up, Herr Fabel?'

'Yes.'

'And?'

'And you've got a cannibal on your patch, in my opinion,' said Fabel.

'Shit . . .' said Scholz. 'So the piece of arse he takes away . . . it goes straight into the pan, you reckon?'

'I would have put it a little more technically than that, Herr Scholz, but effectively yes. He's probably cooking his trophy and consuming it. There are contradictions in his offending pattern, but my guess is that he is a sexual cannibal. His consumption of the flesh is probably accompanied by either involuntary ejaculation or active masturbation.'

'I guess that would be enough to get you chucked out of McDonald's.' Scholz laughed at his own joke. There was silence on the other end of the line. 'Have you had experience of this type of offender before, Herr Principal Chief Commissar?' Scholz adopted a more sober and official tone.

'Similar,' said Fabel. 'But your killer seems fixated on the run-up to Karneval. I'm guessing it has some symbolic significance for him.'

'Him and the entire population of Cologne, Herr Fabel. You don't have Karneval up there in Hamburg, do you?'

'No. We don't.'

'Karneval is more than you see on the television. It's not just fancy dress and reciting lame *Büttenrede* comic monologues in front of the *Elferrat*. Sorry, the *Elferrat* is the eleven elected members of the Karneval committee . . .'

'I know what the *Elferrat* is, Herr Scholz,' said Fabel drily. 'I'm from Hamburg, not Ulan Bator.'

'Sorry . . . anyway, my point is that Karneval defines what it is to be a *Kölner*. It's part of our soul. It's an emotional experience that can't be explained, only experienced. The fact that this nut-job focuses on Karneval is no surprise. It just tells me that he's a born *Kölner*.'

'I think there's more to it than that,' said Fabel. 'But we can discuss this when I come down to see you.'

'Oh?'

'I've cleared it with the Polizei Hamburg. I'll drive down on Friday. I should be there sometime between two and three p.m. Can you fix me up with a hotel? Nothing too fancy. I'm afraid your people will be picking up the tab.'

What else could you expect from a northerner? thought Scholz. 'Fine . . .' he said cheerily. 'No problem.'

3.

After he hung up from his call to Cologne, Fabel used his cellphone to reach Anna Wolff and asked her to meet him at Maria's flat.

'You know that bunch of keys you keep in your drawer, Anna?'

'Yes?' she said hesitantly and with a hint of suspicion.

'Well, bring that with you.'

'Do I detect a whiff of illegality about this?' Anna said. Then, more seriously: 'Is Maria all right?'

'That's what I want to establish, Anna. And yes, this is probably illegal, but I dare say Maria won't file charges.'

'I'll meet you there in half an hour.'

Maria shared the floor of her apartment building with two other flats. Fabel rang the buzzers for both but only got an answer at the second, which had the name 'Franzka' by the bell-push: a small woman in late middle age and with a weary expression came to the door.

'The Mittelholzers are both out at work at this time of day,' explained Frau Franzka.

Fabel showed her his Murder Commission ID and told her there was nothing to be alarmed about. Frau Franzka's countenance suggested it would take a lot more than Fabel's presence to alarm her. 'I'm Frau Klee's boss,' he explained. 'She's been unwell recently and we were a little concerned about her. Have you seen her lately?'

'Not for a while,' Frau Franzka replied. 'I saw her take some luggage down to her car. It was a Wednesday, so exactly two weeks ago today. It looked like she was going away on business. She had a computer bag and a briefcase with her.'

'Thanks,' said Fabel. He and Anna went across to Maria's apartment door. Frau Franzka watched them from her doorway, then shrugged and went back inside. Anna had brought her collection of keys: a wire coat-hanger bent into a circle with a hundred or more keys attached, like some improvised tribal necklace. Fabel remembered that in the days before central locking and keyless remotes, every uniformed station had the same arrangement for car keys. He decided not to ask Anna why she felt it necessary to have such comprehensive means of illegal entry; he had always suspected that Anna bent the rules a little too far at times. Until today, he had pretended to be unaware of her key collection. After about five minutes and countless keys, they were rewarded by a click. Anna paused and looked over her shoulder at her boss.

'Does Maria have an alarm system?'

'I don't know . . .' Fabel looked uncertain for a moment, then nodded decisively.

Anna shrugged and pushed open the door. There was a loud electronic beeping from the alarm keypad inside in the hall.

'Bollocks . . .' she said. Fabel brushed past her and typed

in a sequence of numbers. The display flashed ERROR CODE and continued to beep. He hit the clear button and typed in a new sequence. The beeping stopped.

'Her date of birth?' Anna sighed.

'The date she joined the Polizei Hamburg. I checked both in her file.'

'What would you have done if neither had worked?'

'Arrested you for housebreaking,' said Fabel and headed along the hall.

'You probably would . . .'

They stood in the living room of Maria's flat. It was, exactly as they had expected, pristine, ordered and furnished with immaculate taste. The walls were painted white but were hung with brightly colourful paintings. Oils, and originals. He guessed they would be by up-and-coming artists on the cusp of saleability. Maria was the kind of person to temper her art appreciation with acumen.

'I always envied Maria, you know,' said Anna.

'In what way?'

'Wanted to be like her. You know . . . Elegant, cool, together.'

'She's not together now.'

'Do you never feel that way?' Anna asked Fabel as she examined Maria's CD collection. 'You know, wish that you could be someone else? Even for a little while?'

'I don't give myself as much to philosophical musings as you do,' he lied, with a smile.

'I always thought of myself as too impulsive. Chaotic. Maria was always so disciplined and organised. Having said that . . .' Anna indicated the CD collection. 'This is bordering on the anally retentive. Look at these CDs . . . all ordered by genre and then alphabetically. Life's too short . . .'

Fabel laughed, mainly to disguise the unease he felt at seeing how similar Maria's taste and way of living were to his. They went through to the flat, checking each room. Fabel found what he was looking for, but had hoped not to find, in the smallest of the three bedrooms.

'Shit . . .' Anna gave a low whistle. 'This is not good. Not good at all. This is obsessive.'

'Anna . . .'

'I mean, this is the kind of thing we've come across with serials . . .'

'Anna – that's not helping.'

Fabel took in the small room. The walls were covered with photographs, press cuttings and a map of Europe with location pins and notes attached. There wasn't a square centimetre of clear wall space. But this was no chaos. Fabel could see four defined areas of research: one related to Ukraine, one to Vitrenko's personal history, one to people smuggling, one to organised crime in Cologne.

'Maria hasn't been spending her time recuperating,' said Anna. 'She's been working. On her own.'

'You're wrong. This isn't work. This is vendetta. Maria's planning her revenge on Vitrenko.'

Anna turned to Fabel. 'What do we do, *Chef*?'

'You take the desk. I'll go through the filing cabinet. And Anna . . . this stays between us. Okay?'

'You're the boss.'

Fabel and Anna spent two hours going through Maria's files and notes. They were full of contacts with whom she had spoken, probably using her position as a Polizei Hamburg officer to gain access to otherwise confidential information: the Anti-Trafficking Centre in Belgrade, Human Rights Watch, a people-smuggling expert at Interpol. There were notes on all aspects of current people-trafficking in Europe, a full dossier on Ukrainian Spetsnaz units and a file of even more cuttings that hadn't made it to the wall display. Among them were articles about a fire in a container truck in which several illegal immigrants heading for the West had been burned to death; about a model in Berlin who had been murdered with acid; about a bloody underworld feud in the former Soviet Republic of Georgia; about a Ukrainian-Jewish crime Godfather who had been found murdered in his luxury apartment in Israel.

'What have you got?' he asked Anna.

'A list of hotels in Cologne. Nothing to say which one she's going to use, but I'd say it was a shortlist. She's been corresponding with someone in the Interior Ministry of Ukraine. Sasha Andruzky.'

Fabel nodded. What they had been looking at was detailed but peripheral. The solid core of Maria's research had gone with her to Cologne. He scanned the small bedroom-office for a bag or holdall. 'Help me pack up some of these files. Then I've got a few calls to make.'

4.

Fabel broke the four-hour journey to Cologne under a slate sky at a *Raststätte* on the A1 and filled up his BMW. A few unconvinced fluffs of snow drifted into his face as he did so. Instead of going into the service-station restaurant, Fabel bought a coffee and a salami roll to take out. He sat in the car with the heater on and consumed his lunch without tasting it, reading through the notes he had made on the information that Scholz had supplied. For Fabel, this process was not unlike reading a novel. It took him to a different time, a different place and a different life. He had all the details of the night when the first victim had died, two years ago. The strange thing was that Fabel found it difficult to place himself in the context of Karneval. The Cologners seemed obsessed with its forced jollity and irreverence. He read about the first victim's movements on the night she had died. Sabine Jordanski had not officially been working that day, but had spent most of it doing exactly the same kind of thing that she would have done if she had been at work. As it was Women's Karneval Night she and a group of female friends had planned to take part in a procession through the city before hitting a few of the bars where exuberant *Kölsch* bands would be playing. Sabine had spent the day colouring first her friends' hair, then her own. The dyes differed from the ones she normally used: vivid pinks, reds, electric blues and yellows, and often more than one colour was used on a single head. There seemed to be an element of becoming someone else at Karneval, a belief that true release from everyday order only came with a mask, a costume or a radical change of look.

Sabine Jordanski seemed to be a typical Cologner: exuberant, friendly, fun-loving. She was twenty-six and had been working at the salon for four years. There was no boyfriend at the time of her death, or at least no permanent boyfriend who could be traced, but it would have appeared that this was a strictly temporary situation. Sabine had enjoyed the attentions of several young men. On the night of her death she had been seen talking earlier to three men, all of whom had been traced and eliminated from the police's inquiries. The group of six girls had visited four bars that night. All had been drinking but none was drunk. The girls had walked together to Sabine's apartment in Gereonswall at about two in the morning and had said goodnight to her outside. There had been several people milling around, but no one whom the girls particularly noticed. No one had seen Sabine go into her apartment, but all had assumed that was what she had done.

She was found the next morning in an alley only two hundred metres from her apartment building. She had been strangled with a red tie which had been left at the scene, partially stripped and 0.468 kilos of flesh had been removed from her right buttock. Time of death had been estimated at around the time her friends had said goodnight to her.

Someone had been waiting for her, or had been following the group around the city, stalking them like a lion waiting for a straggler to become separated from the herd.

Sabine Jordanski had been a cheerful, uncomplicated girl who had not demanded much from life. Fabel bit into the salami roll and looked at the scene-of-crime photographs again. Sabine's heavy, white buttocks lay exposed. The excised trench in the right buttock stood out with violent vividness against the paleness of the skin. Scholz had been right: the killer had executed his butchery with a swift precision. There was no raggedness, no tentative first cuts. This guy had known what he was doing. Fabel suddenly realised that he was chewing a mouthful of salami while looking at images of a mutilated corpse. In that moment the reasons he had sought escape from the Murder Commission crystallised. What had he become?

Fabel closed the file, finished his hurried lunch and headed back out onto the autobahn towards Cologne.

5.

Ansgar's expression was one of anguish. He sat, knowing what he was going to do but trying to persuade himself that he was not going to do it. He knew he had times of weakness. Times like this, when he had half an hour to spare before he started his shift at the restaurant.

As he had sat down in front of the computer, Ansgar had told himself that he wouldn't visit the website again. He had promised himself that the last time he had been on it. And the time before that. But his computer's screen glowed malevolently, opening up a window on another reality for Ansgar. A way into abandonment and chaos.

Ansgar let his fingers hover above the keyboard. He could still walk away. He could switch off the computer. He struggled so hard to keep the chaos within himself contained.

Karneval was coming. And during Karneval . . . well, everybody let themselves go. But this little screen was dangerous: it allowed the chaos within to connect with a greater, wider chaos. Ansgar realised that this didn't satisfy his hunger. It sharpened it. Turned it ravenous.

His fingers trembled with delicious anticipation, disgust, fear. He typed in the website address and gave an anguished cry as the images opened out before him. The women. The flesh.

The biting teeth.

6.

The first thing that struck Fabel about Criminal Commissar Benni Scholz's office was how untidy and disordered it was. The second thing was the large dummy head that sat in the corner. Fabel found himself looking at it involuntarily, as he tried to work out exactly what it was. He decided it was some kind of moose.

'I cannot tell you how pleased I am that you could come,' said Scholz, beaming as they shook hands. Scholz was about ten years younger than him, Fabel reckoned, and about ten centimetres shorter. But what Scholz lacked in height he made up for with a stocky, muscular frame. 'I see you were admiring the bullhead for our Karneval outfit. I'm organising it this year.'

'Oh . . .' said Fabel, suddenly enlightened. 'It's a bull! I thought it was a moose . . .'

Scholz scowled at the dummy head and muttered something that Fabel couldn't hear but thought might have been 'Fuck.' Scholz let his scowl go. 'Please, Principal Chief Commissar, take a seat.'

'Call me Jan,' said Fabel. 'We are colleagues.' There was something about the ebullient Scholz that Fabel found immensely likeable. Fabel also resented him a little, in the same way that he resented his brother Lex for being so at ease with strangers, for being so laid back about life. It was then that it clicked what it was he liked about Scholz: he reminded him of a younger Lex.

'Okay . . . Jan,' said Scholz. 'I'm Benni. Have you eaten?'

'On the way down.' Fabel's expression commented on the quality of his repast.

'Oh . . . okay. I thought I'd take you out to a typical Cologne restaurant tonight, if you're up for it?'

'Sure . . .' said Fabel. 'But maybe we should see how we get on going over this case . . .'

'Oh, we'll have time . . .' Scholz made an expansive gesture. 'It helps me to think. Eating, I mean. Can't think on an empty stomach, I always say.'

Fabel smiled.

'Talking of which,' continued Scholz, 'I've been thinking about what you said about our guy being a cannibal. You know something . . . I think maybe you're right. It was some-thing that was suggested before. To be honest, we've tried to play down the angle, just in case the press get hold of it.'

'I'm pretty certain I am right,' said Fabel. 'I also think you have a very valid point about the killer having experience of cutting flesh. A surgeon, or a butcher or slaughterman . . .'

'He doesn't muck about, does he? Knows what he's doing.' Benni leaned forward, resting his elbows on the desk. 'Is it true you're English? You don't have an English accent. Someone told me they call you *the English Commissar* . . .'

'I'm half Scottish,' said Fabel. 'Half Frisian.'

'My God,' laughed Benni. 'That's a thrifty combination. Bet you don't get your round in too often!'

Fabel smiled. 'Did you have any strong suspects? The file seemed devoid of anyone you particularly had your eye on.'

'Nope. It was a real bugger. Women's Karneval Night is mad. Like so much of Karneval. People running about demented, little bastards being conceived all over the place.

Anonymity is part of the whole thing. You can lose your identity and do things that you otherwise wouldn't do. It's the perfect environment for topping somebody.'

'I see.'

'But that's a theory I have about this case. About anonymity and doing things that you wouldn't normally do. I told you on the phone that I'm pretty sure that this guy is a local. Well, I also think that he may be Joe Normal the rest of the year. Karneval is all about letting go. We always say that we Cologners are more sane than everyone else the rest of the year because we go mad during Karneval. Maybe our chum has got this pervy thing going on that he keeps wrapped up in his pants all year, and he needs Karneval to let it loose.'

'That's actually pretty good psychological profiling,' Fabel laughed. 'Although again I would normally couch it in more technical terms.'

'Anyway,' continued Benni. 'Even the divorce courts take a lenient view of Karneval behaviour. Adultery on Rosenmontag is considered to be excusable . . . that you're not really guilty of it the same way you would be the rest of the year. And, of course, there's the Nubbelverbrennung . . . the fire of atonement at the end of Karneval in which all the sins committed during the Crazy Days are burned. What if our guy believes he has an excuse for doing what he does just because it's Karneval?'

'More than that, I think there is a deeply misogynistic element to these murders. He hates women.'

'You don't say . . .' Scholz smiled wryly.

'Okay . . . you worked that out. Both victims were reasonably slim, but had a tendency to be heavier around the hips and backside. I think that may be his selection criterion. Particularly given the fact that he removes flesh from that part of the body.'

'So why is he selecting them?' asked Scholz. 'Is it because he feels sexually attracted to that body shape, or is it simply because he's picking out the best cut of beef?'

'Both,' said Fabel. 'Let me tell you something about canni-balism . . .'

7.

He shouldn't have visited the website again. Now the hunger burned in him and he could not bear to look in Ekaterina's direction. He could tell she had picked up on a tension in the kitchen and she obviously thought she or her work had somehow displeased him, which made matters worse because she now sought every opportunity to speak with him. But Ansgar could not bear her presence. However, within the confines of the kitchen, close proximity, even brushing against each other, was unavoidable. Sometimes she was so close that he could smell her.

Ansgar felt cursed. He wished that he were like other men, normal men. It would be all so uncomplicated. She would let him fuck her. Or not. But the sweetly obscene images, the dangerous, delicious fantasies, would not plague him. Ansgar's work didn't help, either. To see Ekaterina handle meat, split a joint with a cleaver, trim the fat from it with a knife, fillet a breast of chicken, pulling apart yielding flesh; all these simple, innocuous acts became an erotic torment for Ansgar. But what tormented him most of all was the forbidden, dangerous, ineffable idea that maybe, just maybe, he might actually be able to fulfil his fantasy. That he might be able to do what he wanted with Ekaterina.

As his mind wandered so did his eyes. They fell on Ekaterina. They caressed every inch of her voluptuous, curving figure. Then his stare found hers. She was looking directly at him. And smiling.

As if she knew.

8.

The restaurant to which Scholz took Fabel to was in Dagobertstrasse, in the Altstadt area of Cologne. It was housed in the ground floor of an elegant gable-ended building.

'What do you recommend?' asked Fabel.

'This place has quite a reputation. A new chef came in a year or so ago and has worked wonders. And they're starting their Karneval menu . . . but I suppose you'll want fish,' said Benni, frowning as he searched the menu. 'We're big on meat dishes here . . .'

'Believe it or not,' said Fabel, with a smile, 'we do eat things other than fish in the North.'

'And we eat fish here. Did you know that Cologne used to be the biggest fish market in Germany? Because of the Rhine running through it like a sort of medieval motorway. It was a distribution centre for the whole of central Germany. Okay, then, how about the ragout of lamb with figs? It's very good here. And what do you fancy – a nice Rhine wine or an even nicer *Kölsch* beer?'

They agreed on a bottle of Assmannshausen Spätburgender red and placed their order.

'It's nice here,' said Fabel. The restaurant lay beneath a white plastered vaulted ceiling and arched double doors looked out onto the street. He could see that it had started to snow a little more earnestly.

'Yeah . . .' Scholz surveyed the restaurant appreciatively. 'Yeah . . . it's not bad. Cologne is packed with cool places to eat. Almost any type of cuisine in the world. Even vegetarian. We're a big conference and convention city now and we get all kinds of rich business types. I like this place, but sometimes I like to go somewhere a bit more . . . well, basic, I suppose you'd say. I like my food well cooked, not well designed if you know what I mean. You said you were going to tell me all about cannibalism,' said Scholz.

'Sounds like something you know a thing or two about.'

The waiter came with the wine and Scholz asked Fabel to taste it. He obviously expected Fabel's knowledge of wine to be greater.

'That's very nice,' said Fabel and the waiter filled both glasses. 'To be honest, I did a bit of boning up on it before I came down,' said Fabel.

Scholz shook his head. 'I still can't wrap my mind around it. Why would someone get off on eating someone else?'

'Human sexuality is a very complex thing, Benni. I'm sure you've dealt with enough weird cases to know that. There are perversions that revolve around fantasies about eating a sexual partner or being eaten by one. Our mouths are secondary sexual organs. You could almost say that oral sex it a type of cannibalistic behaviour.'

'We obviously date different types of women . . .' Scholz grinned.

'Anyway, there are several forms of cannibalism. Motives for it, if you like. But anthropologists and psychologists break it down into two main groups: ritual and nutritional cannibalism. In nutritional cannibalism you have straight-forward epicurean cannibalism – people who eat human flesh simply for the taste of it or for the experience . . . but without getting a sexual kick out of it. By far the most common form of nutritional cannibalism is for survival, when there's no other food source available. For example, I was reading about the Holodomor before I came down here: the forced starvation of Ukrainians by the Soviets in the nineteen-thirties. Food became so scarce that canni-balism became relatively common.'

'So what's this endocannibalism and exocannibalism I've heard about?' asked Scholz.

'Exocannibalism is when you eat a stranger, endocanni-balism is when you eat someone from your own tribe or culture.'

'So endocannibalism is having granny for dinner . . .' said Scholz. 'But all this is very rare, isn't it?'

'Not as rare as you'd think. We've all done it, every culture, at some point in our history. Ritual mortuary endocannibalism was a European thing in the Stone Age.'

'And what's that in plain German?'

'When a relative died, for example, there would be a sort of funeral feast, except it was the dear departed, specifically their brain, that was the main course. Archaeologically it was a significant discovery. It shows that as early as the Stone Age we had the idea that the mind, or the spirit, was seated in the brain. Close family members would eat parts of the brain to *absorb* something of the spirit of their ancestor. It makes sense, I suppose, in a sort of pre-scientific way. And if, in plain German, you want evidence of people eating people, you only need to go a hundred or so kilometres from where we're sitting. The caves near Balve on the Hönne River. Archaeologists found evidence of it there.'

'So what motivates our guy to cut out such a precise amount?'

Fabel was about to answer when the food arrived. 'This looks good,' he said. The lamb ragout with its fig-and-vegetable dressing had been arranged on the plate like a work of art. He took a mouthful. 'Mmmm . . . tastes good too. Good choice, Benni.' The lamb melted on his tongue. After a moment, Fabel continued. 'Anyway, to answer your question . . . the Karneval Killer takes a precise amount of flesh because that's the *portion* he wants. Just as we go into a butcher shop and order a kilo of mince. The other thing is that our killer doesn't have an *abstract* connection with food.'

'What do you mean?'

'Take this meal,' explained Fabel. 'You and I are sitting here eating lamb ragout . . . but the word "lamb" in this context conjures up only the idea of a type of food. We don't think about a young sheep, or particularly about it being

killed, skinned and gutted. Even in a butcher's shop, we see
a cut of meat and don't really visualise it as an animal's body
part. Similarly, when you see a cow or a lamb in a field, or
a duck in a pond, you don't start salivating and thinking,
oh, I'll have some of that.'

'I'm sorry, said Scholz, his mouth full. 'I don't see your
point.'

Fabel looked at Scholz's half-empty plate and realised that
he was going to have to talk less and eat more to catch up.
'We used to have a more immediate relationship with our
food. But now we live in an age when a particular type of
exotic bean or berry or herb is flown halfway around the
world just so that it can be a garnish on a dish. It's difficult
to imagine that for most of our history simply having enough
food to survive has been our main preoccupation. That also
includes our history of cannibalism. Like I said, we've all
done it – every culture in the world has had some experience
of eating human flesh. Yet it remains the greatest social and
cultural taboo.'

Scholz lifted his fork and contemplated the chunk of lamb
impaled on it. 'I wonder what it tastes like . . . human flesh,
I mean.' He shrugged and popped the lamb into his mouth.

'It's similar to the taste of veal, I believe. Or pork,' said
Fabel. 'Anyway, our killer doesn't have the same lack of
connection with his food source. The links in his food chain
are all too solid. He sees these women, assesses their shape
and selects them. He can *taste* them just by looking at them.'

'So what are you saying?' Scholz spoke through a mouthful
of lamb. 'That he eats them for the taste?'

'No . . . or not just for that. I think he gets off sexually.
But there's a lot of other stuff mixed in. With military cannibalism, you kill a formidable foe on the battlefield and you
eat him to absorb some of his strength. With ritual cannibalism, you eat part of the sacrificial victim to become
connected to the divinity or the spirit of the victim . . . that

symbolism is still there in Christian communion, a hangover from pagan beliefs. And, like I said, funerary cannibalism involves eating part of a deceased loved one so that they would live on through you.'

'Or *in* you . . .' said Scholz.

'I think our killer has abstracted his sexual perversion and believes that he is enjoying a relationship with his victims far more intimate than he would by just having sex with them.'

'By eating a slice of the victim's arse he absorbs their spirit and becomes their soulmate?' Scholz's expression was earnest. Fabel laughed.

'Something like that. But he had to start off somewhere. There is a chance that to begin with our guy was simply a sex offender . . . committing rapes, that kind of thing. Through time he might have added the cannibal element. Remember the Joachim Kroll case? In Duisburg in the late seventies?'

Scholz nodded.

'Kroll was a rapist-murderer and he had an undetected career going back two decades. Then, at some point along the way, he decided to try some of his victims' flesh. Interestingly, he took flesh from exactly the same part of his victims' bodies – the buttocks and upper thighs.'

'Do you think we have a copycat?'

'No. Kroll wasn't exactly an inspirational figure. He had a near-idiot IQ and was a pathetic loser type. He died in 'ninety or 'ninety-one. The similarities are coincidental. But I do think there's a chance the Karneval Killer started off small. Assaults on women. Particularly involving biting.'

'Yeah . . .' Scholz poked his lamb thoughtfully with his fork. 'You could be right. One of my officers, Tansu Bakrac, has a theory about that.'

'Oh?'

'I'll let her explain tomorrow. Basically she's put a question mark over a couple of cases in the past. One in particular. I'm not so sure, though.'

There was a pause and the two men concentrated on their meals.

'I was surprised when you turned up, Jan,' said Scholz at last. 'I was told you were packing the job in.'

'That's the idea,' Fabel said. Suddenly he felt like talking about it. There was something about Scholz's open, honest demeanour that invited confidence. A good thing to have if you were a policeman. 'Officially I'm working out my notice. But I really don't know if I'm doing the right thing. It all seemed so straightforward. Now I'm not so sure.' He told Scholz about his experience on the way down: eating the salami roll while examining the photographs of Sabine Jordanski's disfigured body and it not even crossing his mind that it wasn't normal behaviour.

'I get that all the time,' laughed Scholz. 'I put it down to being accustomed to it all. I say I benefit from professional objective detachment. Everyone else says it's because I'm a pig.'

'But that's exactly what bothers me,' said Fabel. 'I've become *too* accustomed to it all. *Too* detached.'

'But it's what you do . . .' said Scholz. 'Think about what it's like to be a doctor, or a nurse. It's supposed to be all about saving lives, but the truth is that medicine is all about death. Every day a doctor will deal with a patient who is on their way out of this world. Some of them suffering terribly. But it's their job. If they got emotionally involved with every patient, or spent their free time thinking about the inevitability of the same thing happening to them, they'd go mad. But they don't. It's their stock in trade. You can't beat yourself up because you've become used to murder.'

'That,' said Fabel, with a grin, 'would have been a very well-put point, if it weren't for the fact that, as we both know, the medical professional comes right at the top of serial-killer occupations. Statistically, anyway. Also alcoholism . . . suicide . . .'

'Okay . . .' said Scholz. 'Maybe not a good example. But you know what I mean. You're a professional policeman. That's what you are. And the reason you're here is because you are considered the best in Germany for cracking this kind of case. Maybe it's a mistake to deny that.'

'Maybe . . .' said Fabel. He sipped his wine and looked out of the window at the lamplit street, now decked with snow. Out there was a city he didn't know. And in that city Vitrenko conducted his violent trade in human flesh. Maria was out there too. Alone. 'Maybe you're right.'

9.

They had just finished dessert when Scholz's cellphone rang. He held up his hand in apology to Fabel and then engaged in a short exchange with the caller.

'Sorry about that,' he said as he slipped the phone back into his pocket. 'Another case I'm working on. That was one of the team letting me know that we've hit another dead end.'

'A murder?'

'Yep. Gangland stuff. A kitchen worker was sliced up with a meat cleaver.' He laughed. 'Don't worry – it wasn't this restaurant.'

'You get a lot of organised-crime killings?'

'Not particularly. And especially not of late. This one is Russian or Ukrainian mafia.'

Fabel felt an electric tingle at the back of his neck. 'Oh?'

'Yeah. The Vitrenko-Molokov gang muscled their way in here about a year ago. Secretive bunch – all ex-army or special police. We think that the poor schmuck who got killed was caught passing information on to an official. But that's the problem. We can't find any department which was talking to the vic.'

'Why do you think he was involved with an official?'

'He was seen talking to a smartly dressed woman the day

before he was topped. It was clear that she was immigration or police. But that's what the call was about. She definitely wasn't one of ours.'

'Oh . . .' Fabel sipped his coffee and desperately tried to look relaxed as he watched Cologne through the window. Maria. He turned to Scholz and held his gaze for a moment.

'Were you about to say something?' asked Scholz.

Fabel smiled. And shook his head.

Chapter Seven

4 February

I.

Fabel got up early the next day and arrived at the Cologne Police Presidium before Scholz. He waited in the huge entrance atrium, a visitor ID badge clipped to his lapel. It was strange for Fabel to be in another Police Presidium. It was very different from the Hamburg headquarters and Fabel found it odd to see uniformed officers still dressed in the old green and mustard uniforms, yet the Hamburg police had worn exactly the same until just two years ago. It was, he thought as he waited, so strange how quickly one adapts to change.

Scholz apologised a little too profusely for being late and took Fabel up to his office. Fabel smiled when he saw that the old prototype Karneval head had gone and someone had pushed files, phone and computer keyboard to one side and placed a new version square in the centre of Scholz's desk. A yellow Post-it note with nothing but a large question mark had been stuck on the snout.

'Very funny,' said Scholz, turning it to face Fabel. 'Better?'

'Different . . .' said Fabel.

Scholz looked at the head again appraisingly, sighed, and placed it in the corner where its predecessor had skulked.

'I'd like you to meet the team I've got working on the Karneval Killer case,' he said at last. He beckoned through the glass door and two officers came into the office. One was a young man who Fabel knew must have been in his late twenties to be a Commissar in the Murder Commission, but his skinny frame and pale, acned skin made him look more like a teenager. The other officer was a young woman of about thirty. She had a full figure and her hair was a mass of coppery-red coils.

'This is Kris Feilke,' said Scholz indicating the young man, 'and Tansu Bakrac.'

Fabel smiled. From her name, Fabel knew that the female officer must be Turkish-German. He found himself wondering if the rich copper in her hair came from the ancient Celtic tribes who had settled in Galatia. The two officers shook hands with Fabel and sat down. Fabel noticed the informality between Scholz and his junior officers and wondered how disciplined they were as a team.

'Okay, Jan,' said Scholz. 'We have only three weeks to go until Karneval. And as sure as bears crap in the woods, our guy is going to come looking for some more meat. For once I have the opportunity to prevent a murder rather than solve one. Or should I say *we* have the opportunity to prevent it. I'm afraid I just keep coming up blank. So we're open to anything you have to suggest.'

'Okay, I hope you don't mind, but I took the liberty of getting a few things in motion before I came down,' said Fabel. 'You remember the Armin Meiwes case?'

''Course . . . the Rotenburg Cannibal?' said Scholz.

'Meiwes advertised for his victim. On the Internet. Gave himself the online identity of the *Master Butcher*. Twenty years ago, Meiwes might have gone through life with his fantasies remaining just that, fantasies. But Meiwes had the Internet. The Internet is the great facilitator. The great anonymous meeting place where you can share your fetishes and perversions with others. The exceptional becomes ordinary and the abnormal normal.'

'You think there's an Internet connection with this case?' asked Tansu.

'I think it's possible that there's some direct link. Before we go any further I think we need to understand how our killer thinks.'

'God knows,' said Kris. 'He lives in a fantasy world, probably. A psycho.'

Fabel shook his head. 'That's where you're wrong. Criminal psychologists and forensic psychiatrists don't use the description "psychopath" or "sociopath" the way they did. These labels have become so common in the media that they've lost all value. People bandy around the word "psychopath" the way they used to use "axe murderer". What we call a psychopath is better described as someone with an antisocial personality disorder. They tend to be devoid of feelings, of emotions, of empathy for other human beings. They never feel remorse. Most of them are easily identified because they've exhibited symptomatic behaviour since childhood.' Fabel paused. He thought of Vitrenko: someone completely empty of anything human. 'Serial killers generally exhibit personality disorders, but rarely are they psychotic. They know what they're doing is wrong. A psychopath doesn't. In fact, many psychopaths who have been successfully treated for their condition end up getting a truckload of remorse delivered at once and they commit suicide, unable to live with what they've done.'

'So this killer isn't a psychopath?'

'I'm not saying that for sure,' said Fabel. 'But I think it's unlikely. Serial killers tend not to have a single, solid personality but drift between identities to suit the situation, who they're with, etc. Not multiple personalities, as such, but their own personality isn't anchored. One thing they do tend to have is an enormous ego. The universe revolves around them alone. And that, along with the loose personality, *is* something they share with psychopaths. But the important thing is they're not mad. I think your Karneval Cannibal needs to feel that he is not a freak. That he is part of a community.'

'And that's where you see an Internet connection?' asked Tansu.

'It's a possibility. He needs a place where he can exchange fantasies, even compare notes or advertise for victims. I think that it is highly unlikely that your guy has never sat alone in the evening, huddled over his PC, and typed the word "cannibal" into a search engine.'

'Granted,' said Scholz. 'But how does it help us?'

Fabel produced a file from his briefcase. 'Before I came down, I got one of the experts in our technical section to give me a list of possible sites and forums that might interest our killer. Or at least those we know about. There are countless dark corners on the web to hide in. Anyway, I asked them to focus particularly on sites in German, and especially anything hosted from the Cologne area.'

'Is that significant? I thought geography meant nothing on the Internet.'

'It doesn't. But if we find someone uploading a site with this kind of content in the area, then we've located a member of this . . . *exclusive* little community. Someone who might be able to give us a way in.'

Scholz examined the file. He winced a couple of times at some of the images. 'My God . . . there are some sick fucks out there.'

'And the Internet brings them together. That said, our killer may keep a very low profile indeed. He may regard himself as unique. But I reckon he has visited at least one of these sites.'

'But?' Scholz read the caution in Fabel's expression.

'But . . . Andrei Chikatilo, the Ukrainian cannibal in the eighties, Fritz Haarman in Hanover in the twenties, Joachim Kroll in Duisburg in the seventies, Ed Gein in the United States in the forties . . . all these cannibal killers existed before the advent of the Internet. There is always the possibility that he has ripened his fantasies in isolation. But I hope not.

Everybody feels safe on the Internet. They think they're anonymous when in fact they're far from it.' Fabel turned to Tansu Bakrac. 'I've already explained to Herr Scholz, my feeling is that this killer may have had practice runs in the past. He tells me you have a theory about that.'

'More than a theory. There are a couple of cases that I think are linked.'

'Or maybe not . . .' Scholz said doubtfully. 'There's nothing other than a Karneval connection to link them.'

'What cases?' asked Fabel.

'A girl called Annemarie Küppers was found murdered in two thousand and three. She had been beaten to death. Whoever did it had been in an inhuman fury and had pulped her head.'

'But she wasn't strangled,' interjected Scholz. 'And there was no flesh removed. In fact, her underwear hadn't been removed or interfered with either.'

'You said there was a Karneval connection,' said Fabel. 'Was she killed on Women's Karneval Night?'

'No . . .' said Tansu. 'The day after. I'll get you a copy of the file. Both files, in fact.'

'What was the other one?'

'This attack did happen on Women's Karneval Night. In nineteen ninety-nine. A young medical student called Vera Reinartz was beaten, raped and partially strangled – wait for it – with a man's necktie.'

'She survived?'

'Yes. And the really creepy thing is that her attacker was a clown. I mean someone dressed up as a Karneval clown.'

Fabel rubbed his chin thoughtfully. 'It's tempting to see a connection. But you say this girl was raped. Our Killer doesn't have sexual contact. Was semen recovered?'

'Yes. But the clincher for me isn't just that the attempted strangulation was done with a man's necktie . . . there were also bite marks all over her body.'

'Okay, then,' said Fabel, 'I take it you've reinterviewed the victim?'

'Sorry,' said Tansu. 'Another dead end, so far. Vera Reinartz dropped out of her medical studies at Cologne University. In fact she dropped out of sight too – about a year after the attack.'

'But we must have a new address for her,' said Fabel. 'She'll have had to register with the local police if she moved town.'

'No trace of anyone with that name. But I'm still following it up.'

'Maybe she's dead. Shouldn't this be a missing persons inquiry?' asked Fabel. Kris had made coffee and handed him a mug. It had a printed clown and the motto *'Kölle Alaaf!'* emblazoned on the side. Fabel knew this was Kölsch for 'Cheers, Cologne!'.

'She's not dead,' said Kris. 'She's written to her parents a few times to let them know she's alive and well but living, as she puts it, "a different life". The letters have no return address but carry Cologne postmarks. The parents live near Frankfurt. That's where she was from.'

'Okay,' said Fabel. 'I think Tansu may have something with one or both of these cases. Let's make finding Vera Reinartz a priority.'

'What else did you do before you came down?' asked Scholz.

'I had profiles done.'

'On the killer? Of course we did that . . .' Scholz's expression clouded.

'I don't mean on the killer. I have had psycho-social profiles done on the victims. I take it you checked out any possible points of convergence?'

'Yes. Their paths never crossed, as far as we can see. Unless you can tell me something different.' The clouds still hadn't cleared.

Fabel smiled disarmingly. 'Listen . . . I haven't been going over the same ground as you because I think that you haven't done your jobs properly. I've done all of this because you asked me to get involved and I have to do my own home-work. Also, my perspective is different.'

Scholz nodded. 'Fair enough, Jan.'

'I know you'll have done something similar,' said Fabel, 'but I've also had a psycho-geographic assessment done.'

'Yes . . . we did the same. With only two killings to go on, our profilers said there wasn't enough to plot a pattern. But they expressed an opinion that we're not looking far from the city's Altstadt.'

'Did they pick up on the proximity of churches?' asked Fabel.

'It was mentioned, but dismissed. There are so many churches in Cologne. If there's some religious significance, then I would expect the cathedral would figure. But even that would be difficult to assess. Cologne Cathedral is at the heart of the city and the layout of the streets radiates from it. You think this is a religious nut?'

'Maybe. Not especially. It could be churches as buildings, rather than as institutions. As you say, Cologne has more than a few.' Fabel grinned. 'How do you three fancy being Cologne city tour guides for the day?'

2.

It had been a week. Nothing. Maria had listened to the radio, watched the TV news, bought a *Kölner Stadt-Anzeiger* news-paper every day. She had probably taken the life of another human being, or at least seriously wounded him. Yet there was no mention anywhere of a body being found, or even of a BMW full of bullet holes being uncovered in a ditch somewhere. The Ukrainian had vanished into thin air. What she did find in the paper was a small piece about the murder in the kitchen of the Biarritz restaurant. She had made Slavko Dmytruk think that he could trust her. That she would keep him safe. Instead he'd been butchered because she had coerced him into talking to her.

The body of the Ukrainian had probably already been disposed of by his own people, or he had survived and they were nursing his wounds. In either case, they would be looking for her. But as long as she didn't go near the bar or Viktor's apartment, she reckoned she should be okay. And if they really had no idea about her identity or where to find her, then there was always the chance she could slip out of the city. Back to Hamburg. Back to her job. Back to her own identity.

But there had been a value in coming here: becoming someone else, something other than the object of self-loathing she had been for months, had allowed Maria to step out from under the phobias and neuroses that had piled one on top of the other until they had threatened to crush her to death. All around her were reminders of the forthcoming Karneval in Cologne, and only now was she beginning to understand how these people revelled in a few days of insanity, of chaos. The city became something else, the people in it became someone else. And after it was all over and they stepped back into their normal lives, they seemed to keep something of Karneval alive inside them. Maybe, she thought, that was what she had achieved.

God knew she had achieved nothing else. Whatever had possessed her to think that she could come here alone and track down one of the most dangerous and sophisticated organised-crime bosses in Europe? She saw now how hopeless and half-baked her pathetic little crusade had been. She would drop out of sight for another week or so; stay in her friend's apartment, then go back to Hamburg. She would find a decent hairdresser and dye her hair back to its normal colour. She would don the clothes and personality of the old Maria, but without the neuroses. No one in Hamburg need ever know she'd been here.

Maria had to deal with the car. This second hotel was just off the Konrad-Adenauer-Ufer by the river and she had left the Saxo parked in the lot around the corner from the first. She would then drive it back to the garage she'd bought it from and let them buy it back for a fraction of what she'd paid. It had been an expensive car rental.

Maria was about to dress in one of her cheap guises but she checked herself and donned instead a smart designer suit that she had brought down with her. She was amazed at how well it went with her newly dark hair. She made up her face and looked at herself again in the mirror. Almost the old Maria. Except she made up her mind to pick up a late breakfast on her way to the car dealership.

Maria headed out of the hotel and walked with a renewed vigour and confidence. She had gone about two blocks when she became aware of someone close to her side and slightly behind her. Suddenly he was leaning into her and his fingers closed like a vice around her upper arm. Something that was unmistakably the barrel of a handgun was rammed into her back, above her hip.

'Do exactly what I say.' Maria felt a cold, hard fear rise in her as she recognised the accent as Ukrainian. 'Get into the back of the van up ahead.'

The door swung open from inside as they approached the large panel van. Maria was bustled in by the gunman while a second figure, inside the van and unseen by Maria, swiftly pulled a blackout hood over her head. Something stung her arm and she felt a chill surge as something was injected into it.

3.

'This is where Melissa Schenker, the second victim, was found. Weiberfastnacht, last year,' said Scholz. He, Fabel, Kris and Tansu stood at the alley mouth, hunched against the cold and drizzly sleet.

Fabel looked along the street. It swept around at the end but he could see a spire puncture the sky above the rooftops. He pointed in its direction. 'What's that?'

'St Ursula's Church.'

'But the first victim, Sabine Jordanski was found near there.'

'Yep. On the other side. Her apartment was on Gereonswall. But as I said, the significance is difficult to read. There are tons of churches throughout Cologne. And standing here we're within range of at least four of the city's twelve Romanesque churches – St Ursula's, St Kunibert's, St Gereon's, St Andreas's and, of course there's . . .' Scholz turned to indicate the other direction and held his arm out as if announcing a cabaret act. Fabel saw the massive, domineering twin spires of Cologne Cathedral soar menacingly grey-black above the city.

Fabel looked again at the place that just under a year ago had been a murder crime scene. It was a narrow alley between two four-storey apartment buildings. It was cobbled and swept clean. A row of recycling and waste bins lined one side, allowing room for only one person to pass. The bins had been there at the time of the murder. Fabel had seen the scene-of-crime pictures. Being there in person confirmed the instinct he had had when looking at the photographs.

'It has always been assumed that the killer followed the victims. Picked them out from the Karneval crowds because of their physical forms fitting his agenda. But I think the selection has been made long before that. Weeks. Maybe months. Maybe he was on their trails during the evening, but my reckoning is that he knew exactly where they lived and overtook them or predicted their movements. I think he was waiting here for Melissa Schenker when she came home. In the dark, in this confined space, like a trapdoor spider.'

'So he selected the locus well in advance? Not just the victim?'

'Yep . . . and that makes him a whole different proposition,' said Fabel. 'Serial killers come in two types: the impulsive and the organised. The impulsive types simply respond to their appetites. They scratch when they itch. Cannibalistic serial killers tend always to be impulsive and that is what I thought we were perhaps dealing with here.'

'Does it make that much of a difference?' Kris Feilke's acne stood out even more vividly against the blue-white of his chilled skin.

'Yes, it does,' said Fabel. 'Both types commit a series of murders, both often take trophies, both have borderline personality disorders, both tend to be loser types . . . but there is a huge difference between them. Impulsive serial killers have below average IQs. Often significantly below.'

'Like Joachim Kroll . . .' Scholz referred back to their discussion in the restaurant.

'Like Joachim Kroll. But organised serial killers usually have IQs way above average. And they know it. They are smart, but they're never quite as smart as they think they are. Anyway, I'm beginning to think that our Karneval Killer is an organised type. A planner. Especially in this case. Melissa Schenker was an almost total recluse. That was something else that I noticed in the files you sent me. Schenker had practically no social life other than the two friends who were always trying to draw her out of her shell.'

'That's right. They were the ones who persuaded her to come out with them on Weiberfastnacht. Poor girls. I interviewed them. They were completely distraught and riddled with guilt. They felt that if they hadn't cajoled Melissa to come out she would still be alive.'

'They're probably right. But what I don't get is the selection of Melissa. Our killer is a tracker and hunter. He must have seen her somewhere outside her apartment.'

Scholz shrugged, as much against the cold as anything. 'We checked. She was a very regulated person. She worked with computers. Designed games, apparently. Made a small fortune from it, not that you would have guessed that from her apartment. It's the big thing these days, apparently. Everybody wants to get into it.'

Fabel looked down the street along the top storeys of the buildings. Melissa Schenker had lived on the top floor. The sky glowered back at him.

'Is her home occupied?'

'No. It lay empty for more than six months and then was sold. A property company bought it and they want to rent it out. Word gets around, though. People around here can be a superstitious bunch.'

'Have they renovated or redecorated it?'

'Not yet.' Scholz grinned.

'I'd like to see it,' said Fabel.

The grin stayed in place as Scholz's glove dipped into his leather jacket. He raised a bunch of keys and dangled them as if ringing a bell. 'I thought you might . . .'

The apartment was pleasant and bright even on a day like this, but without furniture it was impossible for Fabel to place in it the personality he had got to know through reading Scholz's file. The walls were white. The ceiling was high and dotted with downlighters which cast bright pools on the highly polished light wood of the floor, the gloomy blue-grey day outside pressing itself against the arch-topped windows. The main living area was a good size: open plan with a wide step up to a raised area.

'That's where she worked,' said Scholz, who had followed Fabel's gaze. Fabel nodded. There was a bank of power and data points along the wall of the raised area.

'It looks expensive enough to me,' said Fabel.

'I didn't say it wasn't expensive,' said Scholz. 'It's just that her earning bracket was *way* above this. She cleared over three hundred thousand Euros a year. It was her own business and even after she sold the games on to the big games producers she retained the copyright and earned a royalty for each game sold. Her friends said she loved her work. Too much.'

Fabel, who had been looking out of the window along towards the twin spires of the cathedral, turned to Scholz. 'What do you mean?'

'They were beginning to get worried about her state of mind. Melissa built alternative realities for her games. Invented worlds. Her friends said that she spent far too much time in this alternative existence. They were worried she was losing her grip on reality. When she wasn't working on developing other worlds she was *living* in them, playing online games.'

Fabel nodded. 'It's called data addiction. Or hyperconnected disorder . . . Messing up your mind by spending too much time interfacing with technology and not enough interacting with reality and real people. It creates real mental problems. Interestingly, it is particularly rife amongst people with poor self-image, particularly poor body image. It's their way of existing beyond the confines of their physical selves . . . the selves they are dissatisfied with.'

'It would fit with what we know about Melissa . . .' said Tansu Bakrac. She was standing under one of the downlighters and the copper in her hair burned redder. 'The stuff we were able to access on her computers revealed a lot. She reviewed other games on forums, online stores, that kind of thing. Most reviews were a hundred to a hundred and fifty words long.'

'Well, she was in the business . . .'

Tansu laughed. 'We counted two thousand reviews over a period of two years. That's about three hundred thousand words. And there was a lot of venom in some of them. Sarcasm and trying to sound smart. I can imagine she pissed off a few people.'

'Oh?'

'No . . . that's a dead end. All her reviews were done through aliases. And anyway, it was easy to read between the lines. Her stuff had the mark of someone with no life venting their fury anonymously. And on top of that were the hours she spent playing games. We still have her stuff in the evidence room. You name the gadget, she had it. Like you said, anything she could use to avoid the real world. I didn't think there was a name for it, though . . . I thought it was just a case of her being a saddo . . .'

'But I don't see a connection between that and what happened to her,' said Scholz.

'Maybe not. What happened to her computer equipment?'

'We've still got it in evidence storage,' answered Kris Feilke. 'We thought we should hang onto it just in case she had met someone online. You know, given the kind of life she led.'

'Had she?'

'No. Not that we could see. I had one of our technical guys go through her computer files. I had to take him off it. It was eating up too much time and looked like a dead end. The main problem was that a lot of her stuff was protected by secure encryption which we couldn't break. But from what we could see of her Internet history there was no hint of her meeting someone online.'

'With someone as techno-savvy as Melissa, that means nothing. You would be amazed at what goes on. It's my guess that if we could break her password security, I would bet that we would discover that Melissa had a very active social and sex life. Online. What about family?'

'One sister. I don't think they had much to do with each other. The sale of the flat was all handled through lawyers. No surviving parents.'

'Current and former boyfriends?'

'Nothing here. Melissa wasn't from Cologne. She was brought up in Hessen. Very few boyfriends in her history. We had them all checked out. Nothing.'

'I'd like to see her stuff. Later, I mean.' Fabel looked around the flat again. This had been Melissa's safety zone. Her secure space where she could live out her life by proxy in some digitised version of reality. Nothing bad could happen to her in here. Danger and fear were outside.

As they left the flat and headed back down to the street from which Melissa Schenker had been snatched and murdered, Fabel dwelt on how right she had been.

4.

Andrea waited. Her head thudded with a headache brought on by deliberate dehydration: she had slashed her fluid intake over the last week to a cupful of water a day so that her body would burn the slightest reserve of fat to keep hydrated. There were half a dozen chairs in the dressing room but she sat on none. This was not the time to rest. It was the time to switch on every cubic millimetre of her body; to hard-wire her will into her flesh. Her heart hammered and electricity coursed through every sinew, every nerve, every swollen fibre. Andrea had pumped up with dumbbells five minutes ago, but now she ran through her routine, the poses she would strike on the stage, each an exposition of a specific muscle set. It wasn't that Andrea needed to rehearse to get it right: it was that running through them ensured the optimal muscle tone.

First the mandatory poses: Double Front Bicep, Front Lat Spread, Abdominals and Thighs – one of Andrea's best, because of the definition of her serratus anterior and obliques – Side Chest, Side Triceps, Rear Double Bicep. Then was the weak spot in Andrea's routine, when she had to turn her back on the judges to do her Rear Lat Spread. It was then that the lack of definition on her glutes let her down. But she had put a lot of thought into the outfit she was performing in: it made the most of the lateral sweep of her shoulder-to-hip taper, drawing focus from her glutes. Her last mandatory would be the Most Muscular. From that she would segue straight into Crab Most Muscular, her first optional pose.

She heard the cheers of the crowd. The British Bitch had finished her set and it sounded like it had been a good one. Whistling. Stamping. The crowd bellowing. Calling Maxine the British Bitch wasn't an insult, it was Maxine's professional nickname, just as Andrea's was Andrea the Amazon. Andrea and Maxine had taken part in a number of competitions together. When Andrea had done a tour of England, Maxine had put her up in Nottingham and Maxine would be staying at Andrea's flat tonight. They had trained together. They had put on non-competitive exhibitions together. They were friends.

Except on the competition podium. On the podium you had no friends. Out there you needed no one and nothing except raw adrenalin and aggression. Anger, even. All hidden behind the broadest, brightest, most brainless grin. Out there, Andrea's friend Maxine became simply the British Bitch. The one to beat.

Andrea heard more cheers as the next competitor was up. She would follow her. She needed the aggression. The anger. Andrea knew where to find the anger: it was a switch she could turn on at will. All she had to do was remember. As Andrea waited to be called to do her routine she allowed the raw fire of her hate and anger to fill her body in huge surges.

The knock came and one of the exhibition-hall staff swung wide the door for Andrea to exit. It was like a lion being released into the Colosseum. As Andrea the Amazon took long powerful strides past the attendant she heard a defiant, animal roar. And realised she was hearing her own voice.

5.

Maria guessed she had been bundled into the trunk of a car. Or a van. But even that idea had seemed to drift away from her. The fact was that they had tied her wrists and ankles, gagged and blindfolded her, then put some kind of bag over her head. Finally, they had placed what she reckoned to be a set of industrial ear-defenders over her ears. It was all classic special forces stuff: total sensory deprivation to befuddle the victim. Time ceased to exist. Maria was aware that her mind had been cut adrift from her body; she was losing the concept of arms, of legs, of being connected to her nervous system. She wriggled and strained against the bonds so that the rope would burn at the skin of her ankles and wrists. It worked for an instant and the connection to her flesh was re-established, then faded and the pain became a vague ache lingering on the periphery of her being.

Maria had had no idea how long she'd been in the trunk, or even that the car had stopped moving, until she felt hands on her body, lifting her from the van. She was placed on a hard chair and left for a few minutes, a new bond tight around her chest and binding her to the chair. The tightness of the rope around her wrists had numbed her hands and the ear-defenders and the blindfold and hood deprived her of any sense of whether she was indoors or outdoors. She thought of how people were executed like this. Deprived of sight and hearing, she wouldn't even hear the cocking of the gun or sense the presence of her executioner. It would be sudden and immediate: her existence snuffed out in an instant. Probably not the worst way to go, she had thought, but still her heart pounded. Only a few days ago Maria had been surprised at how little she feared death. But she had learned to live again by being someone else; her life had regained some value for her. She wondered if they would ever find her body. She imagined Fabel frowning as he looked down on her corpse, her hair bizarrely dyed.

The ear-defenders were suddenly gone. The hood was snatched from her head. Someone behind her untied the gag.

Maria's pulse quickened even more. Maybe torture would come before death. The blindfold was removed. The sudden restoration of her senses disoriented her and she sat, her head tilted down, blinking in the harsh light.

Her eyes adjusted. A man and a woman sat opposite her.

She appeared to be in a small empty warehouse or industrial unit. The whitewashed walls were naked and broken by a double door at the far end and a large thick sliding metal door to Maria's right. There was a track system suspended from the ceiling, punctuated by pendant metal hooks. She guessed it was some kind of disused meat-packing factory.

The woman stood up and snapped a glass vial under Maria's nose. Something powerful hit her system and she was suddenly and painfully alert.

'I want you to listen to me.' The man spoke first. His German was thick with a Ukrainian accent. 'I need you to concentrate. Do you understand?'

Maria nodded.

'We know who you are, Frau Klee. We also know why you're here – and that you are acting on your own and without the knowledge, support or sanction of your superiors. You're completely isolated.'

Maria said nothing.

'You may be an accomplished police officer, Frau Klee, but when it comes to this line of work you're a complete amateur. It takes more than a cheap hair-colour job to turn you into a surveillance expert.'

Maria looked at the woman. She was young and remarkably beautiful with bright, pale blue eyes. She wasn't someone who could merge easily into a crowd. The man frightened Maria. He had the same kind of green eyes as Vitrenko, with that strange, penetrating brightness that so many Ukrainians seemed to have. His hair was almost black, and his pale skin was drawn particularly tight over the Slavic architecture of his face. He had an efficient, lean-muscled look, but Maria got the impression that he was tired.

'So what happens to me now?' said Maria. 'Why have you brought me here instead of just dumping my body in the woods somewhere? Nothing I know is of any use to you.'

The Ukrainian exchanged a smile with the woman next to him.

'Frau Klee, we have absolutely no intention of doing you any harm whatsoever. As a matter of fact we *intervened*, to put it mildly, because you were going to get yourself killed. And very soon. Did you really think that Kushnier didn't know you were on his tail within minutes of him leaving the bar?'

'Kushnier,' said the Ukrainian woman. 'Maxim Kushnier. Former Ukrainian paratrooper. Low-level operative in Vitrenko's organisation. That was as far as you got . . . a street-level captain who has probably never met Vitrenko face to face. How the hell did you expect to have Kushnier lead you to Vitrenko?'

'I didn't. I thought it was a start.'

'And it was very nearly the end,' said the man. He stood up and nodded to the woman who came round behind Maria and cut through her bonds. 'We were tailing you. Not that you or Kushnier would have noticed. You were both two busy performing that waltz on the Delhoven road.'

'If we were dancing,' said Maria massaging her now-free wrists, 'then I was leading.'

'Yes . . .' said the Ukrainian, with a conciliatory nod. 'That was impressive. But while you were wandering about lost in the Rhineland countryside, we tidied up your mess.'

'Dead?'

'You got him with three shots. Shoulder, neck and one through the kidney. The kidney shot would have caused him agony. Fortunately for him he bled to death from the neck wound.'

Maria felt suddenly sick. She knew she must have hit him, but not finding the car had meant, until now, not confronting the fact that she had taken another human being's life.

'So, you see,' the Ukrainian said, 'you're now officially working outside the law. As are we.'

'Who are you?' Maria took the glass of water offered by the woman.

'We are your new partners.'

'Ukrainian intelligence?'

'No. We're not SBU. Technically, we're police officers. I am Captain Taras Buslenko of the *Sokil*. It means "Falcon" . . . we are an anti-organised-crime Spetsnaz. And this is Captain Olga Sarapenko of the Kiev city militia, similar to your *Schutzpolizei*. Captain Sarapenko is part of the Kiev police's anti-mafia unit.'

'You're after Vitrenko?' asked Maria.

'Yes. And he's after us. What you see here are the remains of a seven-strong special unit put together to come here and . . . *deal* with Vitrenko.'

'You're planning to carry out an illegal assassination on German soil?'

'Isn't that exactly what you had planned to do yourself, if you got the chance?'

Maria ignored the question. 'You said there were seven of you. Where are the others?'

'Three dead. There were two traitors in the group. We met at an isolated hunting lodge in Ukraine. No one knew about it. By the time we worked out it was two of our own and not an attacking force, we were already exposed. Only three of us made it out of the woods, then Belotserkovsky took it in the back.'

'My fault . . .' The pain showed on Olga Sarapenko's face. 'I was injured and he was helping to get me out.'

'I was supposed to be providing cover,' said Buslenko. A

silence fell between them and Maria could see that they were somewhere and sometime else. She knew what it was like to live and relive an experience like that.

'So why didn't you re-form a complete unit?' she asked.

'No time and no point,' said Buslenko. 'Time's on Vitrenko's side. We have to get to him before he gets to us. Hopefully, Vitrenko will have assumed that we have aborted the mission . . . that Captain Sarapenko and I are running scared. We couldn't be sure that if we did rebuild a unit that we wouldn't have infiltrators again. But we know we can trust each other. There's only one other person we can rely on . . .'

'Who?'

'You,' Buslenko said, handing Maria back her handgun.

6.

The crowd went wild. Andrea stood before them, her body dark and sleek with fake tan and body oil, her hatred and anger hidden behind a searchlight-white smile that beamed across the expanse of the hall. The music Andrea had chosen thudded hard and harsh in the hall and all the time she thought about the stupid, soft little tart she had once been. This, now, for all to see, was the real Andrea Sandow. Andrea the Amazon. Each pose drew a roar of appreciation from the crowd. She improvised a final optional pose at the end of her routine: Overhead Victory. Her biceps, which were bigger than those of any of the other competitors, bunched high with a rippling topography of vein and sinew. The crowd cheered and many rose to their feet. She stood down to Relaxed Front and bowed low to the audience. She turned sideways with a bounce and moved quickly to the side of the stage where the other competitors waited. Maxine smiled a broad smile and nodded respectfully through her applause. And with that Andrea knew she had won. All the pain, all the anguish and sacrifice had led to this point. What no one in the auditorium knew was that it wasn't just her competitors she had defeated.

Maxine hugged her warmly and genuinely as soon as the judges announced their decision. Andrea felt like crying but, of course, the tears wouldn't come. The other contestants congratulated her, but she could see that only Maxine was genuinely pleased for her. Andrea felt bad, knowing that if things had been the other way around she would not have been so generous.

'We'll get pissed tonight,' Maxine said in English. 'Competition's over . . . a week of indulgence before getting back to the grind?'

'The champagne is definitely on me,' said Andrea and they entered the dressing room. Three people waited for them, one of whom she recognised as Herr Waldheim, a member of the competition's organising committee.

'This is Herr Dr Gabriel and his nurse, Frau Bosbach.' Waldheim introduced the other two. 'They are here on behalf of the bodybuilding association to do a random blood test, if you have no objections.'

'Of course not,' Andrea said and felt her jaws ache from the effort of keeping her smile in place.

7.

At Fabel's suggestion they left the car parked and he and Scholz walked to St Ursula's. The church sat in a small square, hemmed in by neighbouring buildings. There was a bar restaurant at one end of the square and a parochial house jammed against the flank of the church.

'Where was Sabine Jordanski found?' Fabel asked.

'Over there, behind the church.'

Fabel and the others followed Scholz round the side of the

church. As with the scene of Melissa Schenker's murder, it was concealed from view. Another hidden death trap.

'Where did she live?'

'Her apartment was around the corner and over on Gereonswall.' Scholz indicated the street that swept away from them.

'Something doesn't make sense . . .' Fabel looked back in the direction of the city.

'What?' asked Scholz.

'I'm convinced that the killer lies in wait for his victims. But the church is on the wrong side. She wouldn't have passed by here.'

Scholz smiled grimly and shook his head. 'She was with friends when she came home. They split up here and headed off. Even if she had come this way, the killer couldn't have grabbed her. She was with witnesses.'

'Then he must have either persuaded or forced her to come up here.'

'Must have.'

'That could mean that this specific church *does* have a significance. There was no sign of sexual contact?' Fabel asked although he knew the answer.

'None,' answered Tansu. 'No semen, no evidence of sexual assault.'

The four detectives stood looking at the ghost of a murder scene. The second they'd examined that day. Fabel was beginning to understand the dynamic of this small team: Scholz acted as if he wasn't the boss, Kris and Tansu called him Benni and never *Chef*, but the truth was that he steered his team probably more strictly than Fabel did his. Kris was the apprentice: quietly gathering the gems of wisdom from Scholz's feet. Tansu was strong-willed and intelligent, but still unsure of her feet and unwilling to challenge Scholz. It was clear that he had closed his mind to Tansu's theory about the rape victim in 'ninety-nine. Fabel, on the other hand, could see her reasoning.

'There's something you've got to see.' Scholz hunched up his shoulders against the cold and led Fabel towards the vast dark doors of St Ursula's. Fabel followed him into the church, gazing up at the vaulted ceilings and the stained glass that burned dully against the winter light beyond.

'Very nice.'

'That's not what I wanted to show you.' Scholz guided Fabel to a vast reinforced door immediately to the right of the main entrance.

'We'll stay here,' said Tansu. 'It gives me the creeps down there.'

Fabel and Scholz went down stone steps into the crypt of the church.

'This is open to the public during the day, but it's monitored constantly by CCTV. And that massive door you saw is shut tight and time-locked at night.'

Fabel stopped in his tracks. The vaulted ceiling was white-washed, with gilded details. Apart from that, it was as if the whole space had been lined with gold. But it was what the gold covered that fascinated Fabel.

'The Golden Chamber . . .' explained Scholz. 'St Ursula's is the second-oldest Romanesque church in Cologne. As you saw, the city has kind of encroached on its space, but there used to be an extensive graveyard outside dating back to Roman times.'

Fabel stared all around the chamber. The details on the walls were of bones and skulls. Real bones and skulls, pressed into the mortar of the walls and arranged in geometric patterns. Hundreds of them. Thousands. All gilded. The art of death. There were small alcoves pressed into the walls of the vault. Each contained a plaster bust.

'Do you know the legend of St Ursula?' asked Scholz.

Fabel shook his head. He was still taking in the detail of the chamber. So many dead. Gilded human remains used as ornament. It was awe-inspiring. And gross.

'Ursula was a British princess who travelled here with eleven thousand virgins. Unfortunately, when they arrived Cologne was besieged by a horde of horny Huns from the East. Ursula and her virgins all died rather than lose their honour, or something like that.' Scholz laughed. 'You'd be pushed to find eleven thousand virgins in Cologne these days. Anyway, the story started out that there were eleven virgins with St Ursula, but you know what we're like here in Cologne . . . we started off by bumping it up it up to eleven hundred, then eleven thousand. Anyway, there's every reason to believe that there was some kind of martyrdom involving virgins around the fifth century. Story goes that they were buried in the graveyard here. When the graveyard was dug up, the Golden Chamber was built to house and display the remains. The truth is more likely to be that these bones date from across a couple of centuries. There are also dozens of ossuaries, and these plaster busts contain the remains of those wealthy enough to have a special place put aside for them.

'It's morbid . . .' said Fabel.

'It's Catholicism.' Scholz smiled. 'We're very big on memento mori. Have fun when you're alive but remember that death and eternity is waiting for you. Like I said, it's a concept we've refined and concentrated into Karneval.'

'Why did you want me to see this?' asked Fabel. 'Do you think there's some significance? The virgin legend and the Golden Chamber? According to Tansu, the rape victim seven years ago was attacked at the back of this church. And she was a virgin.'

'I suppose it's possible there's a connection between that case and the killings. But I thought you'd want to see this. Both murders were in close proximity to St Ursula's. Maybe all this,' Scholz encompassed the Golden Chamber with a sweep of his hand, 'has some special significance for the killer. Maybe he assumed that Melissa Schenker was a virgin. Certainly her lifestyle seemed to be pretty celibate. But Sabine

Jordanski strikes me as someone who would have given up that status pretty enthusiastically some time ago.'

Fabel nodded. 'But there must be *something* that brought these girls to his attention. Not just the fact that they had his particular taste in body shape. He's seen them before the night he killed them. Somehow and somewhere there is a commonality.'

Fabel stared at one of the ossuary wall panels. It stared back at him from the dark sockets of a gilded skull. He turned from its hollow gaze and made his way to the steps out of the Golden Chamber. 'When we get back to your office, I'd like to go over the files again. I know we're missing it.'

8.

'What we are talking about is committing murder.' Buslenko leaned on the table and held Maria in a searchlight gaze. She hated his eyes. Bright and hard like diamond-cut emeralds. So like Vitrenko's eyes. 'Let's be clear on that. We're here to break the very law that it is your duty to uphold. You are a Murder Commission detective, Maria . . . you should know more than anyone that there is nothing that legally justifies the homicide of Vasyl Vitrenko.'

'It's morally justifiable . . .' she said.

'That's not the issue. If we're caught, you'll go to prison. I just want to make that clear. If you want to walk away from this, then you can do so now. But go back to Hamburg . . . I don't want you getting in our way here.'

'I know the stakes,' said Maria. 'I'll do anything to nail that bastard. He finished me as a police officer so I don't see why I should act like one when it comes to bringing him down.'

'Okay . . .' Buslenko rolled out a street map of Cologne. It was no ordinary driver's city guide and Maria guessed it was the kind of map that every intelligence agency in the world would have of cities in every other country. There were a number of small red squares glued to the map. 'These are the centres – or at least the ones we know about – from which the Vitrenko outfit operates. We have good intelligence on these, but we know these aren't the key locations. We know nothing about those. And we can be pretty sure that Vitrenko has changed his appearance significantly. He could be right under our noses and we wouldn't know it. But we do have intelligence on *this* piece of shit . . .' Buslenko laid a photograph on the table. 'This is Valeri Molokov, the Russian. In fact, in many ways Molokov is a Russian version of Vitrenko. The main difference is that Molokov is not quite as smart, not quite as deadly. And where Vitrenko sees himself as something other, something better, than a common criminal and still thinks he's running a military operation, Molokov, despite having a police Spetsnaz background, is quite comfortable with his role as a common or garden mafia boss.'

'Molokov was a police officer?' asked Maria.

'Again, not in the way you think of it. Molokov served with *OMON*, the Russian Special Purpose Police Squad, but was kicked out, ostensibly for corruption. With so many special-forces police on the take in Moscow, that takes some doing. Molokov did three years in Matrosskaya Tishina prison in Moscow for offences linked to people smuggling. Another difference from Vitrenko, who's never been arrested, far less faced trial and imprisonment. The truth is that Molokov built his reputation as a contract killer. He's now officially wanted for a whole range of crimes. Molokov hates Vitrenko but can't do anything about the situation. He and Vitrenko were on a collision course and Molokov knew he'd come out worst. So Vitrenko was able to force Molokov into partnership with him, with Molokov very much the junior partner.'

'Why hasn't Molokov been extradited from Germany?' asked Maria.

'Molokov and Vitrenko are both living here under assumed names. The difference between them is that Vitrenko is better at it – living in someone else's skin, as it were. But the German police still don't know what identity Molokov's using or where to find him. And that's where we're ahead of the game.'

'Oh?'

'We have a location for him. More by accident than by design. Our main interest in Molokov is that he's the highest-ranking member of the Vitrenko organisation who we can observe. Unlike you chasing around after small fry like Kushnier, Molokov could really give us a fix on Vitrenko.'

'It sounds like there's no love lost between them.'

'There isn't, particularly on Molokov's side. Vitrenko has the power to keep him in check, but Molokov is a deadly son of a bitch. But there is a specific stress-point in the Vitrenko-Molokov marriage. Your Federal Crime Bureau here in Germany has a source of information within the organisation. Our intelligence suggests that Vitrenko believes the leak is from Molokov's side. I took part in a failed operation to nail Vitrenko back on Ukrainian soil. One of Molokov's top men, a thug called Kotkin, ended up dead, as did a member of our team who was supposedly on the Vitrenko payroll.'

Olga Sarapenko cut in. 'What we need to know is if you are with us in this. Will you help us nail Vitrenko?'

Maria sipped her water. She noticed her hand trembling as she did so. Her wrists still ached from the rope they'd been bound with.

'What if we were to do this legally? Locate him and get the BKA to arrest him?'

'You know that's not an option, Maria,' said Buslenko. 'That would give him a chance to slip through our fingers. You for one should know how easy that is. Anyway, that is not our objective. We are here to put an end to Vitrenko. Literally.'

Maria looked at the Ukrainian. He held her gaze, leaning forward in his chair, his elbows resting on his knees. This man claimed to be a policeman, knew that she was a police officer, yet was asking her to cooperate in a murder. There again, that had been the conclusion she had envisaged for herself. But how did she know that he was genuine? He could be anybody. He could be one of Vitrenko's killers. But if that were the case, wouldn't she be dead by now?.

'Like I told you,' she said. 'I want to be there when Vitrenko is brought down. I'm in.'

9.

Ansgar, so unused to the ballet of courtship, fumbled clumsily for the right words. Ekaterina, like a city guide helping out a tourist who had found himself on the wrong side of town, had had to help him with his halting and mumbled proposal that she should come with him to the Karneval procession in a few weeks' time. Ekaterina made it easier for him by suggesting that they go out for an evening first; to a Ukrainian restaurant she knew.

Ansgar was no fool. He was, after all, at least fifteen years older than her and by no description a catch. And he knew that marriage to a German national would assure her permanent residency in the Federal Republic. However, he also believed that Ekaterina really did like him. But did she really know about his true nature? His secret desires?

The Rhine divides Cologne in more than the geographical sense. Since the very first settlements the river had represented first an ethnic and then a social and cultural border. The inhabitants of the left bank, of which Ansgar was one, had always thought of their side of the river as the true Cologne, as opposed to 'over there'. The Ukrainian restaurant that Ekaterina had suggested was 'over there', in the Vingst area of the city. The food was authentically Ukrainian.

Ansgar also guessed that a large proportion of the clientele, and probably the management, was authentically Ukrainian mafia. He noticed several huddles of large men in black Armani, the regulation uniform of Eastern European gangsterdom.

The menu was in both Cyrillic and German but Ansgar allowed himself to be led in his choice by Ekaterina. As far as Ansgar could see, the Ukrainians had as many styles of *Borsch* as Eskimos had words for snow. Added to this was *pechyva, pampushky, halushky, varenyky, bitky* meatballs and a whole range of desserts. Ekaterina recommended that they should start with goose-breast *zakuska* followed by a starter portion of *hetman borsch*, then pork ribs stewed in beet *kvas* with *halushky* dumplings.

'You can't get more Ukrainian than that,' she enthused and Ansgar could see that she was genuinely proud to introduce him to her culture and cuisine. When the waiter came over to take their drinks order, Ekaterina engaged in a lively exchange in Ukrainian with him. The waiter smiled and nodded.

'I hope you don't mind,' she said. 'This is something you've got to try . . .'

The waiter returned with a chilled champagne-style bottle. He popped the cork and Ekaterina again took the lead and tasted it, nodding enthusiastically. After the waiter had filled his glass, Ansgar took a sip. His mouth filled with a fragrant effervescence.

'This is beautiful,' he said, and meant it. 'Really beautiful.'

'It's *Krimart*,' she said, gratified. 'It's from the Artyomovsk winery in the Donetsk region. It was founded by a German, you know. A Prussian. It was what Stalin and all the communist bosses liked to drink.'

Ansgar watched Ekaterina eat and talk. Naturally, she did most of the talking, her German charmingly accented, but most of all Ansgar watched her eat. During the meal,

Ekatherina worked hard to coax out of Ansgar some of the details of his childhood, family, what had made him want to be a chef. Ansgar found himself wanting to be more conversational; easier, more interesting company. Most of all, he wished he could sit here in this Ukrainian restaurant with an attractive young woman and be someone else: someone with a normal life and normal urges.

Ekatherina didn't seem to worry about Ansgar's taciturnity. She talked at length about her childhood in Ukraine; about the astounding beauty of the land and the warmth of the people.

Ansgar listened and smiled. Ekatherina was dressed in what he guessed was her best outfit. It clearly wasn't expensive but it showed an element of taste. The white blouse was open to the third button and when Ekatherina leaned forward Ansgar could see the full swell of her breasts, pale and smooth. He appreciated the effort she had made. But all through the meal he sought to keep from his mind those dark fantasies that he had formed around her.

They took a taxi from the restaurant. The food, Ansgar had to admit, had been interesting. It was always a strange, even difficult thing for Ansgar to enjoy a meal in another restaurant. To start with, he was never treated as an ordinary customer: he had a reputation and anyone who knew anything about Cologne's food scene knew who he was. Ansgar had been sure he had heard his name amongst the babble of Ukrainian words exchanged between Ekatherina and the waiter. The other problem he had was the way he had to try to leave his professional self outside and simply enjoy the experience for its own sake. The truth was that Ansgar analysed every mouthful, judged flavour combinations, assessed layout on the plate. Ansgar was an artist, and he liked to compare the brushwork of others to see if there was anything he could learn from it. Many subtle nuances that had been added to some of his most highly regarded dishes had been inspired by a cruder expression in some second-class eatery.

But tonight, as he slid into the back seat of the taxi next to Ekaterina, he felt his belly too full. For Ansgar, food was about quality, about the experience, rather than the quantity. He felt the heat of Ekaterina's body as she leant against him. Ansgar was also aware that he had had more to drink than usual. It made him nervous: he felt braver; more likely to act on his impulses. On that greatest of all impulses. He also sensed carelessness and ease in Ekaterina's movements. It was a dangerous situation and he fought to keep those images from his mind. Images of a fantasy that now seemed possible, even if only remotely.

Ansgar had intended to drop Ekaterina at her apartment. He had declined her offer of a coffee: an early start, he had explained. But she had leant across and kissed him, slipping her tongue into his mouth. It tasted of coffee mingled with the raspberry flavour of the *malynivka* liqueur they had drunk to end the meal.

He paid the taxi driver and followed Ekaterina into her apartment building.

10.

'I used to go out with this girl who liked to be tied up, you know,' Scholz leaned back in his chair and raised a bottle of *Kölsch* beer to his lips. 'I mean really tied up. Really tight. Every time we did it. She couldn't, you know, *enjoy* it properly unless she was trussed up.'

'Thanks for sharing that . . .' Fabel smiled wryly and took another sip of *Kölsch* himself. He started to feel that little bit light-headed. He felt the usual fear of losing control kicking in and made a decision to slow down with the beer.

'I mean, it was like she couldn't get off without it,' continued

Scholz. His frown cleared and he grinned. 'There is a point to this, other than offering a window on my sordid personal life. What I'm getting at is that I have come across a lot of weird stuff in my professional life and a fair bit in my personal, if you know what I mean, but no matter how I try I cannot imagine how some sicko gets pleasure from eating other human beings.'

Fabel sat on the sofa and picked fussily at the pizza that Scholz had ordered for them on the way to his flat. It had been Scholz's idea to collect the files, pick up a take-out meal and go over to his apartment. It was, he had said, going to be a long evening and there was no point in being uncomfortable.

'I can honestly say there's little I haven't seen over the years,' continued Fabel. 'Professionally, I mean. That's one of the reasons I wanted to get out of the job.'

Scholz smiled as he watched Fabel continue to pick at the pizza. 'Sorry,' he said. 'They didn't do a herring topping . . .'

Fabel laughed. 'It's funny,' he said. 'You lot down here make a joke about us in the North eating nothing but fish. Truth is, we tend to eat fish because we're coastal people and that's the most immediate source of food. And the way we connect with other cultures plays a part. You know there's a Hamburg dish called *Labskaus*?'

'I believe I've heard of it,' said Scholz with a straight face.

'Scandinavian sailors brought it to Hamburg. Then we took the recipe across to England. The British don't have a clue if you ask them about *Labskaus*, yet they call people from Liverpool *scousers* because it was so popular there. My point is that our diets are shaped by what's available and the contacts we have. Obviously nowadays you can go into any supermarket and buy whatever type of food you like, but the old, generations-long traditions tend to stay in place. It's like we inherit a prejudice for or against certain foods. Which brings me back to our Karneval Cannibal . . . what I find strange is that we have always had a concept of taboo foods. Take pork. Even here, where you eat so much meat, and further south too, there are many people who have a problem with eating pork.'

'What?' Scholz looked dubious. 'South of the "White Sausage Equator" . . . ?'

'Even there, amongst dedicated meat-eaters there are those who will not eat any part of a pig. Pork is the most common taboo food on the planet. The Muslims won't eat it, the Jews are forbidden it, and there was even supposedly an ancient injunction against it amongst Highland Scots. It must have something to do with the similarity between pork and human flesh. I mean, we live in an age of xenotransplantation where genetically modified pig organs are being transplanted into humans. Tribes in Papua New Guinea talk about human flesh as "the long pig".'

'So you think it's because it's like eating human flesh?'

'I think we maybe have some deep cultural memory of cannibalism. And our rejection of cannibalism is a part of how we define ourselves as civilised. Nineteenth-century European colonisation was often justified as saving the natives from themselves. And cannibalism was cited as the prime example of savage behaviour.'

Scholz sipped his beer. 'We've deliberately kept the details of both murders away from the press. We told them there were elements that only we and the killer would know. We haven't even confirmed a definite link. Like you say, there's something about the whole concept of a cannibal being on the loose that scares the shit out of people. And the press would just love it.'

'So you really had considered the possibility of the killer being a cannibal before I mentioned it?'

'Yep,' said Scholz. 'But I wasn't as sure of it as you were. I thought the weight of the flesh was perhaps the significant thing. *A pound of flesh.*' Scholz said it in heavily accented

English. He paused and contemplated his beer. 'Do you think there's any chance that our guy is motivated by something other than sexual cannibalism? Given that there's no semen found at the scenes.'

'Lack of semen doesn't mean he didn't ejaculate. Just that he's been careful not to leave forensic traces. Or maybe he masturbates later, away from the scene. But let's say we're not dealing with a case of sexual cannibalism. Maybe he just likes the taste. The experience of eating human flesh.'

'What's to like?'

'Well, there is one theory that because of the complex proteins in human flesh some people actually get a high out of eating it. A sort of euphoria. Others believe that they gain life-giving complexes that can't be obtained from other meat sources. But there's a natural imperative against cannibalism. In both humans and animals it tends to cause prion diseases . . . mad-cow disease, kuru, that sort of thing.'

'Could it just be that the killer is simply experimenting? That he just wanted to find out what it was like to eat human flesh?'

'I like a nice steak now and again,' said Fabel. 'But I don't think I could go into a field and slaughter a cow to get one. We tend to keep the source of what we eat at a moral arm's length. An American journalist bribed a mortuary attendant in Paris to get a piece of fresh human flesh and wrote about the experience of cooking and eating it. Tasted like veal, he said. Anyway, it's a hell of a leap to kill – and kill twice – just to satisfy your epicurean curiosity. I would put my money on him fulfilling some kind of sexual fantasy with these murders.'

Scholz gathered up the pizza boxes. While Scholz was in the kitchen, Fabel took in the Cologne detective's apartment. It had all the hallmarks of a bachelor's apartment: a combination of the practical and the slovenly. There was a range of house plants dotted around in various stages of dehydration and death: Fabel had to resist the temptation to ask for a watering can. The bookshelves, however, were packed but orderly and Scholz had a spectacularly wide range of DVDs, arranged in alphabetical order by title. This meticulous organisation shouted out from the chaos of Scholz's flat. There were a handful of surprisingly tasteful art prints on the walls and a poster for a Cologne production of *Macbeth*. Fabel recalled the Shakespearean reference in his report. Scholz came back with two more beers and cleared room for the files on the coffee table.

'You like Shakespeare?' Fabel asked.

'Some. Never in English. My English isn't good enough. But I love the story of *Macbeth*. I remember seeing the Orson Welles version dubbed into German, when I was a kid. I just loved the character. So totally evil and ruthless. But given the case we're looking at *Titus Andronicus* would be a more appropriate text.'

Fabel smiled. Scholz's impressive knowledge of Shakespeare was at odds with his appearance and demeanour.

'At one time I thought about becoming an actor,' Scholz said, almost embarrassedly. 'The idea of playing at being other people appealed to me more then being myself, I suppose.'

'It's a strange leap from acting to police work.'

'It was never a serious idea,' said Scholz. 'My dad was a policeman and a very . . . well, *practical* sort of man. He kinda killed the idea and I sort of drifted in to being a cop.'

'Theatre's loss . . .' Fabel smiled. He tried to conjure up the unlikely image of Scholz playing Macbeth, his ultimate villain. Suddenly another ultimate villain came to mind and Fabel felt something heavy in his gut. 'How's your other investigation going?' He tried to make his tone as conversational as possible.

'The Biarritz thing? It's not, really. To be honest, I'm taking

a bit of a back seat on that one. Other interests, you see . . .
the BKA and Organised Crime are all over it like a rash.'

'Oh?'

'I mean, I'm still *involved*. Anything they find out that's
germane to the actual murder will be passed on to me, but
I get the feeling there's a much bigger picture. From the
involvement of the BKA task force I reckon it's to do with
the Molokov-Vitrenko outfit.'

'I know it well. Particularly Vasyl Vitrenko. Our paths have
crossed.'

'Really?' Scholz raised his eyebrows. 'A dangerous path to
cross, from all accounts.'

Fabel smiled grimly. It was difficult to assess how much
Scholz knew about his history with Vitrenko and he didn't
want to point him in Maria's direction. At least, not yet.

'This woman your victim was seen talking to . . .' Again
Fabel tried to keep his tone chatty. 'You know, the one the
witness said was talking to the victim a day or two before
he was killed. You said she seemed to be official. Police or
Immigration. Did you ever get to the bottom of that?'

'That's the strange thing,' said Scholz. 'We still can't link
her to any official body. Maybe she just *looked* official.'

'Yeah . . .' said Fabel, taking a sip of his beer but watching
Scholz's face as he spread out the files on the coffee table.
'Probably nothing to do with anything . . .'

'Oh, I don't know . . . This BKA Vitrenko-Molokov task
force seems pretty desperate to find her. Or for me to find
her for them.'

II.

Andrea's post-competition, pumped-up toning made it easy
for the doctor to access a vein. The nurse then accompanied
Andrea to the toilet and waited outside the cubicle until she
came out again with her urine sample. Throughout the process

Andrea maintained a friendly demeanour which was as genuine as the big, stupid grin she used when she was on the posing stage. She even joked with the dour little nurse, although Andrea actually felt disgust and hatred for her weak, flaccid face and formless body.

Andrea wasn't too fond of the doctor, either. He was an arrogant, unsmiling little man who did not speak to Andrea other than to order her to hold out her arm.

'When will I get the results?' asked Andrea with a smile, although she felt like twisting the smug little doctor's head from his shoulders.

'*You* don't get the results. They go directly to the governing body. They will advise you of the results. But I do give you half of each sample so that you may have them tested independently should you wish to contest the results.'

Andrea crushed the impulse to smash her manicured fist into the smug face. 'There won't be anything to contest.'

The doctor stood up, placing his accoutrements back into his case. 'My dear lady, I am a physician. I have been involved in testing for the governing bodies of a number of sporting organisations. And I will tell you something that is an absolute and undeniable medical fact – not an opinion, a fact – and it is this: muscular hypertrophy is a male phenomenon. Specifically muscular hypertrophy such as yours. Women can build muscle through weight training, but to a much lesser degree. Only men can achieve the kind of muscle mass you have developed without resorting to banned substances. Even men in middle age lose the mass and definition capacity they had in youth. Why? Because their testosterone levels begin to sink. Testosterone, Frau Sandow. The kind of quantities that only occur naturally in younger men. Men have nearly ten times the testosterone level of women.'

'Are you accusing me of cheating?' The smile had now gone from Andrea's lips. Her muscle-widened jaw set hard.

'I am accusing no one of anything. I am merely stating a medical fact. You could not have achieved your build without taking considerable quantities of testosterone. All this test will ascertain is if there is sufficient in your system to test positive. But, I dare say, you have calculated it all out. I mean, with this competition coming up.'

Andrea stood up suddenly, raw anger burning in her gut. The doctor snapped shut his bag, unperturbed. 'Unusually high levels of aggression are a common side effect, Frau Sandow.' He looked her up and down. 'And I have to say you are a singularly unhealthy individual. I can tell from your halitosis, the dandruff from your scalp and the inflamed rims of your eyes that you are very seriously dehydrated. Please take my advice as a physician: take fluids, and plenty of them.'

Andrea pulled herself to her maximum height, drawing in her abdomen and flexing her shoulders. 'I suppose you think this is being unfit?' she laughed.

'As a matter of fact, I do. You have already done serious harm to your internal organs. The regular dehydration alone will have done God knows what to your liver and kidneys. My guess is, Frau Sandow, that you have used testosterone as the base of a steroid stack. But given your pronounced vascularity,' he said, pointing to the veins bulging on her forearms and biceps, 'my guess is that you thought you could get away with using boldenone. The bad news is that boldenone has a detectable half-life of nearly six months.'

'What you don't know,' Andrea smiled masculinely, 'is that I am infinitely more knowledgeable about human physiology than you imagine. Like I said, you won't find anything in those tests. And what if I have taken steroids in the past? It should be legal. It's part of what we do, like a high-protein diet.'

The doctor and the nurse headed towards the door. Dr

Gabriel turned and shook his head mournfully. 'You are a disgrace to your namesake, Frau Sandow. And I am hoping that Eugene Sandow is no direct ancestor of yours. His vision for this sport was to replicate the ethos of classical gymnasia. To achieve perfect symmetry and balance. To shape – not to misshape. What people like you have done is to take a great sport and turn it into a freak show. As I said, the organising body will notify you of the test results.'

Andrea was left alone with Maxine, who placed an arm around her huge shoulders. 'Don't you worry about it, love,' she said in English. 'You'll pass these tests, no problem. What was that old guy going on about, anyway?'

'Nothing,' said Andrea and smiled. 'Nothing at all. Let's go out on the town tonight, just like you said.'

But deep down inside the dark fire roared. She thought of the pompous little doctor and, worst of all, that snotty cow of a nurse standing there silent, reproachful and so submissive. They were so sure of themselves. But what they didn't know was that she was as smart as she was strong. There would be nothing to find in the sample.

She would go out on the town tonight with Maxine. But soon, very soon, she was going to have to release the heat of her anger.

12.

While Scholz went into the kitchen to get himself a beer and make Fabel a coffee, Fabel laid the photographs of both victims side by side on the coffee table: images in life and in death.

'I was talking to this anthropologist before I came down here,' he called through to the kitchen. 'He was an expert on the ideal of female beauty through the ages. Not so much what is beautiful but what we regard as beautiful. There was a time when these two women would have matched that ideal perfectly: slightly pear-shaped, slim upper body with a little flesh around the hips and belly. Right up until the First World War, in fact. Then came the flapper, then the hourglass, then the skinny.'

'So what's your point?' Scholz emerged from the kitchen and handed Fabel his coffee.

'These women had the wrong shape for today. They might have wanted to do something about it.' Fabel started to rummage through the files.

'What are you looking for?' asked Scholz.

'Gym memberships, diet clubs . . . any hint that they were considering cosmetic surgery . . . liposuction, that kind of thing.'

'But there was nothing really wrong with them . . .' Scholz joined the search. 'I mean, their shapes weren't that unusually heavy around the backside.'

'You would be amazed at what lengths women are prepared to go to over the slightest flaw.'

Ten minutes later they had assembled a selection of options, all for Sabine Jordanski. She went to a private gym twice a week, took regular beauty treatments at the salon, went swimming every Wednesday when she had the afternoon off. There was nothing at all for Melissa Schenker.

'There has to be something.' Fabel ran his hands through his hair.

'Maybe Melissa Schenker wasn't so obsessed with her shape,' said Scholz. 'She spent her life in her own little electronic universe where what she looked like didn't matter. A world without form.'

'Okay.' Fabel read more of Melissa's file. 'What's this . . . *The Lords of Misrule*?'

'Her biggest hit. A role-playing computer game she developed. Very complicated. Apparently she was working on a sequel to it when she died.'

There was an image of the game's cover. Three mythological types – a warrior, a priestess and some kind of warlock – stood on a mountain, a fantasy landscape swirling around them.

'*The Lords of Misrule* . . .' Fabel read the English title aloud again. 'The world turned upside down. The Days of Chaos. The Fool Made King. It's all very Karneval. Maybe this is where our connection lies. Melissa spent so much of her time in an electronic world, maybe that's where she crossed paths with our killer and Sabine Jordanski.'

Chapter Eight

6–9 February

1.

Ansgar lay in Ekatherina's bed and watched her sleep contentedly. Their lovemaking had been dramatic, violent, almost frenzied. Ekatherina had clearly taken it as the release of Ansgar's pent-up passion for her. She was, of course, in part correct: he had been totally consumed by her flesh and had stood breathless before her nakedness, but what she hadn't realised was that it had been only part of his passion that had been released.

The sex had been good for him. Or at least as good as any normal sexual activity could be for him. But, as he lay in the half-dark, looking at the shadowy sweep of Ekatherina's hip, he felt the frustration of someone who had enjoyed an appetising starter yet had been denied the main course. But that first step had been taken. They were now intimate. Perhaps, just perhaps, in time he might be able to fulfil his darkest fantasy with her.

It was Sunday morning and Ansgar's day off. Ekatherina left for her shift. She told him he could spend the day in her apartment and they would have Sunday night together. When she returned after her shift, tired, flushed from the heat of the kitchen and her skin shiny with sweat, Ekatherina said she would shower before coming to bed. Ansgar told her not to bother and the passion of the night before returned, redoubled.

They breakfasted the next morning on orange juice, coffee and bread rolls filled with a meat paste that Ekaterina said had come all the way from Ukraine. Sitting there at Ekaterina's breakfast table, Ansgar felt suddenly melancholy. He saw himself as if through the window of the flat: sitting with a pretty girl several years his junior, breakfasting together like a normal contented couple. What pained him most was the fact that at that exact moment he *was* contented.

They agreed to arrive separately at work and to keep their daytime relationship professional, but Ansgar could tell that Ekaterina was going to have very great difficulty in keeping this new romance to herself. He kissed her goodbye and headed up to the wholesalers on An der Münze to pick up some stuff they were low on in the restaurant.

The gloom of the last few days had lifted and the winter sun hung bright and low in the sky. Ansgar felt good. It seemed impossible for the darkness within him to surface into the brightness of the day, added to which he had, for the first time in years, a sense of normality. Of living a life as others lived theirs.

Ansgar took a taxi across the Zoobrücke and picked up his car. He was very fussy about where he sourced his meat for the restaurant and never bought main ingredients from the wholesalers, but he did stock up on everything else there. It was handy for the restaurant and they always delivered his orders accurately and on time, which was important to Ansgar and his unyielding desire for order in his kitchen.

He took a flatbed trolley and loaded it up with cleaning materials, hand-wash, surface-wipes and other non-food items for the wholesalers to deliver. Then he headed for the drinks section. Ansgar always bought his wine directly from vintners along the Rhine and from several small vineyards in France, but he used the wholesalers to stock up on beers and spirits.

He saw her. He just happened to glance into the food

section and she was there. He froze for a second, then shrank back behind one of the ceiling-high stacks of shelves. She hadn't spotted him. Ansgar had only caught the briefest glimpse, but there was no doubt it was her. He recognised the bright blonde hair, the intense red lipstick, the deep tan even in February. Most of all he recognised her from her build: broad-shouldered and dense, as she had effortlessly pushed a heavily laden cart towards the checkout.

Another trade customer muttered complainingly behind Ansgar, who responded by pulling his trolley closer into the shelves and allowing them to pass. His heart pounded. He had always dreaded this moment. He had hoped it would never come. Yet he thrilled at the thought. He had hoped that she had left Cologne in the time since he had last encountered her. It had been so long ago. And in total the experience had lasted no more than a few minutes. But she had seen. She had seen his true nature.

2.

Maria found that now when she woke up each morning she felt disconnected from herself; from reality. It frightened her to feel that she was watching herself as if she were a character in a film, or some distant figure in a landscape. She knew she wasn't well, and not like before. It was as if something was broken inside her. It frightened her to think that she was now capable of almost anything; that she was more or less prepared to do all that the Ukrainians asked of her. Yet something held her back.

Maria had been with them for three days now. They met each morning, early, at the small former meat-packing plant which Buslenko had rented in the Raderberg area of the city. Maria continued to spend her nights at the cheap hotel and drove down each morning. Something warned her to keep the location of Liese's apartment secret and she decided not to move into it for a few days. Where Buslenko and Sarapenko slept was unknown to Maria, and she didn't ask. For a two-man operation, the Ukrainians seemed extremely well equipped. It highlighted to Maria how inept her attempts and how half-baked her planning had been. Buslenko and Sarapenko had brought masses of electronic equipment, as well as two weapons bags. Maria reckoned that her involvement in the illegal movement of guns and military hardware into Germany was in itself enough to guarantee her a prison term.

The strange thing was that she was now physically stronger than she had been for months. Since she had started to eat normally again, her frame had begun to fill out and her limbs no longer felt leaden. Her resolve, like her hunger, had returned. The way to make up for Slavko's death was to kill Vitrenko. The way to make up for everything was to kill Vitrenko.

'We've set up twenty-four-hour surveillance on Molokov,' Buslenko explained.

'How? There's only the two . . . the three of us . . .'

'Molokov's got a place out in Cologne's leafy suburbs, between Lindenthal and Braunsfeld. It's a huge villa that's supposed to be owned by a Russian importer-exporter called Bogdanov. Whether he exists or is just an alias for Molokov or Vitrenko we don't know. We have set up remote cameras outside his villa – it's on the edge of the park and the street is lined with trees so it wasn't too hard.' Buslenko grinned. 'I worked for the City of Cologne's Parks Department for a day. Anyway, they're safe and undetectable but not as close as we'd like. Ideally, I'd like to get a listening device or camera into his place, but that's impossible.'

Olga Sarapenko had helped Buslenko set up a bank of three monitors. She tuned them in and different views of a large modern villa appeared on the screens. Olga adjusted the zoom and focus on each with a joystick.

'Even if we could get a device inside,' continued Buslenko, 'it's a safe bet that Molokov has his house electronically swept every couple of days.' Buslenko laughed bitterly. 'That's the problem with being on our side of the fence. Molokov's electronic hardware isn't restricted by government budgets. I'll bet his kit is far superior to ours.'

'The thing is,' said Maria, 'I didn't come to Cologne for Molokov.'

'Believe me, Maria, nor did we.'

'What can I contribute here?' she asked, with a sigh. 'Why did you make yourselves known to me? God knows there was no way I was going to get anywhere near Vitrenko. It would probably have been easier and more secure for you to operate invisibly. I really don't see what I can bring to the table.'

'We left three dead behind us in Ukraine,' said Olga Sarapenko. 'What you mean to us is an extra pair of eyes. And an extra gun if we need it.'

'But your true value to us, Maria,' said Buslenko, 'is the connection you offer. The potential access to intelligence that we can't get at ourselves. There's a dossier on Vitrenko. In fact there are two, but one of them, the more comprehensive one, is held by your Federal Crime Bureau on a secure computer. Hard copies are on very restricted circulation. The Federal Crime Bureau task force dedicated to Vitrenko obviously has access to inside information. We only had sight of the Ukrainian version which misses out key intelligence.'

'Vasyl Vitrenko is obsessive about security.' Olga Sarapenko took over. 'He is driven mad by the idea that he can't get at the dossier. He suspects that the informer is on Molokov's side of the operation, maybe even Molokov himself. But he can't prove it. We want you to try to get us a copy of the Vitrenko Dossier. The full one. If we can identify the informer, we can pressure him into setting Vitrenko up. It gives us someone on the inside whose survival would depend on us taking Vitrenko out of the picture.'

'But I don't have access to the Vitrenko Dossier. In fact I'm probably the last person they'd allow to see it.'

'But you have access codes and passwords for the BKA computer system,' said Buslenko. 'That would be a starting point. It's not practical to think that we can carry out a complex mission like this in just a few days. It could be that the best thing for you to do is to go back to Hamburg in a few weeks and ideally resume your duties with the Murder Commission. The information you can obtain for us is of much more value to us than your presence here,' Buslenko explained.

'I'm here to see this through. To see Vitrenko get what he deserves,' Maria said defiantly. She was willing to do almost anything to bring down Vitrenko, but Buslenko was asking her to access government files on behalf of a foreign military unit operating illegally in the Federal Republic. It would be a betrayal of her office. It would probably be espionage.

'I understand your hunger for revenge,' Buslenko explained. 'But this is not a Hollywood western. Your value to us is to pass on to us everything that the German authorities know about Vitrenko's operation. I'm sure you'll find a way,' Buslenko said, not unkindly. 'In the meantime, you may stay here with us and help us set up our surveillance of Molokov.'

Maria took her shifts watching the monitors, logging the activities: who visited the Molokov villa, when they arrived, when they left, the licence numbers of the cars that came and went. Always waiting for the arrival of anyone who could have been Vitrenko. Although she refused to supply the Ukrainians with the access codes they needed, she did share what intelligence she had been able to gather. She felt that this, in some way, could be regarded as the legitimate exchange of information between law-enforcement agencies.

Their situation, Buslenko explained, was like two hunters in the forest at the same time. It was up to Buslenko, Sarapenko and Maria to make sure they got to the game before the BKA

Federal Crime Bureau, and without detection. All he wanted the access codes for was to pinpoint where the other hunter lay hidden in the forest. Maria knew it was only a matter of time before Buslenko became more insistent.

It was on the third day of sitting at the monitors that Maria noticed a huge black Lexus pull up at the villa's gates. It was admitted immediately. Buslenko's surveillance camera was set up so far from the house that it was difficult to see clearly the men who got out of the vehicle. But the final figure sent a chill through Maria.

'Olga!'

Sarapenko ran over. 'What is it?'

'Him . . .' Maria felt her throat tighten, as if the name would choke her if she said it out loud. 'It's him.'

'How can you tell? It's just a shape from this distance.'

'That's him, I know it. The last time I saw him he was just a shape in the distance, like now, only then he was running across a field. Where's Buslenko?'

'He's collecting some stuff. Our contact here . . . it's best if you don't know.'

'Get hold of him on his cellphone. Tell him we've found our target and he is in Molokov's place right now.' Maria watched the figure on the monitor. At last. At last she had him in her sights. It gave her an enormous sense of power to know that she was watching him and he was unaware of her observation. The dark, indistinct figure whose identity Maria knew with absolute certainty turned to speak to one of his heavies, then disappeared into the villa.

Maria watched with a cold, hard expression of violent hatred as Vasyl Vitrenko disappeared from view.

'Now,' she said in a voice not much louder than a whisper. 'Now I've got you.'

3.

The television flickered mutely in the corner of the hotel room. A row of *Funkenmariechen* dancing girls in red-and-white microskirted versions of eighteenth-century Prussian military uniforms, complete with tri-cornered hats, performed a clumpily synchronised chorus-line high kick to unheard music. In the background the *Elferrat*, the Karneval Council of Eleven, presided with forced jollity over the proceedings. Karneval was beginning to build up to its Rose Monday climax. Fabel lay on his hotel bed, gazed blankly at the screen and reflected on the fact that the Karneval Cannibal too was probably building up for showtime on Women's Karneval Night. Fabel had just finished talking to Susanne on the phone; it hadn't gone well. After he had been unable to give her a clear idea about when he'd be back in Hamburg, they had fallen into a silence. Susanne had ended it by saying she would talk to him whenever he got back and had then hung up.

He stared at the silent TV, not taking in the grinning dancing girls who sidestepped their way in unison off the stage and were replaced by a man dressed in a barrel who delivered a comic monologue.

Fabel switched on his bedside lamp and picked up the file on Vera Reinartz, the girl who had been beaten and raped on Women's Karneval Night in 1999. There was a photograph of Vera, taken with a couple of fellow medical students. She was a smallish, mousy-haired girl but pretty. She stood uncertainly at the edge of the group, clearly uncomfortable at having her photograph taken. The second photograph had been taken on a sunny day in a park or garden. Her light-coloured summer dress revealed her figure: slim but slightly pear-shaped with a fleshiness around the hips. Just like the Karneval Cannibal's victims. Again, she had the look of someone who didn't like to be the focus of attention.

Fabel went through Vera's statement, doctors' reports

and the stark hospital photographs, the vividness of her bruises and the rawness of the abrasions and cuts on her face and neck emphasised by the severe lighting. Fabel couldn't recognise the swollen mass of bruised flesh as the girl in the earlier photographs. There were images of the wounds on her body. Including bite marks. Bite marks were by no mean unusual in rape cases, but Fabel felt that Scholz had been far too dismissive of a potential link with the murders. Tansu Bakrac clearly struggled to assert herself in the shadow of Scholz's seemingly relaxed but highly personal leadership.

Again Fabel reflected on the unknown city outside his hotel window, with its strange customs, its Karneval, its dancing girls and costumed clowns. Its killer stalking women on the one night of the year when they were supposed to be free of male tyranny. And Maria, putting herself in mortal danger by stumbling around in the dark. And that made him think about his appointment. The one he had made for the next day. The one Scholz mustn't know about.

Tansu had added a lot of background information on Vera Reinartz. She had been bright; brighter than her peers and destined for a significant career in medicine. She had the kind of intellect that tended to be steered into specialism or research. She had had boyfriends but the medical examination had confirmed her own statement that she had been a virgin. Where are you now, Vera? Fabel thought to himself as he read. How could you just disappear?

Fabel breakfasted well. He had muesli with fruit and yoghurt, a couple of bread rolls with Leberwurst and a soft-boiled egg with fruit juice and coffee. He left the hotel early but did not head for the Police Presidium. It was the first opportunity Fabel had had since he had arrived in Cologne: Scholz had to go to a Karneval police committee meeting that would go on all morning. To start with, Fabel had assumed it was a strategy meeting to discuss the massive but delicate task of policing Cologne's Karneval.

'No such luck,' Scholz had said gloomily. 'It's about our Karneval float for Rose Monday. They're after my head because the finishing of the float and costumes is so far behind schedule.'

Fabel walked into town from his hotel and climbed the cathedral steps above the Bahnhofsvorplatz, the main square that sat between Cologne Cathedral and the city's central railway station. Ahead of him was the Collonaden shopping mall attached to the station. The winter sun was knife-sharp in the cold air and scarf-muffled crowds milled around the square. This was the heart of the city. It had been for nearly two thousand years and the concentric circles of Cologne's main thoroughfares radiated from it like ripples in a pond. Maria was out there somewhere on some half-baked revenge mission. She was here to catch up with Vitrenko. The chances were that she would. And that he would kill her.

He had only been waiting for ten minutes when a tall man with greying hair approached him. Fabel noticed that Ullrich Wagner was much more casually dressed than he had been the last time they had met, in van Heiden's office in Hamburg.

'I see you got my message,' said Fabel. 'I'm glad you could come.'

'After what you told me on the phone the other day, I could hardly not come.' Wagner looked up at the dark mass of the cathedral. One of the spires was encased in scaffolding that looked toothpick-fragile compared to the spire's mass. 'There's always scaffolding somewhere on it . . . it took three hundred years to build and it looks like it'll take an eternity to repair.' He smiled. 'I must say it's very Graham Greene . . . meeting at the cathedral and everything.'

'I didn't want to meet at the Police Presidium. I'm working this Karneval case with Benni Scholz. I didn't want, well . . . to *confuse* things. I didn't have time to head out to BKA headquarters, and you said you would be in Cologne . . .'

'Listen, it's not a problem. By the way, I just wanted to ask you . . . your decision . . . you know, what you said on the phone. Is that your final decision?'

'Yes . . .' Fabel thought back to his phone call to Wagner from his office in Hamburg immediately after he had heard from Dr Minks about Maria's absence.

'I have to say, I agree that we have to get Frau Klee out of the picture. Not just because she's compromising our operation again, but for the sake of her well-being. But I have to be frank, Herr Fabel . . .'

'Call me Jan . . .' Cologne's informality seemed to be affecting Fabel.

'I have to be frank, Jan: I think Frau Klee is finished as a police officer.'

'Let's concentrate on saving her life first, then we'll see about saving her career.'

Fabel had only been in the cathedral once before and as he and Wagner stepped through the double doors into the main body of the building he recalled his previous awe. It had to be one of the most impressive buildings ever built. The vast vaulted space that opened up before them seemed too huge to be sustained in the fabric of the building. For a moment the two men remained silent as they each took in the majesty of the cathedral and its enormous stained-glass windows. On the way in Fabel and Wagner passed a shortish, stocky man with thick sand-coloured hair and a dense bush of moustache. He appeared to be wearing several layers of woollens under his stockman coat. His spectacles were perched on the top of his head and he was peering up, frowning, at one of the detailed stained-glass panels. He had a pen and a thick notebook clutched in one hand and a guidebook in the other.

'Excuse me . . .' He turned and spoke to them in English as they passed. 'Could you tell me . . . there is a coat of arms up there. You see . . .'

'It probably signifies one of the wealthy merchant families in Cologne,' said Fabel.

'That is the strangest thing,' said the man, perplexed but smiling. 'That is quite definitely . . . absolutely definitely . . . a *rhinoceros* . . . But the guide states here that this panel dates back to the Middle Ages. I thought in Germany you would not know of such things at this time . . .'

'Are you Spanish?' Fabel spoke his mother's language like a native and had an ear for foreign accents in English.

'I live in Spain, but I'm Mexican, actually. Paco is my name,' said the tourist and smiled broadly. 'I am a writer and such things interest me.' He shook his head in awe. 'And this is a most interesting city . . .'

'I'm afraid I have no idea. I'm from Hamburg myself . . .'

'Maybe it was a family who traded with Africa,' said Wagner. 'But Cologne started off as a Roman city and had contacts throughout the Empire. It's always been a trading centre for the rest of Europe. For the world. But I'm afraid I can't tell you what the significance of the rhinoceros is.'

'Thank you, anyway,' said the tourist.

They were about to walk away when Wagner checked himself. 'Oh, there is one meaning it might have.'

'Oh?'

'There was a lot of symbolism borrowed from pagan times to represent the various aspects of Christ. They were big on bestiaries in the Middle Ages and used exotic animals as symbols for Christ or the resurrection. The Phoenician myth of the phoenix and the image of the pelican were both used to represent the resurrection.'

'Why the pelican?' asked Fabel.

'Back then they thought pelicans ripped open their own chests to deliver their young.'

'And the rhinoceros?' asked the tourist.

'The rhinoceros was a symbol of Christ's wrath. Righteous vengeance.'

'Most interesting . . .' said the Mexican. 'Thank you.'

Fabel and Wagner left the tourist still looking up at the stained-glass window, shaking his head in wonder.

'Impressive . . .' said Fabel, with a smile.

'I was brought up in a very Catholic family,' said Wagner wryly. 'A lot of it sticks.'

Fabel and Wagner sat on a pew near where the immense stained-glass window soared high and wide, splashing the floor's flagstones with puddles of red, green, blue.

'Amazing, isn't it?' said Wagner. 'Did you know that Cologne Cathedral was the world's tallest man-made structure until the end of the nineteenth century? It was the Eiffel Tower that replaced it, I think. Or the Washington Monument.'

Fabel nodded. 'So much stone. No wonder it took three hundred years to build.'

'This isn't simply a place of worship: it's a physical statement. A big statement. Big God and little us.'

'I take it that despite your Catholic upbringing you're not the most religious person, Ullrich?'

'After going through the Vitrenko Dossier it's pretty easy to believe in the Devil, if not in God.'

'I'd like a look at the dossier. Would that be possible?'

A cathedral guide in a monk's habit, with a cash box and a guidebook dispenser strapped to his belt, walked past. The monk paused to ask an American tourist to remove his baseball cap.

'This is still a place of worship,' the monk-guide said in English.

'It's on strictly controlled release,' said Wagner after the American and the guide were out of earshot. 'You have to sign a register to even look at it. But I'll see what I can do, Jan. However, if you are getting involved in this, we need you to get involved professionally. One renegade Hamburg cop trampling all over this operation is enough.'

'Fair enough. Were you able to run the checks I asked for?'

Wagner's expression suggested it had not been an easy task. 'Hotel Linden off the Konrad-Adenauer-Ufer. She checked in three weeks ago. The nineteenth of January. Stayed a week and checked out on the twenty-sixth. You do know that getting this information was not entirely legal?'

'You'd make a good spy, Ullrich.' Fabel smiled. He remembered that the Linden was on the list of hotels that he and Anna had found in Maria's apartment. 'Could I have a look at the Vitrenko file tonight?'

'Tonight?' Wagner pursed his lips. 'I'll see what I can do. I'm not supposed to take a hard copy out of the office . . . I'll come by your hotel about eight.'

'Thanks. I really appreciate it.'

'That's okay, Jan. Just remember what we agreed.'

'I will,' said Fabel. 'See you tonight.'

He watched as Wagner walked towards the west door of the cathedral, past the Mexican tourist who still stood writing notes and studying the stained-glass window detail of a rhinoceros that should not have been there.

4.

Olga Sarapenko spoke to Buslenko on her cellphone while Maria kept her gaze fixed on the monitor screen, focused on the indistinct grainy image of the front door to Molokov's villa, waiting for Vitrenko to re-emerge.

'Taras says we've to stay put,' Olga said after she hung up. 'He's going over to Lindenthal. It'll take him at least twenty minutes to get in position. If Vitrenko doesn't leave before he gets there, Taras will pick up the Lexus and tail it.'

'Alone. Buslenko's taking the same risk I did.'

'Taras knows what he's doing.' Olga made an apologetic gesture. 'Sorry, you know what I mean. He's specially trained.'

'So are the people he's tracking.' Maria spoke without shifting her attention from the screen.

Olga pulled up a chair next to Maria and they both sat watching the lack of activity. Two guards. One on the door, the other patrolling the house. It seemed an age before Olga's cellphone rang. The exchange was brief.

'He's in position. We have to let him know which way the Lexus turns when it comes out of the gates.'

5.

Fabel ate on the way back to his hotel. He sat in a corner booth on the ground floor café-bar of an old brewery close to the cathedral, drinking the traditional Cologne beer which, like the unique dialect of the city, was called *Kölsch*. *Kölsch* was always served in the small, narrow, tube-like glasses called *Stange* and Fabel noticed that as soon as he drained one another was brought without him ordering it. Then he remembered it was a Cologne custom that, unless you placed your drink mat on top of the glass, you would be continually supplied with fresh *Kölsch*. The way he felt at that moment, Fabel found the arrangement more than satisfactory. He thought about how good it would be to sit in the cosy brewery café and get quietly drunk. But of course he wouldn't. Fabel had never in his life been truly, falling-down drunk. To do so would mean losing control, allowing himself to become subject to the random, the chaotic. A waiter in a long apron appeared and said something completely unintelligible. Fabel stared at him uncomprehendingly then laughed, again remembering Cologne traditions. In a place like this the waiters were called *Köbes* and spoke in thick *Kölsch*, usually peppered with colourful phrases. The waiter grinned and repeated his question in High German and Fabel placed his order.

Cologne was so different to Hamburg. Was it possible,

Fabel wondered, to change your surroundings and change yourself to suit? If he had been born here, instead of in the North, would he be a different person? The waiter arrived with his meal and a fresh glass of beer and Fabel tried to put it all from his mind. For now.

6.

It had been four hours but Maria had turned down Olga's offer to take over watching the monitors. It was getting dark and the villa was reduced to a dark geometry broken up by the brightness of the windows. Suddenly two lights came on above the front door, illuminating one of the guards.

'Tell Buslenko they're on the move . . .' Maria barked at Olga.

The door swung open and Vitrenko's bodyguard emerged. The Lexus door opened for someone still inside the villa and out of sight. Then a tall dark figure was framed in the bright doorway. Again a shudder of recognition. He might have changed his face, but at this distance some primeval instinct identified a form burned into Maria's memory. He stopped, his silhouetted head angled. Maria felt ice in her veins: it was as if Vitrenko were looking through the camera, directly at her.

He stepped forward and into the Lexus, out of view.

Maria followed the car as it drifted silently down the drive and out of the gate. 'They're turning right.'

The Lexus was gone. Vitrenko was gone.

'Taras has picked them up,' said Olga Sarapenko. 'They're heading out towards the autobahn. He wants you to help him with the surveillance.' She tossed Maria a walkie-talkie. 'Channel three. Taras will guide you in. I'm to man the command post here. I'll liaise between you and Taras and update you on any developments.'

'Wouldn't it be better for you to go?' asked Maria. She

suddenly felt very afraid and ill-equipped to deal with the consequences of catching up with Vitrenko. 'Aren't you better trained for this?'

'I'm just a police officer like you. The difference is that you're a *German* police officer. Taras thinks that might be useful if things get complicated.'

'But I don't know this city . . .'

'We've got all the geopositioning kit we need to direct you. Use your own car. You'd better go. Now.'

It was dark, wet and cold. Cologne glittered bleakly in the winter evening. It was a straight drive to Lindenthal through Zollstock and Sülz. The radio lay mute on the passenger seat. After ten minutes and as she approached the Stadtwald park, Maria picked it up.

'Olga . . . Olga, can you hear me?'

'I hear you.'

'Where am I supposed to go?'

'I'm on the autobahn heading north . . .' It was Buslenko's voice. 'Head for the Kreuz Köln-West junction and take the A57 and head north. I'll let you know if we turn off. Olga, guide Maria through Junkersdorf onto the autobahn. Vitrenko's car is not moving fast, but Maria won't catch up to us till we stop. Olga . . . any idea where this takes us?'

'Hold on,' said Olga. There was a pause. 'It looks like Vitrenko's heading out of the city. Could be that he's heading back up north. Hamburg.'

'Unlikely at this time of night,' Buslenko said. His voice over the radio a universe away. Maria felt isolated, cocooned by the darkness and the thick, sleety rain against the windscreen. How had she got herself into this situation? She had taken so much on trust with these people. Who was to say that they were who they said they were? She shook the thought from her head: they had saved her life; they had found Maxim Kushnier's body and disposed of it; they had

given her ill-planned, half-assed mission some kind of coher-
ence and at least a hint of viability.

Maria pressed the call button of her radio. 'Tell me where
I've got to go . . .'

7.

The Hotel Linden was only a few minutes from where
Cologne's Hansaring joined the Konrad-Adenauer Ufer which
ran along the Rhine's edge. It somehow gave Fabel hope to
sense something of the old Maria in her choice: the Linden's
situation gave her as central a base as possible without being
conspicuous. He told the taxi driver to wait for him and
trotted up the steps into the hotel's small lobby. A pretty
dark-haired girl smiled at him from behind the reception desk.
Her smile gave way to a frown when he showed her his
Polizei Hamburg ID card.

'It's nothing to worry about,' he reassured her. 'I'm just
trying to trace someone.'

Fabel showed the receptionist a photograph of Maria. 'Ring
any bells?'

Her frown deepened. 'I can't say that it does . . . but I've
been off the last week. Let me get the duty manager.'

She disappeared into the office and returned with a man
who was too young to wear such a serious expression. There
was a hint of suspicion in the way he eyed Fabel.

'What's this all about, Herr . . . ?'

'Principal Chief Commissar Fabel.' Fabel smiled and held
out his ID again. 'I'm down from Hamburg looking for this
woman . . .' He paused while the pretty receptionist handed
the photograph to the manager. 'Her name is Maria Klee.
Our information suggests that she stayed in this hotel. But
she might have used another name.'

'What has she done?'

'I don't see that has anything to do with your answer to

my question.' Fabel leaned forward on the reception desk. 'Have you seen her or not?'

The duty manager examined the photograph. 'Yes, I have. But she doesn't look like that now.'

'What do you mean?'

'She checked out of here a couple of weeks ago.' He typed something into the reception computer. 'Yes, here it is, the twenty-sixth. But when she checked out her hair was cut really short and dyed black. The other thing was her clothes.'

'What about them?'

'They were always different. I don't mean just a change of outfit . . . I mean completely different styles of clothes. One day really expensive, the next scruffy and cheap.'

Surveillance, thought Fabel. She had a lead and was following it. 'Anything else? Did she ever meet with anyone here?'

'Not that I'm aware of. But she did park her car in the hotel car park without registering its licence number with us. We nearly had it towed away, but one of the porters recognised her as a guest. I was going to have a word with her about it but she checked out before I had a chance.'

'Did you get the number?'

'Of course . . .' The prematurely pompous duty manager again referred to the hotel computer. He scribbled something down on a pad and handed it to Fabel.

'But this is a "K" plate . . . a Cologne licence.' Fabel looked at the number again. 'What kind of car was it?'

'Cheap and old. I think it was a Citroën.'

'Would you have any idea where she was going from here?'

The duty manager shrugged. Fabel scribbled his cellphone number on the back of a Polizei Hamburg business card.

'If you see her again, I need you to phone me on this number. Immediately. It is very important.'

Back in the taxi Fabel examined his list of Cologne hotels. He had to try to think like Maria. He guessed that she had left this hotel because she had checked in under her own name. She would seek out somewhere even less conspicuous. He leaned over and handed the list to the taxi driver.

'Which of these would be the best if you wanted to book in somewhere under a fake name and pay cash without too many questions asked?'

The taxi driver pursed his lips in consideration for a moment, then took his pen and circled three names.

'These would be your best bet, I reckon.'

'Okay . . .' Fabel leaned back in his seat. 'Let's start with the nearest.'

8.

'They're stopping . . .' Buslenko's voice broke the radio silence that seemed to have gone on for hours. 'We're at some kind of disused industrial building next to a reservoir or a flooded quarry or something. There's another car here. They're obviously meeting someone.'

'Can you see who?' Olga's voice crackled across the airwaves.

'No . . . no, I can't. Where are you, Maria?'

'I'm on the A57 north of the city, near Dormagen.' Maria felt sick. She realised she was retracing the route she'd taken the night she had played cat and mouse with Maxim Kushnier.

'Right . . .' Buslenko sounded hesitant. 'You'll be here in about fifteen minutes. Head out along Provinzialstrasse towards Delhoven and you'll come to a bend in the road. Take a left and you'll come to a farm track that leads off of that. I've hidden my car, a black Audi, up the track. I'll see you there in quarter of an hour.'

'Okay,' said Maria and found her mouth was dry.

'Olga.' Buslenko transmitted again. 'I'm going in for a closer look. I want to see who Vitrenko's meeting with.'

'Wait, Taras,' said Olga. 'Wait until Maria gets there. I

think you should get in touch with the local police. This is our chance to nail him.'

'That's not how we're going to deal with it. I'll be fine. But I'm switching off my radio until I get back to the car. Vitrenko has probably posted guards.'

'Be careful, Taras,' said Maria. She put her foot down a little more on the Saxo's accelerator. Now, she thought. Now it's going to be over for once and for all.

Olga guided Maria to the position Buslenko had last given. The roads became narrower and the houses fewer. Maria found herself in a landscape of open fields punctuated with scattered, dense clumps of naked trees. The inky blueness of the darkness outside yielded to a deeper black as she drove, marking the subtle change from late afternoon to true night. The rain stopped.

'I've reached the junction on Provinzialstrasse,' she radioed in to Olga Sarapenko. 'Where now?'

'Take a right and follow the road for about a kilometre. Then you should see the bend Taras talked about and the lane where he's hidden his car.'

To start with, Maria drove past the entrance to the lane: it was crowded in by dense thorny bracken and she had to reverse to turn into it. After about twenty metres she discovered Buslenko's Audi. She got out and shivered in the cold winter air. That old shiver. There was something about the lane, about the night, that gave her the darkest form of déjà vu.

'I've found the car,' she said into the radio, her voice low. She peered in through the rain-speckled side window. 'But no sign of Buslenko.'

'Sit tight,' Olga responded. 'He'll still be doing his recon. He'll be back soon.'

Maria checked her watch. He had said fifteen minutes. It had taken her twelve to get there. Something caught her eye on the passenger seat of the Audi.

'Olga . . . he's left his radio in the car.'

There was a static-crackled pause, then: 'He said he was maintaining radio silence.'

'But wouldn't he have just switched the radio off instead of leaving it here?'

'Maria. Just sit tight.'

Maria slipped her radio into her coat pocket. She made her way back along the lane to the road, the mud yielding beneath her boots. Once out onto the road she checked, her body still concealed by the bracken, for cars coming in either direction. She heard nothing, but the chill breeze rustled as it stirred the naked branches. She made her way along the road to the bend. On the other side she could see an exposed field with a barn-type building at one edge. There were two cars parked outside. Maria felt the nausea well up inside her again and her heart hammered in her chest. The scene she looked upon was like some landlocked version of the field and barn near Cuxhaven. The place she'd last encountered Vitrenko. She found herself looking up at the starless, cloud-heavy sky and at the winter barren field as if to assure herself that she had not travelled back in time. No stars, no swirling grasses. Maria crouched low as she ran back along the road, the lane and into her car. She slammed the door shut and gripped the steering wheel tight. She looked at the keys in the ignition, still with the label of the garage she'd bought the car from attached. She could turn that key, reverse out onto the road and in minutes she'd be on the autobahn heading for Hamburg. She could put it all behind her. Start again.

Maria snapped open the glove compartment with a sudden decisiveness and took out both her service SIG-Sauer auto-matic and the illegal 9mm Glock and slipped them into her pockets. She reached over again, grabbed her binoculars and headed back out on foot along the lane.

There was no cover in the field. It would be almost impos-sible to cross undetected. Buslenko knew what he was doing.

Vitrenko and his team certainly knew what *they* were doing.
But Maria didn't have the kind of training for this kind of
stealth. She moved quickly and quietly to the corner of the
field where a thin, wind-bowed tree and some leafless shrub-
bery offered meagre cover. She scanned the field, the parked
cars, the barn with her binoculars. Nothing. No guards, no
signs of life. There wasn't even any hint of a light inside the
barn. And no sign of Buslenko. She sat down on the damp
grass, leaning her back against the tree. Apart from the wind,
there was no sound. No hint that another human being shared
Maria's dark, frightened universe. She took one gun, then the
next, and snapped the carriages back, placing a round in each
chamber and snapping off the safety. She put her service SIG-
Sauer back in her pocket. She could see the fumed ghosts of
her hard, fast breathing in the chill air.

Maria took a deep breath and set off across the field
towards the barn, bent over as much as she could while
running, the Glock automatic held stiffly out and to one side.

She was about halfway there when the light came on.

9.

Maria's instinct reacted faster than her brain could process the
fact that a light had come on in the building and cast a yellow
shaft across the field. She threw herself onto the cold, damp
earth and lay perfectly flat for a moment, her arms and legs
spread, her head down. Realising she could still be seen, she
rolled swiftly on her side and back into darkness. She looked
up. The barn window was an empty yellow square in the dark.
Then a figure appeared briefly, but long enough for Maria to
feel that same terrifying sense of recognition. She aimed her
9mm Glock at Vitrenko's silhouette, but then it was gone. She
got to her feet, keeping her gaze fixed on the window, and
closed another twenty metres before dropping to the ground
again. She scanned the field, the illuminated window and the

perimeter of the barn. No one. This was too easy. And where the hell was Buslenko?

With a wave of raw panic, Maria suddenly remembered her radio. She had left it on and there had been no communication between her and Olga for several minutes. Olga could radio her at any moment and give away Maria's location to Vitrenko's goons. She scrabbled desperately in her inside coat pocket and clumsily pulled out the radio, dropping it on the ground. She placed both gloved hands over it to smother any sound and her finger found the off button. She breathed a sigh of relief, letting her forehead rest on the cold earth.

Maria was now too close to the barn to make the rest of the crossing upright, so she commando-crawled over the field. Eventually she reached the stone wall of the barn, pressing her back against it. She looked back across the empty field, fringed with bracken and hedge. Every instinct in her body was now screaming at her. This was wrong. So wrong. It all looked too much like that other field and barn. It had been too easy to cross the field undetected, just like it had been that other night, when Vitrenko had felt so secure that he had posted the minimum security. Surely he wouldn't make the same mistake twice. There was one significant difference between that night and this: this time Fabel wasn't around to save her. Maria felt so cold. She checked her gun again and began to edge towards the window.

Maria realised that the stone-built structure was more some kind of workshop rather than a barn. The window was glazed with a reasonably new pane, but the glass was thick with grime which had gathered in particular density around the corners. Maria strained to hear anything from inside, but the wind had picked up and the glass muted any sound. Cradling the butt of her automatic with both hands, she eased forward, craning her neck to see through the edge of the window. She snapped her head back from the window and stood with her back to the wall. Her mind raced to analyse the split second's worth of information she had taken in. Molokov was in there, with at least three henchmen. No sign of Vitrenko, but that didn't mean he wasn't in there, hidden from view. Maria fought to keep her breath under control and her thoughts in order. Now was the time to start thinking like a police officer again. Fabel had always told them that the first duty of a police officer was to stand between the innocent and harm, between chaos and order. Maria knew that someone was about to die, probably horrifically, and within the next few minutes.

Maria's snatched glance through the window had picked up someone who should not have been there. A man sitting on a chair in the middle of the room with his hands out of sight, presumably tied behind his back. He had been surrounded by the others, including Molokov. Torture would come first. Then death.

Maria pulled the radio from the inside pocket of her thick black coat. She would have to risk using it. She turned the volume as low as was practical, given the increasing whine of the wind.

'Olga . . . come in, Olga . . .'

Silence.

'Olga . . . come in . . .' Maria's voice was now desperate.

'Maria – where the hell have you been? I've been trying to get you. Taras's radio is still dead too . . .'

'They've got him, Olga . . .'

'What?'

'They've got Taras. I think they're going to kill him.'

'My God – what are we going to do?'

'We're out of our depth, Olga. I need to become a police officer again. We need to do this right. I want you to phone the Cologne police right now and tell them that you're a Kiev militia officer and that a Hamburg Murder Commission Commissar needs urgent assistance at this location. Tell them that we've got Vasyl Vitrenko pinned down here and the BKA Task Force will want to be here as well. But for God's sake tell them to hurry.'

'I've got it . . . I'll do it now, Maria. Are you safe?'

'For the moment. But I'm going to have to do something if the local police don't get here before these bastards start on Taras. Do it now.'

Maria switched the radio off again, eased back along the wall and checked through the window. Molokov was shouting, ranting at Buslenko, gesticulating wildly. Occasionally he would look across to something or someone outside Maria's field of vision.

Vitrenko.

Maria crouched beneath the sill and worked her way to the other side of the window and to the far end of the wall. She stole a look around the corner. A door, two heavies. Sub-machine pistols. No way in that way. That made things diffi-cult: she wouldn't have direct access to the room they were holding Buslenko in. She retraced her steps to the other corner.

She needed to get in there. She felt tears sting her eyes. She thought about all that she had been through in the last three years, about that night in the field near Cuxhaven, about Fabel, about Frank. Maria knew why she was crying: she was mourning. She was mourning the person she had been before it all happened. And she was mourning the life she knew she was about to lose. The local police would take too long to get here. She and Buslenko would both be dead and Vitrenko would probably once more vanish into the night. But she had to do this. End this. She would find her way into that room and use the one shot she would have before they gunned her down to take out Vitrenko. She was certain he was in there with them. She knew that she probably would not recognise his face; that would be changed totally by now. But his eyes. And his presence. Those she would recognise in a split second.

Maria steadied herself against the wall. She sniffed hard and wiped the tears from her face. She paused for a moment in the vain hope that she might hear the approach of police cars. The wind rustled through the bare trees and hedgerow behind the workshop with a strangely soothing sound. Maria took her service automatic from her pocket and now stood with a gun in each hand. She gave a small laugh. Like a movie. But it doubled her chances of hitting Vitrenko before they gunned her down.

With that thought she stood clear of the wall and walked calmly around the corner. Again alarm bells began to ring. It was too easy. This side of the workshop looked completely unguarded. There was a window into another room: this time the glass was broken and the room was in darkness. Maria looked at the luminous dial of her watch. Seven minutes since she had radioed Olga. It would be maybe another five or ten before the local police arrived. Again she hesitated. They wouldn't come with lights and sirens, of course. She looked out back across the field to the road. No headlights, no movement. She peered in through the shattered window. The room was empty except for a couple of broken chairs and a grimy desk pushed against one wall.

Maria eased her hand through the broken glass and undid the latch. The window protested at having its decades-long rest disturbed by creaking loudly as she eased it open. It took a couple of minutes for her to ease it open enough for her to squeeze through. Again she paused and strained the night for the sounds of approaching rescue. Nothing. Where the hell were they? Maria tried not to think of the sound she inevitably made as she stepped in through the window and onto the debris-strewn floor. Despite the cold of the winter air, she felt beads of perspiration break out on her upper lip. She stood stock-still. There were sounds from outside the door. She aimed both guns at the grubby wooden panels but the door didn't open and the sounds faded. Maria reckoned that the workshop was only big enough for the two rooms, both off a corridor. She crept across to the door; it was ill-fitting and a gap allowed her to see part of the hallway. She heard low voices, from the room next door. No screams.

Maria made the decision to act swiftly. She swung the door wide and swept the hall with the guns held in each hand, ready to shoot anyone she found there. The hall was empty but the light still issued from the room just over two metres away. They must have heard her. The voices in the room continued talking. She moved up the hall. The outer door was directly in front of her but she couldn't see the two goons posted at it: presumably they were outside. Whatever happened in the room, she would have to be ready for them coming in at the sound of gunfire. Two highly trained Spetsnaz with machine pistols against an anorexic, neurotic cop on sick leave, armed with two handguns. Shouldn't be a problem, she thought. She felt no fear. It had left her with her first step towards the open doorway of the room. She had heard that certainty of death can do that to you. With it came a new strength and determination.

Maria rushed forward and stepped into the doorway, swinging her guns round to bear on whomever she found inside.

10.

Ullrich Wagner was ten minutes late. Fabel had positioned himself at the bar from where he could see the hotel lobby and Wagner as he arrived.

'Drink?' he asked as he steered the BKA man into the bar.

'Why not?' said Wagner. They took their drinks and sat down on a sofa over by the window with a view across Turinerstrasse, towards the railyards and the spires of the cathedral. 'Should we do this up in your room?' he asked, taking a thick file from his briefcase. 'There are some unpleasant images in here. By the way, I need you to sign the register to view it.'

Fabel surveyed the hotel lounge. There was a huddle of business types at the far side of the bar. A group of six, all in their twenties, talked and laughed with loud, youthful energy. A couple two sofas away were too engrossed with each other to notice even if the hotel had caught fire.

'We're okay,' said Fabel. 'If it gets busier we can go up.'

Wagner snapped back the binding on the dossier.

'This is heavy, heavy stuff. We are dealing with the forces of evolution here. Vitrenko has changed. Adapted. He is without doubt the major figure in East-to-West people smuggling. Added to that, he controls much of the illegal prostitution racket in Germany. But he has focused on a specialism. A niche operation, you could say.'

'What do you mean?'

'There are a lot of people out there who have, well, let's say *special* requirements. Vitrenko's prostitution businesses are there to fulfil that need. I don't think I need to draw a picture for you . . . we're talking about very unpleasant stuff indeed. And most of the prostitutes are not voluntary. He sells people like meat, Jan. Everything we've got so far is summarised in there. I have to tell you that there are a lot of people who are not very happy that you have this information.'

'Others know? Do they know why I want it?'

'No . . . if I had mentioned Frau Klee's involvement I dare say there would be a warrant out for her arrest. I told them that I was trying to involve you in this investigation in order to persuade you to reconsider setting up a proposed Federal Murder Commission.'

'So you haven't told them about my decision either?'

'No . . . time enough for that.'

Fabel read through some of the file. It was filled with horror. Scores of murders initiated by Vitrenko across Central

Asia and Europe, ranging from simple assassinations to killings of spectacular cruelty, intended to warn others of the price of crossing him. There was a detailed account of Vitrenko's activities in Hamburg, including the attack on Maria Klee. There were details of the mass murder that Maria's notes had referred to: thirty illegal migrants burned to death in a container lorry on Ukraine-Poland border. Fabel read about how a Georgian crime boss had refused Vitrenko's offer of partnership, saying that his only partners would be his three sons when they were older. Vitrenko had sent the Georgian three packages, all arriving on Father's Day, each containing a head. There was an account of how a beautiful Ukrainian girl forced into working as a high-class call-girl had tried to break free from Vitrenko's grasp by contacting the Berlin police. She had been found tied to a chair, facing a full-length mirror. She had died from asphyxiation: her airways inflamed as a result of the sulphuric acid that had been thrown into her face. It was unlikely that she would have been able to see much of her own reflection. But she would have seen enough, thought Fabel, to satisfy Vitrenko. There was the assassination of a Ukrainian-Jewish crime boss in Israel that had Vitrenko written all over it. Fabel shook his head in admiration of Maria as he read. She had mentioned all of these in her notes. Without the resources of the BKA Federal Crime Bureau, she had been able to read Vitrenko's hand in far-flung and seemingly unconnected incidents.

'You won't be surprised by any of this, I suppose . . .' said Wagner. The file had included an account of how Vitrenko had murdered his own father; and the fact that Fabel had been a witness to it.

'We've got to get Maria out of Cologne,' Fabel said without looking up from the file. 'If Vitrenko gets wind of the fact that she's got a personal crusade going against him, he will make a point of amusing himself with her death.'

'I agree, Jan, but the first priority has to be nailing Vitrenko.

Maria Klee has got herself into this situation by her own actions.'

'For which she is not entirely responsible . . .' Fabel turned over another page and was faced with photographs of even more victims. He looked up and checked that none of the hotel guests was near enough to see the horror in his hands. 'What's this?'

'Ah . . .' said Wagner. 'What you're looking at are the remains of an elite task force made up of Ukrainian Spetsnaz specialists. Operation Achilles. The official story from the Ukrainian government was that they were going to approach us about liaison and try to nail Vitrenko in Ukraine. Our guess is that this was a last desperate attempt to take Vitrenko out of the picture by illegal assassination inside the Federal Republic.'

'Is this in Germany?' Fabel looked at the forest in the background of the photographs.

'No. It's outside a place called Korostyshev, to the west of Kiev. They were assembled there for a pre-mission briefing. At a hunting lodge. Get it?'

Fabel looked at the photographs again. 'Very ironic. And very Vitrenko. No survivors.'

'Oh yes,' said Wagner with a knowing smile. 'Like you said, it was all very Vitrenko. The bodies you see there were more than likely taken out by the other members of the team. All of whom have disappeared from sight. It took the Ukrainians a few days to put it all together, but they reckon they know who the infiltration-team leader was. There had been an attempt to grab Vitrenko a few days before on one of his rare trips to Kiev. The Ukrainian government had an inside man on the job, a Sokil Spetsnaz commander called Peotr Samolyuk who was playing triple agent. He pinpointed where and when Vitrenko would appear. But Vitrenko's mole betrayed Samolyuk and he ended up castrated. And when this task force was assembled, the chief mole and two other infiltrators were in place. It looks like a couple of the team nearly made it to Korostyshev and safety before they were killed and dragged back to the lodge and . . . well, you can see.'

Fabel examined a picture of a man in his thirties who, like the others, had been stripped, gutted and hung outside the hunting lodge on the frame used for hanging the deer and boar killed by hunters. There was something painted in red, it looked like blood, on the wall behind the gutted corpse. It was written in Cyrillic.

'What does that say?' Fabel tilted the photograph towards Wagner.

'Hmm . . . I wondered about that too. Very esoteric. "Satan has craft to be in two places at once." Obviously Vitrenko being whimsical. I'm guessing it had some significance for the poor schmuck they ended up gutting.'

'Who was he?'

'He was in charge of Operation Achilles. A good man by all accounts,' said Wagner. 'Vitrenko's chief mole in the operation is thought to have been a female Kiev militia officer called Olga Sarapenko. She probably had orders to give this guy really special treatment before he died. He'd been after Vitrenko for years.'

'What was his name?' asked Fabel.

'Buslenko.' Wagner sipped his drink. 'Taras Buslenko.'

II.

Maria stood framed in the doorway. She swung her aim into the part of the room she had not been able to see from outside, expecting to find Vitrenko there. It was empty. She swung back. There were the two goons standing, Molokov and Buslenko seated. No Vitrenko. She had given up her life for nothing. Everyone in the room had turned to face her. She felt the guns kick in her hands. Two bullets hit Molokov in the throat and his right eye popped as a round passed through it and into his brain. He was still dropping when Maria swung her guns onto the first heavy. Some bullets smacked into the wall of the workshop but three caught him in the chest. She sensed the second man move but didn't have time to react.

Buslenko threw himself from his seat and Maria was surprised to see that he hadn't been bound. He slammed into the ex-Spetsnaz who looked shocked at Buslenko's sudden attack. He recovered sufficiently to swing a boot at Buslenko, who feinted and rammed his own boot hard into the other man's groin. He followed up with a slash with the flat of his hand across the man's throat. There was the sound of something snapping and the heavy sank to his knees and started to claw at his neck, his face turning blue. Buslenko grabbed the man's lower jaw and forehead and wrenched his head sharply to one side. A louder snap. The heavy's eyes glazed immediately and Buslenko pushed him away and he crashed onto the grimy floor. Buslenko looked at Maria and nodded grimly. She spun round to deal with the guards rushing in from outside. No one appeared at the doorway. She stood, both automatics held at full stretch from her body, her hands now shaking violently.

'It's all right, Maria . . .' Buslenko's voice was calm, soothing. He reached out to her shaking hands and took the guns from her. 'It's all right. It's all over. You did well.'

'The guards . . .' she said desperately. 'Outside . . .'

'It's all right,' again Buslenko soothed her. 'It's taken care of.'

Maria heard someone coming in through the door.

'Olga?' Maria gazed confused at Sarapenko, who stood in the doorway. She was carrying a sniper's rifle that looked more like a piece of scientific equipment than a weapon. It had a heavy night-vision sight mounted on it and its barrel was elongated by a flash eliminator and silencer.

'I don't understand,' said Maria. 'The police . . . where are the police?'

'We clear up our own mess,' said Buslenko, pocketing Maria's automatics. He placed his arm around her shoulders and guided her towards the door.

'Vitrenko . . .' Maria's voice was faint and shook with the tremors that were beginning to take control of her body. 'Where is Vitrenko? He was supposed to be here . . .'

Maria started to shake uncontrollably. She felt as if her legs could no longer support her. The story outside the door was easy to read. Both guards lay dead, each with bullet wounds to the body and head. The second guard still held his machine pistol and his eyes gazed up dully at the dark clouded sky. Maria had read somewhere that that was how snipers always took out a victim: a bullet to the body to bring them down, then one or two to the head to finish them. She looked at Olga, who still held the precision tool of her sniper's rifle. It was an odd skill for a Kiev city policewoman to have.

'Stay here,' said Buslenko. 'I'll fetch my car. Olga, I'll drop you at Maria's car and you can drive it back to Cologne. I want no evidence that we have been here.'

'What about housekeeping?' asked Olga, nodding at the bodies.

'We'll get these two inside. I'll send someone out to clean up. But we'd better get away from here first.'

'You'll send someone?' Maria's voice was weak. She sounded dully confused. 'Who do you have . . .'

'You're in shock, Maria,' Olga handed the sniper's rifle to Buslenko. She took a syringe from her pocket and removed the protective sheath from the needle.

'Why have you got that with you?' asked Maria, but she was too shaken and weak to resist as Olga bunched up the sleeves of Maria's coat and the jumper underneath. Maria felt the sting of the needle in her forearm.

'What . . . ?'

'It'll relax you,' said Olga and already Maria felt a warm sleepiness swell through her body. She felt as if she were already asleep, but remained on her feet. Her shaking had stopped.

'I thought I was going to die . . .' she said absently to Olga, who didn't answer.

'I'll get the car,' Buslenko said and ran across the field towards the road.

Maria felt completely relaxed, devoid of any fear or anxiety, as she watched Buslenko's shrinking figure and realised that she had seen him run across a field very like this one, a long time ago. It was funny, she thought as she felt Olga's grip tighten on her arm, that she hadn't recognised him before; that it was only from a distance, like on the surveillance monitor, that she knew for sure who he was.

I am going to die, after all, thought Maria and turned to Olga Sarapenko, smiling vacantly at the irony of it all.

Chapter Nine

9–11 February

1.

Fabel was surprised to look up and find Benni Scholz standing next to him.

'What are you doing here?' Fabel said, closing the dossier. 'Oh, this is Herr Wagner of the BKA . . .'

Wagner stood up and shook hands with Scholz.

'We've met before,' said Scholz. Wagner frowned. 'That Internet fraud case – two years ago . . .'

'Oh yes . . .' said Wagner. 'Of course . . . How are you?'

'The best,' Scholz grinned, but looked at the blank covered dossier on the coffee table. 'Sorry, am I interrupting something?'

'No . . . not at all,' said Fabel. 'I was just taking the opportunity to chat with Herr Wagner about a Hamburg case we're both involved with. Can I get you a drink?'

'Well . . . as a matter of fact I called by on business. As you know I was tied up almost all morning in this bloody Karneval committee meeting, but I got Tansu and Kris to check out some of those leads on Internet sites your technical guys put together But you weren't around this afternoon . . .'

'Ah, yes . . . sightseeing, if I'm honest.'

'I see . . . anyway, we've got something. There's a website hosted from here in Cologne. It's called *Anthropophagi* and it's devoted to all things relating to cannibalism. Not overtly sexual content, but if you dig deeper there is some pretty sick stuff in there. And there's a chat room. We don't know who actually runs the site, but we know the company that provides the server space, design, etc. I thought we could go over there tomorrow.'

'Sounds good. Sure you won't have a drink?'

'No, thanks. You see, that's not all. I wondered if you wanted to take a little trip with me. You'll be pleased to know that we've also followed your suggestion and trailed every reported assault or incident involving biting. There's something you and I should take a look at . . .'

The hotel contrasted sharply with the plush and trendy one they had just left. It wasn't that it was shoddy or seedy, rather that it was at the budget end of the market. The kind of place where tourists on a tight budget or the lower class of business traveller would overnight. It was, as Fabel realised he already knew, also a place where you could pay in cash and not be asked too many questions. Scholz pulled up outside the main door and as he and Fabel got out a doorman approached, clearly to complain that he wasn't allowed to park there. Scholz silenced him with a flash of his Criminal Police ID. He turned for a moment when he noticed Fabel pause and look up at the hotel.

'Everything okay, Jan?'

'What? Yeah . . . sure.'

'There was the report of a disturbance here a few weeks ago,' Scholz explained to Fabel. 'The patrol car was effectively turned away – the hotel said it had all blown over and their own people had dealt with it. Sorry to have troubled you and all that crap. Truth is these places don't want their clientele to see the lobby full of uniforms. Puts them off their dirty weekends.'

Scholz slapped his gloved hand down on the chest-high reception desk and grinned at the male receptionist.

'Cologne Criminal Police,' he said. 'I want to speak to Herr Ankowitsch, the manager.'

A tall, slim man appeared at reception. 'Can I help you?' he asked Scholz. Then, seeing Fabel: 'Oh, hello again, Herr Fabel . . . I didn't expect to see you twice in one day. Is this about the same matter?'

'No . . . not related at all . . .' Fabel said. He ignored Scholz's frown.

'We're here about an incident on January twentieth,' said Scholz, turning back to Ankowitsch. 'You called the police about a disturbance.'

'Oh, that . . . that was all dealt with at the time. Something and nothing. A woman was heard to scream from one of the rooms and came running out. But she didn't want to press charges.'

'Yes, I know all that. What I want to know about is what she said had happened to her. According to the police report, she claimed someone had bitten her in the arse. Bitten her badly.'

Ankowitsch grinned. 'Yes, she did, as a matter of fact.'

'This isn't a laughing matter. We're here in case this event is connected to a couple of murders we're investigating. Now, no bullshit – was she a hooker?'

Ankowitsch leaned over the counter and craned his neck to check there were no guests on the stairs. 'Yes. Yes, she was. I've seen her before. We don't encourage it but we do turn a bit of a blind eye. There are a lot of ships passing every night of the year here. So long as there is no trouble, and that it is contained and discreet, we don't delve too deeply into whether the relationships between our guests are personal or professional.'

'Who was with her?' asked Fabel.

'A man, about thirty-five . . . Well-dressed. Good-looking. I got the impression that they'd been somewhere, well, *swankier* than here beforehand. She was smartly dressed too.'

Ankowitsch gave a small laugh. 'Although I must say I thought her choice of costume was a bit ill-advised.'

'In what way?' asked Scholz.

'Well, she was wearing this figure-hugging skirt. Like a nineteen-fifties pencil skirt. It looked expensive, but it was really inappropriate for her.'

Scholz made an impatient face.

'She had this enormous backside. Huge. She was a really attractive girl otherwise. But it was almost as if she was trying to attract attention to it. That's why we thought it was so funny . . . you know, when she came running out later screaming that the guy had bitten it.'

'Was she badly bitten?'

'Oh yes . . . there was quite a lot of blood and one of our Polish girls here, Marta, had to help her. Marta said the bitten girl was Ukrainian, but she understood everything that Marta said to her in Polish. They can understand each other, apparently. Anyway, Marta said it was a really bad bite and told the girl that she would have to go to hospital, but she didn't want to.'

'Where was the man while all this was happening?' asked Fabel.

'As soon as the commotion started he must have grabbed his stuff and made a run for it. Down the stairs – he didn't use the lift. I went straight up to the room with a porter but the guy was gone when we got there.'

'And the room. Did he pay for it or did she?'

'He did. Cash. He said he had left his credit-card wallet at home. We usually ask for a credit card so that we can charge anything taken from the mini-bar, but he gave us a hundred-Euro deposit instead.'

'Let me guess: he didn't pick up the deposit,' said Fabel.

Ankowitsch reddened. 'No.' Fabel guessed that the deposit would have gone into the manager's pocket.

'We need to find this girl,' said Scholz. 'You say you have seen her before?'

Ankowitsch looked uneasy. 'Yes. She's been here once before. Maybe twice.'

'And the man?'

'No. I can't say I ever saw him before that night.'

'Do you have any idea where we could find this girl?' asked Fabel.

Ankowitsch's unease seemed to intensify. He got the phone directory from under the counter, flicked through it and noted down some details on a pad. He tore the sheet out and held it out to Fabel.

Scholz took it from his hand. 'Thank you for your cooperation,' he said.

'I suspect Herr Ankowitsch has a liking for big bums himself,' Scholz said to Fabel on the way back to the car. 'He seemed to be pretty sure which escort agency she worked for.'

Fabel sat back in the passenger seat of Scholz's VW and suddenly felt very tired. It had been a long day and he had probably had more *Kölsch* beer than he should have had earlier. He found himself grateful that Scholz was uncharacteristically taciturn as he drove through the city. Fabel watched Cologne go by as they drove, glittering in the blue-black night. Fabel began to realise that it was taking them longer to get back to his hotel and that he didn't recognise the area they were in. All of a sudden they were down by the Rhine. There was a lot of building going on by the river and the superstructure of two vast buildings, shaped like oversized shipyard cranes, loomed above them. Scholz braked hard as he parked his VW on a concrete slipway and got out, slamming the door and walking to the water's edge where he stood illuminated in the car headlights.

Fabel got out and stood beside Scholz. There was a moment's silence as the two men watched a long barge drift by, a flag at the stern flapping in the dark.

'Are you going to tell me what this is all about?' Scholz said quietly, without taking his eyes off the barge. 'I walk in on you and that guy from the BKA and you look as if I've caught you with your trousers around your ankles . . . Then I find out you've been carrying out private investigations in my city while I'm otherwise occupied. I'd like to know what the fuck is going on, *sir*.'

Fabel sighed. 'When I told you that I'd crossed paths with Vasyl Vitrenko you said it was a dangerous path to cross. Well, it was. It ended up with two officers dead and one very seriously injured. She only just made it. Her name is Maria Klee and she was my top officer . . . in fact, she should have been in line to take over from me. But although the physical stuff healed she's had mental problems. Maria's on extended sick leave. She's had a major breakdown and was supposed to be receiving treatment. The problem is that I think she's down here trying to find Vitrenko single-handed.'

'I see . . .' Scholz turned to Fabel. 'Why didn't you tell me this before?'

'You have your own priorities.'

'Yes. Yes, I do. And I am not fucking about here. I have a murderer to catch. This guy is going to kill again, in just over two weeks' time, unless I can get to him first. I called on your expertise in good faith.'

'I know that, Benni.'

'But you've had this other agenda going on all the time. To be honest, I feel sorry for your officer, but it's really not my problem. I thought I had your undivided attention on my case.'

'Let's get this straight, Commissar . . . I am here to give you all the support you need. But I am also concerned about my officer and I *will* continue to try to locate her. That doesn't mean you're only getting a half-hearted effort from me.'

'Oh, wait a fucking minute . . .' Scholz's face became suddenly animated. 'I get it now . . . this *is* my business, isn't it? No wonder we couldn't trace the female cop or immigration officer who was questioning Slavko Dmytruk before he got hacked to bits in the restaurant kitchen. That was her, wasn't it?'

'I think it might have been. That doesn't mean it was.'

'Right . . .' Scholz turned and headed back to the car. 'First thing tomorrow, you and I are going to have a chat with my boss.'

Scholz had said nothing on the five-minute drive back to Fabel's hotel. Fabel paused before getting out of the car.

'Listen, Benni,' he said. 'I meant what I said. I'll help you nail this serial, and I can't stop you going to your boss about Maria. But all that will do is hold up both cases.'

'Your personal missing-person hunt isn't a *case*. Mine is.'

'Whatever way you want to put it. But we are beginning to make progress in this Karneval Cannibal case. Do you really want me to be tied up in some inquiry?'

'What are you proposing?'

'My priority here is just the same as yours – to catch this lunatic before he kills again. But your resources would make it much easier for me to track down Maria before she gets herself into serious trouble. But the deal is that we nail this son of a bitch first.' Fabel grinned. 'Come and have a drink at the bar and we can discuss it.'

Scholz stared ahead, his hands still resting on the steering wheel. 'Okay . . . and you're paying.'

2.

As he had done every morning, Fabel took a taxi from his hotel across the Severinsbrücke bridge and into the Kalk area of the city where the Cologne Police Presidium was situated. It was a brighter morning and, as the taxi crossed the Rhine,

Fabel was able to look along the river's length to the iron-work arches of the Südbrücke rail bridge. Several long barges drifted along the Rhine, some heading south into the heart of Europe, others north to Holland and the rest of the world. He tried to imagine a time before cars, high-speed trains or lorries: Scholz's analogy of a medieval version of an auto-bahn was fitting. There was something timeless about this river, today's barges carrying on a tradition that was almost as old as European civilisation.

When Fabel arrived at the Presidium, the security-desk officer smiled and sent him straight up without an escort. He found it odd to walk into a different Murder Commission without being fully a visitor any more. It was almost, but not quite, as if he worked here and the thought brought to mind the offer that Wagner and van Heiden had made: is this what it would be like to have a Federal Republic-wide brief?

Tansu was on the phone when Fabel arrived. She had gath-ered her rich coppery curls up in a clasp on the back of her head and it exposed the line of her neck. Tansu was not particularly pretty and her figure was more than full, but there was something about her that Fabel, in spite of himself, found attractive. Sexy. She indicated Scholz's office with a jab of her head and covered the mouthpiece of the phone for a second.

'He's waiting for you,' she said. 'But make sure neither of you leave until I have a chance to talk to you.'

'Okay,' said Fabel.

Scholz was on the phone but gestured for Fabel to take a seat. From what Fabel could gather from Scholz's side of the telephone conversation, it had to do with the Cologne Police Karneval float and Scholz was still not at all happy with its progress. It struck Fabel that this subject, more than the murders he was investigating, seemed to have Scholz wound up tight. He was not someone that Fabel would otherwise imagine ever becoming stressed.

'Morning . . .' Scholz said gloomily as he came off the phone. 'You ready to talk to these Internet people?'

'Yep. But Tansu said she wants to talk to us before we go out.'

Scholz shrugged. 'There's another call we should make today. I did a bit of checking into the escort agency our chum at the hotel gave us last night. I think this will interest you quite a bit.'

'Oh?'

'The *À la Carte* escort agency is operated by a certain Herr Nielsen, a German national. Tansu's looking into his background. But the real owners are a couple of Ukrainians called Klymkiw and Lysenko. No criminal records but they are suspected of heavy involvement in organised crime. Particularly people-smuggling. So you won't need three guesses who the organised-crime division reckon Klymkiw and Lysenko work for?'

'Vitrenko.'

'Exactly. The boys at organised crime have asked that we handle this with extreme care.'

'You spoke to organised-crime division? I take it you didn't say anything about Maria Klee?'

'For now. And it was just our organised-crime guys. The Federal Crime Bureau don't know we're talking to Nielsen. But there's a limit to how long I can withhold that. Anyway, as far as we can see, *À la Carte* Escorts operates legally and its girls pay the regulation tax. Or at least the ones who are officially on their books.' Scholz grinned. 'The trade in human flesh was first made fully taxable in Cologne, as you probably already know.'

Fabel nodded. Cologne had been the first German city to levy income tax on sex-industry workers.

'We're quite proud of our role in pioneering a tax on sex. At first it was impossible to assess exactly how much any given prostitute earned . . .' Scholz continued. 'I mean, can you imagine a federal tax form with a section on how many blow jobs you performed and for what price in the last fiscal year? The tax boys calculated a possible range of earnings and came up with an average. So now there's a flat-rate tax of one hundred and fifty Euros per month per hooker. I can tell you, even with all the undeclared earnings, Cologne has been raking it in. What I've always tried to work out is: does that make the Bürgermeister a pimp?'

Scholz's musings were interrupted when Tansu came into the office.

'At long bloody last I've got somewhere with Vera Reinartz, the medical student who was raped in 'ninety-nine.'

'You've tracked her down?' asked Fabel.

'Yes . . . well, technically no, not Vera Reinartz, I suppose. But I now know why we couldn't find her on any registered change of address. Vera Reinartz really doesn't exist any more. She changed her name six years ago. A full legal change of name.'

'She obviously wanted to put as much distance as possible between herself and what happened to her,' said Fabel.

'That's the strange thing,' said Tansu. 'I would have thought that she would have wanted to move as far away as possible. But she's stayed right here in Cologne. Why change your name but not your location?'

'I take it you have an address for her?' asked Fabel.

'Yes. I thought I'd try to see her today,' said Tansu.

'If you don't mind, I'd like to be there, too,' said Fabel. 'And Herr Scholz, of course.'

'Okay.' Fabel thought he detected a little defensiveness in Tansu's tone.

'I'm pretty sure you're maybe onto something and it could be the best lead we've got.' Fabel turned to Scholz. 'I've read what Tansu has put together on the case and I agree with her. I think there's a strong chance that attack is linked to these murders.'

'And the killing the year after? Annemarie Küppers, the girl who was beaten to death?' asked Tansu.

'That I don't know about. It ties in with the savagery of the beating that Vera Reinartz took, but sits at odds with the other two killings. But I'm not ruling it out. The main thing is that if Vera Reinartz *was* a victim of our guy and survived, then she's probably the only person who's seen him.'

'I'll pin down her whereabouts and we can see her this afternoon or evening,' said Tansu.

They took Scholz's VW. The address Scholz had for *À la Carte* Escorts was in Deutz so it took them only a matter of minutes to get there. The street was a mix of small businesses and apartment buildings. There was a restaurant, a bar, a delicatessen and a computer sales and repair store. Scholz referred to his notebook and led Fabel to a doorway between the computer shop and the deli. There were a number of business names listed on the buzzer panel.

'Here we are,' said Scholz. '*À la Carte* Escorts. Second floor . . .'

Everything had been done to communicate that this was a serious, professional business. Leo Nielsen was dressed in a sombre business suit and the offices of *À la Carte* Escorts could have been those of a civil engineer. There were no tarty types in reception and the receptionist herself was mousy and conservatively dressed. Nielsen almost carried the whole thing off and could have been any kind of businessman, except that his neck was as thick as his head and his shoulders strained against the material of his suit. In addition, there was a line down one cheek where the skin was paler than the rest of his face. Fabel guessed that Nielsen's human-resource management experience had started with slapping loose change out of drug-dependent whores hanging around the main railway station.

'What can I do for you?' asked Nielsen in an unbusi-nessman-like way.

'There was an incident,' said Fabel. 'In the Hotel Linden. One of your girls claimed that a customer had bitten her. Badly. We'd like to talk to her.'

'We've been all through this already,' said Nielsen with a weary sigh. 'We . . . *she* isn't interested in pressing charges.'

'We understand that.' Scholz sat on the corner of Nielsen's desk and knocked a desk-tidy full of pens and an expensive-looking calculator onto the floor. 'But – how can I put this? We don't give a fuck. I want the name of the girl right now or I will go through every file, every client credit-card receipt and personally visit every punter who has dipped his wick in one of your whores.'

'I don't have to put up with threats.' Nielsen maintained his composure and grinned at Scholz contemptuously.

'No one is threatening anyone,' said Fabel and looked mean-ingfully at Scholz. 'We just need to get this girl's name. She may have some important information relating to a murder case we're working on.'

Nielsen made a show of going through files on his computer. 'Sometimes these girls don't give us their proper names,' he said.

'Well, I hope this one did, Herr Nielsen,' said Fabel, 'or things could get difficult. Listen, we're not interested in you or your business here. We're not even interested particularly in this girl. It's her client we're after. But if you like, we could take a closer look at your operation here. Talk to some of your clients . . .'

Nielsen glowered at Fabel for a moment, then yielded. 'Okay. I'll get her to contact you . . .'

'No,' said Fabel. 'That won't do. We need an address and we need to see her now.'

Nielsen sighed, scribbled an address on his notepad and tore it out, handing it to Fabel. 'She's with a client. She'll be through by the time you get there. I'll tell her you're on your way and to stay put. I'll have her wait in the hotel lobby.'

'I don't think Herr Nielsen liked us,' said Scholz, grinning as they made their way back to the car. 'God, I'd like to take that place apart. I bet there's a bucketload of misery hidden in those files. If our organised-crime guys and the Federal Crime Bureau are right, then À la Carte is one of the end-users of Vitrenko's human trafficking operation.'

Fabel thought back to the Vitrenko Dossier. He couldn't remember seeing À la Carte amongst the list of premises tied into the trafficking operation. But, there again, there had been dozens. Whoever was providing the information to the Federal Crime Bureau was worth his weight in gold. Fabel had asked to see the full version of the Dossier, but the name of the informant and all references that could possibly have given a clue to his identity had been removed.

Scholz's cellphone rang.

'That was Tansu,' said Scholz after he hung up. 'She's done a check on our chum Nielsen. He did a three-stretch in Frankfurt about ten years ago. Serious assault. Drugs-related. Nothing since then but he stinks of organised crime to me.'

'Me too,' said Fabel. 'But not the usual Vitrenko foot soldier. It looks like our Ukrainian friend's business is truly global-ising. Maybe he's franchising some of his operations.'

'Tansu also says she's been unable to speak to Vera Reinartz, or whatever she calls herself now, but she's got both a busi-ness and home address for her. Tansu's asked if we can meet her about four this afternoon. But first I think we should visit this Internet company. The hotel this hooker is in is on our way.'

The hotel was one of the more luxurious kind that line the right bank of the Rhine. Fabel and Scholz waited, as agreed, near the entrance. The entire front of the reception area was glass-walled and Fabel marvelled at the panorama of the Hohenzollernbrücke bridge and, on the far bank, the Altstadt and the tower of St Martin's. Of course, dominating it all was the looming presence of Cologne Cathedral.

'Spectacular,' said Fabel.

'Yeah,' said Scholz uninterestedly as he looked around the reception area. 'This looks like our girl.'

A young woman approached them with an expression on her face somewhere between apprehension and suspicion. She was dressed more soberly than Fabel would have expected but, when he thought about it, this hotel was not the kind of place to encourage her type of enterprise. As she approached Fabel noticed her shape: slim except for the pronounced swell of her hips. Exactly like the Karneval Cannibal's victims.

'Are you Lyudmila Blyzniuk?' Scholz struggled over the surname.

'Yes. But I never use my full first name. I'm known as Mila. What have I done? My papers are all in order.'

'But you also go by the professional name "Anastasia"?'

'Yes. I never give clients my real name. What's this about?'

'Let me see your identity papers.' Scholz held out his hand.

'What? Here?' She glanced nervously at the reception desk. Scholz made an impatient gesture and Mila took her identity card and a couple of immigration papers from her handbag.

'Maybe we should sit down somewhere a little more private . . .' Fabel suggested, indicating a group of low sofas by the window.

'Mila, we want to talk to you about the incident with the client a few weeks ago. The man who bit you.' Fabel tried to sound less confrontational than Scholz. 'This is nothing

to do with you or what you do for a living. We think the
man who bit you is dangerous.'

'You don't need to tell me that,' said Mila, her expression
still hard and resistant. 'Everybody thought it was a big laugh.
Me getting bitten on the . . . I forgotten the German word
for it . . . on my *sraka* . . .'

'Arse,' said Scholz.

'Yeah, big joke. I have a big arse and he bites me on it.
Very funny. But he is a very bad man. Dangerous man. I had
to have stitches. He was like an animal, not a human being.
I saw his face afterwards, covered in blood.'

'Let's take this one step at a time, Mila,' said Fabel. 'Describe
this man to us.'

'He was about thirty to thirty-five, a little less than two
metres tall. Medium build . . . he looked fit, like he worked
out a lot. Dark hair, blue eyes. He was good-looking. Not
the usual sort of client.'

'What type of person was he? I mean rich, poor, educated
or not?'

'He was definitely educated and had money. I mean from
the way he was dressed.'

'He paid cash?' asked Scholz.

'Yes. And he gave me a little extra. I knew he had special
requirements. The agency told me.'

'That he liked to bite?'

'That he liked big bottoms. Like mine.'

'What happened? I mean at the hotel.'

'We went up to the room and he asked me to take off my
clothes. Then he started to touch my bottom.' Mila talked
as if she was describing an everyday occurrence, without the
slightest hint of embarrassment. 'Then he took his clothes
off and I thought that would be it, that we would have
normal sex. But then he pushed me onto the bed, very rough.
I started to get worried, but he talked all calm and asked if
he could bite me on the bottom. I thought he meant pretend

bites. But then he attacked me, like he was an animal. He bit me really hard. I swear he was trying to take a chunk out of me . . .'

Fabel and Scholz exchanged a look. 'Go on, Mila,' said Fabel.

'I started to scream and he stopped, but only to hit me. I pushed him away and screamed more. He had locked the door but I got it open and ran down the hall. Then the Polish girl and others from the hotel came to help. When we go back to the room he was already gone.'

'Why didn't you tell the police any of this when they were called to the hotel?' asked Fabel.

'The manager in the hotel said he didn't want no trouble. And the agency phoned me and said I was to say nothing. They didn't want you, I mean the police, making trouble for them.'

'So you went along with it,' said Scholz.

'I had to. But I didn't want to.' Mila looked out of the window across the Rhine to Cologne Cathedral, dark against the sky. When she turned back there was an earnestness in her expression. 'Everyone thought it was nothing. That he just got – how do you say it? – that he got a little carried away. But they didn't see him. They didn't see his face or his eyes after he bite me. He was not human no more. He was become a . . . I don't know what you say in German. We call such beasts *vovkuláka* in Ukrainian. You know . . . a man who become a wolf.'

'A werewolf,' said Fabel and looked at Scholz.

3.

Ansgar knew where she worked. He had followed her back from the wholesalers on Monday.

He had sat in his car in the car park and waited for her. It hadn't been as if he had had a plan: pure instinct had impelled him along a destinationless course. Maybe he really could have a normal relationship with Ekaterina. Maybe he could keep order in his daily life by allowing himself this little piece of chaos. After all, he had done *that* with this woman before. It was like a sign that he had happened across her again, after all this time. She obviously worked in the restaurant or hotel trade. It was a thought that had never occurred to him, that he might at some time encounter this woman again because she was in the same business as him. Ansgar had shadowed her as she pushed her low bed-cart stacked with purchases across the tarmac to where her small van was parked. Then he had followed her through the city to her café on the north-west fringe of the Altstadt.

And today he had come back. The café had the anonymously trendy look of almost every coffee shop and the name *AMAZONIA CYBER-CAFÉ* was emblazoned above the large picture window. Ansgar smiled at the choice of name. He thought about going into the café: the chances were that she would not recognise him, but he couldn't take the risk. Instead he watched from across the street.

Ansgar looked at his watch. His shift started in two hours.

He had until then.

4.

'Those papers looked pretty genuine,' said Scholz as they drove across the bridge to Cologne's Left Bank. 'But I'd bet you anything you like that they're fakes.'

'I don't know,' said Fabel. Mila had insisted that she was in Germany of her own free will and that she chose to do what she did for a living. She certainly hadn't looked oppressed, but of course it was difficult to tell. Prostitution, legal or otherwise, was seldom a profession of completely free choice. And Mila's reluctance to be seen talking to two policemen had to do with something more than the business she was in. Scholz had treated her with nothing less than contempt. Fabel liked Scholz, his laid-back manner and his friendliness, but the Cologne officer's attitude towards women troubled him. Fabel had always had female officers in his team, but he had never had to make a conscious effort to do so. Everyone was picked on their merits. It bothered Fabel to see how Scholz was almost dismissive of Tansu, who was clearly a capable officer. And there was something about his manner with Mila that bothered him.

The MediaPark on the northern fringe of the Neustadt area was a reasonably new element in Cologne's landscape.

'The Cologne Tower has only been open for about four years. There's still quite a bit of office space to fill,' explained Scholz as they circled through the streets looking for somewhere to park. Eventually they used an underground car park and walked through the chill drizzle to the bright glass and steel of the Cologne Tower. InterSperse Media was on the fifth floor.

There was no reception as such and most of the people milling about the open-plan office space or working at workstations were in their twenties or early thirties. Everyone was dressed in casual sweat-tops or T-shirts and jeans. In environments like this, Fabel always felt he belonged to another era. Despite considering himself to be liberal-minded, he often found such situations provoked the reactionary in him: the northern Lutheran who believed that people should still dress smartly for work; that the only men who should wear earrings were pirates; that tattoos on women were uncomely.

'Cool place . . .' said Scholz, clearly untouched by the same conservatism. A fat young woman came over to them. Despite her near-obesity, she wore jeans and a top that left her too-ample midriff exposed. Predictably she had a piercing, a ring through her nostril.

'Can I help you?' she asked in a tone that suggested she would rather do anything else but help. Scholz showed her his police ID and her cloudy expression dimmed further.

'We want to see David Littger.'

'You'll have to wait – he's in a meeting.'

Scholz smiled indulgently, as if she were a child who had said something cutely naive. 'No, no . . . you see, we don't have to wait. This is a murder inquiry so get him now or we'll walk into his meeting. Clear?'

The young woman stormed off, presenting the policemen with her bustling rotund figure from the rear.

'She should be more willing to help,' said Scholz. 'Christ knows what our guy would do if he ever saw that arse. That would keep him in stew for six months.'

Fabel laughed despite himself. The girl returned after a minute and sulkily showed them into the only meeting room, a glass box in the centre of the office. There was a large conference table with an impossibly thin computer-display screen in the centre, a cordless keyboard and mouse. Three media types stood up and left as Fabel and Scholz entered. Scholz spoke to the remaining man.

'You David Littger?' Scholz asked and sat down at the table uninvited. Fabel remained standing by the door. Littger nodded, eyeing both policemen suspiciously. He was in his early thirties, with cropped-short sand-coloured hair and stubble grown to disguise a weak jaw. 'I'm Commissar Scholz, this is Principal Chief Commissar Fabel. We're here to talk about one of the websites you host and did the design for.'

'I'm afraid I will not divulge any such information. InterSperse Media is bound by strict commercial-confidentiality rules—'

'Listen, pencil-dick,' said Scholz, still smiling as if conducting a perfectly pleasant conversation with an acquaintance. 'I am not here to fuck about. This is a multiple-murder inquiry and in my pocket I have a warrant from the Staatsanwalt's office. If you force me to exercise this warrant, your offices will be closed to your staff, all of your files seized and your operation will be shut down for as long as it takes us to find the information we need. Now, you don't want that and I don't want that, because if I have to do that it will take me much longer to find the sick pervs who run the site. I will also take it as read that you have obstructed us for some reason. Maybe you're into this scene as well and are more "hands-on" than you want to admit. In which case you and I will be seeing a great deal of each other over the next twenty-four hours. And it'll be at my place, not yours.'

'What's the name of the website?' asked Littger in a flat tone. If he was shaken, he didn't show it. Scholz handed him a sheet of paper.

'They call themselves the *Anthropophagi*,' explained Scholz. He referred to his notebook. 'It is, as they describe it, "an online meeting place for individuals and groups interested in the exchange of information on *hard vore* and cannibalism." In other words, Sick Fucks Reunited. And your hip and trendy techno company put this shit on the web for them and designed their website.'

Littger remained unperturbed. 'I remember it. We uploaded them on our server about six months ago. We do no main-tenance on the site – we supplied a general design and a template for them to update. As for its content . . . we're not responsible for that. We simply supply the door, the access to the web. But there is no regulation out there. The Internet is the Wild West. Anarchy. We can't check up on every single site we host.'

'And if someone puts up pictures of kids being raped?' asked Fabel.

'We have a zero-tolerance policy towards that kind of thing,' said Littger. 'But we need to know it's going on before we can pull the plug and call you guys in.' He sighed. 'Listen, I'll give you the name and address, but you're going to have to serve your warrant. I'll have all kind of shit from clients to contend with if you don't. But I'm willing to cooperate, so I'd appreciate it if you don't disrupt my business the way you said. I'll point you to all the right information. I just need to be legally obliged to hand over the information.'

'Ah, well . . . it's not as easy as that, Herr Littger.' Scholz made an *I'd like to help but . . .* face. 'You see, if I do this through the proper channels and you blab to your clients, or even if the press get a hint that your company is part of this investigation, then God knows who's going to find out about it before we're ready. I am prepared to give you my word that no one will know where the information came from.'

'You know something, Herr Scholz?' said Littger. 'I don't believe you have a warrant.'

Scholz's smile disappeared and his expression clouded. 'You want to put me to the test?'

'No one finds out about this?'

'Not unless Tons-of-Fun out there or any of your other employees blab. But they don't need to know that we have had this discussion.'

Littger leaned over the table and typed something on the cordless keyboard.

'This is it,' he said. 'Peter Schnaus is the guy's name. That's his address. It's in Buschbell, a part of Frechen.'

'Okay,' said Fabel. 'I think we'll pay Herr Schnaus a call. I take it we can rely on your discretion? I'd be most annoyed if Herr Schnaus knew in advance of our visit. In the meantime, could you put up the *Anthropophagi* site for us? There are a few questions I'd like to ask.'

Littger shrugged and typed the address into the wireless keyboard. The site appeared. 'What does *Anthropophagi* mean?' he asked as the site loaded.

'It's Greek,' said Scholz. 'It means cannibals. In some folk-lore it refers to headless men, with their eyes and mouths in their chests, who feed on human flesh.'

'Nice . . .'

Fabel took charge of the mouse and navigated the site. There was a picture gallery, a forum and a section devoted to classified advertisements.

'You see this shit?' asked Scholz.

'Yep,' said Fabel. 'Weird stuff, isn't it?'

'Well . . . yeah . . . but I expected to see all kinds of sick porn. But it's just weird. The only thing I could see that could by any stretch of the imagination be deemed erotic was a series of badly doctored pics of some tart in a bikini being swallowed whole by a fish.'

'That, believe it or not, *is* pornography for these people. It's a fetish called voreaphilia. They get off by fantasising about eating someone or being eaten. The picture you described is what's called *soft vore* as in *soft core*. It shows a human or an animal being consumed whole, without blood. *Hard vore* is when it involves the cutting or ripping of flesh with lots of bloodshed. Believe it or not – and this is pretty hard to believe – there are voreaphiles who get off watching nature programmes. You know, lions tearing antelopes apart and eating them.'

Scholz shook his head. 'Shit . . . like I said to you before, I sometimes can't imagine how the hell people get to a place like that, where their idea of sex is so fucked-up.'

'I honestly believe that this kind of crap on the Internet feeds it. It gives them a place to exchange their fantasies and to convince each other that they're not abnormal. Sadists, paedophiles, rapists all do exactly the same thing,' said Fabel. Littger shrugged his shoulders as if to say 'nothing to do with me'. Fabel clicked onto the classified ads section. 'This is what we want . . . yes, here it is.' He read one of the ads out loud.

'"Love Bites" . . . nice title, huh? "Love-hungry predator seeks submissive prey for voreplay. Must not be fat, but should have a bottom ample enough to sink one's teeth into. Genuine replies only. No professionals, only enthusiastic pears ripe for the eating. Apply to Lovebiter, Box AG1891".' Fabel turned to Littger. 'You have any way of tracing who placed this?'

'Only an IP address, and that could be for anywhere. He may even have used a cybercafe or a WiFi hotspot. And you can't trace him through his credit card – he had to pay for the ad but there's no secure credit-card facility built into the site. Advertisers have to send hard copy in to the PO box number listed, along with sufficient funds to pay for it.'

'So this guy Schnaus may have the details of whoever placed the ad?' asked Scholz.

'Not necessarily. The advertiser could have paid by money order or might even have sent cash. But what Schnaus will be able to provide is the access password to get into the virtual mailbox for all the replies he got.'

'We've got to find "Lovebiter",' Scholz said to Fabel. 'He lives in the same dark place as our guy. He may be connected to him.'

'He may even be him,' said Fabel.

5.

Tansu was waiting for them when they got back to the Presidium.

'Productive day?' she asked Fabel. He ran through what they had found out while Scholz went into his office to check his messages and e-mail.

'He's going to be in a really bad mood for the rest of the day,' said Tansu. 'The police Karneval committee is going ape because the float is so behind schedule.' Fabel looked through the glass into Scholz's office and grinned. The Cologne detective was standing talking on the phone, his free hand intermittently running through his hair or gesturing to the empty room.

'Listen, Tansu,' said Fabel. 'While we have the chance, I wondered if I could ask you a favour . . .'

'Certainly, Herr Chief Commissar,' she said, and smiled wickedly.

'This is it,' said Tansu. They had been to the home address Tansu had got for Vera Reinartz and there had been no one home. 'This is her business.'

Fabel looked across at the café. It looked bright and warm in the dull winter street. 'What's the name she uses now?' he asked Tansu.

'Sandow . . . Andrea Sandow.'

As they entered the Amazonia Café, Fabel smiled to himself at the sight of one of the waitresses. She could certainly be described as an Amazon. At first, Fabel wondered if the waitress was in fact a man in drag. She was massively built, with muscles bulging on her exposed arms and straining at the material of her T-shirt, yet her make-up was heavily applied and the platinum blonde of her hair was as synthetic as the bronze of her midwinter tan. He found himself wondering where she would fit in with the theories of female beauty that Lessing, the anthropologist-cum-art historian, had expounded.

'Excuse me,' Fabel asked the waitress, 'I'm looking for Andrea Sandow . . . I believe she owns this café?'

'I am she.' The Amazon pulled herself to her full height and regarded Fabel coldly with her brilliant blue eyes. 'What can I do for you?'

Fabel found himself speechless. He thought of Vera Reinartz, the pretty if mousy girl in the photographs; of the bright medical student always reluctant to have her photograph taken.

'Frau Sandow,' Tansu intervened. 'Can you confirm that you were originally known as Vera Reinartz?'

The mascaraed eyes narrowed in the masculine face. 'What's this all about?'

Fabel took in the café. There were about a dozen customers scattered around the tables. 'Listen, we're police officers . . . is there somewhere private we could talk?'

'Could you cover for me for a minute or two, Britta?' Andrea turned back to the three detectives. 'We can talk in the kitchen.'

'If you don't mind me saying, Frau Sandow, you've undergone a considerable change,' said Fabel. He eased sideways to allow Tansu and Scholz to follow him into the kitchen. Andrea Sandow, as Vera Reinartz was now called, was a good head shorter than Fabel, shorter even than Tansu, yet her physical presence seemed to dominate the cramped kitchen. 'I wouldn't have recognised you from your photographs.'

Andrea smirked. 'That wasn't a *considerable change*. It was a metamorphosis. Complete and irreversible. Now, what is it you want?'

'We want to talk to you again about the man who attacked you,' said Tansu. 'I know it was a long time ago, but we think he's attacked other women.'

'Of course he has.' Another contemptuous grin. Andrea's jaw tightened with it, wide and strong, her cheeks creasing with deep dimples. 'I know why you want to talk to me. I've been expecting you. It's about those killings, isn't it? The last two Women's Karneval Nights?'

'You think it's the same man?' asked Tansu.

'I know it is the same man. So do you. That's why you're here.'

'Why didn't you come forward, then,' said Fabel, 'if you were convinced it was the same man?'

'What would be the point? You won't catch him. Ever.'

'Why did you change your name?' he asked.

Andrea stared hard at Fabel. A man's stare. 'What's that got to do with you?'

'I just wondered if it was a reaction to the attack. And if it was, why didn't you move away from Cologne? You're not from here originally, are you? Your parents live in Frankfurt, don't they?'

'You haven't told them where I live?' The sudden fore-shadow of anger clouded Andrea's expression.

'No, no . . .' said Tansu reassuringly. 'We wouldn't – couldn't – give out information like that without your consent.' Tansu cast a look in Fabel's direction. He knew why. For some reason there was an atmosphere of hostility between him and Andrea. Mutual hostility. He could understand why she resented the intrusion of the police into the new life she'd built for herself. What he couldn't understand was why *he* felt hostile towards *her*.

'When did you get into bodybuilding?' he asked.

'It started after the attack. I had to have a lot of physio-therapy. I needed to build my strength up and the physio involved some weight work. It was then that I got the idea. To rebuild myself. To create someone new.'

'But there was nothing wrong with the old you,' said Tansu. 'You were a victim. Do you blame yourself for what happened?'

'No,' said Andrea defiantly. 'I know it was that bastard who's to blame. But pretty little Vera Reinartz was too soft and weak, too pliant. She was too afraid. Maybe that's why he picked her. Because she had victim written all over her.'

'But your medical career . . .' said Tansu. 'According to what I've read you showed enormous promise. You could have excelled as a doctor.'

'There are other ways to excel,' said Andrea. 'That was all part of the past. Of Vera Reinartz. Now I excel at something else. I started bodybuilding in 2000. I mean seriously. I am an expert on it, you know. Not just the sport or the techniques – the history, too. The philosophy of it. Do you know that the father of modern bodybuilding was a German? Eugen Sandow. He started out as a circus strongman and ended up setting the standards for all bodybuilding. He organised and judged the world's first bodybuilding competition. His fellow judge was Arthur Conan Doyle, the British author who invented Sherlock Holmes.'

'Sandow . . .' said Fabel. 'That's the name you took . . . Why?'

'I needed to be someone else. That's why I became a bodybuilder, Herr Fabel. Like I said, a total metamorphosis. I needed a new name for a new body.'

Andrea leaned back and braced herself against the kitchen counter. As she did so, the veins in her upper arms protested hard and blue against the brown skin. Fabel saw the spasmodic twitch of a bicep, as if it had a life independent of its host body. Andrea caught him looking.

'Do you find me repulsive?' she asked. 'Do you find the shape of my body a real turn-off? Most men do. But others . . . oh, you would not believe what other men are like. They come to the competitions, a lot of them. They come to watch me and the other girls. Do you know that perfect muscle tone disappears within an hour of each workout session? We pump up before each contest, then run through our routines. Not rehearsal – it's to maintain that perfect tone till we go on stage.' She leaned forward even more and lowered her voice conspiratorially. 'Do you know that some of our male fans come backstage before or after the contest. Little men who ask if they can *touch* us. Our bellies. Our thighs. Our arms. Just so they can feel the muscle at perfect tone. They do it out of admiration of the sport. Reverence, almost. But that doesn't stop them having a little stiffy in their pants. You see, Herr Fabel, one man's meat is another man's poison . . . What, exactly, would *your* meat be?'

'You said you knew the Women's Karneval Night killer was the same man who attacked you,' said Fabel, holding Andrea's gaze. 'Why? Is there anything about the night you were attacked that you've remembered over the years that maybe isn't in your original statement?'

Andrea laughed bitterly. 'Do you know, Herr Fabel, that even after all this time he still comes back to haunt me? The clown?'

'I'm sure,' said Tansu. 'You can't go through an experience like that without post-traumatic stress.'

'No . . . I'm not talking about that. I dealt with that. All of this . . .' She stood up straight and flexed her physique. 'I created this to put that behind me. It wasn't just the rape. That bastard beat me so badly I thought I was going to die. Well, I did, in a way. Vera died and I survived. He left a broken body behind and I fixed it. I don't have nightmares about the Clown who attacked me. No post-trauma panic attacks. I'd love to meet him again . . . then I'd break every bone in his body. That's not what I meant when I said he still comes back to haunt me. The sick bastard writes to me.'

'What?' Fabel exchanged looks with the others. 'How? E-mail?'

'No. Letters. They arrive every few months.'

'Wait a minute,' said Scholz. 'Do you mean he puts pen to paper and sends it through the mail?'

'That's usually how letters arrive,' said Andrea.

'But that's physical evidence. That's a chance for us to track him down.' Fabel couldn't contain his frustration. 'Why on earth didn't you get in touch with the police?'

Andrea shrugged. 'When the first one arrived, not long after the attack, I was terrified. But I was still *her* then. Soft, timid, pliant. Too scared to do anything. Then I decided to change my name and the rest all fell into place. Then the other letters arrived. Even after I'd changed my name and moved apartments. They don't come often. But they did come.'

'Have you kept them?' asked Scholz.

Andrea shook her head. 'I burn them now without reading them. But the ones I did read were all the same. Mad ravings. How much he wanted to do it again, how he was biding his time.'

'And this doesn't bother you?' asked Tansu incredulously.

'No. He's lost his power to frighten me. Maybe we will meet again, but he's the one who should be afraid.'

'I need you to think hard about what was in those letters, Andrea,' said Fabel firmly. 'I need you to take the time to write down everything you can remember. Do it tonight and we'll send someone to pick it up from the café tomorrow. Like I said, anything that might give us a handle on his identity.'

'What about his name?'

It took a moment for Fabel to realise that Andrea was being serious. 'He signs them?'

'Every one. The name he uses is Peter Stumpf.'

Fabel heard Scholz groan. 'Does the name Peter Stumpf mean anything to you?' Fabel asked Andrea.

'Nothing.'

'It obviously does to you,' he said to Scholz.

'It sure does. But we'll talk about that later.'

As they walked back towards Scholz's car, someone on the other side of the street caught Scholz's attention.

'Hi, Ansgar!' Scholz called over. Fabel and Tansu followed him across the street.

'Remember the restaurant I took you to – the Speisekammer?' Scholz said to Fabel. 'This is Ansgar Hoeffer, the chef. The best in Cologne if you ask me and that's saying something. How are you, Ansgar?'

'I'm fine . . . you?' Ansgar answered. He was a tallish man with a high-domed head. His sparse hair had been trimmed bristle-short. His eyes seemed large and doleful behind his glasses. But what struck Fabel most about him was that he looked decidedly uncomfortable.

'The best,' said Scholz. 'What are you doing in this part of town?'

Ansgar again looked flustered for a moment. 'Oh, I had a few things to do. How was your meal the other night?' Ansgar addressed his question to Fabel.

'Oh, I'm sorry, I meant to introduce you . . .' said Scholz. 'Ansgar, this is Principal Chief Commissar Fabel of the Hamburg Police. He's down here . . . on a course.'

Fabel and Ansgar shook hands. 'It was excellent,' said Fabel. 'We both had the lamb ragout. Delicious.'

After a brief exchange of more small talk they went their separate ways, Ansgar walking off towards the city centre with a purposeful stride.

'Great cook,' said Scholz as they reached his car.

'Mmm . . .' said Fabel, but he looked back in Ansgar's direction and noticed that Tansu was doing the same.

In the car Scholz didn't start the ignition.

'Well, that was on the bizarre side of weird,' he said. 'She looks like some kind of bad drag act. What the hell is all that about?'

'What she went through would be enough to knock anyone off kilter,' said Tansu. 'My guess is she's rejecting her own femininity. No matter what she says, I think she blames herself for what happened to her.'

'No,' said Fabel. 'She blames Vera Reinartz for what happened. As though Vera was a different person. Did you notice how often she referred to her past self in the third person?'

'It's the name these letters were signed with that interests me,' said Scholz. 'Peter Stumpf. I'm now convinced that whoever attacked Andrea is our killer. You were right all along, Jan.'

'Actually, it was Tansu who came up with it first.'

'This is a nice lyrical touch,' said Scholz, ignoring Fabel's correction. 'A local reference. Out to the west of Cologne there's a town called Bedburg. Peter Stumpf was Bedburg's most famous resident. Or infamous. He lived there in the sixteenth century. The Beast of Bedburg – one of the first serial killers recorded in Germany. He also had the most horrific execution ever recorded.'

'So Andrea's rapist and tormentor is referencing this Peter Stumpf. Why does that make you believe he's our Karneval Cannibal?'

'Because that's exactly what Peter Stumpf was. A cannibal. He was supposed to have eaten dozens of victims. He also claimed he was a shape-shifter who had sold his soul to Satan for the ability to turn into a wolf. Stumpf said he preferred to remain in human form to rape his victims before turning into a wolf to eat them. Maybe our killer believes he has transformed a rapist to a cannibal.'

'I think that's stretching it, but I agree – he may be trying to say he undergoes some kind of transformation. Maybe it's the clown disguise. What's more important is that it means we have his DNA from the attack on Vera . . . or Andrea. You said Stumpf had the worst execution on record. Is that significant?'

There was something grim in Scholz's wry smile. 'Our priest told us about it in Sunday School. A little horror story to lighten the catechism lessons. Peter Stumpf was a rich farmer who confessed freely and without torture to having been a necromancer and black wizard since childhood. He claimed to have been visited several times by the Devil who gave him a magical belt that would give him superhuman strength in exchange for his soul. The price of this superhuman strength, however, was more than Stumpf's soul – the belt turned him into a wolf. He admitted to tearing apart and eating scores of victims: men, women, children. He had a particular taste for pregnant women, apparently. Two meals in one. After the trial they strapped him to a wheel and broke his arms, legs and ribs with the blunt side of an axe. You see, they believed that, as a werewolf, there was a danger of him returning from the grave, so breaking his limbs would prevent him doing that. Then they ripped chunks of flesh from his body while he was still alive, using red-hot pincers. As a finale, they beheaded and burned him. True mortification of the flesh.'

'But it didn't work,' said Fabel grimly. 'It would appear that Peter Stumpf *has* come back to life.'

6.

Fabel got the impression that Scholz had allowed Tansu to come along for the Peter Schnaus interview only because it would have been out of the way to drop her off at the Presidium first. Scholz had called ahead to make sure that Schnaus would be in before heading along Aachenerstrasse. Buschbell was to the north of Frechen, he had explained, and therefore it was easier to avoid the town itself.

'Incidentally,' said Scholz, 'Bedburg is out this way too – the home of the infamous Peter Stumpf.'

Buschbell and Frechen were only nine kilometres from the city centre and Fabel had been aware of a continuous urban landscape. Buschbell, however, was more open and tree-lined and clearly on the edge of the Cologne conurbation.

'How did Schnaus sound on the phone?' asked Fabel.

'Guilty,' said Scholz. 'What of I don't know yet, but he sure was sheepish to hear that the police were coming out for a chat.'

They pulled up outside a reasonably expensive-looking

house with more garden than Fabel had seen in Cologne since he first arrived. It was the home of a high-middle-income earner. Not the dwelling of a millionaire, but substantial enough to indicate a respectable bank balance. Added to which there was the regulation Mercedes E500 in the drive.

As they made their way to the front door, it was clear that Scholz's mind was on something else. 'Listen,' he said. 'I don't really like this idea the two of you have come up with . . . It's far too risky . . .'

'My idea,' said Fabel. 'I asked Tansu if she would do it as a favour—'

'Like I said, I don't like it,' interrupted Scholz, 'but I'll go along with it. But I've got a few conditions. We'll talk about it after we're through here.'

The front door opened before they had a chance to knock. A man of about forty stepped out, drawing it to behind him. He was a little under two metres tall, athletically built and reasonably good-looking. A perfect fit for the description given them by Mila, the escort who'd been bitten.

'Commissar Scholz?' he asked Fabel.

'No, that's me,' said Scholz. 'Herr Schnaus?'

'Yes. What's this about? My wife and kids are here and—'

'It's about the website you run,' said Fabel.

'Oh . . .' Schnaus looked crestfallen. 'I rather thought it would be. Listen, I've told my wife this is to do with business.'

'What exactly is your business?' asked Fabel.

'Computer software.'

Fabel looked over at the car in the drive and at the house once more and considered the decision he'd taken about his future.

'Okay, we'll play along. For now. Is there somewhere private we can talk?'

'My study . . .' Schnaus led them into the house and along

a wide hall. The study was roomy, bright and contemporary. There was a large desk with two expensive-looking computers on it. Two more sat on workstations on the other wall.

'You run your site from here?' asked Fabel.

'Listen, it's a hobby more than anything else . . . I don't do it for the money . . .'

'Just for pleasure,' Scholz sneered. Schnaus's face reddened.

'Listen, I can't explain it. It's just something . . .' He let the thought die. 'What is it you want to know?'

'For a start you can tell us where you were on the evening of Friday the twentieth of January.'

Schnaus typed something into his computer. 'I was in Frankfurt. At a conference.'

'Can anyone confirm this?'

'About a hundred people. I gave a talk there to introduce a new product.'

'You stayed overnight?'

'Yes. Three days in total.'

'What kind of new product?' asked Fabel. 'I mean, what kind of software do you sell?'

'We're distributors for gaming software. Other stuff too, like interactive software for training, that kind of thing.'

'Have you ever heard of a game designer called Melissa Schenker?'

'No . . .' If Schnaus was lying he was covering it up well. 'I can't say I have.'

'What about a role-playing game called *The Lords of Misrule*?'

'Oh yes . . . more than heard of it, we distribute it.'

'Melissa Schenker designed *Lords of Misrule*,' said Fabel.

'Oh. I wouldn't know that. It's not part of the portfolio I represent. And anyway, I'm not always familiar with who designed or conceived the games.'

There was a pause.

'Why do you do this, Herr Schnaus?' asked Fabel. 'I mean

you have a good job, a family. Why do you feel the need to run a website like this?'

'Inside each of us is a little chaos. Some have more than others. I have an orderly life here. I am a good husband and father and my wife knows nothing of my . . . well, the stranger side of my nature . . . If I kept that chaos completely bottled up then there's a chance it would explode. Destroy all the order and stability in my life. So I run a harmless, non-pornographic website relating to voreaphilia and cannibalism.'

Fabel thought of another ordinary businessman with an ordered, stable life who had tried to keep the chaos within bottled up tight. Right up until he had blown his brains out in front of Fabel.

'Where the hell do you get the idea that anything relating to cannibalism – particularly sexual cannibalism – is harmless?' Fabel asked.

'I don't mean any harm . . .' said Schnaus weakly.

'I'll tell you why we're here, Herr Schnaus,' said Scholz. 'We have a complete nutter who is running about biting chunks out of women. He may also have murdered several. That, my friend, does not strike me as being a bit of harmless fun. I've looked at your website. I'm not surprised that you want to keep all of that filth away from your wife. My guess is that if she were to find out about your little hobby you wouldn't see her or your kids for dust. Now I am quite prepared to get a warrant and turn this place upside down. It may be your home but your little website is run from here and that puts it right at the heart of a major murder investigation. I promise you that by tomorrow morning this place will be crawling with forensic technicians, uniformed police officers and, if anyone were indiscreet enough to tip them off, with members of the press.'

Schnaus looked as if he was about to be sick. 'No . . . please, no . . . I'll do anything you want. I'll give you any information you need. And I promise I'll shut down the site. Just tell me what you want me to do . . . I just don't want my wife and kids to know.'

'Well, one thing we *don't* want you to do, Herr Schnaus,' said Fabel, 'is to shut down the site. Not yet, anyway.'

Chapter Ten

13–14 February

I.

Maria rolled onto her side and her body was racked by involuntary, empty retches. She eased herself up onto her knees and elbows, head still down, her shrunken gut still in spasm. She felt the dirt and grime beneath her skin and realised she was naked. It was then that the intense, freezing cold hit her like a glacial wave. A second wave collided with her, as chill and harsh as the cold: raw terror. Vitrenko. She couldn't believe it: Buslenko had been a fiction. Taras Buslenko was Vasyl Vitrenko. She had been right about his eyes. It was the one thing he couldn't change. Vitrenko had completely convinced her with his fiction of a Ukrainian government mission. He had been true to form: Vitrenko liked to get in close for the kill. He liked to mess with his victims' minds. He had been playing with her all along. And now it was endgame.

Maria tried to work out how long she'd been unconscious. Shuddering with cold, she checked her arms and saw a number of puncture wounds. They'd kept her out for hours; or days; even weeks. She dragged herself up into a sitting position, drew her knees up to her chest and wrapped her arms around them. The spasms that convulsed her body went beyond any description of shivering. Great racking muscular convulsions. Her naked skin had puckered into gooseflesh and had lost all its pigmentation. It was now going past white and had started to look like frosted glass shot through with a cobalt bloom. So it was true, she thought bitterly, you really do go blue with cold. She looked around her confinement. Even the light was cold: a wire-caged neon strip flooded the space with a sterile and cheerless light. No window. No sound. Outside it could be any time of day or night. They had achieved the all-important first stage of interrogative torture: the complete disorientation of the subject.

They had put Maria in the cold-meat store and turned the refrigeration on. The cold-meat store that Buslenko . . . no, that *Vitrenko* had told her wasn't working any more. Had he known, even then, that this was where he was going to kill her? She scanned the meat store for anything, any scrap or rag with which to cover her nakedness; to try to delay her death by slowing the rate at which her core body heat was being dissipated. There was nothing. She hugged herself even tighter. But this wasn't Vitrenko's style. Death in here would be too easy. True, she was experiencing agonising cold now, but she knew how hypothermia worked: very soon she would stop shivering; then, perversely, she would actually start to feel warm again, along with a gentle, sleepy euphoria as her brain flooded her body with endorphins. It would be at that peaceful point that she would quite contentedly fall into a sleep from which there would be no waking.

No. It didn't fit with Vitrenko. There wouldn't be enough pain. Enough horror. Enough fear.

Maria got her answer some time that she couldn't measure later. There was a loud metallic clunk and the door of the cold store slid open. Vitrenko stood there with his new face but his old, cold, hard eyes. Next to him, armed with a handgun, was Olga Sarapenko. They both wore their outdoor coats. Vitrenko looked at Maria impassively.

'If I talk to you, can you understand what I'm saying?'

Maria's nod was almost lost in her convulsive shivering.

Vitrenko walked over and dragged her to her feet. She

struggled to cover her nakedness and he slammed the back of his hand across her face. Again. And again. Maria felt her mouth fill with blood and was alarmed at how cool it was. Vitrenko pushed her away from him and she crashed onto the gritty, cold floor. The heat from the grazes on her skin was almost welcome.

'If I talk to you, can you understand what I'm saying?' he repeated.

'Yes.' Maria heard the quiver in her voice. She wanted to tell him it was because she was cold, not because she feared him.

'You are alive only because I have some use for you. If you cease to be of use to me, I will kill you. Do you understand?'

Maria nodded again and Vitrenko's heavy boot crashed into her ribs.

'Do you understand?'

'Yes!' she screamed at him in defiance. Something had cracked inside her but she didn't care. 'Yes, I understand.'

'You are pathetic . . .' Vitrenko said. 'You think that because I made a big impact on your life you could make a similar impact on mine. Yet you are a nobody, a nothing. You think you have some importance, some worth, but you have none. You have gone out of your way to be a nuisance to me. I make examples of nuisances, you do know that, don't you?'

'Yes,' Maria said dully.

'There are two functions you can now serve. The first is as a key to the information I need on the informants inside my organisation and the extent of the intelligence on me gathered by your Federal Crime Bureau.'

'I don't have that kind of access . . .' said Maria.

'I didn't say you could provide that information or offer direct access to it. I said you offer a means to that end. The other purpose you can fulfil is more final . . . I intend, when I'm finished with you, to make an example of you. As I have done with others, including Buslenko, I will show through you what I do to anyone who sets themselves against me. What did you think you could have achieved?' Vitrenko looked down on Maria as if he could not understand her stupidity. 'I let you live. That night in the field when you tried to stop me. Did you think it was an accident that my knife missed your heart? Have you any idea how many hearts I have punctured? Sliced open like an apple?'

Maria struggled to her feet. She tried not to think how her emaciated blue-cold body must have looked. 'Why don't you just get on with it?' she said defiantly. 'Why don't you just kill me?'

Again Vitrenko's hand slashed across Maria's face. She felt dizzy and staggered from the force of the blow. Something trickled down her temple and cheek.

'Weren't you paying attention to what I said? I want access to the so-called "Vitrenko Dossier" held by the BKA.'

'Why? You don't need those – I can tell you everything there is to know about you. You think you're Genghis Khan, or Alexander the Greek or shit like that. Do you know what they say about you in those files? That you're nothing more than a nut-job. A former junior officer with a Napoleon complex. You're no soldier, Vitrenko. You're a common crook.' Maria felt good that her voice hadn't betrayed how frightened she was.

Vitrenko smiled. 'Well, thanks for the insight, Frau Klee, but I am much more interested in what intelligence has been gathered by the task force about my operations. I need access to this dossier. Not the one we took from Buslenko. The full German version.'

'Tell me this, Vitrenko: if you're such a criminal master-mind, how come you let me kill your deputy?'

'Molokov?' Vitrenko grinned. 'I didn't *let* you kill him . . . I *made* you kill him. And I did so because I believe Molokov was doing a deal with the German authorities. I think he planned to deliver me up to them. I don't know for sure, but

I think he was the one passing on information. He was ambitious and treacherous. I needed to dispose of him and, well, it *amused* me to have you do it for me. And it fitted with our little charade. Tell me, Frau Klee, your willingness to lose your life when we were back there in the workshop with Molokov . . . was that your enthusiasm to save me, as Buslenko, or kill me, as Vitrenko?'

'Work it out yourself.'

'Did you like the location, by the way?' Again the cruel smile that was as cold as the meat store itself. 'I mean, the field and everything. I arranged the meeting there with Molokov because I knew you would appreciate it. I really did mess you up in that field in the North, didn't I, Maria? I know all about your psycho boyfriend, all about your sick leave, about Dr Minks and his treatment. I don't think you're in any kind of position to call anyone a "nut-job". Anyway, let's start with all the access codes and passwords you know for accessing the Federal Crime Bureau system.'

'Those won't get you far,' said Maria.

'Oh, don't worry – we know you are a very, very small fish indeed. That's not how you're going to help us get into the dossier. But, in the meantime, what are the access codes and passwords you hold? Do you have them memorised or written down somewhere?'

'Close the door on your way out,' said Maria, now unable to restrain her shuddering. 'There's a terrible draught in here.'

'Oh, I'm not going to let you freeze to death, Maria.' Vitrenko nodded to Olga Sarapenko, who left the cold store for a moment, handing her pistol to Vitrenko as she passed him. She returned carrying a large bucket. Maria had only enough time to register that the bucket's contents were steaming when they hit her. She screamed as the scalding hot water seared her naked skin. Her face, her arms, her chest all felt as if they were alight and she writhed on the dusty floor. The agony of her scalding seemed to last an eternity.

Eventually she prised her hands from her face to inspect the damage. She looked at her arms, her legs, expecting to find the skin blistered and scarlet. It wasn't. Where the water had hit, her flesh had bloomed pink, but no more. Yet still the pain seared through her. Vitrenko gave Maria a moment as she cowered, taking gasping breaths.

'A little trick I learned along the way,' he explained. 'The water was merely hand-hot. Does no damage to the victim, but if you have chilled them sufficiently beforehand it feels like being hit with acid.' Sarapenko had brought in a second bucket and doused Maria with its contents. Again she felt pain, but this time less intense and only where the first bucketful had missed. Now the warmth was almost welcome. 'You see?' he said. 'Now you're accustomed to it.' Sarapenko returned with a third bucket which she handed to Vitrenko.

'You see, the central nervous system is very easy to confuse: it finds it difficult to distinguish between extreme heat and extreme cold.' He threw the third bucket over her.

This time Maria's world exploded into white searing pain. She screamed an animal scream as every nerve ending seemed to surge with burning electricity. She was immersed in an agony she could see no way through. Now, she thought, now she would die.

2.

Oliver knew he shouldn't have done it. This was far too risky, but the risk gave his appetite an added edge. And when he thought about it, maybe it wasn't any more risky than going through an escort agency again. After his last encounter there would always be the danger that word had got around. The next time he turned up he could find the police waiting. This was easier. And, unlike when he paid a whore, there was a real chance he might meet someone through his ad who reflected his passion: someone who would *want* him to do what he did.

A different bar, a different variation on the expected retro-cool, the same anticipation and reflection as he waited for her to arrive. Her answer had been perfect. 'Suzi22' had, of all the replies to his advertisement, been the only one who had sounded right. It was clear that she was genuine, and the photograph she had uploaded with her reply looked genuine too. It was a poor digital beach shot and she had been wearing a bikini, but her face had been deliberately obscured. She had a full figure: not as heavy around the hips as Oliver would have liked, but it was a face-on shot and therefore he couldn't see her backside which could, of course, be gloriously fleshy. And there was also the fact that she had expressed very eloquently where her desires lay.

'Hans?' Oliver turned. She was not too tall and not as full-figured as the photograph had promised. But she had a certain sexiness about her and her backside was a decent size. Enough to get his teeth into.

'Yes . . . Suzi?'

'That's me. Or it's not really, just like I suppose you're not really Hans. But let's see how the evening goes and we can take it from there.'

Oliver smiled. She was smart too. And knew what she wanted. He just hoped that she understood, fully, what it was that *he* wanted.

Suzi declined Oliver's offer of dinner.

'Let's just go somewhere private,' she said and smiled a wicked crimson smile. 'I think we both have an appetite that pasta isn't going to satisfy.'

Oliver felt his heart pick up the pace and a stirring in his groin. 'Let's go to my hotel room.'

'No,' she said. 'Not your hotel. My place. I feel safer there and we won't have to worry about . . . well, *noise.*'

Oliver thought it over. He didn't like the idea of an unknown location. His hotel had, again, been carefully selected. And he had to be very careful. He knew that, if things didn't go his way, he would not be able to control his temper and it could get messy. He needed to know his way out of wherever he was.

'Are you sure?' he asked. 'I thought a hotel room was, well, neutral ground, I suppose.'

'Listen, *Hans*,' Suzi said, still smiling but with resolve in her voice. 'We both know what we want. We are different from others. Our needs. But I need to have my things around. For after. You know, to fight infection, that kind of thing. Trust me, Hans, I think this could be the start of a beautiful friendship. Now, are you coming or not?'

Oliver looked at her for a moment, then said decisively: 'Okay. Let's go . . .'

3.

The last bucket had been filled with iced water. The shock after the hot water had robbed Maria of her breath – and, for several seconds, of her consciousness. When she came round her heart was hammering and intense pain shot through her left arm and across her chest. She had heard of people dying from heart attacks in cold plunge pools after too long in the sauna. What she had experienced had been the same experience amplified a hundredfold. The pain eased, but she knew that her heart probably would not withstand many more of these temperature shocks. Maria was also aware that she had lost even more body heat. Her mind was becoming fuzzy.

Vitrenko stood over her. She looked up at him and, for a second, saw his former face and gold-blond hair. Then the illusion faded. His hair darkened, his face reshaped around the unchanging eyes. He crouched down and grabbed a handful of her short dyed-black hair, snapping her head back and forcing her to look at him.

'How did it feel to be someone else, Maria?' Vitrenko's emerald eyes glittered hard and cold in his new face. 'It's liberating, isn't it? For a while you actually do become the person you pretend to be. You thought you had got to know Taras Buslenko. Oh yes, he does exist. Or at least he did. Like you, Buslenko took everything far too seriously. This is just business. But Buslenko was an eager young fool. A patriot. He was full of all kinds of romantic ideals about what Ukraine could be. And, just like you, he made it his personal mission to find me and kill me. So everything I said to you . . . all that really was him. He lived again through me. In a way, you really did get to know the real Buslenko. What's it like to get to know a dead man?' Vitrenko let go of Maria's hair and her head fell forward. 'You wanted to kill me too, didn't you, Maria? You wanted it so badly that you were prepared to sacrifice your life to take mine. But the real Maria Klee wasn't up to the task, was she? First you had to become someone else. And the reason you had to do that is that you were too broken and too afraid before. But I'll tell you something right now: the old Maria was right. You should have stayed afraid.'

'I need to sleep . . .' was all Maria managed to utter.

'Okay,' said Vitrenko. He smiled and suddenly his voice became warm and friendly. Vitrenko became Buslenko again. 'I'll let you sleep, Maria. With blankets to keep you cosy. Out there, outside the cold store, in the warm. I'll give you a hot drink before you sleep. The access codes . . . all you have to do is give me the access codes or tell me where they are and I'll allow you out of here and let you get some sleep.'

Maria became aware that she had stopped shivering. She was beginning to feel warmer. Even more sleepy. Her leaden eyelids slowly succumbed to gravity. She was going to cheat Vitrenko. Her eyes snapped open as he slapped her hard across the face.

'Maria – stay awake. If you fall asleep in here, you'll die. Out there . . . out there you can sleep and live. Tell me the access codes.'

'I forget . . .' Maria's eyes started to close again. Vitrenko started to shout and Maria vaguely thought that that was what swearing must sound like in Ukrainian. She felt his boot smash into her ribs, but she was too sleepy and already too distant from her own flesh to feel any pain.

Maria closed her eyes and slept.

4.

'This is it . . .' Suzi said. She had insisted that they take her car, which suited Oliver in one way because there had been no taxi driver to identify him. But it also meant that he had no quick getaway. Suzi led him up the stairs and into her apartment. There was a small hall with a number of doors off it, all but one of which were closed. The open door, he could see, led into the bedroom. He waited for her to show him into the lounge, but she guided him directly into the bedroom.

'What?' He grinned mischievously. 'No preliminaries?' He took in the bedroom. It was surprisingly characterless, almost functional, which was odd, given the size of Suzi's personality.

'Maybe a little chat first,' Suzi said. She sat down on the edge of the bed and patted the spot next to her. 'And then we'll have some fun.'

Oliver sat down. Suzi was beginning to annoy him. He had always seen himself as a predator, but it was almost as if she was leading their dance. Suddenly the situation seemed less appealing to him and Oliver was aware that he was being robbed of much of his enjoyment. He had never fully considered how much of his gratification came from his power over them. And from their horror. Their shock. Their fear.

No, he thought, I will lead this dance. Oliver felt the rage rise inside him. If she did not succumb to exactly what *he* wanted, then he would smash her face. This was not about her, or her needs: it was about him and his.

'Have you done this before?' asked Suzi. Her hair had been coiled up behind her head and she undid it. A glorious red, but much deeper than Sylvia's, the girl who had introduced him to his own hunger, so many years before.

'Of course I have,' he said. 'Lots of times. Why don't you get undressed? Let's get started.'

'Not yet,' said Suzi. 'I want to know if you've done this with other girls.'

'Yes, sure. Loads of them. I told you.'

'And they enjoyed it?'

'Well. Maybe not as much as you will. They misunderstood.'

'They didn't want you to do it but you did it anyway?'

'I don't know . . . yes, I suppose so. What does that matter?' Oliver frowned. This was ruining it. What did the stupid bitch have to talk for? He grabbed her roughly by the shoulders. 'You said in your reply that this is what you wanted. Let's do it.'

'You want to bite me?'

'Yes,' Oliver said, breathless. Lust and anger robbed him of oxygen. 'I'm going to bite you.'

'You want to make me bleed and tear flesh from my buttocks?' Suzi drew closer to him. He could smell her body, her hair. 'Like you bit the others?'

'Yes . . .' He started to pull at her blouse. He saw the swell of her breast. Full, warm flesh.

'Not yet,' she said firmly and pushed him away. 'Tell me about them . . .'

'I hurt them.' Oliver felt the rage surge in him. 'I really fucking hurt them and now I'm going to hurt you, you fucking slut!' he screamed at her. 'You're just a tease and a whore, but now I'm going to teach you a real lesson. I'm going to bite you and fuck you and if you're not quiet I'll kick the shit out of you.' He lunged at her, swinging his fist into the side of her face.

The blow didn't connect. There was a sharp pain on the inside of his forearm where she had blocked the blow, followed by an agonising explosion in his groin as her knee slammed into it. The rage changed to confusion and then to fear as he realised that she had twisted his arm round behind him and slammed him against the wall. He couldn't move. He couldn't see much either, with his cheek pushed hard into the wall. There were other noises. Crashes. Shouting. The room filled with dark figures. They had guns. There were other hands on him now. Handcuffs. Suzi spun him around. She pushed the thick copper coils of hair from her face.

'Now, *Hans* . . . now I'll tell you my real name. Just like I promised. It's Tansu Bakrac. Criminal Commissar Tansu Bakrac. And you, you perverted piece of shit, are under arrest.'

As they led him out of the flat, Oliver noticed that the doors off the hall were now open. Empty rooms. No furniture. That was where all the other police had been waiting; that was why she had led him directly into the bedroom: it was all a masquerade. They had probably recorded every word he had exchanged with 'Suzi' since they met in the hotel.

There were two other plain-clothes police officers waiting in the hall. Of course, Oliver knew the shorter dark-haired one who now looked at him in shock. 'Suzi' turned to the taller, blond-haired officer whom Oliver had not seen before and grinned.

'That was some favour you asked . . .'

5.

'What's up with you, Benni?' Fabel asked as Tansu and the uniformed officers led 'Hans' out to the waiting police cars. 'You look like you've seen a ghost.'

'Shit . . .' said Scholz, his expression still one of shock. 'Bloody hell . . .'

'What's up?' Tansu's triumphant grin gave way to a frown.

'Don't you know who that is? You've just arrested Herr Dr Oliver Lüdeke.'

'The forensic pathologist?'

'One and the same. Now the crap is really going to hit the fan.'

'A forensic pathologist . . .' said Fabel. 'Someone who would be an expert at excising an exact quantity of human flesh.'

Scholz had led the questioning but had asked Fabel to partner him. Not that it had done any good. Fabel's dislike of Oliver Lüdeke had been instant and intense. He knew that he would have felt the same disdain for Lüdeke if he had met him at a cocktail party instead of as the chief suspect in an inquiry into two, and potentially three, horrific and brutal murders. Lüdeke had refused to answer any questions at all and had only been vocal in complaining about his unjustified detention.

'I don't need a weatherman to tell me that there's a shitstorm heading our way,' said Scholz to Fabel after they had terminated the interview. 'He's already been in touch with his lawyer – and you can bet the first calls his lawyer's made have been to the State Prosecutor and the Police President. We've got to nail him quick.'

'So you're convinced he's our man? Even although you know him personally?'

Scholz snorted. '*Especially* because I know him personally.'

'You don't like him?' asked Fabel.

'Oliver Lüdeke is good-looking, charming, rich, clearly highly intelligent, has a highly paid, prestigious job and is regularly seen in the company of a string of beautiful women. Of course I hate the bastard. But putting that aside, there are a whole lot of other reasons why I've never liked Herr Dr Lüdeke. He's an arrogant son of a bitch. No – more than that. He has this way about him . . . I don't know, it's difficult to explain. He doesn't fit in Cologne. I know that doesn't make sense but class means nothing here. Karl Marx was from Cologne, but he said he could never start the international revolution here . . . it would never catch on in a city where the labourer and the factory manager drink in the same pub. Take the other state forensic pathologists: great guys to work with. Great guys to get pissed with. But Lüdeke looks down his nose at you every time you speak to him.'

'So you're saying he's a good suspect because he's a snob?'

'Snobbery doesn't come close, Jan. With Lüdeke it's more like we are all lower forms of life. It doesn't take a stretch for me to see him as someone who believes others have been put on this Earth to provide him with what he wants out of life. And that would fit with a sexual predator who doesn't give a damn about inflicting pain on those he uses to fulfil his needs. Or even killing them.'

'He's certainly the strongest suspect we've got so far. But if he's as connected as you say he is, then we're going to have to move quick to prevent him walking. What's the situation with a warrant to get a DNA sample?'

'Tansu's chasing the State Prosecutor's office,' said Scholz. 'We should get one in a couple of hours or so.'

'Okay,' said Fabel. 'Let's have another go at chummy.'

'Oh shit . . .' said Scholz, looking over Fabel's shoulder. Fabel turned to see a heavy-set man in his fifties coming along the corridor towards them. Fabel recognised the attitude of

authority about him. When he reached them Scholz introduced Fabel to Cologne's Police President, Udo Kettner.

'This is an awkward situation, Benni,' said Kettner.
'Potentially very embarrassing. You don't seem to have a lot
to go on.'

'He was about to attack Tansu,' said Scholz.

'You'll find that difficult to prove.'

'We have it on tape,' said Fabel.

'What you've got on tape, Herr Fabel, could be construed
as entirely consistent with the nature of the advertisement he
placed. He's going to argue that the manner of his arrest
amounts to entrapment. Added to which, he can claim that
he did nothing wrong other than, as an unmarried man,
meeting a young woman to explore a mutually consensual
sexual encounter.'

'I smell lawyer talk,' said Scholz.

'They're on the way in . . .' Police President Kettner said
wearily. 'I got a call within thirty minutes of Lüdeke being
arrested. They're going to challenge the legitimacy of the
arrest and the set-up behind it.'

'So what do we do?' asked Scholz.

Kettner grinned. 'Lüdeke's lawyers aren't the only ones who
can use a phone.' He handed Scholz a document. 'I thought
a little leaning on the State Prosecutor's office might speed
things up. Here's your warrant to obtain DNA. But for Christ's
sake, Benni, make sure you do everything by the book.'

Fabel, Tansu and Scholz sat in Scholz's office. The latest 'bull'
head watched them from the corner. Scholz contemplated it
dourly.

'We have only eight days until Women's Karneval Night,'
he said. 'I hope to God Lüdeke is our guy. If that DNA
doesn't check out then we're screwed.'

'Even if it does,' said Fabel, 'it only ties him into the rape
and battery of Vera Reinartz. He's clearly a sexual sadist with

a cannibalism fixation, but without a confession or other corroborating evidence we'll never get him for the murders. And given Lüdeke's arrogance and the hourly rate he's paying his lawyers, we're never going to get a confession.'

'Forensics have turned up nothing. His office and apartment are both clean,' said Scholz glumly. 'The annoying thing is that the very weapon he's used to slice chunks out of his victims may well be right under our noses. I've never had a suspect whose job it's been to cut up human beings. It's a forensic nightmare. If only Vera Reinartz or Andrea Sandow or whatever she wants to call herself had kept just one of those bloody letters.'

'Even then that would only tie him directly in with the attack on her,' said Fabel. 'All we've got to link him to the murders is the similarity of m.o.: the necktie around the victims' necks and the biting. Circumstantial. Listen, Benni, we may never nail him for the killings, but if we get him for the Reinartz rape and assault, we can at least be content that we've taken him off the street for Women's Karneval Night. We get a conviction and it'll be a few Karnevals before he sees the light of day again. Only, of course, if we get a DNA match.'

The thought was interrupted by the pale schoolboy face of Kris Feilke appearing around the door.

'We've got the bastard, Benni!' Kris beamed. 'We've got a perfect match. Oliver Lüdeke is the man who raped Vera Reinartz.'

6.

Andrea opened the door of her apartment to Tansu and Fabel. She was dressed in a short skirt and loose black blouse. There was also a cluster of heavy costume jewellery at each wrist and her face was even more made up than the last time Fabel had seen her. She could not have presented herself more femininely, yet the sheer stockings only served to accentuate the heavy musculature of her thighs, the blouse the breadth of her shoulders and the make-up the masculine angularity of her features. What was it about Andrea Sandow, thought Fabel, that provoked such hostility within him?

'I was just about to go out,' she explained.

'This won't take long,' said Fabel and made to enter the apartment. Andrea did not move.

'I have an appointment. I can't be late.'

'We've got him, Andrea,' said Tansu. 'The man who attacked you eight years ago.'

'You sure it's him?' Whatever Andrea was thinking, it didn't penetrate the mask.

'Positive,' said Fabel. 'We've got a perfect DNA match. It's a man called Oliver Lüdeke.'

The mask shattered. Andrea gazed at Fabel in disbelief. 'Oliver Lüdeke?'

'You know him?'

Andrea stood to one side. 'You'd better come in. I have to make a call – see if I can put back my appointment . . .'

7.

Again, Maria found herself anchorless in time. She had no idea how long she had been asleep or unconscious. It could have been a few minutes or a few days. Her first awareness on awakening was pain: in her ribs, in her face, and a hot, sharp tingling on her rasped skin. Maria grabbed onto the pain. It was the lesson that Vitrenko had taught her: that pain meant life.

She awoke to find herself lying on a mattress on top of a metal camp bed. They had dressed her again and her clothes smelled musty and dirty. There were several blankets over her and she saw that she was still in the cold-meat store. No, not still; she realised that they must have taken her out of the store to warm her up and stop her terminal decline into a hypothermic death. That would have taken time and skill. Maria rolled up the sleeves of her coat and jumper. She found what she was looking for on her left arm: a fresh puncture wound into a vein. Her brain was still running sluggishly and her head pounded but she knew what this meant: they would have administered a warm dextrose and saline drip to increase her core body temperature, and they would probably have put a mask on her to administer warm, humidified oxygen.

Maria knew that she was already a dead woman. And before she died there would be a lot of pain: both for Vitrenko's enjoyment and to extract whatever information he could from her. But Maria was aware that what she knew was not enough for him to keep her alive. He was going to use her somehow to gain access to the dossier he was obsessed with. She had to escape: it was the only way for her to survive. And to stop Vitrenko from winning.

Maria still felt chilled to the core. She sat up on the edge of the bed and gathered the musty blankets around her. She removed her glove and waved her naked hand through the air. The temperature in the cold store was tolerable. It would have taken a long time to remove the chill from the air. There were no heaters in sight but she surmised that they must have been used. Maria's guess was that she had been taken out, treated for hypothermia and kept sedated somewhere until the temperature in the store had risen sufficiently. This was no longer a torture chamber, merely a place of confinement. For the moment.

Maria tried to stand but an electric shock of pain from her cracked ribs jolted her. She allowed her fingers to explore gingerly beneath her jumper. Her ribs had been strapped. She eased back on the camp bed and thought about Buslenko, someone who had existed for her only through Vitrenko's masquerade. She lay still, looking up at the ceiling with its bleak, relentless neon light and mourned a man she didn't know.

The door opened and a tall heavy-set man came in, carrying a bowl. Maria didn't recognise him but he had a distinctly Russian or Ukrainian look. His hair was cropped short and his nose showed signs of an ancient break. He placed the bowl next to her bed and left the cold store without speaking. So there were others now. For all she knew, Vitrenko had left and was going about his more important business. Maria made a mental picture of the guard who had delivered the food. I'll call him The Nose, she thought. She ate the stew. It was so hot that it burned her mouth but she didn't care. She relished the scalding heat in her chest and belly and consumed every morsel.

She had been surprised to find a metal spoon in the bowl. When she finished the stew she licked it clean and rubbed it against the stone floor next to the camp bed. After a minute or two she ran her thumb along the edge of the spoon: yes, she could sharpen it; create a weapon. She picked at the stitching of the mattress and concealed the spoon inside. She pulled the blanket over her eyes as a shield against the perpetual light from the neon strip. She couldn't sleep. Her head buzzed as she conceived, elaborated and then rejected one plan of escape after another. She might not be fed again that day, but that was the only opportunity for escape. Even when she was fully fit she would have been no match for The Nose. She would have to take him by surprise and kill him quickly. If she worked at sharpening the edge of that spoon, she could maybe have a go at slashing the artery in his neck. She would have only one chance.

The door opened. Maria feigned sleep beneath the blanket. She heard the sound of heavy boots approaching. There would be no surprise attack now. It would need at least another day of preparation, of sharpening the spoon into a killing edge. The blanket was ripped from her head. She turned, blinking, to look up at The Nose who had collected her food bowl. He held out his hand, moving his fingers in a 'give me' gesture.

Maria frowned as if confused. He repeated the gesture and she shrugged. The Nose sighed wearily, put the bowl back down and unholstered his heavy automatic. He snapped back the carriage, clicked off the safety and rammed the barrel of the gun into Maria's cheek. He then repeated the 'give me' gesture with his free hand. Maria reached into the pocket she had fashioned in the mattress and removed the spoon. She handed it to The Nose with a cynical grin, which he returned, simultaneously slashing her across the forehead with the barrel of his automatic.

Maria glared defiant hate at The Nose, focusing on staying conscious and feeling the blood from the gash on her forehead trickle down the side of her face. Neither of them were in any doubt that she wanted to kill him, but The Nose simply gazed back at her impassively before turning and leaving with the bowl and the spoon. After he left, the light went out. Maria remembered there was a switch just outside the door. She was grateful for the sudden total darkness. She could sleep without cowering beneath the stinking blanket. She lay back in the pitch black and vowed not to touch the wound on her head.

Something was happening to her. It was as if the pain was shaping her resolve, sharpening her mind. She felt new clarity, a new purity of thought. Mortification of the flesh, they called it. The pain became like a background noise: the further she placed herself from it the more dislocated from her physical being she would become. Maria focused all her energy on her thoughts. There had to be a way out of this.

8.

'You know Oliver Lüdeke?'

'Yes . . .' Andrea looked into the air as if seeing into the past. She shook her head. 'I can't believe it. Lüdeke. You're sure?'

'Yes,' said Tansu. 'There's no doubt about it. How did you know him?'

'We were medical students together.' Andrea crossed her legs and the hem of her skirt rode up a little. Fabel noticed that a few centimetres of the top of her thigh were exposed above her stocking, the skin tanned dark over a ripple of muscle.

'Where are you going tonight?' he asked. 'I mean, if it's an important appointment, then we could come back later, or even tomorrow.' Fabel used the word 'appointment' just as she had. Not 'date'. Not 'meeting with friends'.

'No, it's fine. I've explained that I'll be delayed.' She turned back to Tansu. 'When I say we were medical students together, I mean he was a couple of years ahead of me. But we all knew him. He was a bit of a heart-throb for a few of the female students.'

'You too?' asked Fabel.

Andrea fixed him with her hard, masculine stare. 'I suppose. I was like that back then. Soft. But he never seemed to notice me. I can't believe that he . . .' Her expression hardened even more. 'The bastard. Leave me alone with him for half an hour and I'll save you all a lot of time and trouble. Why? Why did he do that to me?'

'It would appear that Lüdeke is a very sick individual,' said Fabel. 'You're probably not his only victim, and some of the others didn't survive. But it looks like we're going to have some difficulty proving that.'

'But if we can convict him of the attack on you,' said Tansu, 'then we'll be able to put him away for a long time. Hopefully long enough to build a case against him for the murders.'

'Are you prepared to give evidence against him?' asked Fabel.

'Of course I am.'

'It's just that it may be an ordeal for you. In court, I mean.'

Andrea laughed bitterly. 'Do you think that that shit can scare me now? I'll look forward to facing him across a courtroom and telling everybody exactly what he did to me.'

'Good . . .' Fabel paused for a moment. 'You say you knew him by sight. As a student, I mean.'

'Yes.'

'But you didn't recognise him that night?'

'No – he was all made up. As a clown.'

'I have to ask this,' said Fabel. 'There's no way Lüdeke is going to be able to claim consensual sex, is there? I mean, if you knew him and had a thing for him.'

'Are you mad?' A vein throbbed visibly in Andrea's neck. 'He nearly killed me. Didn't you see the state he left me in?'

'Listen, Frau Sandow . . .' Fabel made his tone as conciliatory as possible. 'You have to trust me when I say I know exactly how sick and perverted this creep is. But I just need to know if things had maybe started off consensual and then got out of hand. It's an angle his defence may take.'

'No. I was at that party that I told you about. When I came out there was a clown in the street. He seemed to just stare at me, not moving. I started to walk home, then I realised he was following me. I ran and he ran after me. I thought I'd lost him in the crowd, then he appeared out of nowhere at the church. St Ursula's. Then he raped me, beat me, then raped me again. All the time he had his tie pulled tight around my neck, half strangling me.'

'And he bit you?'

'Over and over again.'

'We've got the forensic photographs of the bites,' said Fabel. 'We'll get a match from an impression of his teeth. Trust me, Frau Sandow, he's going to prison for a long time.'

'I would never have thought of him. I thought it was a stranger. Some psychopath who happened to pick on me.' Andrea looked as if she was lost in her memories, then she became galvanised as a thought hit her. 'Maybe he was at the party! When I was questioned, they asked me for the names of all the men there but I couldn't give them many. I mean it was Karneval and everybody was in disguise. You know, fancy dress and stuff. So he could have been there. I know they questioned all the male students in my year.'

'It was a medical student party?' asked Tansu.

'Mainly. But not exclusively. Tell me, will he be released pending trial?'

'Not if we can help it,' said Fabel.

'Don't worry, Andrea,' said Tansu. 'We'll keep him away from you.'

'I'm not worried,' said Andrea, again with the hard, male stare. 'Like I said, it's he who should worry if we were ever to come across each other again.'

On the way back to Tansu's car, Fabel looked back at Andrea's apartment building as if he could read an answer from it.

'What's up?' asked Tansu.

'Did you see the way Andrea was dressed?'

'She looked like she was going out on a date. To be honest, without the muscle behind it I would have called that outfit almost tarty. What about it?'

'That's it,' said Fabel. 'She looked as if she was dressed for a date but she kept on talking about an appointment. Like it was business. I have the weirdest idea . . . Don't laugh, but I think our musclewoman moonlights. As a hooker.'

Chapter Eleven

Women's Karneval Night. 23 February.

I.

The world had gone mad by the time Fabel walked into the Cologne Police Presidium. Today was Women's Karneval Day and even the security officers were wearing fancy dress. In the Murder Commission, Benni Scholz was sitting behind his desk wearing full uniform – except, Fabel noticed, it was a female officer's uniform.

'Now, Principal Chief Commissar Fabel,' said Scholz in warning. 'Don't start getting ideas . . .'

Tansu Bakrac came in wearing an all-in-one catsuit, complete with fluffy ears and painted-on whiskers. Fabel found himself noticing her curves. Kris Feilke was dressed as a Wild West sheriff. The rest of the officers were similarly attired, including – rather inappropriately, thought Fabel – several dressed as clowns.

'I must say, Jan,' said Tansu in mock reproach, 'you could have made an effort.'

The truth was that Fabel did feel rather out of place without a fancy-dress outfit. Instead, he was dressed in his usual Jaeger sports jacket, black roll-neck and chinos. At least he'd remembered not to wear a tie.

The team assembled in Scholz's office.

'Okay,' Scholz said, summoning as much seriousness as his outfit would allow. 'All of you are on duty until midnight, after which we're all going to the pub where we're going to show our Hamburg colleague here what a real party is like. Until then, however, I want you to stick to the routes you've been allocated and keep your eyes peeled. The Karneval Cannibal has always struck before midnight on Women's Karneval Night. Of course, we have our number one suspect banged up and if we make it until midnight without incident, then it proves we've got the right man.'

Scholz spent a further ten minutes confirming which teams were covering which routes and repeating his order that no one was to touch a drop until they got the all-clear from him.

'You sure you want to take the duty you've asked for?' Scholz asked Fabel afterwards. 'I could put a uniformed unit on that.'

'No . . . all I ask is that I can borrow Tansu for her local knowledge,' said Fabel.

'So long as that's all you borrow her for,' said Scholz and nudged Tansu. 'She looks pretty sexy in that cat outfit.' For a moment Fabel couldn't think of a response and there was an awkward silence. 'Anyway, keep in touch,' said Scholz. 'If you need anything just shout. I hope to God we've got the right guy, Jan. Women's Karneval Night is insane – it's the first big event of the climax of Karneval. There's a dozen processions throughout the city, along with more parties than you can shake a stick at. From tonight until Rose Monday the city will be crazy. Not the ideal conditions for catching a psycho on the loose.'

'Everything points to Lüdeke,' said Fabel. 'The cannibal fetish, the necktie used to strangle the victims, the violent aggression towards women . . .'

'Why do I get the feeling that you're not convinced?' Scholz frowned.

'There's clearly a link between his attack on Vera Reinartz and the killings. It's just that something's missing. Why rape one victim and none of the others?' Fabel sighed. 'Forget it, I'm just overthinking things. I'm sure Lüdeke's our guy.'

'So am I,' said Scholz. He winced and pulled at his skirt. 'Now, if you'll excuse me I need to adjust my tights before I hit the streets.'

Tansu parked across the street from Andrea's apartment.

'You still think this is necessary?' asked Tansu.

'Just a feeling I've got. If we keep an eye on her for Women's Karneval Night I'll feel a lot happier.'

'Well, I suppose it won't do any harm and we've got a party to go to afterwards. I think we'll feel like celebrating.'

The street began to fill with revellers moving from party to party. Fabel was glad to have Tansu's protection as he noticed bands of gaudily clad women roaming the street. He felt strange to still be in his own country yet have everything around him seem so foreign.

'You find this all a bit much, don't you?' Tansu read his thoughts.

'No . . . well, yes.' Fabel laughed. 'I've never seen anything like it.'

'Well, you're not a *Jeck*, you're not even an *Imi*. It takes getting used to.' Tansu read the confusion of Fabel's face. 'It's *Kölsch* dialect. A *Jeck* is someone born in Cologne. A true Cologner. That would be me or Benni. There's an expression in *Kölsch* that defines what it is to be a Cologner: *Mer sinn all jet jeck, äver jede Jeck es anders* . . . it means that all Jecks are crazy but each in his own way. An *Imi* is someone who lives in Cologne but was born somewhere else in Germany or abroad – like Andrea up there.'

'So what am I?' asked Fabel with a smile.

'You're a *Jass*, a guest.'

A group of women came down the street, singing loudly in *Kölsch*. Fabel had heard the song before but couldn't place it. They passed the car noisily and stopped at the corner of the street where they ritually accosted a group of young men.

'This is nothing, by the way,' said Tansu. 'Wait until Rose Monday. That'll really confuse you. Nothing is what it seems and nobody is who you think they are. For example the whole of Karneval is headed up by the Three Stars . . . there's the *Prinz Karneval*, the Master of the Carnival who's addressed as His Craziness, the *Kölsch* Peasant and the *Kölsch* Virgin. And, of course, the Virgin is always a man in drag.'

Fabel laughed. 'I've noticed you're big on that down here. I thought Benni looked less than virginal.' He looked up at Andrea's apartment. The blinds were up and the lights were on. 'That's one person who's not going to get into the spirit of things tonight. No matter what she's done to herself physically or her aggressive attitude, Andrea Sandow is still Vera Reinartz. A broken individual.' Fabel's gaze fell back to the street.

'What is it?' asked Tansu.

'Over there . . . that man.' Fabel nodded in the direction of a figure standing across the street from Andrea's apartment. He too was looking up at the lit window and was all the more conspicuous because of his lack of any Karneval attire. 'I've seen him before.'

'Yes, you have,' said Tansu. 'That's Ansgar Hoeffer. He's the chef at the Speisekammer. He was hanging around outside the café when we first talked to Andrea. Now this is more than a coincidence.'

They watched as Ansgar crossed the street towards the entrance of Andrea's apartment building.

'I think we should have a word . . .' said Fabel, his hand on the door handle. They had just got out when a knot of revellers swamped the car. Tansu and Fabel struggled to get through but one large lady grabbed Fabel and planted a kiss on his lips, to the cheers of her companions.

'Let me through,' shouted Fabel. 'Police!'

Still he struggled through the knot of revellers. He saw that Ansgar had turned in his direction. A scared recognition registered on his face. Shit, thought Fabel, he's going to run. 'Herr Hoeffer!' he called over the shoulder of an obese Snow White who stood in his way. Hoeffer turned and ran towards the far end of the street. Fabel and Tansu shoved their way through the crowd.

'Stay here,' shouted Fabel. 'Call for back-up but stay and watch Andrea.' He tore off down the street after Hoeffer. He rounded the corner only to be faced with a throng of revellers. He stopped in his tracks and scanned the crowd. It was only because Ansgar was hatless and in everyday clothes that he caught sight of him pushing a path through the mob. Fabel sprinted after him but collided with the same wall of flesh. He barged his way through and was met with the occasional jeer as he roughly shoved revellers out of his way.

'Police!' he shouted repeatedly into the faceless throng. He felt immersed in communal madness. Fabel rammed into something solid. He looked up to see a two-metre-plus tall, 120-kilo ballerina with a beard. The ballerina grabbed Fabel by the neck of his jacket.

'What's the rush?' boomed the ballerina's baritone. 'You trying to spoil everyone's fun?'

Fabel didn't have time for explanations and slammed his knee into the ballerina's tutu and the grip on his jacket was released. He broke through the crowd and caught sight of Ansgar running around the next corner. The cold air seemed to sear Fabel's lungs as he sprinted to the corner and around into the next street. He thought about radioing in but, without Tansu, he had no idea where he was. Suddenly he found himself in a dark, quiet side street. It was only wide enough to allow cars to park along one side, leaving clearance for a single stream of one-way traffic. Fabel stopped. He had seen Ansgar run into the street and had closed the gap enough to be sure that the chef hadn't had time to make it to the far end. He was here somewhere. Hiding. Fabel walked slowly down the roadway, checking between the parked cars.

'Give it up, Herr Hoeffer,' he called breathlessly. 'We know who you are and we'll track you down sooner or later. All I want to do is talk to you.'

Silence.

'Please, Herr Hoeffer. This will do you no good . . .'

A dark figure rose from between two parked cars, about ten metres further down the street.

'I didn't mean any harm . . .' Ansgar's voice was high and pleading. 'I didn't. She let me do it before. I just wanted to do it again . . . I'm sick . . .'

Fabel moved closer. Slowly. Reaching into his belt, he removed his set of handcuffs. 'We can talk about it, Herr Hoeffer. I want to talk about it. To understand. But you need to come with me. You understand that, don't you?' Fabel eased between the parked cars. There was a flash: a glint of sharp steel as Ansgar took something from his coat pocket. Fabel reached for his gun which was not there. As a visiting officer from another city's force, Fabel was unarmed. Ansgar held the blade in front of him, shaking.

'I'm sick,' he repeated. 'A pervert. I don't deserve to live . . . I can't stand this chaos . . .' The blade flashed in the dim street light as it arced first upwards, then down – towards Ansgar's abdomen. Ansgar was hurled off his feet as Fabel slammed into him. The impact threw Ansgar against the wall and the knife fell with a clatter.

'No, you don't,' said Fabel as he turned Ansgar onto his belly and twisted his arms behind him, clasping the handcuffs shut. 'I've lost one already that way.'

2.

'So who's our killer?' asked Scholz. 'I am seriously fucking confused. We have positive proof that it was Lüdeke who raped Vera-cum-Andrea in 'ninety-nine, yet now we find Ansgar Hoeffer loitering outside her apartment and he's ready to make a confession.'

'A confession to what, we don't know yet,' said Fabel.

'Well, I think we can hazard a guess . . . The search of his apartment has turned up this pile of goodies.' Scholz indicated a cardboard evidence box on his desk. 'And we've done a quick check of his computer. Three guesses what his favourite website is?'

'*Anthropophagi?*'

'In one,' said Scholz.

Fabel looked through the contents of the evidence box. A few magazines, DVDs, older VHS tapes. Fabel read some of the DVD titles, all of which were variations on a theme: *Flesh-Eating Zombie Women, Cannibals of Lesbos, Food for the Demon Women.*

'What's up?' asked Scholz. 'Seen something you want to borrow?'

'There's something wrong here. Doesn't fit. Let's go talk to him. In the meantime, I think Tansu should stay outside Andrea Sandow's place, just until we hit midnight. Have you updated her on what's happened?'

'Yep . . . she says this better not interfere with her going to the party . . . '

Fabel looked Scholz up and down. 'By the way,' he said, with a grin. 'I think you should maybe think about changing out of your skirt before we question him . . .'

Fabel found himself feeling genuinely sorry for Ansgar Hoeffer. He sat in the interview room pale and sad, his cheek bruised from its encounter with the wall that Fabel had rammed him into.

'Why were you outside Andrea Sandow's apartment?' asked Scholz.

'I wanted to see her. I needed . . .' He let the thought die.

'Needed what?' asked Fabel.

'I have this thing . . .'

'About cannibalism?' asked Scholz. Ansgar looked up, surprised.

'How did you know?'

'Don't be stupid, Ansgar,' said Scholz. 'You know what this is all about. You know why you're here. And anyway, we've seen your dirty-film library.'

'I didn't think I was doing anything illegal . . .' Ansgar looked at the detectives pleadingly.

Scholz was about to say something but Fabel cut him off. Everything fell into place.

'Ansgar,' said Fabel urgently, 'do you know who Vera Reinartz is?'

'No . . .'

'I didn't think you would. But you know Andrea Sandow?'

'I only know her as Andrea. Andrea the Amazon. I hadn't seen her since it happened. Then, the other week, just by chance . . . so I followed her. Found out where she worked. Where she lived.'

'When did you first meet her?'

'I only met her the once. Three years ago. I hired her through an escort agency. *À la Carte*. I paid her . . .'

Scholz exchanged a look with Fabel.

'You paid her. What did you pay her to do, Ansgar?'

'I can show you . . .' Ansgar stood up, loosened his belt and turned sideways so that Fabel and Scholz could see as he eased his trousers and shorts down to expose his buttock.

* * *

3.

Tansu sat in the car and watched the lit window of Andrea's apartment. She was bored and could think of a dozen better ways to spend Women's Karneval Night. But this was what she had become a policewoman for: to watch and protect. It gave her comfort that whether it was Lüdeke or Hoeffer who was the killer, the chances were that the streets were safe tonight. Andrea would be safe tonight.

Something, someone passed across the window. Tansu gave a small laugh. She was imagining things. She could have sworn it had been . . . No, that was mad. The light went out. Tansu picked up her radio. No. There was nothing to report. What she had thought she had seen didn't make sense. Andrea was probably just turning in, hoping to put Women's Karneval Night behind her. Tansu decided to check it out anyway.

The street was still thronging with people and Tansu dodged round clumps of revellers to reach the entry of Andrea's apartment building. She buzzed up and waited a minute for a reply that didn't come. She was just about to buzz again when a group of partygoers came down the stairs. Tansu caught the door before it swung shut behind them and made her way up the stairwell.

Tansu knocked on the door. No answer. She knocked louder.

'Andrea!' she called through the closed door. 'Andrea! It's Commissar Bakrac from the Criminal Police. Let me in!'

Again no response, but this time Tansu heard sounds from inside the apartment. Her heart began to pound: what if she had really seen what she thought she'd seen at the window? She unholstered her service automatic, clicked off the safety and held it pointed to the ceiling. 'Andrea . . . I think you are in danger. I'm coming in.' Tansu stepped back and took a deep breath. She swung her boot at the door. Then again. The lock splintered and the door flew open. She could see along the apartment's hall but the rooms off it lay in darkness.

She debated about taking precious seconds to call for back-up. But Andrea could be dead by then. She edged along the hall, her back pressed against the wall. She knocked a hanging photograph from its hook and it crashed onto the floor. Tansu glanced down and saw that it was a picture of a young woman: pretty, with long brownish hair and a floaty summer dress. Vera, before she had made a mess of her body with weightlifting and steroids. Before she had become Andrea. Before that bastard Lüdeke had screwed her up.

'Andrea?' Tansu swung into the door frame of the first room, sweeping the darkness with her gun. Nothing. But she had heard Andrea in the apartment. She had heard *someone*. She stepped quickly back into the hall. The door to the next room was closed. She reached forward for the handle, but the door swung suddenly open and a figure took two strides into the hall and slammed straight into Tansu. The Clown's sudden appearance stunned her for the fraction of a second it took him to grab the wrist of her gun hand. She staggered back but the Clown's grip remained vice-tight. He slammed her hand hard against the door jamb again and again until her grip yielded and her gun clattered to the floor. Tansu swung her free fist at the Clown's painted head but he blocked it with a rock-hard forearm. She struggled fruitlessly to free her other hand. The Clown snatched her by the throat and rammed her against the wall with terrific force. The impact winded Tansu and she struggled to refill her airways. The Clown let go of her throat and slammed his fist into her belly, just below the diaphragm, robbing her of the meagre air she had clawed back into her protesting lungs.

The Clown let go of her throat for a moment and Tansu felt something being looped around her neck. And as he tightened the ligature, all Tansu could do was stare into his face.

His grotesque clown face.

4.

Fabel and Scholz ran along the corridor and took the lift to the car pool.

'It's going to be like driving through sludge,' explained Scholz. 'We'll take one of the big MEK vans and go with lights and sirens. Hopefully the Red Sea'll part for us.' Scholz tried again to raise Tansu. Nothing. 'There are units in the area on their way as well. You knew, didn't you? How did you know?'

'About Ansgar? The porn was all wrong. There are two types of voreaphile – the ones who fantasise about eating another human being and the ones who fantasise about being eaten. Those are much more common. All the DVDs we seized from Hoeffer's place were about women eating men. And now we have the connection between the rape and the murders. Not a link. Cause and effect. I just hope we get there in time . . .'

5.

Tansu punched and kicked at her attacker, but she knew that her strength was failing. She put all her effort into focusing all her concentration, all her effort into one decisive action. She jabbed the straightened fingers of her free hand into the Clown's eye. He clutched his eye and the pressure around her throat eased. She swung her foot and hit the clown in the belly. He staggered back and Tansu aimed a kick at his groin but caught the top of his thigh. She tore the ligature from her neck. A man's tie, just as she'd expected. She threw herself along the hall's floor and reached for where her gun had fallen. Suddenly she felt as if the building had collapsed on her and realised that the Clown had thrown himself onto her back, winding her for a second time. He spun her round and clasped his hands around her throat. But he didn't squeeze.

Instead he yielded to the pressure of the muzzle of Tansu's service automatic, jammed into the flesh beneath his jaw.

'Just give me a fucking excuse,' Tansu said through tight-clenched teeth. 'After what you've done to all those women. Where's Andrea?'

There was the sound of boots running up the stairs and the door of the apartment flew open. Uniformed officers poured into the cramped hall and grabbed the Clown, forcing him to the floor and handcuffing his hands behind his back.

Tansu stood up and composed herself. 'I asked you, where is Andrea?'

'That is Andrea . . .' Tansu turned to see Fabel and Scholz in the hall. She looked down at the Clown. The male physique. The hard-set jaw.

'I don't believe it . . .'

'It's true,' said Scholz. 'That's why we didn't find any semen at the murder scenes.'

'She killed all those women?'

'All of them. But the first woman she killed was herself. Vera Reinartz.'

They stood back as the uniformed officers hauled Andrea to her feet. She stared at them with empty eyes, the only expression her painted smile. The officers led her out of the flat.

'That was the connection between the rape and the murders. Like I said to Benni: cause and effect. Lüdeke raped Andrea and subjected her to his perversion, biting her repeatedly. She hated herself, or rather herself as Vera, and she mimicked Lüdeke's attack on her. Except she took it further. She took flesh from each victim and ate it. A little extra twist she picked up after her encounter with Ansgar Hoeffer.'

'It was Jan who figured it out,' said Scholz. 'We came rushing to your rescue, but from what I hear you didn't need rescuing.'

'It was a close call,' said Tansu, rubbing her throat.

'You need to see a doctor?' asked Fabel.

'No – I need to see a barman. But I suppose we'll have to get some paperwork sorted out first.'

6.

The bar was small, bustling and noisy. It was exactly what Fabel needed. It was three in the morning and the party was still in full swing. Scholz, Fabel and Tansu had to lean forward and shout to be heard above the noise.

Andrea had been processed and was in the cells. Scholz had arranged for a psychiatric assessment to be done as soon as possible. Which wasn't going to be the following day. Even psychiatrists took time off to go insane during Karneval, apparently. Fabel and Scholz explained to Tansu about the wound to Ansgar's buttock and his sexual compulsion to be eaten; how *À la Carte*, with its reputation for catering for clients' more *unusual* needs had recruited Andrea and how Ansgar had become a client for one disfiguring night.

Now Andrea sat in her cell silent, answering no questions, responding to nothing. Fabel thought it was possible that maybe she didn't even know what she had done. They had found a diary in her apartment: the usual egomaniacal ravings, but they suggested that the Clown saw himself as male, and as totally distinct from Andrea's personality. Just as Andrea had forced her third-person, past-tense existence as Vera Reinartz from her identity.

'What, multiple personality?' asked Tansu. 'I thought that was all fake.'

'Dissociative Identity Disorder is the proper name for it,' said Fabel. 'And the Americans are great believers in it. But you're right, it's not accepted to the same extent by psychiatrists outside the US. My guess is, though, that Andrea is going to try to use it as a defence to avoid prison. Maybe the dumb act in the cells is exactly that, an act.'

They sat at a corner of the bar and Fabel found his *Stange* glass filled regularly with *Kölsch* beer without being asked. He grinned at the raucous songs in a dialect he didn't understand and he realised, joyfully, that he was very probably drunk. Tansu was next to him at the bar and every time she leaned into him to make herself heard he could feel the warmth of her body.

'Benni said you had Andrea sussed,' said Tansu. 'How?'

'A combination of things. Like what you said about the *Kölsch* Virgin being a man,' said Fabel. 'Karneval is all about becoming someone else, about letting out what you've locked up inside. There was something about Andrea that bothered me from the start. I was in the cathedral and a tourist asked me why there was a rhinoceros in one of the stained-glass windows. Amongst all those metaphors of resurrection, a symbol of strength and righteous wrath. That's what Andrea built herself to be. Andrea murdered those women because they reminded her of herself, as Vera. She killed Vera as an identity legally, then proceeded to kill her over and over again in the flesh. Oh, and the last clue was the very large slice of backside that Ansgar Hoeffer was missing. You didn't need to be Sherlock Holmes to work it out from there.'

They stopped discussing the case and Fabel felt himself slide further into a pleasant state of drunkenness. It was difficult to hear over the noise in the pub and their conversation became limited. Another group from the Police Presidium joined them and the consensus was that they should all move on somewhere else. Fabel spotted Scholz disappearing through the pub door with a pretty young woman dressed as a nun.

'Simone Schilling,' explained Tansu. 'Our forensics chief . . .'

Fabel allowed himself to be carried out of the pub and into the street by the current of bodies. The streets were thronging with partygoers and Fabel suddenly realised he had become separated from the police group and was cast adrift in an ocean of revellers. The night air made him feel even more drunk and he felt some of his old anxiety about losing control.

'I thought we'd lost you . . .' He turned to see Tansu beside him. 'I think we'd better find somewhere quieter. But first, there is a Women's Karneval Night custom that I insist on – I demand a kiss . . .'

'Well,' said Fabel grinning, 'if it's the law . . .' He leaned forward to give Tansu a chaste kiss on the cheek, but she held his face between her hands and pulled him towards her. He felt her tongue in his mouth.

Chapter Twelve

24–28 February

1.

The light was on and Maria woke up cold and sore. The chills and aches in her body combined like a string section playing a continuous glissando, but then the still not fully-healed wound on her head from The Nose's pistol-whipping took centre stage. For a moment she thought that they had switched the refrigeration back on, then she realised it was just her body's reaction to the abuse it had suffered. For Maria the cold no longer meant death; it meant she could still feel. It meant life.

But they've broken my mind, she thought to herself calmly. She knew there was something different about the way she thought; the way she felt. She lay and thought of Maria Klee as if she were someone she knew rather than someone she was. Maybe Maria Klee was dead, but whoever or whatever was left was determined to survive. She knew, lying bruised and broken in an empty cold store, that her only strategy for survival was to separate herself from her own flesh: to focus her mind and use whatever internal resources she had left on thinking her way out of this situation.

Maria dragged herself to her feet, wrapping the blanket around her body and moving across to the cold store heavy door. She pressed the side of her head against the cold steel, but it was too thick to conduct any sounds from the room beyond. She made a circuit of the meat locker, seeking out anything that might be useful as a weapon. There was nothing. And even if she had found something, she doubted that an improvised weapon would have given her any kind of chance against The Nose and his handgun. She returned to the mattress and sat contemplating her situation. They were feeding her. That meant that, for some reason, Vitrenko was keeping her alive, but perhaps only for a matter of days. She gingerly touched the raised ridge on her head to remind herself that there seemed to be little other consideration for her welfare. She was in a hostage situation. She could not have been kept in more appropriate surroundings: she was just a lump of meat being preserved until she could be put to some profitable use.

The next meal was brought in by Olga Sarapenko. The one after that by The Nose. Perhaps they spelled each other, taking shifts. If she was going to make an attempt to escape, it would be that bitch Sarapenko she would go for. Maria knew that she could never succeed against the Nose. And even fully fit she didn't know if she would have been a match for Olga Sarapenko. But one thing that her years in the Murder Commission had taught her was that anyone could kill anyone else. It wasn't about strength. It was about murderous intent. About knowing no boundaries.

Maria knew that even if Vitrenko intended to use her as a bargaining chip, there was still no way he would let her survive. And when she became surplus to his needs he would kill her in a manner that would fit his perverted sense of natural justice. It would be messy, it would be slow, and it would be painful. She brought her thoughts back to her immediate situation. She would escape Vitrenko and the fate he had planned for her, either by getting herself free or by dying in the attempt. She would escape either in flesh or in spirit.

Her plan began to take form.

There was a chance that either The Nose or Olga Sarapenko was alone in the building. The charade of a surveillance operation had been for her benefit. No . . . that wasn't right. There had been another point to the exercise: Vitrenko had suspected betrayal and had put Molokov under electronic surveillance. Molokov had been marked for death long before Maria had entered the picture. Vitrenko had said that Buslenko's mission had been genuine but had been betrayed. Perhaps Olga Sarapenko really had been part of the operation.

She had seen no other guard. When Sarapenko or The Nose had brought food there had been no sounds of activity outside when the door had been opened. The worst case might be that The Nose would be out there when Sarapenko came in. Maria played and replayed scenarios in her head, running through all the possible ways she could take Sarapenko down. But they would be ready for almost every scenario. Sarapenko or The Nose would anticipate her hiding beside the door, pretending to be ill or dead, or her launching a sudden attack. She had to think of the extraordinary, the unexpected. It would have to be when Olga Sarapenko came in with the meal. Maria was bitterly aware of the irony that food had been the one thing she had avoided and now its delivery offered her the only chance of survival. She thought about all the times she had made herself vomit to void her body of food. How she had perfected the technique. It was then that the idea started to take shape.

She reckoned she would have about four or five hours until the next meal. Time that she had to spend wisely.

2.

Fabel blinked at the light that cut slices across the room from between the blinds. His head hurt and his mouth felt thick and furry. He eased himself up onto his elbows. He was alone in a wide, low bed. There was the smell of coffee in the air, but a richer, darker aroma than he was used to. He stared at the poster on the wall opposite him. It was of a landscape that looked as if it belonged to another planet: slender rock towers capped with darker conical stone. A setting or rising sun had painted the towers red-gold and windows had been carved into some, giving the impression that elves or some alien race lived in them.

'Cappadocia,' said Tansu as she came in from the kitchen. She was wearing a silk robe which clung to her curves. 'The Fairy Chimneys. You ever been to Turkey?' She sat on the edge of the bed and handed him a coffee.

'Thanks,' said Fabel. 'No . . . I've never been. Listen, Tansu . . .'

She smiled and held her fingers to his lips. 'Drink your coffee. You'll feel better. Hangover?'

'A little . . . I'm not used to drinking so much.'

'That's the thing about Karneval – you can let go a little.' She stood up decisively. 'I'm going to take a shower. Help yourself to breakfast.'

'I'm fine,' said Fabel. 'I'd better get on my way soon. I thought I'd buy something for my daughter. A souvenir from Cologne.'

'You married?' said Tansu in a way that suggested it didn't matter to her one way or the other.

'Divorced.'

'You'll be lucky to find a store open. There might be a couple on Hohestrasse.'

The daylight was cold and bright and turned the throbbing in Fabel's head up a notch or two. When he got back to the hotel, he found the reception staff were all wearing bright red wigs and false noses. He allowed himself the curmudgeonly thought that these people never knew when to stop. He wanted to be home. Back in Hamburg. He wanted to talk to Susanne and put everything behind him. Including Tansu. But first he had to find Maria and bring her home too.

He showered and changed into a fresh cashmere roll-neck and cord trousers. His sports jacket smelled of cigarette smoke and he hung it up outside his wardrobe to air, pulling his coat on before going out again. He tried phoning Susanne at her office but, when he got her voicemail, he decided not to leave a message. He rang Scholz on his mobile: Scholz told Fabel they should meet the Presidium and have lunch in the canteen. Taxis would be difficult so Scholz would send a patrol car to pick Fabel up.

When Fabel arrived at the Presidium he was guided by security to the car pool, where a vast wheeled structure was in the process of being decorated. Scholz was involved in a heated debate with a tall lean uniformed officer. At least, the debate was heated on Scholz's side: the uniformed officer leaned against the float and nodded wearily.

'Bloody Karneval,' muttered Scholz as he greeted Fabel. 'Enjoy yourself last night?'

Fabel studied Scholz's expression for any hint of sarcasm. There was none and Fabel couldn't help feeling grateful that Scholz had disappeared earlier and had not known what had transpired between Fabel and Tansu.

'Great. I think we all deserved to celebrate a bit. Are you ready to reinterview Andrea Sandow?'

'Let's grab some lunch first.'

As they walked towards the lift, Fabel turned back to look at the float. 'It looks like some medieval war machine. You could hide an army under that. Maybe you should have made your theme "The Trojan Horse".'

Scholz's grim smile revealed that the police Karneval float was not a subject for humour. 'We're still getting nothing from Sandow. Prepare yourself for a fruitless afternoon. I've actually managed to get a shrink to come in later to do a psych assessment.'

They sat down by the window in the canteen. Fabel had ordered a coffee and split roll with ham. He found it difficult to eat. His hangover combined with an aversion to meat that had grown over the course of this case. He sat at the window that looked out over the alien life of this strange city. His longing to go home was still there, but he knew that he would come back to Cologne. He would have to. It was a city that got under your skin.

'Listen, Benni,' he said at last, 'I've kept my side of the bargain. I've helped you nail your cannibal. Now it's your turn. I'm worried about Maria Klee. I need your help to find her. And forget the need to be discreet. I'm going to talk to the Federal Crime Bureau as well. If we don't find her soon she's going to end up revealing herself to Vitrenko and get herself killed.'

'I'm already on it.' Scholz smiled. 'You see? I do keep my promises. I've sent out uniformed teams to check all the hotels. I've had copies made of the photograph you gave me and told the uniforms that she may have dyed her hair black.'

'Thanks, Benni. I need to get out there too.'

'I'm going to need you here. At least for the next couple of days, to help me question Andrea Sandow. But that won't take up all our time, mainly because I don't think we're going to get a word out of her. In between we can coordinate the search for Maria.'

After lunch they headed down to the interview room. Andrea Sandow was brought in, washed clean of make-up and with her hair scraped back severely. Her face naked of cosmetics looked even more masculine. Scholz led the questioning, but Andrea never broke her silence and kept her fixed, hard gaze focused on Fabel. After twenty fruitless minutes they gave up.

'We'll see what the shrink has to say later today,' said Scholz. 'But I have to say that Andrea seems to have something going on with you. It was as if I wasn't there.'

'Yeah,' said Fabel. 'But I got the idea that my presence was making things worse.'

'Why don't you take the rest of the afternoon off? You look pretty washed out after last night.'

'Maria . . .'

'By the time you get back I'll have chased up the uniforms and we'll see if we've got any leads on her whereabouts,' said Scholz. 'In the meantime, why don't you chill out? After all, you've just completed your last murder case.'

Fabel smiled wearily. 'Maybe you're right. I could do with a rest.'

Fabel accepted a lift in a patrol car back to his hotel.

'Can you drop me at the end of Hohestrasse?' he asked the driver. 'I'd like to do some shopping.'

Although some stores were open, the spirit of Karneval had seized the city fully and Fabel understood why these were called the 'Crazy Days'. He quickly gave up hope of finding a souvenir for Gabi, his daughter.

His cellphone rang.

'I've had a report from one of the uniforms,' said Scholz. 'It seems that Maria Klee checked out of a second hotel on Saturday the fourth. No joy with any of the other hotels. She seems to have dropped out of sight completely. Are you sure she's not back in Hamburg?'

'Hold on a minute . . .' A noisy group of street entertainers bustled past and Fabel edged out of their way. 'No, there's no way. I've got Anna Wolff, one of my team, checking regularly that Maria doesn't resurface . . . wait a minute . . .' The entertainers had gathered around Fabel, one of them juggling three gold balls. 'Do you mind?' said Fabel. 'I'm trying to have a conversation.' He noticed that they were dressed all in black, each wearing exactly the same type of mask: not the usual Karneval mask but more like the type worn during the Venetian Carnival: full-face, gold, genderless and empty of expression. The juggler gave a mime-artist shrug and moved back.

'As I was saying,' said Fabel, 'I would have heard if Maria

had resurfaced in Hamburg. I'm getting really worried, Benni.'

'Don't be – I'll keep on it.'

Fabel snapped his cellphone shut and the group of entertainers swamped him again. The juggler leaned in close, tilting
his blank gold mask from side to side as if examining Fabel.

'Clear off – I'm not interested.' Fabel was now annoyed.

'Want to see a good trick?' asked the juggler. Fabel thought
he detected an accent in the juggler's voice. Suddenly he felt
the others grasp his upper arms tight and push him against
the wall.

'I know a very good trick . . .' Still the mime-act tilting of
the mask from side to side. 'I can make a mad-bitch Hamburg
cop disappear.' Fabel struggled but the others, laughing
jovially, gripped him tight. He felt a knife point pressed into
his side, beneath his ribs. He looked past the masked jugglers
at the shoppers walking past in Hohestrasse. There was no
help to be called for. He would die before his cry was heard.
You always die alone, he thought.

The jugglers did a jester dance in front of him. Fabel
couldn't work out if it was to keep the pretence going for
the sake of passers-by, or if it was for his benefit.

'I can make anyone disappear,' said the juggler through the
gold mask. 'Anyone. I could make *you* disappear, right now.'

'What do you want, Vitrenko?'

'Why do you think I am Vitrenko? We are many here.'

'Because you're an egomaniacal fuck and this is how you
get your kicks,' said Fabel. 'Because you have to make a big
show of everything. Just like the way you killed all those
people in Hamburg. Just like the way you made sure I was
a witness to you murdering your own father.'

The juggler leaned his mask into Fabel's face again. 'Then
you know your bitch friend will suffer before she dies. I've
got her. I want the dossier. Deliver a copy, complete and unex-
purgated, or Maria Klee will be delivered to you piece by
piece.'

'I can't just get a copy of the dossier. It has to be signed out before anyone can even read it.'

'You're a resourceful man, Fabel. You are finished with the police – what does it matter to you? But if you fail to deliver a full copy of the dossier to me, I will deliver Maria Klee to you in one-kilo pieces. And I will use all my skill to make sure that she will be alive for most of the butcher work.'

'When?' asked Fabel.

'Let's keep things festive. Rose Monday. During the processions. Wait on the corner of Komödienstrasse and Tunisstrasse and someone will collect it from you. They will be wearing a mask like this.'

'I'll only give it to you.'

'You don't even know what I look like now. It could be anyone behind one of these masks.'

'I'll know. Just like I knew today. If it isn't you, then I won't hand over the dossier.'

The juggler's laugh was muffled by the mask. 'You want me to walk into a trap that's so obvious?'

'You're sick enough to see it as a challenge. There'll be no trap. Give me Maria and we'll both stay out of your business. For good.'

'Do not disappoint me, Herr Fabel. If you wish I can have a portion of Frau Klee delivered to your hotel to prove that I have her. And to underline my intent . . .'

'I believe you've got her. Don't hurt her and I'll do as you ask.'

'Good. But let me warn you that if there is *any* suggestion of a police presence, Frau Klee will be carved alive. No metaphor. You understand?'

Fabel nodded. He was shoved violently and crashed onto the ground. A couple of passers-by helped him to his feet in time to see the last of the masked men skip into the mass of the crowds.

3.

Maria's heart began to pound as soon as she heard the heavy clunking bar mechanism of the cold store door. It all depended on whether it was The Nose or Sarapenko who came in with the meal. Not that it could be called a meal: they had kept her on the minimum calorie intake to dull her mind and weaken her resistance. The near-starvation diet combined with the irregular switching on and off of the light was intended to disorientate her. The door slid open. She didn't look to see which of them it was. The decision to act or not act, to kill or not kill, would have to wait until the very last moment. She knew the routine: the tray would be left outside on the floor and whoever had brought the meal would stand back from the doorway, sweeping an automatic round the room before training the gun on Maria.

Maria remained on her knees, clutching the hollow of her belly, gasping for breath.

'I'm sick . . .' she said, still not looking up. It was the only way to go: she knew that Vitrenko would have given them strict orders to keep her alive until whatever use he had for her had been fulfilled. She heard the sound of boots approaching.

'I have medicine . . .' gasped Maria. 'In my coat . . . please help me.' She didn't want the door to close; for her guard to contact Vitrenko for instructions. She was presenting a problem and a solution at the same time. She was counting on her stuff still being there. The tablets in her coat were the anti-anxiety pills that Dr Minks had given her. The boots didn't move: feigning sickness was an obvious ploy. Maria had predicted this doubt of the guard's and she clamped her hand to her mouth as if about to vomit. Unseen, she slipped her ring finger into her mouth and throat. The hair-trigger reaction. There was little left in her stomach from the meagre meal of God knew how many hours before, but enough splashed onto the cold store floor to suggest that she was genuinely ill. Maria slumped onto her side, her eyes closed. She heard the footsteps approach again and a boot jabbed her in the ribs. Maria had so detached herself from her body that she didn't even flinch at the kick. A pause while the guard calculated the risk: just how much of a threat could Maria pose, even if she were conscious? Then the sound of a weapon being reholstered. She felt fingers jab into her neck to check her pulse.

It was then that Maria opened her eyes. Wide. She stared directly into Olga Sarapenko's face. Maria saw the alarm in Sarapenko's eyes as she realised that she was looking at something that was no longer human.

4.

Fabel's hotel room had the expected brightly coloured abstract print hanging on the wall. He sat on the edge of his bed and stared at it as if it would yield the knowledge or the strength to help him work out what to do next. His head ached. It was Vitrenko's sheer arrogance that astounded him: grabbing a senior police officer on a busy street and demanding that he betray everything he believed in.

As Fabel stared at the painting, he thought of *The Nightwatch* hanging in his mother's parlour; about how he had forgotten what he had seen in the painting as a small boy. The protection of others from harm.

Fabel knew what he had to do but dreaded doing it. It went against every instinct he had. He picked up the phone and dialled.

'Hello, Ullrich, Fabel here. About the Vitrenko Dossier . . .'

5.

Maria had realised, in those cold, dark, isolated hours, that she needed a sharp cutting edge to succeed in any attack. She had planned to sharpen the spoon, but that had been taken away along with, for a while, all hope. Then she had realised that, of course, she did have a sharp-edged weapon. It was just that using it had taken her to a place that was beyond human.

The grey-white walls were splashed with arcs of arterial blood. Sarapenko now reached out to Maria, desperate to touch another human being as she died. The spurts from her neck weakened: the outstretched hand dropped onto the grubby floor. Shakily, Maria dragged herself to her feet and wiped the blood from her mouth and face with the back of her sleeve. She took the automatic from its holster on Sarapenko's body, trying not to look at the face stripped of its beauty. The face that she had ravaged. But Maria felt no horror. Again, it was as if she were unreal; simply watching herself. She staggered out into the main part of the unit, swinging Sarapenko's automatic wildly around. There was no one. No Nose. Maria saw where the row of surveillance monitors still sat: now blank dark eyes. She ripped drawers from their runners, tore open cabinets until she found three more clips for the automatic, plus the two guns they had taken from her. There was a wastebasket in the corner and she frantically tossed its contents out onto the floor. She found a half-eaten roll, sodden with discarded coffee, with a shred of meat left inside. She stuffed it into her mouth and swallowed it half chewed, its stale flavour mingling with the lingering taste of Sarapenko's blood in her mouth.

The Nose came in through the main door at the end of the unit, carrying a large box. The instant he saw Maria he dropped the box and reached into his leather jacket. Maria walked deliberately and unhurriedly towards him. She heard several gunshots and felt Sarapenko's gun kick in her outstretched grasp. The Nose sank to his knees, hit in his chest and left flank. His hand cleared his jacket and Maria fired twice more into his body. His gun clattered to the floor. Maria kicked the automatic out of his reach. He looked up at her, his breath coming in short gasps. Maria knew that he was seriously wounded and would die if he didn't get hospital treatment immediately. She guessed he knew that as well. He tried to stand up but Maria shoved him back onto the floor with her boot.

'Where's the swap supposed to take place?' she asked.

'What swap?' he said between laboured breaths.

Maria lowered her aim and fired again. He screamed as his right kneecap shattered, his jeans turning black-red as the blood soaked into them.

'I'm supposed to be swapped for something,' said Maria, still calm. 'My guess is the Vitrenko Dossier. Where's the meet and who with?'

'Fuck you . . .'

'No,' Maria said wearily. 'Fuck you.' She leaned forward and aimed the muzzle at his forehead.

'Near the cathedral,' said The Nose. 'On the corner of Komödienstrasse and Tunisstrasse. With Fabel.'

'Jan Fabel?'

'He's supposed to hand over a copy of the Dossier in exchange for you.'

'When?'

'Rose Monday. When the procession is passing.'

'Thank you,' said Maria. 'You'll die if you don't get help. Do you have a cellphone?'

'In my pocket.'

Maria shoved the gun's muzzle into his cheek while she dug into his leather jacket with the other hand, retrieved the phone and put it into her own pocket. Then, with all her remaining strength and ignoring his screams of agony, she dragged The Nose by the collar of his jacket across the floor and into the storeroom. She dumped him next to the body of Olga Sarapenko and left him there.

'Like I said . . .' Maria regarded the Ukrainian coldly as she slid the cold-store door shut. 'Fuck you.'

6.

Fabel stood on the corner of Komödienstrasse and Tunisstrasse, the spires of Cologne Cathedral looming behind him, and watched as float after float drifted by. Crowds of organised chaos. Fabel looked up Tunisstrasse and recognised Scholz's Cologne Police float approaching. He stood watching the procession but not seeing it. Instead, he ran through every possible outcome. He even wondered if he would die here: if Maria was already dead and if Vitrenko would finish him off as soon as he got his hands on the dossier. Fabel gripped the plastic carrier bag tight.

'It's nothing to do with roses, you know,' Scholz had told him. 'The *Rose* in Rose Monday comes from the Old Low German *Rasen* – to rave or run around madly.' Now Fabel stood on the corner of a Cologne street on Rose Monday and watched as the city's population turned the world on its head. A giant papier-mâché model of the American President George Bush, his bare buttocks being spanked by an enraged Arab, drifted by. It was followed by another depicting the new German Chancellor, Angela Merkel, dressed as a Rhine Maiden. A group of German TV personalities were depicted on the next float, stuffing their pockets with cash. Everyone was cheering and scrabbling to catch the candies thrown by the costumed members of each float.

The procession slowed and came to a temporary standstill, as it did periodically to maintain the regulation distance between floats. Undaunted, the crowd continued to cheer. Fabel scanned the faces around him: clowns, oversized floppy hats in stridently jolly colours, face-painted children hoisted on the shoulders of parents. Then he saw him: the same gold mask and black outfit, standing four or five rows back. Fabel edged through the crowd towards the figure, then became aware of another gold mask. Then another. And another. There were five . . . no, six of them scattered throughout the crowd. All the gold masks were watching Fabel, not the procession. He stopped and tried to weigh up which was Vitrenko. Two of the figures made their way over to him. Fabel and the two gold-masked men stood, an island in an unseeing sea of revellers.

'I said I'd only hand this over to Vitrenko,' said Fabel. Neither masked man moved but Fabel heard Vitrenko's voice.

'And I said I wouldn't walk so easily into a trap.'

Fabel spun around and came face to face with another identical gold mask. The other two men closed in behind him.

'You have it?'

'I have photocopied pages from the original. Where's Maria?' said Fabel. The crowd around him cheered another passing float.

'Safe. She'll be released when I return with the dossier.'

'No, she won't. That wasn't our deal. You said we would exchange here. If I let you walk away with the dossier you'll kill her. Or she's dead already.' A shower of candies rained down on them, thrown by a passing float with the ritual *Kölsch* cry of '*Alaaf . . . Helau!*'. The crowd responded with '*Kölle Alaaf!*'

'You're right, Herr Fabel, I don't have her to exchange any more. But that doesn't matter, because you've brought the dossier. Thank you. And goodbye, Fabel.'

Vitrenko seized Fabel by the shoulder and pulled him close to the expressionless gold Venetian mask. One of the others snatched the carrier bag from his grasp. Vitrenko's other hand thrust a knife upwards and into Fabel's abdomen. Fabel doubled over, gasping for breath.

At that moment a flood of police officers burst out from under the curtain of the Cologne police float. Benni Scholz, who had been riding on top, leapt from the float, still dressed in his comedy police costume. The crowd cheered enthusiastically, thinking it was all part of the act until the officers barged into the crowds. Vitrenko looked down at Fabel, then at the knife in his gloved hand. He dropped it and ran, disappearing into the crowd.

'Get after them!' Scholz screamed at his men. He pushed through the crowd to where Fabel had fallen.

7.

Scholz put his arm around Fabel's shoulders and gently eased him up.

'You okay?'

Fabel looked down at his punctured coat and jacket. 'Just winded.'

'It's a good job you were right about his weapon of choice. If he'd brought a gun that stab-vest wouldn't have helped much.'

'Let's go,' said Fabel.

The uniformed officers had already grabbed two of the masked men and pulled their masks from their faces. Fabel, Scholz and half a dozen uniformed officers pushed on through the crowd which thinned out the further they moved away from the procession.

'There!' shouted one of the uniforms and pointed to where a dark figure had cleared the crowd and ran off in the direction of the Rhine.

'No . . . wait,' shouted Scholz. 'There's another one.' He pointed to a second figure, heading off towards the railway station. 'And another . . .' A third gold mask flashed in the winter sunlight as it turned in their direction before running towards the back of the cathedral.

'We'll have to split up and go after them all,' shouted Fabel. 'But a minimum of three men on each. These are dangerous bastards. Benni, we'll take the cathedral guy. You armed?'

Benni reached deep into his oversized outfit and produced his SIG-Sauer automatic. He ordered one of the uniforms to come with him and Fabel and they sprinted off in the direction taken by the third masked man. They came round to the south side of the cathedral and suddenly they were alone. The cheering of the crowd was still loud but seemed to Fabel to belong to another universe. They stopped and caught their breath.

'He can't have got round the rear,' said the uniformed cop. 'He didn't have time.'

Fabel strained his neck to look up at the immense looming mass of the cathedral. They were on the south side and a row of massive flying buttresses, each tipped with a spire, flanked the cathedral's nave like a rank of soldiers. His eyes fell to street level and caught sight of a side door.

'Is the cathedral open today?' he asked.

'Not to the public,' said Scholz. 'But there's a special *Fastenpredigt* pre-Lent Mass later. They're probably preparing for that.'

'He's gone inside,' said Fabel. 'The cathedral is like a crossroads itself. He's trying to lose us and come out on another side. Come on!'

The heavy door yielded, then slammed echoingly behind them. There was a man lying on the flagstones immediately inside the door. His white hair was dishevelled and was stained red with blood on one temple.

'Are you all right?' Scholz bent over the elderly security man.

'I . . . I tried to stop him. Told him the cathedral was closed. He hit me . . .'

'You – stay with him,' Scholz ordered the uniform. 'Radio in. I want men at each portal of the cathedral. Jan, you stick with me. Chances are this is one of Vitrenko's decoys, but it's better to be safe.'

Fabel unholstered the automatic that Scholz had issued him with before the meet with Vitrenko. They walked down the centre of the aisle, past the window where Fabel had discussed rhinoceroses with a Mexican writer.

'This place is the size of a football stadium,' he said to Scholz. 'The bastard could be anywhere.'

'You check along the pews on the left, I'll take the right.'

They worked their way up the aisle, the sounds of Karneval outside now even more remote. They reached the crossing of the transept and Fabel found himself looking through the retrochoir to where the Shrine of the Three Kings, a huge golden reliquary, gleamed behind its glass. There was a sound to his left.

'Over there, behind that screen . . .' he hissed to Scholz and swung his gun around. Scholz put a restraining hand on Fabel's arm.

'For Christ's sake don't shoot. That *screen*, as you call it, is the Klaren Altar. It's priceless.'

'So's my life.' Fabel nodded past the triptych screen. 'You go that way.'

Fabel kept his aim locked on the screen and moved towards it, taking slow steps and ready to fire. He checked that Scholz was in position. Fabel swung around the edge of the screen. Something slammed hard into him and he toppled sideways. He heard his gun clatter across the flagstones and felt cold steel pressed against his cheek. He looked up at a gold mask.

'Now why don't you stand the fuck up and drop that gun,' Fabel heard Scholz say calmly but firmly. 'Or I'm going to have to pop one in your head.'

'Let me go or I'll kill him,' said the masked man. 'I'll do it.'

'And then you'll die,' said Scholz. 'And nobody comes out of this on top, Vitrenko.'

The man took his automatic away from Fabel's face and laid it on the flagstones. He stood up and pulled his mask from his face. He was dark-haired and younger, thought Fabel, than Vitrenko would have been.

'It's not him,' said Fabel. 'I don't think it's him.'

'Are you sure?' asked Scholz. Fabel scrambled to his feet and recovered his automatic. He stood beside Scholz and also locked his aim on the figure.

'Drop it. Now!'

'You're right, Fabel. I'm not Vitrenko. He'll be long gone by now. He told you that he wouldn't walk into a trap.'

'Who are you?'

'Pylyp Gnatenko. As far as you're concerned, a nobody.'

'A nobody prepared to die or go to prison to buy your boss a few minutes to escape?' asked Fabel.

'If that's what it takes. You still know nothing about our code, Fabel.'

'Step out of the shadows. I want to see your face properly.'

There was a sound from behind them and Fabel spun around.

'Maria?' Fabel stared uncomprehendingly at the figure before him. Maria was dressed in cheap black clothes and looked painfully thin, her face pale and pinched. Almost grey. There was an ugly swollen welt across her forehead. Her blonde hair had been cropped and dyed black, just as the hotel clerk had told Fabel. She was aiming two automatics directly at the Ukrainian. Scholz swung his aim round onto her.

'It's okay! It's okay!' shouted Fabel. 'It's Maria. The officer I told you about.'

'If it's not too much trouble,' said Scholz, 'could you tell me what the fuck is going on?'

'That's him,' said Maria. 'The devil is here.'

'We don't know if it's Vitrenko,' said Scholz. 'He says he's just one of his stooges. I think you'd better give me those guns, Frau Klee.'

'His eyes, Jan. Look at his eyes. He couldn't change his eyes.'

'Step out of the shadow. *Now!*' Fabel kept his gun trained on the figure.

He smiled as he stepped into the light. He was too young, too dark to be Vitrenko. But Fabel knew, as soon as the emerald eyes glinted in the light cast from the high windows, that that was exactly who it was. 'I thought my new face might fool you, but unfortunately Frau Klee has already seen it.'

'He told me he was a Ukrainian called Taras Buslenko.'

'The policeman they sent after him?'

Maria nodded.

Vitrenko placed his hands on his head. 'I am your prisoner,' he said. 'No tricks.'

'You'll give in that easily?' said Fabel. 'I don't believe it.'

'There are many ways to escape,' said Vitrenko. 'As Frau Klee has already discovered. We found the remains of the guards, Maria. Poor Olga. It would appear your bite is worse than your bark. Anyway, like I said, there are many, many ways to escape. And I know that your Federal Crime Office will want to negotiate over what information I can give them. After all, I've given them a lot already.'

'I know,' said Fabel. 'The dossier you took from me was blank pages, but you knew I wouldn't hand it over, didn't you? And you didn't really need to see it at all.'

'May I repeat my request of earlier?' Scholz, his gun still aimed at Vitrenko, frowned angrily. 'Could someone tell me what the fuck is going on?'

'The so-called Vitrenko Dossier is all crap. The mole inside the organisation was Vitrenko himself. Misinformation. A few scraps of genuine intelligence and the rest was all bollocks. This whole idea that he was desperate to get his hands on it was to convince the Federal Crime Bureau of its authenticity.'

'Buslenko died for a lie?' The question cracked in Maria's throat. 'Everything you did to me? It was all a masquerade?'

Vitrenko shrugged. 'What can I tell you? I became caught up in the spirit of Karneval. But the lie Buslenko died for was that Ukraine was worth dying for. A patriot. A fool. Now, if you don't mind, if you'll handcuff me and deliver me to a cell somewhere. Of course there's a lot of evidence against me. It's all in the Vitrenko Dossier – oh, wait, that's all fake, isn't it? I wonder how long you'll be able to keep me . . .'

'There's the murder of the policeman in Cuxhaven. The attempted murder of Maria. The container full of human cargo that you let burn to death. I think we'll find something.'

'And I think my lawyers and their medical experts will have a lot to say about Frau Klee's psychological credibility as a witness.' Vitrenko grinned. 'You see, Fabel, I'm getting away again. Just like the last time. It's just that I'm taking a different route.'

'No . . .' said Maria, her voice dull. 'Not like the last time.'

Fabel and Scholz didn't have time to react. Maria fired both guns, squeezing the triggers until the magazines emptied. The shots hit Vitrenko in the chest and gut and he staggered backwards until he hit the wall. His emerald eyes became dull and unfocused and he slid down the stone surface, leaving a smear of blood behind him. Maria let the guns fall. At the same time Fabel saw something empty from her face.

Even in the midst of his shock he knew that what had left her would never return.

8.

It was already dark when Fabel walked slowly up the grassy mound in the Marienfeld park to where the bonfire raged and sparked into the night sky.

'I didn't think we'd see you here,' said Scholz. He handed Fabel a bottle of *Kölsch*.

'I wasn't doing much good at the hospital. I've arranged for Maria to be transferred to Hamburg. After you've completed your case, that is.'

'I don't think it matters where her body is. Truth is, she's not in it any more. I'm sorry, Jan. I really am.'

'Thanks, Benni.'

Tansu Bakrac came over to them. Fabel noticed that Scholz moved off discreetly to leave them to talk.

'You okay?' Tansu asked. She placed a hand on his arm.

'No. Not really. I'm going to head back to Hamburg. I'll be back in a week or two to tie things up with Benni. Listen, Tansu, about what happened . . .'

She smiled and nodded towards the bonfire. 'This is the Nubbelverbrennung. All the sins and foolishness of the Crazy Days get burned up. Here. Tonight. Have a good life, Jan.'

'You too, Tansu.' Fabel kissed her and then watched as she walked back to her friends, the firelight etching the outline of her body.

Epilogue

Hamburg.

Fabel sat with Maria, by the window. He held her hand and looked into her eyes but she simply looked past him and out of the window. Through the glass lay the shapes of the hospital extension, the outbuildings, the large triangle of grassed grounds and the green froth of bushes that marked the hospital boundaries. Beyond that lay the roadway that rumbled continuously and faintly with traffic. But Fabel knew that although Maria seemed to be looking at this unremarkable view she was not seeing it. He didn't know what she was seeing. Maybe it was that field near Cuxhaven. Maybe it was a garden or a favourite place from her childhood in Hanover. Wherever it was, it was visible only to Maria; it existed only in the world that she had withdrawn to. But what frightened Fabel was the all too credible thought that Maria might have been seeing nothing at all: that she had withdrawn to a void.

Fabel talked to Maria. He talked about getting her better now that she was back in Hamburg. Dr Minks was going to help with her treatment. The Polizei Hamburg had arranged it all. Maria still didn't answer but continued to look out of the window at the view across to the road, or at nothing at all. Fabel continued to talk about the recovery that he knew would never come, or at least not completely. He talked about the colleagues that he knew she would never work with again.

He talked with the same forced calmness with which he had spoken to her so very long ago as she lay close to death in the field by Cuxhaven. Except this time, he knew, he could not save her.

Every now and again Maria would smile, but Fabel knew it was at nothing he had said, rather at something in the deep and distant inner world that she now inhabited.

It rained in Hamburg that day. Fabel met Susanne in the bar around the corner from his apartment in Pöseldorf. Neutral territory.

'Susanne, I wanted to talk,' he explained. 'I think we need to straighten things out.'

'I thought we had,' she said flatly. 'At least, I thought *you* had. I mean when you phoned me before you went off to Cologne.'

Fabel pushed his beer bottle around the table top contemplatively. He thought back to those three calls he had made weeks before: to Wagner at the Federal Crime Bureau, to Roland Bartz, and to Susanne.

'Listen, Susanne,' he said gently, 'when I was down in Cologne things were supposed to be confused. The whole point of Karneval, I suppose. But they weren't for me. They weren't for me as soon as I found out Maria had gone off on this personal crusade that's cost her her sanity. Down there I was surrounded by people who were being someone else . . . Vera Reinartz who had become Andrea Sandow who claims to become this killer clown whom she has no control over . . . then there was Vitrenko, stealing one identity after another and manipulating everyone around him. But me . . . I knew who I was. The funny thing is I didn't know who I was before. Or I denied it, I don't know.'

'So who are you?'

'I am a policeman. Just like that poor kid Breidenbach who got shot rather than let a gunman walk onto the street . . . just like Werner or Anna or Benni Scholz in Cologne. It's who I am. It's *what* I am. It's my job to stand there between the bad guys and the innocent. What I didn't realise until now is that it's more than a job. It's often ugly and it's invariably unrewarding, but it's what I was meant to do. I've always pretended to myself that I'm a historian or an intellectual who's stumbled into this job and who doesn't really fit. But that's wrong, Susanne. Whether I found the job or the job found me, it was meant to be.'

'So you've accepted this nationwide brief? This Super-Murder-Commission thing?'

'Not really. I've said I'll help out elsewhere if I'm needed. Lend my "expertise". But that's the other thing I've learned. I belong here. Hamburg is my city. These are the people I want to protect.'

'So where does that leave us?' Susanne's voice was cold and hard. Fabel reached over the table and took her hands in his.

'That's rather what I wanted to ask you . . .'

Cologne. Six months later

Andrea sat on the edge of the bed. No make-up, no lipstick, platinum hair scraped severely back in a ponytail and dark at the roots.

There was nothing in the cell other than the bed and the combined desk and bench, all of which were bolted to the floor. No free weights to work with. That would be a major problem for as long as they kept her confined in this cell. But Andrea was, she knew, on suicide watch and she would be moved from this empty space eventually. Until then, she could use her own body weight to exercise the main muscle groups. She knew that without free weights she would lose mass, become leaner, but at least she could maintain tone.

She stood up and went to the corner of the cell, braced her feet against the wall to maximise the load borne by her arms, and started a set of push-ups. She knew that a nurse was watching her through the spyhole in the door. They wouldn't deny her access to a gymnasium for her entire confinement. There would be weights or resistance machines in the gym. Then she could start building muscle again. And strength. In the meantime she would do her press-ups: sets of twenty, six sets a day, three days a week. A total of nineteen thousand press-ups a year. Every other day, while her arms and upper body rested, she would run through a similar routine with sit-ups.

She would time her routine so that it would not conflict with therapy sessions, work details, meal breaks, communal exercise. She would be a model patient – or prisoner – whichever it was she was supposed to be in this place. They would let her out one day. Not for a long time, perhaps, but she would convince them she was healed and no longer a danger. That she had, once more, become someone else.

One thing that Andrea had learned during her earliest days of bodybuilding was that to focus your body you had to focus your mind. Set a goal. Concentrate on it. She clenched her teeth as the final repetitions of her set strained her arms. When she had first started, it had been the face of the Karneval clown who had beaten and raped her, half-strangling her with a necktie. She had burned that image into her mind with each exercise, every day for seven years. It had given her the focus that she had needed.

But now she had another focus. With each push-up she repeated in her head a new mantra: the words she would say into herself with every exercise, every day of her confinement.

Jan Fabel.

When she was released, she would still be strong.

Acknowledgements

I would like to thank the following people for their help and support: Wendy, Jonathan and Sophie; my agent Carole Blake; from Hutchinson, my editor Paul Sidey, Tess Callaway and my copy-editor Nick Austin; Bernd Rullkötter; Erste Polizeihauptkommissarin Ulrike Sweden of the Polizei Hamburg; Dr. Jan Sperhake, chief pathologist of the Institut für Rechtsmedizin; Udo Röbel; and Anja Sieg.

I would also like to thank all of my publishers around the world for their enthusiasm and support.